ARCADIA

JONATHAN D. CLARK

Praise for ARCADIA

Jonathan D. Clark's voice is unlike any other. Each sentence is deliberate and rich with prose and insight. *Arcadia* was a roller-coaster of emotion, oftentimes dark and heavy, other times, nostalgic, with hopes and dreams emanating from the characters. He can bring out your worst nightmares, but there's a warmth present, too, which is rare in my opinion, to find a balance of both.

—Eve Corso, author of *Spellbound* and *The Fallen Starlet*

[E]asily one of the best books I've read in a long time . . . I thoroughly enjoyed every page. . . .

—E.K. Lloyd-Williams, author of *How to Cure*

Clark's exceptional artistic ability is showcased in *Arcadia*. His writing style is outside of the typical, but dive in and you'll find yourself pouring over the intricate imagery and insightful characterization as you weave together all the pieces to find yourself mesmerized by Clark's understanding of the human condition. Simply put, this novel will blow your mind. It'll have you questioning reality, all the way to the end.

—Destiny Eve, author of *Her Heart in Chains*

author manipulated & gaslit these women, but
still uses their praise on his books

Also by Jonathan D. Clark

NOVELS
Division Street
In Perfect Lines
False Cathedrals

About the Author

Jonathan D. Clark (the pseudonym of Jourdan D. Dunn) was born in Redding, California, in 1990, where he currently resides with his son. He self-published his debut novel, *Division Street*, in 2016. He is also the author of *In Perfect Lines* and *False Cathedrals*.

For Waman Clark (1928-2011)
a man who never lost the gift of laughter,
even in the last moments of his life

ARCADIA

a novel

01010100 01101000 01100101 00100000
01110111 01101111 01110010 01101100
01100100 00100000 01100101 01101110
01100100 01100101 01100100 00100000
01101111 01101110 00100000 01001010
01100001 01101110 01110101 01100001
01110010 01111001 00100000 00110010

Part I: The Awakening

00110001 00101100 00100000 00110001
00111001 00111001 00110101 00101110
00100000 01000101 01110110 01100101
01110010 01111001 01110100 01101000
01101001 01101110 01100111 00100000
01111001 01101111 01110101 00100000
01101011 01101110 01101111 01110111
00100000 01101001 01110011 00100000
01100001 00100000 01101100 01101001
01100101 00101110 00100000 01010111
01100101 01101100 01100011 01101111
01101101 01100101 00100000 01110100
01101111 00100000 01000001 01110010
01100011 01100001 01100100 01101001
01100001 00101100 00100000 01111001
01101111 01110101 01110010 00100000
01101110 01100101 01110111 00100000
01101000 01101111 01101101 01100101
00100001 00100001 00100001 00100001

Time has always had the upper hand—humanity's attempts to outmaneuver its cunning nature proving themselves futile as a dying Earth continued to spin, with little regard to their survival.

T HERE IS NOTHING *more detrimental* toward the idea of progress than that of a lie—the on-going promise of change for the better only growing thinner as the years press on; the world continuing to go on without even the *smallest* sign of improvement. We've seen it with politicians. We've seen it with lawyers—essentially politicians in their embryonic stage. We've seen it with writers, doctors, company executives, university professors, even the people we've grown up with and love dearly; their false promises of a better future for the generations to come having saturated us for as long as we can remember. For most (if not all) of what we've heard growing up has been a well-constructed lie blended with enough 'half-truths' so nobody—not even the original perpetrators of the lie—can tell the difference between what is false and real anymore.

One would hope as the state of the world grew progressively worse over time that we, as a species, would eventually grow tired of living off of the tall-tale filled oxygen which has filled our lungs since birth. Unfortunately, we have become dependent upon these false pretenses to continue to try our best to press *forward* in this world; no matter how futile our attempts have become. Pierce continues to tell me to trust in his judgment; that, eventually, the surviving cities of the world will rise from the ashes of its past and become a place of beauty once more.

However, in order for any *true* progress to come about, one should not only speak about wanting to improve the state of the world, but also make the appropriate actions necessary to make those promises sound. Personally, I feel Dian Fossey explained it best when she said, "When you realize the value of all life, you dwell on what is past and concentrate more on the preservation of the future."

Perhaps, one day, someone will finally reveal themselves unto us; bringing the world back to its fabled original state and can keep it going strong like we've been promised all those years ago. All we can do these days is hope (pray even) that *that* day comes sooner rather than later—we've waited long enough, to be honest. However, my fears are beginning to choke the very idea that such a hope exists. I sit here, in my office, continuing to work with the very people who have filled the world's head with the ideas of hope and the endless string of lies of a salvation still to come; continuing to spin the web until there is *no way to unravel it*. . .

- Elizabeth Hestler

1

A HELICOPTER LOOMS overhead in the distance, its searchlight roaming the streets below—with no real sense of urgency. Up in the sky the city looks peaceful—up there one can't tell the city streets are overcome with decadence: a drug deal taking place in an all-but-forgotten alleyway, homeless junkies (most of them veterans from either the Vietnam Era or the *recent* military debacle known as Desert Storm) suffering another winter's night without food, while a poor old lady finds herself getting mugged (and murdered—left for dead on the sidewalk of Towne Avenue) for seventeen dollars and some change; from up here, someone could take a candid photograph of the city and the unknowing individual would find it beautiful; majestic, even. Continuing in a random fashion, the helicopter's searchlight finds its way to a lone automobile traveling down the city's lonely night-time streets.

Even with there being no other traffic on the road at 11:20pm on a Tuesday, Gordon Jones found himself afraid to merge on the Los Angeles freeway. He'd never felt this way about driving in any other city. Only in the sprawling, neon-soaked landscape of La-La Land would a competent driver, which Gordon presumed he was, find themselves consumed with such a high amount of anxiety that even the act of *merging onto the Interstate* became a difficult task; one which demanded applause upon achievement. Hoping to calm his fears, he rolled the windows down and turned the volume up to his car radio; the slow-paced instrumentation of Soundgarden's "Black Hole Sun" now screaming from the worn out speakers of his '87 faded blue Ford Mustang GT LX; his troubled mind continuing to haunt him. *Coming here was a mistake,* he thought. *I should have listened to Alexis and just stayed in Nebraska; taken her father's job offer at his law firm.*

Gordon had come to Los Angeles to pursue his dream of becoming a famous Hollywood screenwriter—the relentless reality of Los Angeles hitting him square in the face, unfortunately. After five *grueling* years of hopelessly sending out his manuscript to various studios throughout town (even sinking to the point of reworking his entire script to work as an adult film; still unable to find *anyone* to pick it up)—being forced to find employment as a cashier at a local Target—Gordon had given up entirely. He took his eyes off the road to stare down at the cursed stack of papers he had spent six years on prior to coming to this *cursed* town; eleven years down the fucking drain, his mind attempted to belittle his work—succeeding with little to no effort. *Great . . . I've been reduced to insulting inanimate objects . . . fucking fantastic.*

Out of nowhere, it seemed, another vehicle zoomed past him, cutting him off—a young female screaming into the air as they continued onward; the sudden appearance of another vehicle on the road causing Gordon to swerve a bit in the confusion. *Fucking teenagers,* he assumed—who else would be driving *that* recklessly on a Tuesday night? After all, it wasn't that long ago that *he* was the one speeding down a city freeway to feel the rush of adrenaline coursing through his veins. As the other car disappeared in the distance, leaving the road desolate once more, Gordon found himself at ease. Picking up speed, the car's speedometer reading 75mph, the sounds of Stone Temple Pilots' "Interstate Love Song" having taken over the stereo (Scott Weiland's voice bleeding over the other instrumentation), the rumbling purr of the Mustang's engine allowed Gordon to return to a state of nostalgia; imagining the Los Angeles wind was a Nebraskan breeze—Alexis sleeping in the passenger seat as they drove aimlessly until either the sun came up or they ran out of gas; it didn't matter which one came first.

A wave of sadness washed over him after a while, knowing those days were behind him. He found himself wondering how Alexis was these days. Was she doing okay? Had she started seeing someone else; it had been five years, after all—he wouldn't blame her if she had, but he couldn't deny he would feel relieved if he found out she were still single; working as a florist. *I could always drive back home*, he dreamed as the road continued to pass him by, *see if that job offer is still available. Maybe—if she's still single, or just as friends (I guess we'll find that out down the road)—ask Alexis if she'd like to go see a movie, sometime; the third Die Hard film looked promising—based on the trailer I saw not that long ago.* Wanting to avoid lingering on the thoughts of a life no longer his, having only filled his mind with an endless trail of regret, Gordon looked up toward the sky, hoping to calm his nerves.

What he saw, however, was mildly unsettling. Above him he saw what appeared to be falling debris coming down toward the City of Orange. Gordon's imagination ran wild with what the foreign objects could be: scrap metal from an old Cold War satellite finally falling back to Earth, a meteor shower which had gone unnoticed by local astronomers—it was hard to tell from a moving vehicle. Whatever it was, it traveled toward downtown Los Angeles with violent determination.

A blinding flash of light came first. Moments of hushed monotone passed afterward. An awkward silence; his car's stereo now only playing white noise. Bringing his vehicle to a complete stop, Gordon watched as the car that cut him off moments earlier came to a screeching halt, turned around in one swift motion, and began speeding in the opposite direction—three mushroom shaped clouds billowing over the horizon. *Fucking Christ!* he screamed as he shifted his car in reverse to turn around and follow the other driver's instincts to get as far away from the blast as possible.

When his foot hit the gas, however, the car refused to move. *You've got to be fucking kidding me, right now!* he continued to press his foot down on the gas, flooring it, with no response from the vehicle. He watched as the other vehicle zoomed past him, going at least 95 down the open freeway. In the distance, the once looming helicopter came falling to the ground; a small explosion coming alive upon impact. If he had learned anything from watching *Terminator 2: Judgment Day* countless times since its theatrical release (and if James Cameron, like he usually did when it came to the art of cinema, did his homework), Gordon knew a heat wave would surely follow the initial explosion, and by the look of things, he was within the blast radius.

Not a place one wanted to be with an immobile vehicle.

Thinking fast, he unbuckled himself and got out of the driver seat; lifting himself into the back-end of the vehicle. Clearing out the trash which had collected along the floor in the past few months, he made himself as comfortable as possible while he waited for the blast to come for him; hoping his makeshift shelter would keep him from being annihilated.

I should've just stayed in Nebraska. . .

• • •

SITTING BEHIND A TABLE stacked with books in the back corner of the Barnes & Noble in Redding, California, Tom Dolin silently waited for the store to open so he could welcome his fans; holding a book signing for his latest book, *A Lost Legacy*; the last in a series of novels that had become known among fans as the *Transmigration Trilogy*. Honestly, he had grown to dread the public that would swarm him with each location he visited. The excitement of being the 'new and upcoming author' having faded years ago after his first and second novels (*Discord Avenue* and *In Flawless Strokes*) were printed in hardback for their second editions. This time being published using his actual name, for he had used the pseudonym of J.D. Clark for their first publications for personal reasons not even his agent and close friend Lauren Anderson knew of. The only thing Tom looked forward to these days was when he could finally go back to his hotel room, call up his wife and kids to see how they were doing, and fall asleep; dreaming of one day being back home in Santa Ana so he could start work on his newest idea for a novel; a police procedural crime thriller currently under the working title *Modus Operandi*.

The lights flickered on one row after the other—letting Tom know the store would be opening soon; allowing what would be an endless wave of customers to come spilling in at any moment. Preparing himself for the onslaught of people he took a few deep breaths and forced a smile he'd become all too familiar with in the past decade; a smile he swore he was done faking when he quit his retail job at Chump's Plus all those years ago. It's just another day in paradise, he thought to himself; taking one last sip of his complimentary Starbucks coffee before any sense of tranquility became lost to the endless drone of *"I've read all your books Mr. Dolin"* and *"I think your work would improve if you (insert unimaginative suggestion from a fan who believes their ideas are actually worth a damn to him)"* which he knew would consume the next two to four hours of his life—if not longer. It's just another day in paradise, Tom, he told himself once more, and you're only along for the ride. . . Enjoy it while you can; forcing the smile back onto his face.

After the first fifty-something *devoted* admirers had passed through the line Tom found a steady pace which would—at least he hoped it would —make his day go by a little bit faster: grab the book, sign the inside cover page while trading a few pleasantries with the person, and hand the book back; telling them he was glad they enjoyed the book and to look out for his next upcoming release. Occasionally, he'd be forced to break his pace when the person (usually a female in their early to mid-twenties) would want him to go into a well-detailed breakdown of one of the many plot points in the novel he was signing—the novel in question for these type of fans usually being *Discord Avenue*; the novel seeming to strike a chord with the female audience more than his male readers. Although, after a while, he even began to conjure up a few quips to go in response to such loaded questions which he didn't have the time to go into full-detail with them on. Had today's book signing event been a reading where there would be an allotted amount of time for in-depth questioning, he would've gladly gone into detail on such questions. But this being Redding, California (his hometown; one he'd tried so desperately to escape, only to come back to as part of this book tour)—he wanted (nay, needed) to wrap up this particular book signing event before he felt the clutches of the city taking its hold on him once more.

"Excuse me," a soft voice spoke as the next person approached the table. Tom looked up to meet the gaze of a young woman (early to mid-twenties, he assumed, by her trendy style of dress; reminiscent of the early noughties—when he was still in high school. Jesus, he thought, I never thought I'd witness the day when outfits comprised entirely out of *denim* would make a comeback); carrying a first-edition copy of *In Flawless Strokes*—still printed with the J.D. Clark pseudonym instead of his own name; the spine worn and pages sun stained yellow. The book had seen better days.

"Yes?" Tom said as he—unknowingly, as a reflex—held out his left hand to take the book from her so he could sign it.

The girl, however, kept the book close to her chest and, instead, leaned closer to the table and whispered, "You remember the part of *In Flawless Strokes* where Jackson and Allison hook up?"

Tom, confused, nodded in response to her question. Why wouldn't I remember a section of a book *I* wrote, he thought.

"Well," she continued, lowering the volume of her voice to a hushed whisper. "Every time I read that part of the book, I can't help but touch myself."

"I'm glad I could help," he said awkwardly; hand still outstretched, hoping she'd hand him the book so he could sign it and carry on with the rest of the crowd—he still had (he leaned to take a quick glance of the line) thirty-or-so more people to go through before he could wrap up and leave. "Who am I making it out to?" he asked, hoping if he asked the question the woman would *finally* hand over the book.

"Oh," she laughed while pressing the book against her breasts. "You've already signed my book. I just wanted to come see you *in person* and tell you, eleven years later, that *your* book was the first thing I ever masturbated to; being twenty-five now, I *finally* felt comfortable coming to a book signing—without my mother—to tell you how important your work is to me." Tom, left speechless upon hearing this, simply smiled; cringing on the inside that he—his work, at least—was motivation for someone's *alone time*. He'd never look at another copy of *In Flawless Strokes* the same ever again.

I can't wait to go home, he thought as the next person walked up to the counter. Just keep smiling, he told himself; having not shaken the disturbing images of a fourteen (now twenty-five) year old girl using a —according to him, poorly written—sex scene from a book he wrote when he was twenty-six in such a pornographic nature.

Just twenty-something-more people to trudge through, he reminded himself, hoping the gentle reminder would help lift his spirits enough to keep the worn-out facade going until he could breakdown in the privacy of his car and be the anti-social version of himself once more; it wasn't helping. If I had known *this* was part of the deal, his mind spoke —signing his name on the front page of his third novel, *Ascension* (the first in the *Transmigration Trilogy*) for a fan (male, fresh out of high school) who couldn't help but voice his opinion that the series felt like a derivative mashup of the 1999 sci-fi classic, *The Matrix*, Philip K. Dick's *Ubik* and *Dr. Bloodmoney*, along with Thomas Pynchon's *Against the Day*. (He had to admit, for a kid, he was well read for his age; he knew his science fiction well enough to know when, yes, other people's work took *fragments of influence from other pieces of work*.) Whether or not he would claim it as derivative, as the kid had postu-lated, was another topic of discussion he didn't have time to discuss with him—I would have *never* considered showing Lauren the first draft of *Discord Avenue* back in the spring of 2015 had he worried about such things.

The store, now void of anyone who had shown up for the book sign-ing event—only high school kids and college students writing term pa-pers having remained in the cafe, the persona known as Tom Dolin gathered his things, what little he had brought with him on this trip—it being Redding after all—and made his way for the front door.

"Wait," a voice cried from behind him, causing him to turn around to find a Barnes & Noble associate darting toward him; a copy of *The Lurid Traversal of Interstate 5* (the second in the *Transmigration Tril-ogy*) underneath her left armpit. "Sorry," she managed, out of breath. "I was working in the backroom during your signing event and wanted you to sign my copy of this." She held the novel out to him as she con-tinued to take in one deep, labored, breath after the other.

"It's no problem," he told her; taking the book from her shaking hands and, without looking at it, opened it to the first page so he could sign it for her. "Who am I making it ou—"

He couldn't finish his sentence, dumbstruck by what he saw on the front page. From top to bottom, the young woman had written down the basics of neurobiology; a topic discussed *throughout* the first two books of the series. He flipped through a few more pages of the book to find she had written among the text of the novel as well; not a space left unmarked.

Impressed by the girl's intellect and dedication to double-check his work, Tom lifted his gaze from the pages of the novel to find the young woman—having recovered from her bout of exhaustion—was now fidgeting; nervous, it seemed; like a student waiting in anticipation while their professor graded their mid-term paper in front of them; hoping they got a decent grade.

"Where would you like me to sign," he asked, continuing to flip through the pages—hoping to find an unmarked section. "It seems you were captivated by the sections of the book which dealt with the neurobiological properties of bringing a human being out of cryogenically induced suspended animation."

"The back of the book, under your brief biography. It was the only part of the book I managed to leave untouched," she brought herself to say, shyly. "Sorry," she continued, "I've always found the concepts of neuroscience and cryoconservation *fascinating*. When one of my friends told me there was a set of novels which discussed the hypothetical properties of reversing the process in a post-apocalyptic setting I knew I had to give it, as well as your other works of fiction, a read. And, to be honest," she paused, taking a breather, "I prefer this set of novels over your other work. Your first two novels felt esoteric in nature; too personal and self-obsessed that only a particular group of people—the people the novels mentioned—would understand the pain behind the material."

Tom couldn't help but laugh. She was right. While *Discord Avenue* was a rather successful release (especially for a debut novel from an—at the time—unknown writer), the material of the novel was, as she had elegantly put it, esoteric in nature.

"Not that my opinion matters," the young woman continued, still quiet and bashful in execution. "But if you write any more novels in the future, could you stay away from writing something like your first two bodies of work ever again. That particular style of writing doesn't suit you. From what enjoyment I got out of *Ascension* and *Interstate 5*, if you were to *ever* return to your roots, might I suggest adding a didactic element for those of us who enjoy the use of academia in fictional works; leave the mundane, minimalist, self-absorbed rantings to such authors like Chuck Palahniuk and Gordon Lish. My name is Maggie by the way; Maggie McGuffey," she ended as Tom finished signing his name underneath the short paragraph which was the publishing houses poor excuse for a *brief* biography. "Just in case you were wondering who you were making it out to." she smiled as she looked down at the floor. Unbeknownst to Maggie, Tom preferred it when his 'fans' were a shy, neurotic mess; they reminded him of himself when he first started out as a professional writer; shaking uncontrollably at his first book signing; hoping each question would be the last for the afternoon.

Maggie's literary advice stayed with Tom during his entire drive home to Santa Ana; still amazed at her intellect—having taken notes throughout the *entire* novel. He may never write another piece of work on the properties of entropy, but he'd make sure he did as much re-search as he had for *Ascension* and *Interstate 5* (*A Lost Legacy* not having *any* academic properties in it) before deciding to sit down and write the first few pages of his next novel.

• • •

HOURS LATER, NIKOLAI SOKOLOV'S ears were still ringing from the blast the transport vehicle took upon its arrival to the military outpost where his basic training to become a soldier of the USSR's Spetsnaz GRU; inspired to join (instead of avoiding the draft like his father had in the '60s) when he heard of the 154th Separate Spetsnaz Battalion's involvement in Шторм-333 (Shtorm-333) as a youth of fifteen years of age—wanting (nay, hoping) to see the same kind of (in his eyes, honor-able and glorified) action the generation of soldiers before him had the pleasure of taking part in. He hoped, if he had a chance to play his cards right, to advance to the rank of Lieutenant General before the turn of the century—if not by the turn of the decade. Lieutenant General in eight years? It seemed manageable, he thought. This speculated path for his successful military career was the only thing (currently) getting him through—what would be—the most rigorous part of it all; recruitment training. "Сделайте свое самое худшее," he said as he lay in his cot; waiting for the sun to rise. "Do your worst."

"Встаньте, мудак," an officer screamed; standing over Nikolai's cot. Before he had a chance to respond to the officer's demand, Nikolai felt the pull of gravity drag him to the floor; another officer pulling the cot from underneath him. It couldn't possibly be sunrise, he thought—he had only closed his eyes for a moment, it seemed. "I said get up, asshole," the officer repeated as Nikolai got to his hands and knees. "What, do you not speak Russian? Idiot!"

Nikolai looked up to find the other recruits were experiencing the same treatment; responding to their wake up call with an energy one could only exude when they were experiencing the combined biological reaction of a lack of oxygen to the brain due to a lack of sleep (delirium) while reacting to an unknown, potential threat (adrenaline); rising to their feet in a matter of seconds—finding the threat to be an officer—and snapping to attention; hoping their response time was in a reasonable enough manner. Nikolai, having remained on the floor—on his hands and knees—felt his awaking officer's steel-toed boot kick him square in left side of his ribs; his body falling limp to the cement floor; gasping desperately for air. "Look, everyone," he yelled, grabbing the attention of everyone else in the room. "We have ourselves a pizda; a kiska mal`chik—get up, pussy boy!"

"отвяжись," Nikolai breathed as he rose to his feet.

"What did you say to me?"

"I said *fuck off*," he repeated. "What's the matter, are you deaf?"

The shift in gravity (the officer, not taking Nikolai's insubordinate remark lightly—refusing to allow a recruit to humiliate him on the first official day of training—grabbed Nikolai by the neckline of his shirt and kneed him in the stomach) was sudden; the weight of his body meeting the cement floor a second time. Throughout the room, he could hear the hushed whispers of the other recruits talking about him; some of them making small bets on how long he would last before he was either thrown out or *killed*. He laughed. Compared to what his father used to do to him growing up (they couldn't see the scars on his back from the countless lashings he had received in his younger years whenever he got home from school nor the cigarette burns from when he was a small infant), this was child's play. Do your worst, his mind repeated; refusing to get up from the floor; the officer continuing to bark his incessant demands for Nikolai to join the other recruits—a smile finding Nikolai's face as he got to his feet and joined the others outside on the field. Off to a good start, he thought. For the rest of recruitment training the officer (whom Nikolai would, later that day—during chow—come to find was *actually* Grigory Stepanov; an old classmate from his childhood days; a couple years older than him but was held back due to his inability to get along well with others at age five) kept his eye on him. Despite their first impressions of each other, Grigory grew to appreciate, and (to a small extent) admire, Nikolai's disregard for the chain of command. Yes, the point of training was to break the individual down and turn him into a soldier, but Grigory could see the fire which burned in Nikolai's eyes; a fire he had seen in very few people who came through here. Nikolai Sokolov: a man born to live and die on the battlefield; a warrior at heart—with the mouth of a feral дворняжка (mongrel).

"Are you trying to get yourself killed, you *idiot?*" the recruit in front of Nikolai turned to ask him while they waited in line for their first drill of the morning: pain management training; starting off easy with taking full-force punches to the chest from their commanding officers without flinching, to getting burning cinder blocks broken over their stomachs with a sledgehammer—ending the day with each recruit taking turns being dragged through the base while being bound to the tail-end of a combat vehicle. "I hear that officer is well-renown for having the most recruits leaving training in a body bag—and you just got on his bad side; on the first day, even," the recruit continued as the line slowly edged forward.

Nikolai scoffed, turning back to find Stepanov had made his way to the next barracks to awaken the next batch of unsuspecting recruits from their lackluster slumber. "He doesn't frighten me," he replied, returning his attention to the other recruit. "I've honestly had worse growing up with my old-man—the fucker wasn't even a *military man*. He somehow dodged the draft to be with my mother who was pregnant with yours truly. The man was only good at two things: putting away a bottle of vodka and how to make a riding crop effective *enough* to make one bleed for—what felt like—hours. That officer? He can fuck off."

The day had been a long one. Every recruit lay in pain as they attempted to find sleep; today's events having taken a toll on *all* of them. To his left, Nikolai could hear another recruit masturbating underneath his covers—hoping to distract himself from the road rash his lower half had sustained that afternoon. It didn't take long for the rest of the recruits to join in on the unsophisticated act of groping themselves to the point of sexual release. Bringing his own sheet over his head, hoping to block out the obscene smells which would soon consume the entire barracks, Nikolai closed his eyes and prayed for sleep; hoping to pass out before the repulsive smell of semen filled the room.

· · ·

"Pierce, why must you refuse to understand what I am trying to say? I have reason to believe *someone* is sabotaging our work. How *else* would you explain our continuous failures after our miraculous success with Subject No. 2773? It doesn't make *any* sense. Please—my friend—if you can think of another way to explain our misfortune, by all means, go ahead and do your best to convince me otherwise."

"Calm down, Theodore. There's no need for such a paranoid accusation. Perhaps we're—"

"Stay out of this, Elizabeth. There is no need for *you* to get involved between matters which only concern myself and Pierce."

"There's no need for that, Theodore. Elizabeth is in the same line of work as us; if she desires to speak her mind of the subject, please, let her have the floor."

"Thank you, Pierce."

"It's nothing."

"But she's only started working in the field of reverse engineering *four* years ago. Before that she specified in monitoring the temperature levels and brainwaves of the Subjects housed in the old NICU wing of the hospital; the equivalent of learning one's ABC's in comparison to something such as this!"

"If I recall, *Theo-dore*, our *miraculous* achievement which you're speaking about—bringing Cordelia out of her comatose state—didn't occur until *my* involvement with the project. Many might call it a coincidence—perhaps it was—but one mustn't rule out the possibility *I* could have had something to do with the success of her reanimation."

"If that *were* the case, *you* would have been able to undo the undermining of our work. I told you, Pierce, she wasn't ready to be brought in to work on taking down the program. She's still too young, in my opinion; too impulsive and proud to lay aside her ego to *allow* herself to be fully dedicated—with*out* distraction."

"Now, now, you two, there's no need to belittle one's contribution to our efforts nor the need to consider another field of work to be any less important to what we are hoping to—one day—achieve. Now, let's put our animosity toward one another, as well as any half-baked conspiracy theories pointing at sabotage aside and get back to work; Subject No. 2773—"

"Cordelia."

"—Cordelia. Subject No. 2773. In the end, it's all the same. Anyway, as I was saying, she was only the first in, *hopefully*, dozens—if not *hundreds*—of lives we can successfully *unplug* from *Project Arcadia*. Now, please you two, let's get back to work; we've wasted enough time as it is having this rather senseless conversation."

"But—"

"Not another word. Please. None of us have all the time in the world to continue on with this—especially *them*."

Hoping to make his escape before Theodore or Elizabeth had the chance to drag the fruitless exchange of paranoia and insults out any longer than they had already, Pierce rushed toward the door which led to the lobby, taking the elevator up to his office on the twelfth floor; the floors above having been deemed uninhabitable after the war. Normally, he would have stayed and helped the other scientists work toward (re)discovering the solution to *successfully* thawing out the Subjects who—to put it bluntly—lived in the basement of the hospital.

Meanwhile, back on the third floor, Theodore and Elizabeth began rereading—for the Nth time—what was left of a series of textbooks that had survived the initial blast waves from the war which had taken place nearly four-hundred years ago. Elizabeth—having only known the world as it had been since—often found herself wondering what life must've been like before the bombs fell; if the city skyline was as majestic as she had read in what books managed to remain intact: her favorite being the 1939 classic by Raymond Chandler, *The Big Sleep*. She would often catch herself coming back to it during the nights she found she couldn't sleep—even after a long, tiresome day spent working with Theodore and the other self-taught scientists and mathematical engineers; hoping to stumble across the solution to waking up the rest of the Subjects which resided in the underground levels of the facility—having grown fond of the detective story which took place within the worn pages of the novel.

Theodore cursed under his breath, loud enough to bring Elizabeth back to the grim reality which was the third floor of the hospital—designated as the *Quiet Room* centuries ago by the first round of survivors who had holed themselves up in the building to monitor those who chose to place themselves into suspended animation. She turned to find Theodore standing over the corpse of their latest failure: Subject No. 2866, also known as—according to his E.B.C (electronic birth certificate)—Marcus Craven.

"What is it?"

"Excuse me?"

"You still seem distracted, standing over our latest. . .endeavor. . . Are you *that* convinced someone is sabotaging our work? Why would *anyone* do that, though? You've worked with every scientist who's spent time down here. You've seen how diligent everyone has been; having spent—what—thirty years down here, working beside them. It's clear, to all of us, that our goal is to revive *these* people and rehabilitate them so they can live alongside us in this unfortunate, *godforsaken* landscape we have had the misfortune of calling our home."

"Elizabeth. May I please speak my mind; without interruption?"

"If you believe it will help you *focus* on the task at hand, by all means Theodore, speak your damned mind."

Theodore's eyes fell back down to the unfortunate, lifeless body of Subject No. 2866—which still lay on the operating table, taking a moment before letting the words fall from his tongue.

"I hate to say this, but I believe Pierce *might be the one behind* our never-ending streak of misfortune. . ."

∙ ∙ ∙

THE CALIFORNIA HIGHWAY was more rigid than usual; Cal-Trans' funding having been cut by the current administration's state budget cuts; California's roads falling more and more into disrepair with each passing month. Despite the poor condition of the road, it seemed it was during a long and arduous drive—much like the one Tom found himself experiencing during his trip home—one's mind would often drift; drift off (subconsciously) to the part of the mind where it seemed most thoughts would lose themselves; unable to be extracted for later use— no matter how simple or complex the topic in question happened to be; e.g. the number of shots fired during the assassination of JFK; whether or not I left the stove running when I left for work—having slept past my twelve alarms, rushing my way through breakfast; if humans would ever have the capability to travel forward (as well as backward) through space-time—proving many physicists wrong, that the amount of energy required to accomplish the task of bending time to create a space-time loop *would not* dematerialize (ultimately killing) any living thing which tried to traverse through the loop; or—and this was a personal favorite for Tom's unsuspecting mind—whether or not the world would ever experience *absolute silence* ever again. These ponderous, subconscious streams-of-conscious thinking such as this bothered Tom to no end, since he was usually away from his laptop or without a notepad and a pen when such thoughts occurred; today's random thought—which would soon find itself lost until three o'clock in the morning three days later, while he was asleep—was about the possibility one might be living in an alternate reality; one where their life shared little to no similarities to the one they were currently living. Personally, Tom liked to make the joke that *this* life—this version of himself—was the only one where he didn't wind up becoming a serial killer, having found solace in a journal when he was in his early twenties instead of cracking open his father's gun safe—taking every pistol, shotgun, rifle (along with every illegal firearm) his father had managed to collect over the years—and going on a murderous rampage at his local Walmart Super Center.

A flash of light lit up the horizon. Its sudden occurrence going unnoticed at first. Tom, having been distracted by the gag-reel his mind had spun for him to make the road trip back home less insufferable — not a fan of sitting for long periods of time without having a moment to stretch his legs; although, too stubborn to make a quick (unnecessary, he thought) stop at a gas station to allow himself such a break — thought his eyes were playing tricks on him; having driven from Redding to Bakersfield without taking a break other than getting gasoline in Stockton. A second flash. This one grabbing the attention of Tom's distracted mind; bringing his lethargic gaze to the skyline. He blinked. He blinked again, doubting the unimaginable scene which lay before him. In the distance he saw the billowing smoke cap of a mushroom cloud rising from the horizon; near the Los Angeles area. It didn't take long after for a second wall of smoke to make itself known off to the west; Santa Barbara, he guessed as he continued traveling south — too in shock to move his foot to the brake pedal and bring his vehicle to a complete stop.

As he continued to drive southbound, Tom, still in shock, stared on in horror as the scenery ahead of him became engulfed by the aggressive heat blast which came tumbling in his direction. It was surreal. Having watched a countless amount of videos about thermonuclear detonations on YouTube Tom never would have thought, in his lifetime, he would get to be a witness to the end of the world — knowing if one country had decided to launch their nukes, the other wasn't far behind. Before he knew it, he too found himself lost in the ravaging heat blast as it continued to expand outward from *Ground Zero*. The impact didn't seem to affect the trajectory of his car; still moving forward down the 99 — only the glass of his vehicle shattering; exposing him to the effects of radioactive flash burn. However, despite the conditions of his current predicament, he felt fine. This is the end of the world as we know it and I feel fine, he laughed as the nightmare continued, finding the surrealism of the situation a comic affair.

A light tapping on his driver's side window woke Tom from the nightmare, disorienting him, at first, until he found his footing and realized he had fallen asleep in the parking lot of the Stockton gas station where he decided to fill up his tank before continuing his drive home. Paranoia took over; making it impossible for him to move. This wasn't the first time he had had such vivid, detailed imagery play itself out in a dreamscape. After all, it was a *dream* similar to the one he had just experienced which inspired the concept of what would become the *Transmigration Trilogy* six years ago. Timid, Tom managed to look around to find the sun had already begun to set off to the west; a young man—young enough to still be confused for a high school student if no one bothered to ask his age—still tapping on his window, asking if he were okay. He felt embarrassed. During the book tours of *Discord Avenue*, *In Flawless Strokes*, and *Ascension* Tom had been able to shift from one city to the next without feeling the adverse effects from the months of endless travel until his head hit his bedroom pillow back home. Lately, however, he would often find himself dozing off in between flights and during the brief moments when he would have a moment to himself in complete silence; a rarity these days.

Still dazed from the unexpected nap, Tom took another glance at the surrounding cityscape. It had been a little over a decade since he'd visited the city of Stockton, having come down with his uncle and grandmother on an impromptu road trip; a (hopeful?) trip down memory lane for everyone involved, having either grown up or spent a substantial amount of time (summers, holidays, birthdays) in the small, neighboring town of Tracy. If Tom thought the city had become a decadent slum back then, his younger self would be appalled by the amount of degradation which transpired in the forthcoming years since his last visit: the housing market in shambles—having never recovered from the second Great Depression brought on by Trump's border tax and repeal of Obamacare—hate crime/gang-related violence at a record high (you couldn't go a day without hearing about the death of a minority or member of the LGBT community, it seemed; desensitizing the public whenever a news story decided to cover the tragic incident). The world could use a nuclear detonation, he thought. It might actually do the place a favor. . . give it a chance to finally *rebuild* itself.

As the final remnants of the sun slipped behind the horizon, leaving the surrounding landscape in darkness, Tom turned the keys in the ignition, bringing his vehicle to life, and, with a shallow sense of urgency (forgetting about the young man tapping at his window, having not thanked him for the sudden wake up tap), edged his way out of the gas station parking lot and continued his drive southbound toward Santa Ana; toward home.

• • •

THE LIGHTS FLICKERED throughout the building, causing everyone to quit what they were doing and stare up nervously at the ceiling; having suffered the chaos of a blackout earlier that year. As it became apparent the electricity wasn't going to cut out, they all returned to their prior dispositions; hoping to find a copy of whichever film they desired to rent for the weekend. Having not been bothered by the occurrence (having actually hoped the power would go out, allowing him to head home early, finding his job boring) Nathan Luckman turned his attention to the computer screen to find it was only 7:45pm. He sighed, knowing he would be stuck here for another two hours before he could lock up for the night and head home. Having loved the weekly visits to Blockbuster with his father as a child, his father being a cinephile and wishing to share his love for films with all of his children, Nathan had often dreamed of the day when he could get a job so he could apply here and become a Blockbuster associate; helping indecisive families in their quest to find the *perfect* film for Friday Movie Night. The reality, however, wasn't as luxurious as he had pictured — most of his shift being spent ignored by passing customers as they came and went; weekend entertainment under arm as they marched out the door, the child skipping in excitement—eager to place the VHS tape into the VCR and watch the magic unfold before their young, anticipating eyes.

Off in the distance, somewhere in the back-end of the store, Nathan saw a couple of his friends loitering, waiting for the moment he would announce the store would be closing for the night so they could "rescue" him from his "prison" and head over to Katherine's house so they could sneak into her father's liquor cabinet and end the night in a drunken stupor while they got high smoking cheap weed and mescaline and listened to the latest Pearl Jam record, *Vitalogy*; it being rumored to have a song about Kurt Cobain and his suicide earlier that year. Looking around the store, making sure no one was wandering around aimlessly (prompting him, by order of his supervisor, to ask if they needed help finding anything), Nathan decided to leave the front counter and join his friends in the corner—in the Horror/Slasher section of the store. As he approached his circle of friends he could hear Daniel going on about the possibility of the DVD replacing the VHS by the end of the century.

"Shut the fuck up, Danny," Phillip, a film purist—it being his desired major in college—scoffed at Daniel's theory. "The DVD, much like the compact disc, will be a fad; nothing more. The VHS tape has been around for almost two decades, man—the cassette tape, almost thirty. You can't replace the purity of analog with digital. It can't be done. It just can't. Besides, what are they going to do with every film made *before* 1997? The essence of great films like *Jaws* and *The Empire Strikes Back* will be lost during the conversion process. That's *my* theory, anyway."

"Jesus, not this again." Nathan—who had remained quiet during his stealthy approach, snuck up behind Phillip as he kept his eyes on Katherine. "When are you two going to shut up about this topic?"

Katherine laughed as Phillip jumped at the sound of Nathan's question, "I'm certain these two will still be talking about it well into the 21st century; only the context will change—depending on the course of history, whether or not the DVD replaces the *oh so holy* VHS tape." She lifted her arms into the air and waved them frantically, mocking the other two in the group.

After locking up the building, the rest of his shift having gone by rather quick (having spent the majority of his time bullshitting with his friends), Nathan hopped in Katherine's beat-up Toyota Camry—the guitar-driven interlude of "Heresy" from Nine Inch Nails' *The Downward Spiral* pouring from the speakers; the thumping synthetic drums vibrating the entire car as the song carried on. "Still on a Trent Reznor binge, are we?" he yelled over the noise as he buckled himself in. Katherine nodded to the beat in response to his question. It had been months since she'd played what used to be her favorite album, *In Utero*; still finding it haunting to hear Kurt's voice—the lyrics to certain songs having taken on a whole new meaning since his unfortunate suicide back in early April.

As the late night lights of Los Angeles continued to pass them by, the soundtrack of their trip having moved on to the 'lighter-side' with the likes of Sunny Day Real Estate's *Diary*—an album (and band) he had yet to fully warm up to, Nathan found himself lost in a daydream; an often occurrence for him. With this one he found himself and his friends living their lives how they imagined them to turn out: Phillip becoming a high-in-demand low-budget director, joining the ranks of Stanley Kubrick and David Lynch; Daniel's band, Nucleus (Superchunk-lite Katherine liked to call them), having signed to an independent label; picking up steam with their sophomore record *Palinoia*; Katherine's affinity for politics having finally paid off, having been inspired by First Lady, Hillary Clinton, to pursue a career in politics—becoming a representative for the state of California: helping pass legislation which would legalize the use of marijuana; while Nathan found minor success as a talk show host, similar to that of Charlie Rose—interviewing successful actors, writers, musicians, politicians and other forms of celebrity.

It helped to think about the future. To think the years to come held something worth looking forward to kept Nathan from feeling the same as every other young adult around his age felt; hopeless and completely fucked—the previous generations (the Silent Generation and the Baby Boomers) having ruined the American Dream in several ways: the failed War on Drugs, the deconstruction of the *nuclear family* (a majority of Gen Xers being children of divorce), government funding having been diverted away from programs for children and, instead, directed toward the elderly population. . .it seemed the country had lost itself to greed; the Silent Generation feeling entitled (somehow? having won WWII single-handed) to whatever came their way—leaving nothing for the future generations. There were moments where even Nathan had to admit he could feel the weight of the world crushing his spirit. Not even the optimistic daydreams he would attempt to lose himself in could prevent the encroaching cynicism (something his generation had become well known for in the Media) from taking over him for a brief period of time.

A flash of light stretched across the night sky, scaring Nathan back to the humble realm of reality; a yelp escaping his tongue, bringing Katherine's attention to his pale-stricken face.

"Scared of a little lightning, are we?" she chuckled, elbowing him in the shoulder. "Don't worry, little guy," running her hand over the top of his head, messing up his hair. "We'll be home safe so the *big bad lightning* can't come down and get you."

"Fuck you," he laughed as the car continued to carry them onward toward their destination—to her house; Daniel and Phillip waiting impatiently for them so they could begin their late-night activities. The thought of ending the night with the sounds of Jawbreaker (Daniel and Phillip having walked home)—cross-faded and passed out while still spooning Katherine's smooth, naked body until the blinding rays of the Saturday morning sun came pouring through her bedroom window; the quiet hum of the stereo still playing—the cassette having ended hours ago—lulling them both back to sleep; Katherine's right leg wrapping around Nathan's ankle as she pressed her warm buttocks onto his cock; his morning erection mindlessly searching for the opening of her cunt while Nathan continued to sleep, dreaming of James Bond-esque spy adventures: preventing the villain from bringing the world to the brink of nuclear annihilation—driving off into the sunset with actress Talisa Soto; her gentle silhouette disappearing into the seat of the car while she teased him with the promise of road head; a warm summer breeze blowing through her hair—the scene fading to black, epic music playing in the background as the end credits began to crawl. . .

2

ON THE WALL, left of his desk, hung an old prewar portrait of Los Angeles; the city skyline lit up at sunset — the streets teeming with life underneath a violet blue sky; a full moon shining in the background. A life the city hadn't seen in centuries. Pierce Alexandre Needham often found himself admiring it like he used to when he was a child and his grandfather, Alexandre Oliver Needham, was one of the Chief Directors (alongside Theodore's grandfather, Mitchell Emmett Webb); unknowingly having grown envious of the beauty everyone before the war got to marvel at every night as they drove onward toward their unknown destinations. He'd found it hidden deep in a storage closet on one of the lower floors — his father having hated the picture, believing it to be a poor reminder of the way things were; being a progressive man, he believed the residents of the hospital should dispose of any memorabilia which could bring forth false memories of a world long forgotten; feeling the deceptive nostalgia would prevent the idea of *progress*; settling on the illusory misconceptions of the past. Like his grandfather, however, Pierce found the artifact calming; believing (like his grandfather used to) that, one day, those who survived the war would be able to rebuild the world they were left to call theirs; bringing it back to its former glory. At his desk he kept another set of mementos his father would have also deemed *unacceptable* to keep and demand they be stowed away, if not destroyed on sight: a Los Angeles Angels baseball cap, bat, ball, and mitt. Despite not knowing the official rules of the sport—it having been an outside activity from the prewar era and not a single soul having shown any real interest in exploring the ways of their ancestors—Pierce found the four items (much like the portrait of the city of Los Angeles) to be soothing in nature. Had he ever found the time to settle down and start a family in his younger years, he would've found the time to make a trip out to Anaheim Stadium to find a second mitt so they could at least toss the ball back and forth during his off hours. Thankfully, his luck in the foreign (to him) domain of romance had taken a positive turn lately with the slow, progressing relationship with his latest assistant in the Quiet Room—Elizabeth Hestler. She was thirteen years younger than him (a questionable age gap according to the other inhabitants of the hospital, including Theodore), but, despite her age, her intelligence made her seem more mature; making her age irrelevant in his eyes.

A knock at the door, his attention was brought back to the world around him. "Yes? Who is it?"

Only silence met him in response.

Not a fan of being ignored, especially if it interrupted his *office hours*, Pierce left his desk and, doing his best to remain quiet (wearing a well-worn set of cap toed dress shoes; his grandfather's—as well as his father's—at one point), tip-toed to the door; hoping to sneak up on the unsuspecting visitor and ask them to either state their business or leave him to return back to his *work*. His pace was slow, having to forfeit his speed for stealth; the leather soles of his shoes making the task of remaining silent more of a chore than he would have preferred. It annoyed him how long it was taking him to reach his destination; something which would normally take him seconds, had he been able to walk to the door at a *normal*—less ridiculously executed—pace. When he (finally!) reached the door, however, he found no one standing near the entrance or along the hallway. Impossible, he thought. Who in this building (besides a child—their steps lighter than that of a grown up's) could traverse *successfully* down a linoleum floor without making a sound? He called out; his voice echoing throughout the empty hallways of the entire floor.

Still nothing.

The undisturbed silence of the hallway leaving Pierce on edge, he began to quietly hum the melody to a lullaby his mother would sing to help him fall asleep when he was a child; having been afraid of the lightning and thunder storms which would rage during the colder nights of his youth.

> Close your eyes, and sleep tight,
> Pray you'll wake up, come morning.
> Let's pretend the midnight thunder's
> A drifter shooting at the moon!
> So close your eyes now, little angel
> And dream of 1992.

Pierce had always found the date confusing as a child, having not known the calendar year the bombs fell. It wasn't until he started his schooling at the age of eight—having began his educational career two years sooner than the other children—when he was told the tragic (inaccurate unbeknownst to him and everyone who was told) story of the day the world, having fought for decades, reached a point of no return and launched a *Mutually Assured Destruction* nuclear massacre on the entire planet; not a single city was left untouched by the onslaught of thermonuclear annihilation. It was believed Russia was the first to send their rockets off toward the unsuspecting countries, leading the current President of the United States of America, William Jefferson Clinton, to retaliate; sending everything the country had to their preordained destinations; leaving *nothing* for the people of Russia to claim for their own if anyone managed to survive the fallout. Once the teacher, Mrs. Somerset, finished educating the children about the most horrific point in human history, she asked if anyone had any questions. Only two hands managed to rise toward the ceiling: Pierce's and Theodore's.

Amused, Mrs. Somerset chuckled. During her twelve years of teaching the children between ages ten and twelve she'd never encountered curious minds after telling them the destructive tale of the World's final moments before being blown beyond recognition for the initial survivors of the fallout. It didn't surprise her, however, when she saw it was the Directors' sons; Theodore Webb and Pierce Alexandre Needham (she never understood why the Needhams requested they be announced by their *full names*. To her, it seemed superfluous). "Yes, you," Somerset pointed in Theodore's direction—showing favor to the eldest of the two. "What's your question?"

The twelve year old, lowering his hand, declared, "My grandpa says, according to his past travels, there is a good chance there are some cities up north and to the east which remained untouched by the bombs. But, if that's true, why haven't we decided to leave this place and head there?"

"Excellent question," said Somerset. "This will be answered for you next year when you move forward in your educational career with Mr. Holcomb. Yes, you?" this time she pointed at Pierce.

Pierce's eyes widened. Nervous, he lowered his own hand and stammered, "Whe- When did the war ha- happen? Like, how- how long ago was it from today?"

Mrs. Somerset's face dropped into a stoic state. It seemed, to the students, not even *she* knew the answer. It wouldn't be until he was finished with his elementary and secondary years of schooling, studying under his and Theodore's father in the field of neurology, when he would be told, one night—after a night of drinking the building's homemade brew—the date in question when he was eight years old was January 25, 1995. Upon hearing the date, a drunken Pierce couldn't help but laugh. It amused him that the mind of a child couldn't deduce the connection of the numbers relating to a prewar date. Three-hundred sixty-nine years, according to the Tachyon Era based calendar the city and its surrounding settlements had agreed to live by, had passed since the reemergence of the initial survivors who awoke from suspended animation after an equivocal amount of time had passed—later found out to be January 1, 2000 by the building's statistician when his great-great-grandfather (Albert Tobias Booker) was just a newborn.

Circling back to the door of his office, having walked the perimeter of the twelfth floor—having satisfied his paranoid curiosity—Pierce laughed at the mnemonic effect a simple (albeit disturbing upon further reflection) lullaby could have on him; only hoping to calm his nerves, originally, as he examined the hallways, looking for a non-existing trespasser. He refused, however, to acknowledge the knock he had heard, which had led him to take this unnecessary walk, as a hallucinatory occurrence.

A flickering light ahead of him brought Pierce's attention to the ceiling. He couldn't remember the last time Chuck, the building's self-taught mechanic, had been up to the twelfth floor to change the lights —had it been months? a year? longer?—but the hallway's yellowish hue had become apparent to him, thanks to the faltering light fixture. I'll be sure to write up a maintenance chit and have Candice deliver it to him in the early hours of tomorrow, he took mental note as he turned the corner to find Theodore standing outside his office; fiddling with a non-existent piece of chalk as he scribbled imaginary notes into the æther—his mentally projected blackboard—occasionally erasing a mistake (which did not *physically exist*) with exhausted frustration; a nervous tick from his days as an apprentice to his father which he never managed to shake.

"Something bothering you, old friend?"

Theodore turned to face Pierce, his hand still in the air—holding the invisible piece of chalk, awaiting the mental cue so he could continue working on his invisible calculations. "Yes," he replied. "You're needed in the lower levels. It seems we're experiencing *yet another* malfunction with one of the Subjects' temporal mainframe. He appears to be caught in a limbo between consciousness and stasis. Elizabeth and Winsome are looking into it as we speak, but, given your past success with putting a Subject back under and reconnecting them to the *Arcadian Sequence*, we would prefer it if you joined us for this one."

Pierce sighed. So much for taking some time to relax, he thought as he motioned for Theodore to join him at the elevator so they could descend into the lower, underground, levels of the building to (hopefully) take care of the situation before they lost *another* to an unfortunate mishap.

"What the fuck took you two so long?" Elizabeth screamed as she and Winsome continued to do the best they could to keep the Subject's vitals stable. "Friedrich and I have no idea what we're doing, to be honest. Sure, I can monitor a Subject's vitals, but when it comes to code red malfunctions I'm out of my element!"

"See? I told you she wasn't ready to join us," whispered Theodore as he and Pierce marched toward the other two scientists. "She should've stayed in the NICU wing, where she *belonged*."

Pierce kept quiet as they continued toward the situation, throwing a look of contempt in Theodore's direction, silently telling him to hold his tongue before he went any further with his caustic remarks at Elizabeth's expense. Theodore, despite remaining oblivious to Pierce's sharp glare, finished his passive aggressive evaluation of Elizabeth's capability (or lack thereof) to be allowed access in the Quiet Room and *lower* levels of the hospital; interacting *directly* with the Subjects. Romantic feelings aside—going by her academic scores during her internship, Pierce felt Elizabeth could be the most capable out of *all of them* after she had spent enough time among the cryochambers; learning how they worked and how to properly maintain them.

As the two Directors approached the Subject in question Pierce read his designation number to find it was one they had had issues with since the Subject's birth thirty-two years ago: Subject No. 2990. Pierce sighed heavily. If it hadn't been for his father still being the Director on his family's side—Theodore's father having been forced to resign early when he fell ill (later being diagnosed with a malignant brain tumor; rumor spreading among the citizens of the building that Theodore *somehow* was the cause of his father's misfortune)—he would have had the child euthanized, knowing the high probability he would become an issue for him and the facility later in life. It didn't help him, once he became Director, to find Elizabeth had developed an affinity for the Subject while they were both children (he only being two years older than her). If he had decided to pull the plug on him now he would *have* to deal with the unfortunate resentment of someone he'd grown to care for in the past few years. Instead, he chose to put his personal feelings for the Subject aside and help Elizabeth and Winsome steady the Subject's vitals and—once the Subject's mind was at ease—make sure there were no other complications before heading back up to the twelfth floor and *finally* (hopefully!) get a chance to sit back and relax his brain; forgetting about the worries of the small—often claustrophobic—world around him.

"The Subject is finally stabilizing," Winsome, monitoring the dimly lit monitor. "Elizabeth, would you take over while I begin tracking his brainwaves to make sure he's sequencing accordingly?"

Switching positions with Winsome without a word of protest, Elizabeth stood over the Subject; her eyes moving up and down—taking in his quiescent state with a mild, sympathetic gaze. Although he would never admit to such an emotion getting the better of him, Pierce felt jealousy for a man who had yet to live an *actual* day of his life. How could someone, especially someone like Elizabeth, develop such a strong *emotional* bond with a person who had spent their entire life trapped behind a plate of glass. It didn't make sense to him.

Two hours later, as he sat in his office on the twelfth floor (continuing to stare at the portrait of Los Angeles; further fueling his subconscious envy for the people of the past), Pierce's mind couldn't shake the image of Elizabeth holding Subject No. 2990's hand in hers; gently stroking the tops of his fingers with her thumb—having opened the Subject's chamber; a risky maneuver on her part—while Winsome continued to fumble about the room, trying to take accurate readings of the Subject's temporal sequencing; yelling at Elizabeth from across the room when he realized what she had done.

Hoping to distract himself from his jealous thoughts, he turned his gaze to the window—taking in the panoramic view of the world outside; its lack of color (in comparison to the well-adored photograph of the city; consisting only of various shades of gray and scattered traces of vibrant greens and dying browns catching his eye) disgusting him.

• • •

SOAKED IN A COLD SWEAT, Tom rose from his pillow feeling anxious, having forced himself awake from a dream he hadn't had in years; finding himself lost in a rundown facility (unable to move by his own volition), surrounded by a small group of people who were foreign to him while they picked and prodded at his brain. A schizophrenic's nightmare his friend, Jared (a psychology major), would call it one night during a neighborhood barbecue this past summer. Still breathing heavily, he turned to find his wife, Sarah, sound asleep; snoring loudly, lost somewhere inside a dream of her own. Normally, she would have been stirred awake by Tom's sudden movements, but tonight—with her recent decision to begin taking Melatonin—not even a catastrophic tectonic shift of the San Andreas Fault could wake her, it seemed. Hoping to calm himself from the dream, he turned to his alarm clock to see what time it was. It read 4:28am. An exhausted sigh escaped his lungs. He knew he wouldn't be able to fall back asleep right away; only having two hours before his wife's first of seven alarms would begin going off to (attempt to) wake her so she could begin her first day back at her job as a ninth grade Earth Science teacher at their local high school— he *also* taught at the same high school; twelfth grade English.

Before he could get a chance to readjust himself to make the next two hours drift by more comfortably their dog, Daisy, poked her nose through the door (opening it enough for the rest of her mid-sized body to fit through), hopped merrily onto the foot of the bed and, with her tail wagging uncontrollably, began to bark 'Good Morning!' for the entire household to hear. Sarah's limp body managed to mumble, "It's your turn to take her outside so she can go potty." before dozing off again to find solace in her dreamworld once more; Daisy having been silenced by Sarah's soft spoken voice; just the sound of her tail wagging in the air breaking the silence (hitting the edge of the bed with each jubilant stroke). Why not, he thought, it's not like I'll be getting any more sleep this morning. "Alright, Daisy," he motioned her towards the door, feigning excitement, "let's go potty!"

When Tom went to reach for the doorknob his half-formed fist met only wood; the doorknob being on the other side of the fixture. Odd, he thought, I could've swore the knob was on the right side of the door. Not letting the anomaly of the position of the doorknob get to him, taking his drowsiness into account for the mistaken placement, he reached for the correct side and opened the door; Daisy rushing past him to head for the doggy-door so she could go about her business, which included barking at the morning blue jays which would frequent their backyard; waking the neighbors in the process.

The early morning sky of Santa Ana, still dark, the only source of light coming from the waning crescent of the moon (the street lights which *normally* illuminated the scene as well having shut off early, having not been re-calibrated with the time change due to Daylight Savings) was soothing to him, despite Daisy's incessant barking. Like a camera taking a photograph, Tom's eyes and ears captured the minimalist composition the world decided to give him—removing the negative, leaving only a representation of silent grace as the earth continued to spin—the moon falling into the horizon to let the sun have its moment of praise among those who would be waking up soon to go about their day in a zombie-like trudge; hoping the hours fly by so they may (once again) return to their slumber, only to repeat the process for another twenty to thirty years. Had it not been for his time away from home every few years, Tom would find himself in the same banal disposition; existentially adrift in a never-ending flow of time; finding himself drowning slowly as the years continued to press on. . .

"Could you tell your dog to shut the fuck up?" a voice, male, came screaming from an open bedroom window; given the direction, the Holloway household. "*Some of us* are still trying to sleep!"

"Sorry, Quinton," Tom shouted as he clapped his hands together twice and whistled at Daisy—telling her it was time to head back inside. "I'll be sure to have a talk with Daisy; let her know which times it's *appropriate* to bark uncontrollably at the neighborhood birds." He couldn't help but laugh, finding Quinton's complaint insipid and audacious enough to find it humorous. Following shortly behind Daisy Tom could've swore he heard Quinton spout off, "Fuck off, you overly pretentious cocksucker. . ."the violent sound of the window being slammed shut echoing through the crisp morning air.

Making his way back to the bedroom in complete darkness—using the constant thumping of Daisy's tail hitting the wall as she waited by the door—without warning, a wave of drowsiness washed over Tom. "Thanks, Mr. Sandman," he whispered sardonically. "Visit me when I have. . ." he checked his watch, "less than an hour and a half to try and (hopefully. . .) catch a few more Zs before starting my day. . ."

The dry heat of late August met the Dolin family without remorse, the temperature already in the mid 80s before eight o'clock; Tom and Sarah's eldest, Christie (10 years old) attempting to soothe their youngest, Benjamin (9 months old), while Matilda (their middle child —6 years old) sang "It's hot outside, it's so hot outside. . ." as they both loaded up the van so they could drop the youngest at their Aunt Paige and Uncle Daniel's for the day and take the eldest two to their elementary school before heading for the high school so they both could begin their day. Along the way, after dropping Christie and Matilda off, Sarah brought up the topic of Tom's book tour for his latest novel—having come in late last night, everyone else having already headed for bed. Unable to hold back laughter, Tom took a left turn (the road being surprisingly empty for a "first day back" Monday morning. Once the bout of laughter died down, he went to tell her the awkward moment when the young woman approached him to tell him she masturbates to a particular scene from *In Flawless Strokes*.

"Oh good God!" screamed Sarah, smacking Tom on the thigh. "Why would someone tell *anyone* that kind of information? Also, why from *that* book? There were *far more* sensual scenes in *Interstate 5* she could've used for her *inspiration*."

Tom was shocked to hear his wife had *actually* read his novels; having not been a fan of reading anything unless it were a textbook—finding fiction (of any kind) a waste of one's time. "Hold up," he said, turning into the high school parking lot, finding an empty spot in the staff parking, and turning the van off. "When did *you* find the time—let alone the energy—to read one of *my* novels?"

Feigning feeling insulted by her husband's remark, Sarah turned, "I've read every single one of your books! Since *Discord Avenue* and *In Flawless Strokes* were both semi-autobiographical and there were *some* historical aspects—albeit inaccurate for the purpose of your novel's fictional plot—I was able to push through the fact I was reading a thousand-or-so pages of *made up bullshit*." She stuck out her tongue as she opened her door to pout her way up the stairs.

"I love you too, sweetie," Tom replied as he got out of the vehicle as well. "Be sure to save me a seat in the teacher's lounge!" Sarah having already disappeared behind the building's double doors.

Bypassing the teacher's lounge, wanting to set up his desk and write an introduction to this year's curriculum, Tom decided to head toward his classroom; this year he would be on the second floor of the East Wing —a part of the building which no one wanted to be assigned. According to educators of the past, the section of the building had a dark history; a student having committed suicide on the third floor after having been bullied for *supposedly* being a homosexual—having been caught with an erection in the boy's locker room while changing during gym. Even though it had been twenty-six years since the tragedy, the emotional stain of the young boy's death still remained; even students dreaded being scheduled classes in the East Wing, given the tale.

Upon entering his classroom, Tom was surprised to find a student (your typical high school outcast—unkempt attire, horn-rimmed glasses, a Misfits t-shirt underneath a worn flannel, an old pair of Chuck Taylors completely covered in Sharpie) already sitting at a desk; hunched over; burying her nose in a book. Tilting his head to read the front cover, he discovered the young girl was reading a peculiar read for someone in their teenage years: Don DeLillo's 1988 novel, *Libra*. His appearance having gone unnoticed, Tom made his way to the whiteboard to write his name and a few bullet points for discussion.

"A fascination with the exploits of Lee Harvey Oswald and the assassination of JFK, I take it?" without turning away from the whiteboard, Tom broke the silence.

Startled, the young girl looked up from her book, turning her head in Tom's direction and, swallowing the small lump in her throat, she breathed, "Hm?"

Turning to meet the gaze of the student, Tom noticed the right lens of her glasses was cracked diagonally from the left to the right; the bridge being held together with electric tape. "Your choice of literature," he replied. "It focuses on the life of Oswald and offers a speculative account of the events which shaped the events of November 22, 1963, correct?"

The young girl nodded, unable to mouth an actual response; her gaze falling back to her book every few seconds. He could feel how awkward he was (unintentionally) making her, having interrupted her anti-social bubble. Hoping to defuse the situation from sinking into a wormhole of maladroit tension, Tom walked toward her desk to shake her hand and properly introduce himself.

She said her name was Regina; Regina Wilson he would later discover while scrolling down the roll sheet once class started and he was taking attendance. It wouldn't be until later in the day, once school was let out, he would find out she had recently lost her father in a tragic automobile accident; the driver of the other vehicle having suffered a brain aneurysm on the freeway—causing the vehicle to lose control and swerve into her father's left side; forcing his car into the barricade, flipping over on its side and being crushed by an eighteen-wheeler going 60mph. For the entire trip home, Tom checked his mirrors every fifteen seconds, having lost all trust of other drivers who drove alongside him.

As the rest of the students came pouring into the classroom—the bell having rung, herding them in like sheep, Regina quietly put her book away and placed her attention to the front of the class. Despite having been a teacher for eight years and having been on five promotional book tours, Tom Dolin could never shake the anxiety of the first day of school; hoping to make a good enough "first impression" on his students so they would be far more willing to participate in class and *actually* do the homework assignments, unlike the reluctance Mr. Putnam—the 10th grade Chemistry teacher (and kind of an asshole, according to the students; his teaching style having been known to be abrasive, at best [he had tenure, what could you do?])—would have to deal with during the entire school year.

"Alright, everybody," Tom motioned toward the whiteboard—a marker in hand. "I'm Mr. Dolin and I'll be your tour guide, captain, and flight attendant for the duration of this school year. If you look to your right. . .you'll be able to look outside the windows and view the freedom we'll all be denied until 3:40pm."

Only Regina let out a laugh at Tom's attempt at classroom humor. . .

The rest of the school day went as expected, the usual assemblage of students making their way through with each hour that passed: the athletic slacker who would attempt to spend his final year of high school skating by on his facile merits; the "misunderstood" teenager who had discovered the guttural, passionate screams of Black Flag, Minor Threat, and any other cliché hardcore act from the 1980s; along with the occasional writing snob who believed they were the next William Faulkner (while some of them showed the potential to become the next *Great American Author*, most couldn't write anything, even if their lives hung in the balance). During the lunch period of the day Tom and Sarah (along with the other teachers) shared their assumptions on which students would be their favorites and who they believed would eventually become an issue throughout the school year. Overhearing Nancy, who taught Calculus, mention a student she found rather peculiar—a student who couldn't help but bury her nose in a *godawful* Don DeLillo novel the entire period.

"Oddly enough," Nancy, taking the bite of egg salad from her plastic fork, "the young girl was able to follow along. I'm not sure if I like her. I'm sure you'll find her a treat this school year, Tom. You do seem to have a soft spot for students who enjoy indulging themselves with a book; even more if the work of fiction 'happens' to be *one of your own*."

Finding Nancy's last minute (and poorly executed) jab at his ego, Tom laughed, "Don't be so sour, Nancy, just because *you* chose a subject most students find to be soaked in tedium; rendering their attention spans to that of a dying goldfish."

Nancy, having not found Tom's rebuttal playful, left the teacher's lounge in a heated march—her high heels clicking across the floor. Sarah and Putnam quit eating their respected meals to slow clap Nancy's departure from the room.

"Thank God," Putnam muttered, "I could never stand that cunt these past thirteen years, I'm glad someone," he eyed Tom, "finally came along who can put the old hag in her place. Every fucking year, I keep telling myself, 'It's only three more years before she finally retires. Just three. . .more. . .years. . .' hoping they'll go by quicker. I must say, Thomas, your arrival on the scene has made the past eight years go by quicker than they would have without you."

Shuddering at the mention of his full name, something he hadn't heard since the age of sixteen, Tom, having nodded awkwardly at Putnam's attempt at a compliment (having never been able to accept words of praise from anyone—not even from Sarah) turned his attention (finally) to his own lunch; leftovers from last night's dinner: a concoction of chicken parmigiana, Alfredo noodles, Pillsbury pizza dough, fried eggs, and spaghetti sauce which had been thrown together to make a (surprisingly tasty) makeshift casserole. As he continued to eat the meal by the spoonful, he figured he would get a head-start on reading through the stack of papers which rested in his satchel from today's in-class assignment: write a short poem about something you did during the summer months.

Dreadful, he thought. Some of them were downright dreadful. One of the students had written one word in the middle of the page. Drunk. That was it. He couldn't even write down the student's name to make note because they decided to leave the assignment anonymous. He figured he would wait until he read every other student's assignment to eventually discover the mystery poet's identity. The second piece of paper read like a pornographic haiku:

> i masturbated
> into my brother's shampoo
> cuz he's such a (~~fucking~~) dick

Well, at least (he looked at the upper right hand corner of the page) Michael Shaeffer can *somewhat* follow instructions. He swallowed the last bite of his lunch as he marked the student's paper a 10/10 with a note at the bottom letting Michael know of a few (less obscene) ways to get back at one's sibling. The next paper, going by the length, showed promise to *actually* have a poem worth reading in between the blue lines of the page:

> Sleeping, dreaming, but my eyes are still wide open
> While shadows in white talk among themselves, wrapped in unclear conversation
> *"Where am I?"* I ask, but the words won't leave my tongue
> Consolation finds my curious hand; a gentle caress of a thumb
> Echoes come and echoes fade, but the question still remains
> Why do I (finally) feel awake during these odd recurring dreams?

Tom paused, took a moment to recollect himself, and reread the poem three more times before making an attempt to grade it. What struck him the most about the piece was how similar it was to something he had written down (word for word he would later discover when he got home and rummaged through the drawer of his desk) during the outlining stages of his third novel, *Ascension*; the poem itself never making it into the novel because Frank, his editor, had deemed it irrelevant to the plot of the story's arc—despite Tom's reluctant pleas to take his word and reconsider and allow it to be the enigmatic opener to the novel instead of the brief quasi-politically charged rantings of one of the main characters. Curious to find out who could've written the poem, Tom's eyes darted toward the top right corner of the page.

Regina Wilson.

. . .

HAVING ERASED EVERYTHING from his blackboard, finding everything he'd written up to this point unsatisfactory, Theodore took a step back and, while scratching away at his graying mustache, attempted to remember the formula they had used to successfully bring Subject No. 2773 (designated Cordelia Dashkov by her E.B.C.; a fact Elizabeth wouldn't lay to rest until everyone else in the room caved and agreed to call her by her "actual" name instead of her Subject serial number) out of her vegetative state; disconnecting her brain from the *Arcadian Sequence*. Unable to find the answer within the confines of his own brain, he turned to see how Elizabeth and Friedrich (Pierce having retired early for the afternoon) were doing with their calculations. Friedrich, much like himself, seemed to be stuck in a cycle of writing and erasing his progress every few minutes. Elizabeth's blackboard, however, remained covered in—what appeared to be—a seemingly endless collection of varied equations; never taking the same approach twice—the ones she considered no longer relevant having been slashed with a giant 'X' across them to indicate she had moved on to the next *possible* solution. The entire process was difficult enough attempting to theorize the correct sequence to bring someone out of a coma without the use of test subjects; his father having learned the repercussions of testing out their theories on randomly selected *Arcadians* (a term Pierce's grandfather, Alexandre Oliver Needham, coined after reading a prewar book on Greek mythology; considering those who resided within the comatose lucid dreaming state to have been given the gift of living in a

Utopia while they continued to live in the grim reality of a destroyed Earth); Pierce's father, Isaac Octavius Needham, implementing that only Subjects nearing the end of their life cycle be chosen to test each *promising* theory on—leaving little room for error in recent years due to Isaac's liberal use of them during his (and Theodore's father, Raymond Webb) time as Director.

Meanwhile, as Elizabeth continued to bounce from one theorem to the next, in the lower levels of the building, Friedrich helped Meredith monitor seven Subjects' vitals and dream sequencing; each one having shown signs of trouble within the past month. It was puzzling. Lately, it seemed, more and more Subjects were experiencing (one variant or the other of) neurological trauma. Some of them with the inability of having an explanation why their brains were experiencing their form of trauma; one Subject appeared to have developed a minor concussion, but had no written history of experiencing seizures or tremors throughout their lifetime. And without proper surveillance, the cause of these mysterious instances would remain unknown.

"Do you think there will ever be others like me?"

Theodore jumped. "Jesus Christ, Cordelia," the words managed to fumble from his tongue as he recollected himself. "Do you *have* to be as quiet as you are when approaching others? Almost gave me a goddamn heart attack. Fuck. . ."

"Please, forgive me, Dr. Webb," Cordelia replied, bowing her head in self-appointed shame. "During my time with Lieutenant Zavasky and his men at the old Naval Base in Bomb City (what used to be known as San Diego) they taught me to *always* be conservative with announcing my presence—that it could mean *life or death* out in the desiccated wastelands of Southern California. I do sincerely *apologize* for this discrepancy. To avoid any further discord among us, I will try and remember to make myself known next time."

A reluctant sigh left Theodore's lungs. While he understood the necessity of increasing their security (the outer-city limits having become increasingly savage in the last decade; Theodore assumed it was the effects of radiation exposure *finally* taking its toll on those who were either forced or chose to dwell out in the open ruins of the Wasteland), he would have preferred the militant inhabitants of Bomb City (referring to themselves as servicemen; a frail attempt to revitalize an archaic code of ethics from the world before the War) have sent one of their own instead of sending Cordelia—who, in her "previous life" within the *Arcadian Sequence,* was a machinist's mate for the USS *Archimedes* —back to the hospital once she had come to learn the circumstances of her hometown (and acquired a duffel bag of firearms and ammunition). Had it not been for Pierce and Elizabeth's insistence Cordelia stay with them and help teach the doctors and civilians living inside the hospital how to use a firearm, Theodore would have suggested exiling her to the outskirts of the city; to fend for herself against the countless horrors of Los Angeles.

He hated that he felt this way—especially about a Subject whom they had spent months figuring out the one-off solution to bring her out of her coma—but there was something off about Cordelia's demeanor; the way she would talk feeling synthetic in execution (she knew the correct words to say in every situation but the tone of voice was never accurate; always a beat or two *off* from what was considered socially appropriate). Also, the way she would slink around the building, not making a fragment of noise—sometimes, like a moment ago, approaching another person (getting within inches of them) before announcing herself; it wasn't pleasant—nor was it natural—thought Theodore.

"Is something wrong, Director?" Cordelia's voice grated against Theodore's eardrums. "Is there any way I may be of assistance?"

"I'm *fine*, Cordelia. . ." an irritated Theodore spoke through a clenched jaw. ". . .only the weight of fatigue taking its toll on me," he lied, not wanting to offend the only person in the room with a loaded weapon—not knowing how she would react, given her unconventional personality. "The only way you could help would be to head upstairs to the roof and help the current watch keep an eye out for approaching marauders. But, please, remember to hold your fire until they fire the first shot. We don't want to *accidentally* kill a trader or friendly drifter again; if we have another incident like last year, we'll be on thin ice with neighboring settlements."

When he turned to face Cordelia, hoping to get a verbal response from her, Theodore found she had already left; leaving him alone with Elizabeth and an array of blackboards; most of them having been covered in failed (crossed-out) solutions during his brief period away. Jesus, he thought as he bared witness to the amount of work Elizabeth had done in such a short amount of time. While none of the equations proved to be of any use to them, he still found it impressive the rate her mind would race through each possibility. Perhaps he was wrong to make the assumption she wasn't suited for the rigorous amount of work the four walls of the Quiet Room demanded from each individual who chose to dedicate most of their time there.

To think he spent a large portion of his life in front of a blackboard, the tips of his fingers permanently stained white (a stark contrast to his own dark brown skin), saddened him; his marriage and family having faded into obscurity—his wife and two kids having left for the ruins of San Pedro after years of only getting to see Theodore for the occasional meal when he *remembered* to go home instead of calling in from the kitchen staff on the fifth floor. Had he the chance to go back and redo everything, however, he wouldn't change a thing; despite the lack of positive results—refusing to consider Cordelia a *success*, given her lack of human emotion.

"Theodore," Elizabeth, still scratching away at the blackboard, refusing to look back as she asked her question. "What if we can't figure out the solution a second time? What will happen to everyone downstairs?"

A woeful breath escaped Theodore's lips. He knew the answer. That, if the notion Pierce wished to execute were brought to fruition, every single Subject which resided in a sleeping chamber would eventually die—leaving the lower levels of the hospital empty; soon to be forgotten with the passing of time. This, among other various (heavy-handed) topics of discussion, was where he and Pierce could not come to a mutual understanding. While Pierce saw the Subjects as nothing more than a nuisance (a waste of valuable time and resources he would often mutter under his breath), Theodore, much like his father, wished to do all he could to undo the mistakes of the past.

"Theodore?" the young woman said his name a second time, this time turning away from the chalk-ridden blackboard to stare him in the eyes; bringing with her a weight of emotion he wasn't equipped to digest at such a late hour. (was it late? he had lost track of the day, to be honest. Either way, the desperate plea for an answer, which rested behind Elizabeth's vibrant green irises, had begun to make Theodore feel uncomfortable in his own skin with each passing second the Silence remained between them.)

"I honestly can't tell you what will happen to them," he lied. "And I hope, one day (hopefully sooner than later, he thought), that *that* question will no longer have to be asked."

Elizabeth, seemingly displeased with his answer—a small series of tears welling to the surface of her eyes—turned back to face the blackboard, placed the sliver of chalk down, and headed for the door; unable to continue with her work while in a negative mindset. Theodore watched as the door swung back and forth until it came to a complete stop; the quiet hum of the elevator in the distance.

As the elevator took her down to the lower levels, Elizabeth allowed the tears to finally fall down her face and soak into the dirt-stained lab coat she had acquired years ago when she became a medical technician—alongside Dr. Friedrich Winsome. She had hoped moving to the Quiet Room (away from the NICU, where she watched over every Subject through a computer screen) would help alleviate the depression she had come to feel with each passing shift she'd spent watching over the comatose residents' brain activity. The academia behind it all, however (the amount of time and effort everyone put into finding a solution to successfully bring every single Subject out of hibernation; showing little to no results), was far more depressing than it had been to sit in front of a wall of monitors and watch everyone's "lives" pass by her; keeping their vitals stable whenever an issue arose. Trapped. No matter what she did, she felt she wasn't doing *enough*. She often wondered if she would ever feel useful to those around her, instead of a disappointment.

The sound of the elevator coming to a grinding halt brought Elizabeth's attention back to the outside world—leaving her dismal thoughts for another time. Behind the double doors she could see Friedrich and Meredith working diligently; Friedrich following Meredith—fixing any mistakes she happened to make as they made their way through each Subject; checking their vitals and temporal sequencing. As she passed through the double doors a memory from her childhood found itself playing through her brain; one of the few memories she cared to remember because it was the day she realized she wanted to work here, in the lower levels of the facility.

"I hope we're enjoying ourselves down here," Chief Director Needham spoke jovially at the small group of children who had found themselves in the lower levels of the hospital for *Take Your Child To Work Day.* "I know it may seem boring, watching over a bunch of *sleeping* residents, but it's actually not as banal as one would presume."

The old man let out a deep laugh, hoping to make the children feel less shy about being in one of the only rooms without windows—the rows of dormant Subjects wasn't helping matters much, he felt it was safe to assume. The old cryogenics chamber was the one place Isaac Octavius Needham felt reluctant to include in the event. He found it easy to reduce the occupational jargon of the kitchen staff or a chem technician, but to simplify the day-to-day responsibilities of the neuro-technicians to allow the children to understand what their parents were doing—without scaring them by letting them know the *sleeping* individuals would remain that way until the day they died.

"Dad, do I really have to be here? I know I'll eventually be running this place, but I've been coming here since I was seven. I'm more than certain I can do *half* of these people's jobs with my eyes closed. I'm fucking eighteen, dad. Could you let me enjoy my *one year* without school, please?"

"Pierce! Watch your language!" Isaac, not willing to tolerate his son's inappropriate behavior in front of the younger children. "If you truly find yourself *above all of this*, you can head upstairs and help your mother sort through the medical records."

"Gladly!" Pierce yelled back at his father as he turned to head toward the elevator, bumping into his old school friend, Theodore—whose father had volunteered him to work today to be part of the demonstration—along the way, telling him he would meet up with him later tonight, and stared back at his father with discontent as the elevator doors shut; taking him to the old outpatient records wing of the building to help his mother.

As Isaac went on to apologize to the staff and their children, a little girl (she would tell you she wasn't little anymore, having turned five three weeks ago) wandered off on her own; exploring the sleeping chambers of children—hidden in the back left corner of the floor. Curious, she leaned closer, pressing her face up against the glass of one of the chambers. Inside of it rested a boy; not much older than her, but still noticeable since he was several inches taller than her. He seemed at peace, her mind decided; like he was having the most pleasant dream. Beyond the serenity of the young boy's face, the little girl's attention drifted to the horrific scene of tubes attached to his arms; dripping unknown fluids into his system. What happened to him, she thought. Was he going to be okay? Would he ever wake up from his peaceful slumber? Would she ever get to say hello to him; welcoming him back to the real world?

She turned to ask her father, who had lost himself in a conversation with old-man Isaac, if the boy was going to be okay when the room became flooded with the flashing of red lights and a continuous screeching noise pouring from the loud speakers mounted on the ceiling. In the confusion, she turned her attention back to the boy trapped behind glass to find him convulsing about. Before she could react to the horror of seeing the poor boy thrashing his body around, the little girl was pulled away from the scene while a wave of doctors swarmed the sleeping chamber.

"Elizabeth, what were you thinking?" her father cried as he dragged her to safety. "You know better than to wander off on your own down here; it isn't safe for children."

"I'm sorry daddy," the young girl cried as she glanced back at the crowd of doctors—who had opened the chamber so they could attend to the boy appropriately. "Is he going to be okay?"

"He's going to be *fine*," her father reassured, "That little boy has had his share of problems ever since he was born. This little episode isn't even the worst we've seen in the past eight years." He smiled, brushing the tears from his daughter's face. "Now, let's head upstairs. I'm certain your mother is cooking up something special in the kitchen today. After all, it is *Friday*."

"David," one of the doctors yelled, bringing his attention to the wave. "You're needed. Quit consoling your little girl and get over here!"

David cursed at his colleague, telling him he would have to find another doctor to help him with the Subject. He wasn't about to abandon his daughter to the labyrinth that was the hospital's many levels and hallways. "Let's go, Lizzy," he lifted his daughter up into his arms, kissing her left cheek to comfort her. "We're going to go find mommy and have ourselves a nice lunch." He didn't care if he would be written up for insubordination, what mattered more to him was knowing his little girl wasn't traumatized by what she had witnessed today.

As the elevator made its way to the upper levels, little Elizabeth whispered into her father's ear, "Daddy?"

"Yes, Lizzy?"

"Does he have a name?"

"Does who have a name, sweetie?" he asked, finding himself confused by his daughter's vague question.

"That little boy," she replied, her voice having raised half an octave —a child's version of snark; like her father didn't know what she was talking about. "I'd like to know his name. That way, when he wakes up, I can say hello."

David, having felt a kick to his stomach, let Elizabeth down on the elevator floor and explained, "We're not allowed to know their names, I'm afraid. The Chief Directors fear if we knew their names we'd become too attached and wouldn't be able to make the more *brash* decisions; if we were ever forced to face them. Instead, we only know them by their number." He paused, choking on the little boy's number. Despite the Chief Directors' best efforts to keep them unattached, David had grown to care for every single Subject he was tasked to look after; especially the little boy. "That little boy you saw today," he continued, having swallowed the lump in his throat, "*his* designation is Subject No. 2990."

Returning to the present, the memory of her childhood fleeting to the dark recesses of her mind, the old familiar sound of the alarms wailed throughout the room. A Subject was experiencing a seizure. She had a feeling she knew which one. Without hesitation, Elizabeth darted towards the back left corner of the floor's layout. Friedrich and Meredith were already attending to Subject No. 2990 when she arrived to the scene. Even twenty-five years later, the young boy (now a grown man— thirty-two years old) still fascinated her. His mind's noncompliance to remain in a state of serenity—unlike the other Subjects, who, for the most part, remained docile—revealed, in Elizabeth's point-of-view, a strength; a desire to wake itself up from its *Arcadian* prison and venture out into the *real world*.

As Friedrich went through the procedure, step by step, making sure Meredith was taking note for future occurrences, Elizabeth walked over to Subject No. 2990 and, like she had many times before, placed her hand over his and gently rubbed it; *the gesture hadn't failed to calm him down after all these years, why stop now?* she thought.

Something happened that had never happened before; Subject No. 2990's eyes sprang wide open. Elizabeth jumped back. Terrified, thinking her rubbing the Subject's hand had caused the anomaly, called Friedrich's attention to it.

"Fucking hell," cried Winsome, pushing Meredith away from the sleeping chamber, "How long has he been like this?"

"It just happened," Elizabeth, unsure what to do, replied, "I was checking his vitals," a lie, "and his eyes blinked open. Has this never happened before?"

"Only once," Winsome, while recalling the incident, grabbed for a syringe and anesthetic agent. "It was decades ago, long before you and I were even alive, back when Alexandre Oliver Needham and Mitchell Emmett Webb were the Chief Directors. The Subject is still around, actually, I've been told," declared Winsome as he pointed in the other direction, aimlessly. "Subject No. 1937, if memory serves me right. According to the techies upstairs, they say he was never the same after they made an attempt to *awaken* him. They hadn't even begun the process and his eyes just . . .*opened*. . . They also say he never sequenced properly after that day, which—some say—led him to become *paranoid and aware* he was living in a simulated program. Later, Pierce tried to pass the notion along to everyone down here that it would be best to have him *liberated*, but Theodore shot it down before it could gain traction with anyone. To be honest, I'm surprised the motherfucker is still alive. He must be well into his eighties, at this point."

Elizabeth knew which Subject Friedrich was speaking about; she didn't even have to walk to the other side of the room to know for certain. He was a well-known (and appreciated) author of his time, having written several seminal works; at least, that's what he was known for in the world of Arcadia. She remembered following his monitor upstairs before she requested to be moved to the forefront of it all—he certainly was a paranoiac; entertaining, but one had to keep an eye on him most of the time to make sure he didn't cause too much trouble.

At the moment, however, her attention was with Subject No. 2990; his pale blue eyes still staring up at her stoically.

· · ·

ANOTHER BODY BAG, zipped up, carried by two junior ranks, left the barracks while Nikolai finished putting away his shaving kit underneath his rack. He didn't know the recruit well, but he still felt a sadness for the young man's parents, who would soon find out they would have to suffer with the grief of losing their son; especially at such a young age. "Встаньте, мудак" he whispered while the other recruits prepared for the day. Had he known the chances of dying during recruitment training were as striking as they had proven themselves to be, Nikolai would have taken the time to give a proper farewell to his mother and father before getting on the bus. If he happened to perish in the coming (final) weeks of training—which included how to survive extreme interrogation tactics and infiltration by air—Nikolai would hope his parents would still be proud of how far he had made it.

Before he could finish double-checking his entire rack to make sure it would pass Stepanov's rigorous inspection, Nikolai's vision became non-existent; the smell of what could only be a mangy potato sack having made its way over his head—a sharp kick to the back of his knees following suit shortly after; crippling him, forcing him to the floor. He knew he'd be up for *interrogation* eventually, but (going by the usual order of things) he figured he had *at least* three more recruits before his number was up.

They never asked him any questions. Having been interrogation training, he would have assumed they would at least come up with something to ask him during the ordeal. Instead, they (without warning) beat him senseless; potato sack still resting over his head. They started off simple: throwing punch after punch to the stomach, ribs, and face; child's play, he thought as each blow hit their desired target

—nothing my old-man hadn't given me when I had done wrong. It wasn't until they moved on to using high-voltage shock batons that the pain began to become an issue. There was a moment when one of the officers (Stepanov, he assumed) thought it'd be a good idea to jab him in between the ribs and hold it there for a few minutes, causing Sokolov to piss his pants; everyone in the room falling over themselves in innocuous laughter at his misfortune. Once they were done with their *playful* fit of *mild electrocution*, they found it appropriate to move on to a technique most thought was never *actually* used.

The room filled with light as one of the officers removed the potato sack from his head—taking a mound of hair with it. His pupils readjusting to the sudden shift in light exposure, discovering the room's only source of light was a lone light bulb hanging precariously above him, Nikolai found himself facing Stepanov, who fancied himself three Nagant M1895 revolvers.

"I see we have yet to get rid of you," Stepanov's voice echoed throughout the small room. Nikolai watched as he unloaded each cylinder, every single bullet falling to the tile floor. Stepanov let out a sigh, catching the last bullet to fall from the cylinder, smiling, "Maybe today." His eyes gleamed, smiling as he loaded the single bullet into one of the cylinders. Locking each revolver's cylinder back into place, spinning them to allow the bullet to find a new (random) home, Stepanov began to toss them into the air; juggling them like a circus clown would to entertain children. "Let's play a game, shall we? Among these three pistols are twenty-one shots—twenty-one chances for the bullet to say hello to wherever it decides to hit you."

Nikolai stared stoically into Stepanov's eyes, waiting for the *game* to begin.

"Ah, it seems we have ourselves a contender" Stepanov motioned to the other two officers in the room, who had moved into the shadows; hoping to avoid getting shot themselves. "Tell me, Sokolov," Click. "Why is it you desire to be a member of Spetsnaz?"

Silence.

"Was it so you could escape your lush of a father's obsessive beatings? That does seem to be—" Click. "—a popular reason among you fuckers these days."

Still, Nikolai remained silent; he even refused to blink. If he were meant to be shot by a stray bullet, he would welcome it without as much as a flinch. Stepanov didn't deserve the satisfaction.

"Listen, Грызун," Click. Click. "if I had it *my way*, all of you would have been tossed back on another bus and sent back home to your families in disgrace. None of you, I repeat," Click. Click. Click. "none of you deserve the honor of serving the Motherland! But, *unfortunately*," Click. "I'm," Click. "stuck," Click. Click. "training," Click. "*you lazy shits!*" Click. Click. Click.

Bang!

A piercing, high-pitched echo rang throughout the small, poorly lit room; deafening everyone who found themselves trapped inside its four walls. The right side of Nikolai's chest felt a sharp sting course through it, the stray bullet having *only grazed him*, sending a surge of (false) pain response signals to his brain, leading him to believe the wound was worse than it actually was—sending him into shock, passing out, and pissing himself a second time; leaving his limp, soiled body to be held up by his confined, elevated arms. Beyond that, the sound of one of the officers in full panic could be heard screaming at the top of his lungs.

"Holy shit, Grigory, *you fucking shot him!*"

"He seems fine. Now quit being a fucking cunt and take him back to his barracks; both of you!"

"But, Grigory, he could require medical attention. . ."

"I swear to fucking god, Sergei, I will pick one of these damned bullets from the floor and shoot you with it. Now, I'll say it one more time, take this fucking piece of shit and drag his ass back to his *damn barracks!*"

3

OICES COULD BE HEARD in the distance, along with the insufferable sound of a fire alarm going off in every direction. Among the familiar tones of panic within the room, another well-known ritual—the soothing presence of a woman's hand gently caressing his own, hoping to calm him—took place while another voice (male, frantic) barked orders at another, who had yet to speak, telling them to take note for next time, in case this were to ever happen again during her watch. The only emotion able to make itself known was confusion. *Why, after all these years, must I have this damned dream again?* the thought found its way to his subconscious mind; aware he was only dreaming—that none of what his senses were experiencing was real. *And why do I always have difficulty waking myself up from it—*

Tom's eyes opened, the voices still carrying on with their panic-stricken conversation; slowly, they faded into the distance—allowing him to find comfort that he was back in his bedroom. He turned to find a sound asleep Sarah lying next to him snoring away while the dog cuddled at her feet, an episode of *Law & Order* playing on the TV; the volume turned low enough not even the dog's ears could pick up the insipid dialogue of Sam Waterston's character (Executive Assistant District Attorney Jack McCoy) while he rambled on in front of a jury about the case in question. Feeling at ease with his surroundings, Tom closed his eyes once more in search of sleep; refusing to let the recurring dream continue to bother him.

Stirred awake by the sound of Wham!'s "Wake Me Up Before You Go-Go" screaming from the radio alarm clock on his bedside table, slamming his fist down on the snooze button, a wave of confusion met Tom upon opening his eyes. *When did we get an alarm clock?* he thought. *Didn't those stop being popular with the invention of the iPhone?* He turned to ask Sarah when she had the time to purchase and install such a relic (with the kids and work taking up most of their time these days) to find her side of the bed empty—a rather uncommon occurrence, even for the weekend. "Honey," Tom hollered at the bathroom door from the bed, too lazy to get up, "When did we decide we were living in the '80s?"

But there was no response.

Seconds later, an upbeat Daisy came through the bedroom door, tail wagging. She let out a quiet bark when too much time had passed between her arrival in the room and her desire to be patted on the head by her male master. "Good morning to you too, Daisy," Tom rolled over (still too lazy to force himself out of bed), pushing her over onto her back so he could rub her stomach. "You weren't who I wanted, little girl, but I appreciate the greeting, nonetheless."

Daisy licked her master's face in response—putting an end to their conversation.

Finally deciding to get out of bed, having grown curious where his wife could be, Tom (slowly) made his way to the living room/dining room area, hoping to find Sarah and the kids enjoying Saturday morning cartoons. As he walked in to find his family how he imagined they would be, Tom couldn't help but smile at the picture perfect moment transpiring before him; Sarah singing along to Tori Amos' "Cornflake Girl" while she soaked several slices of thick cut bread slices in the egg and cinnamon & sugar mixture; the kids watching *Animaniacs*—their eyes refusing to leave the screen as their father made his presence known with the rambunctious introduction of saying (in his best Foghorn Leghorn impression), " '*I say—I said I say hello, children! And how ah we doin' to-day on this fine and dandy Saturday mornin'?*' " The only response he managed to muster from the children was from his eldest, Christie, "Daddy, why do you have to be so *dumb—like, all the time?*" Sarah could be heard breaking from her vocal performance; consumed by a bout of uncontrollable laughter, finding their daughter's insult toward her father the perfect way to describe Tom's personality seventy-five percent of the time—with or without having the children (or his students, for that matter) as a reluctant audience.

As the day progressed, the two eldest children having lost interest in watching television—showing no desire to watch *Batman: The Animated Series* (deciding to join their mother while she tended to her Galanthus Snowdrops, which were bound to bloom next month)— Tom took advantage of having the living room to himself while his son, Benjamin, slept soundly in his rocker; hoping to start work on his latest idea for a novel. When he went to gather his notes, however, confusion found its way into his thoughts. Where a series of papers with character bios, well-detailed scenes of grotesque and relentless violence, and enigmatic haiku poetry should've been, a black leather-bound notebook rested in its place—opening it, he found its pages were already covered with fevered notes for *another* idea for a novel. A novel he couldn't recall having considered as a future project in his writing career. The handwriting on each page was his though, which he found odd; he couldn't even recall having purchased such a notebook—his preference being the simple yellow notepads one could find in *any* shopping center's office supplies section.

Flipping through the pages of the notebook, Tom was surprised to find himself enjoying the myriad of ideas which he (supposedly) had written down—along with a *seemingly endless* supply of characters which would be used to explore each topic. Among them, Tom found the idea of 'the lack of human connection' the most appealing, since one of the characters which would be used to traverse this existential plane was a schizophrenic woman whose only wish was to get better so she could leave the mental institute where she resided and return to her family and live a normal life once more. What he couldn't figure out, however, was how all of these characters' narratives would flesh out into an actual novel; most of their narratives taking place in various other cities across the United States. What amazed him most, as he continued to browse through the notebook's pages, was he had (apparently) already begun writing the opening passage to one of the characters; the character's narrative being written in 1st person point-of-view—something he had avoided doing for all of his fiction writing up to this point. Curious, he read what he had written so far:

Birds chirp in the distance as a northern wind blows, communicating an *unknown language* to the trees along the shoreline; their leaves billowing in a foreign rhythm as children play underneath them—their youthful screams of delectation joining the jazz-like symphony Mother Nature has beautifully composed; the muffled screams of adults (young, old, and in between) getting drunk on a pantheon of house boats out on the lake; adding to an already cacophonous song. Beyond the scene, lost in the distance, the sound of two strangers playing tennis cry out in response to one another's futile attempts to out-smart their opponent with each swing of their racket; the hollow ricochet of the tennis ball flying back and forth acting as the punctuation to each barbaric call. Above the two friendly combatants, a lone cumulus cloud drifts by—having separated itself from the rest of the group—hoping to see who wins the match before the wind picks back up and blows it back on course; the shadow it casts on the two opponents brings its own sense of urgency. The players' cries become more eccentric with each transitory hit, the sudden shift in sunlight causing them to believe it could rain at any time; leaving their match unfinished and in a draw.

   Not far from the picnic area, down by the water, a small group of teenagers (most of them having graduated from high school only months ago) sit inside the old rundown gazebo and smoke their first collective pack of cigarettes to help celebrate and symbolize their newfound freedom from the banality of the educational system they were forced to endure for the past four years of their lives while another group of teenagers play an impromptu game of beach volleyball; their only form of a net being a two inch thick line carved into the sand; a rectangular perimeter made of four average-sized stones acting as markers for out of bounds. The laughter of a friendly competition finds its way into the æther as the volleyball soars into the sky upon each serve and volley.

   These are the sights and sounds of summertime I've come to know so well; like an ever evolving painting that never ceases to amaze me.

"Daddy, are you writing lies again?"

   Tom looked up to find his younger daughter, Matilda, sitting above him on the head of the couch, making a vain attempt to read his sloppy handwriting. *"Lies?"* puzzled by his daughter's odd word choice. "What makes you think I'm writing lies, sweetheart?"

   "Mommy says you're a fwiction writer and when I asked her what fwiction was she told me it's like writing lies, only the lies are for people to *enjoy or laugh at.*"

Chuckling at his daughter's limited understanding of what it meant to be a fiction writer—based on her mother's poorly worded explanation—Tom thought about everything he'd written since he began writing *Discord Avenue* at the young age of twenty; up to the three short paragraphs which resided in the notebook in front of him. While, yes, some—if not most of his first two novels—were based off of actual experiences he had witnessed or been a part of, the amount of exaggeration added to each piece would have (if he had published them as memoirs instead of works of fiction) given anyone who happened to read his work the opportunity to make the claim that he had written nothing but a dishonest representation of himself and those who were personified within the body of work in question. Re-reading what few paragraphs resided within the pages of the notebook—still unsure when he had had the time to write them (also wondering where the pages of notes for *Modus Operandi* had wandered off to)—Tom felt it was safe to say this production in his fwiction *writing* career would survive without being labeled as a *lie* by his wife and children.

Coming in from outside, her hands covered in Miracle-Gro, Sarah, seeing her husband laboring over his leather-bound notebook, "Finally feeling inspired to write again, are we?" she asked.

"I guess so," Tom said. "You haven't happened to see my *other* notes floating around somewhere, have you?"

Sarah shook her head, a look of confusion finding its way to her face. Wiping her forehead, having forgotten her arms were covered in potting soil, "I don't recall another set of notes, babe. Are you sure you aren't confusing an old set of notes from years ago?"

Refusing to let his wife's inability to recall his (rather extensive) set of notes for *Modus Operandi*—having spent countless hours at the library researching the psychology of serial killers like Ted Bundy, Alexander Pichushkin, Charles Edmund Cullen, Dennis Raider (AKA the BTK Murderer), Jeffrey Dahmer, and John Wayne Gacy—Tom closed the black leather notebook, laid it down on the coffee table, tiptoed past Benjamin's rocker—not wanting to wake him—and headed for his office upstairs; determined to find the *appropriate* set of notes. As Tom edged his way past his son the television went to static for a few seconds before transitioning to the EMERGENCY BROADCAST SYSTEM banner, stopping him in his tracks; "We interrupt your program at the request of the White House" appearing in yellow fine print at the bottom of the screen, almost too small for one to catch if they didn't know to look for it. But before he could reach over for the remote control to turn the volume down, knowing what was about to follow, the loud droning digital bleeps (which he hadn't heard since he was a child and his father would attempt to startup the dial-up Internet: *weeeee woooong weeee woooong de-nuh de-nuh*) followed by an automated warning, letting the surrounding areas know *all* local broadcasting stations would be taking part in the EAS broadcast, that all news stations would be open for civilians to remain updated on the situation as it progressed. After three minutes of the automated voice a young man in a gray suit—his face showing signs of anxiety, despite every attempt to appear calm and collected—appeared on the television screen, standing behind a podium, clearing his throat before speaking into the microphone; beads of sweat forming along his forehead as he continued to prepare himself.

"Good morning . . ." the gentleman cleared his throat, picking up a glass of water, taking a long, slow sip to calm his nerves. "The President has authorized me to make the following announcement as he is being transported to an *undisclosed* location at this time." Another pause, allowing photographers to take snapshots (hoping to make the front page of their assigned newspaper—a pointless endeavor, if the world were to end today, to be honest) of the event. "As you may already know, tensions between the United States and Russia are at a breaking point, which we fear may lead to nuclear war. Let me stress that a nuclear attack is not taking place at this time. However, as a precaution, the President has ordered the evacuation of all cities with a population of over 250,000—as well as communities within a 100 mile radius of a strategic military installation. Once again, these evacuations are only a precautionary measure. Let's face the facts, America. This situation is more desperate than ever. We are doing everything in our power to stop this from escalating any further. But even if this period of tension does lead to war, we will come back fighting as one nation under God. Thank you." Upon finishing his speech the television screen went black for a second before it returned to the EMERGENCY BROADCAST SYSTEM banner for a brief moment.

"This concludes operations under the Emergency Alert System. All broadcast stations and cable systems may now resume your regular scheduled programming. . ."

"That was . . . odd. . ." Sarah remarked, having turned to listen to the announcement while in the middle of washing the dirt from her hands; the faucet still running hot water. "You don't think we'll *actually* have to worry about this situation resulting in a Russian nuclear attack, do you?"

Tom wished he could calm his wife's fears—tell her everything was going to be okay, that this was only a test—but with political tensions being at an all time high for the past eleven years, he found it difficult to come up with something to say. Would Russia decide to send its 200+ missiles over to annihilate the United States? He wanted to say no, that the thought of the world reaching the breaking point of *Mutually Assured Destruction* was an impossibility—that Russia, China, North Korea, and other nuclear capable countries would step down from their threats once the rest of the world promised to follow suit with their own *nuclear attack.* Unfortunately, the state of the world (being in a seemingly endless state of political unrest, with countless wars and conflicts appearing over the horizon as each day passed) proved that we, as a species, were doomed to witness our demise. The only thing which surprised Tom was how long it took for the world to reach this point.

"Babe?" Sarah's voice echoed, bringing his attention back to the outside world. "Do you think we should start packing everything we need and gather up the kids to head to the nearest shelter? I'm getting worried."

It wouldn't matter, he thought. By the time we—the *average American citizen*—were notified that an onslaught of Russian nukes were headed toward us we would only have ten to fifteen minutes to gather the government approved essentials, pack up the car, and race to the nearest shelter; with no guarantee there would be enough room to house us during the attack. If you aren't a government official, economic juggernaut, Hollywood celebrity, right-wing nut job with your own (poorly made) "end of times" bunker, or have connections, you're fucked. Not wanting to frighten his wife, who was already showing signs of experiencing an anxiety attack—having left the living room to fidget in the kitchen; counting food supplies and considering what would last them fourteen days—Tom kept his pessimistic (albeit honest) thoughts to himself. Without warning, startling him and Sarah, the television screen flickered back to an *Emergency Broadcast System* backdrop. This time, instead of reading *Emergency Alert System* at the top of the screen it read *National Alert: Emergency Action Notification*, followed by the automated voice's announcement that a speech from the President would commence shortly.

When the screen flickered to show the President, something seemed off about the presentation of the scene at hand. Unlike the previous spokesman, who had made his appearance in a well-lit, packed room—filled with other politicians and cameramen—as he made the announcement that nuclear war was a *possibility*, the President sat in the shadows; his face obscured in darkness like a villain from a Cold War Era James Bond film—wishing to remain enigmatic until the *appropriate* moment to reveal himself. Moments passed, it seemed, before the President finally spoke—leaving a tension in the air which made both Tom and Sarah grow uncomfortable.

> "My fellow Americans . . . As you know, our attempts at preventing *nuclear war* have failed. There are currently two hundred and fifty Russian missiles heading toward the United States and seventy-five others heading for Canada. I would like to apologize that myself and my advisers were *unsuccessful* in diffusing the situation. The only advice I can give the American public, at this time, is to pray; pray for yourselves. Pray for your loved ones. Pray for forgiveness. Pray for a—"

Cutting the President off mid-sentence, their television screen shorted out for a brief moment before flickering back on—playing only white noise.

Nothing, not even a word (or a heavy-weighted sigh) could manage to escape between Tom and Sarah. They both simply stood in their living room. Stuck in place. Words escaped them—Benjamin still sleeping in his rocker; unaware of the dire situation. Staring down at his son a wave of sadness washed over him. To think, he and his sisters would never get to experience a fulfilling life like he and his mother had had the chance to. They would spend the last moments of their childhood —a period of life which should be spent *drowning in naive innocence*— not knowing if tomorrow were certain. He wouldn't deny the world wasn't a utopia, far from it, but a parent wants the best for their children, regardless. It depressed him, knowing his children (along with his wife and himself) would be dead in half an hour.

Without the television as a warranted distraction, silence penetrated the entire house. Had it not been for the constant annoying buzz of static coming from the TV, it would have gone unnoticed. Looking around, it came to Tom's attention that everything around him seemed to have been put on pause. Baffled, he called out to his wife, telling her to gather up the kids and head to his office space—the only room without a window—finding it to be the safest place in the house (telling himself no irradiation from the nuclear blast could find its way to them in there); his cries being in vain as Sarah and Benjamin, along with everything else in the room, remained frozen in place. *What the fuck is going on?* his mind screamed as it raced for an explanation which would justify why everything (except himself) was experiencing temporal suspension; something he thought was only possible in works of science fiction.

Taking a few steps toward the front door, to see if the rest of the world was experiencing the strange anomaly, each step echoing throughout the house, Tom could feel his heart pounding—loud enough to break the unwanted silence.

As he passed through the doorway, leading him outside, Tom's fears met him at a high velocity—forcing the wind out of his lungs. What he saw was a sight he had only witnessed in his nightmares during the outlining stages of *Ascension*; in the distance, off in the northern section of the Santa Ana skyline, what would have appeared to most to be a jet soaring through the clouds was a Russian Intercontinental Nuclear Missile heading for central Los Angeles—it too being frozen in place above its desired destination; its imminent detonation hanging over the city while nearby residents desperately (hopelessly) attempted to escape the blast radius. With everything at a standstill the scenery felt like an interactive photograph. Deciding to head in the direction of the missile, having come to the conclusion he wasn't in any danger—as long as the world remained suspended—Tom's thoughts began to wander aimlessly. First, he cursed himself for not buying season tickets this year for Disneyland; Sarah being a fan of going there with the kids during winter, when they would decorate sections of the park with *The Nightmare Before Christmas* themed props—loving each child's reaction when they saw a life-sized Jack Skellington and Oogie Boogie looming over them as they approached *The Haunted House*. His thoughts continued to hop from one topic to the next (eventually questioning the realism of the plot of the 1988 classic *Die Hard—with the amount of injuries John McClane accumulated throughout the film, he would've died during his first encounter with Mr. Gray Sweatpants*), the scenery around him began to slowly shift forward in time; the nuclear missile inching its way to detonation.

Continuing to walk toward the inevitable catastrophe, eventually reaching the city limits, Tom watched as the silhouette of the missile disappeared into the horizon. At a slow-paced time lapse, a flash of white light blinded the entire scene for a brief moment; followed by sudden darkness as the horrific sight of the mushroom cloud began to build vertically—reaching for the stratosphere. What happened next struck Tom. An oddity. Instead of a rippling heat wave radiating from the explosion, the skyline became engulfed in cacophonous white noise static; consuming everything in its path as it traveled outward— the screams of everyone in the distance becoming nothing more than a sea of random frequencies—becoming static, themselves. Frightened, Tom went to let out his own agonized scream at the sight which lay before him, but only silence came out as the wall of noise consumed him as well. . .

The sound of children's laughter woke Tom from his nightmare. Still anxious, he refused to move for a moment before turning to see what time it was. His iPod dock read 8:47am, Saturday, August 26, 2028. *Jesus*, he choked as he lifted himself up, *How long have I been asleep? Last I remember, it was only Tuesday. . .* Standing up, still disoriented from his slumber, Tom headed for the living room downstairs to find the kids sitting on the couch; Christie and Matilda sharing one cushion—fixated with their mother's iPad as they watched some obscure kid's show on Netflix. Sitting down next to his two daughters (Benjamin sleeping soundly in his rocker on the right side of the couch) he found his *Modus Operandi* notes which had gone missing during his nightmarish, highly realistic dream. Next to it, however, rested an object which shouldn't have existed outside of his subconscious—the *black leather notebook. . .*

· · ·

A MONTH HAD PASSED since Theodore's exile; whispered rumors still being spread about the hospital's walls, hoping to find an explanation for the unheard act of exiling a *Director*. Some would claim racism, that he was thrown out due to his dark ebony complexion, while another jumped to the drastic conclusion that Theodore had been caught desecrating unconscious Subjects—performing eugenics, removing organs for bizarre tests, etc. Some even made the accusation he was having intercourse with a few of them; men and women, it didn't matter, Elizabeth overheard a resident say as she made her way down the corridor towards the Quiet Room. Despite knowing the truth, Elizabeth kept quiet. Had she revealed the truth behind Theodore's banishment she would have unleashed an uproar among the citizens of this hospital—bringing about a riot which could put Pierce's life in jeopardy. And while she agreed with Theodore on the issue which led to him being cast out into the Wasteland, she couldn't risk banishment as well; being as close as she was to cracking the mystery of the comatose Subjects; freeing them from their *unsuspecting slumber*. It didn't take long for Elizabeth to ignore the preposterous rumors which had made themselves commonplace among the hospital's residents.

With Pierce acting as the sole-Director of the hospital, Elizabeth had been *unofficially promoted* to second in command—Pierce refusing to grant her the title of Co-Director. It didn't feel much different from before, to be honest, having been Pierce and Theodore's brightest, most promising protege (although Theodore would have never admitted it, believing if she knew his true feelings toward her she would cease to improve her efforts), as she walked through each level—every hallway—of the hospital's gray, lonesome walls.

Only Winsome occupied the Quiet Room today, Pierce having called it a day hours ago—claiming fatigue. "You should talk with the Director. Ask him if we could send someone to some of the neighboring settlements and request they send some of their best minds our way. I've been working doubles since Theodore's . . . 'decision' to leave us— Meredith's nothing more than a setback when it comes to *our* work."

"I'll see what I can do, Friedrich, but *you and I* both know Pierce isn't one to ask for help if *he* feels the hospital doesn't need it."

A defeated sigh left Winsome's throat, turning away from the wall of blackboards, having given up for the time being on solving the *unsolvable*. "Do you even think it's worth the trouble?" he asked.

"Feeling pessimistic, are we?"

"It's the truth, Liz," Winsome could tell she hated being called 'Liz'—the mood of the entire room having changed as soon as the monosyllabic nickname left his tongue. "Men. . ." a pause, he glanced over at Elizabeth to find her giving him an unapologetic stare, ". . .*and women* of science have been trying to figure this shit out for well over a hundred years, if not longer. What makes you think we —*we! of all people*—will be able to find the answers to this. . .this mess? And Pierce would prefer it if we shut this entire project down. Even *he* understands what a waste it is on our resources. Theodore was a damned fool to believe we could bring these people out of 'hibernation'; for all we know, they're already dead and we're just prolonging their suffering by keeping them going."

"You don't believe that. You can't."

"And what if I do? I mean, Christ, Elizabeth, what good would it do to wake them up, huh; to be met with immense confusion—possibly depression—the moment they take their first few steps into this grim reality, a reality we've had the 'honor' of calling our own all our lives, having lived *their entire lives* walking around in a lucid dream. *It could drive them insane!*"

"If you really feel this way, Friedrich, then why do you continue to come here, day-in and day-out, and *waste your time* at a gigantic blackboard? Please, tell me, because everything that's coming out of your mouth doesn't make any sense when pressed up against your actions. You claim it to be insanity—to continue our work—yet you choose (*choose! no one here is twisting your arm!*) to come down here and waste your days (and nights!) away supposedly working on a problem you deem unsolvable. *That*, my dear Friedrich, is *actual insanity.*"

Winsome swallowed his tongue. He didn't expect Elizabeth to have such a strong opinion about their work down here; especially an opinion which opposed Pierce's—the man she was in a 'secret' relationship with (and probably fucking senseless each night, he assumed). Had he the nerve to admit why he continued to torture himself by coming down to the third floor of the hospital every day, despite showing no *real* progress since Subject 2773/Cordelia's awakening—that it was her conviction and Theodore's optimism which kept him from quitting and asking for reassignment. With Theodore gone, however, Winsome's attitude toward the Subjects began to slip; moving more toward Pierce's pessimistic views. Impressionable, he was. A trait which many who knew him had claimed would come back to bite him in the ass, eventually.

As Winsome continued to stand still, looking dumbstruck (feeling it as well), Elizabeth made her way to the blackboard to continue her work; periodically taking a break so she could rewrite her solutions into a worn black leather-bound notebook, hoping to avoid the possibility of losing her progress if the mysterious saboteur were to strike again—erasing everyone's work—forcing them to start over. Again.

With the sound of chalk scratching against slate, Elizabeth's thoughts wandered elsewhere; to Theodore and how he was doing in the Wasteland. She knew he would be okay for a while, having gone out on expeditions for medical supplies and to visit nearby settlements, but even someone as experienced with the outside world as Theodore would run into complications eventually.

About a Month Ago. . .

No matter what he did, having tried everything in the hospital's arsenal of medical supplies, the Subject's vitals refused to either spike or slow to the point of cardiac arrest. He was, however, able to induce one of the Subject's *infamous* seizures. Was he proud of his actions? To've sunk to the point of attempting *murder?* No. But the Subject (Subject No. 2990), he felt, had always been nothing more than a liability; causing the hospital to revert far too many of its resources to keeping him stable. *This sack of worthless human shit has been nothing but a pain in the ass since his birth!* his mind screamed as he went on to try the next possible solution to his problem. *Yet my father and grandfather felt the desire to keep him alive. . .* He resented him. Taking the attention he desired from his father and grandfather away from him—all because he (the Subject) 'experienced complications' and was 'unable to take care of himself'; unlike himself—a child born with an active brain. *To think, I had to wait thirty-two years to be able to do this. . .*

"What the hell do you think you're doing?" asked a familiar voice.

It was Theodore.

Turning away from the Subject, his violent gaze landing on his old childhood friend's silhouette, Pierce found himself unable to speak. What could he say that would justify his malevolent actions? (I am at a loss for words, as well, to be honest. . .) Theodore wouldn't understand, would be unable to sympathize with him. Unlike Pierce, Theodore valued the lives of every Subject (much like his own predecessors); Subject No. 2990 being no different. After a brief moment of silence, the two of them still staring each other down in a cold, emotionless haze, Theodore repeated his question; not a fan of being ignored—especially by an old friend. Instead of answering him, he turned back to the Subject and, having run out of options—and, quite frankly, time—placed his hands around the Subject's neck and began to strangle him; hoping to squeeze what little life the bastard had left in him.

Instinct kicked in as an immediate response, adrenaline pumping through Theodore's veins—allowing him the ability to run at a speed he hadn't been able to since his younger years—as he darted toward Pierce. Making contact with his old friend, laying his hands on both of his shoulders, he attempted to pull him off and away from the Subject.

Theodore begged, "Please, Pierce, think about what you're doing. This isn't right. You know it. I know it. Don't let your father's past indiscretion continue to cloud your judgment. Now, please, let him go. I beg of y—"

A swift elbow to Theodore's jaw knocked him back; his grip on Pierce's shoulders having loosened, causing him to lose his footing for a moment. *That's going to hurt come morning.* he thought while he collected himself for another attempt to restrain his friend. Success. Having managed to release Pierce's hold on the Subject's neck, he spun his friend around and, with a tightly closed fist, punched him square in the jaw—*tit for tit, my friend.*

While Pierce attempted to recover from Theodore's retaliatory blow, Theodore stepped up to Subject No. 2990's sleeping chamber to find he was still in critical condition. He noticed an open medicine container and the leftover powder of Lorazepam, assuming Pierce had crushed several tablets to a dust to add to the Subject's IV solution, hoping to kill him in the process. Moving quickly, he elevated the Subject's head with one hand while the other blindly searched the nearest medical drawer for Flumazenil and a clean syringe so he could inject the Subject, hoping to nullify the Lorazepam's effects. And as Pierce cursed in the background, Theodore's jab having caused him to bite his tongue hard enough to cause blood to fill his mouth—spitting out small puddles in-between each curse word, Theodore waited by the Subject's side, hoping he'd have enough time to watch the medication do its work. *Why does Pierce have it out for you?*

Blunt force trauma to Theodore's head knocked him unconscious. Pierce stood over his friend's limp body, still holding his weapon of choice: a bedpan.

Coming to to find himself confined to a chair, startled, Theodore's attention bounced about the room to realize he was being held in the hospital's security wing; the night shift's guard, young Andrew Goodman, sitting behind his desk, filling out paper work.

"I never thought I'd have a Di-Di-Director on the other side of my desk," Andrew's voice echoed throughout the small room. "You must've fucked up real bad to land yourself *here*, Director Webb. Director Needham, naturally, refused to pr-pr-privy me as to why, leaving me at a standstill when it comes to this damned p-p-p-p-paperwork."

Before Theodore could open his mouth to explain the situation—truthfully—Pierce stepped through the door. His lower jaw having developed a lump and a bruise where Theodore's fist had made impact. He could only wonder what *he* looked like, having taken a blow to the chin *and* back of the head. "You may leave us, Andrew." Pierce said in his usual calm and collected demeanor—refusing to let Andrew in on what had transpired between the two of them earlier in the lower levels of the hospital; he found no need to bring a lowly security guard in on their *disagreement.*

"B-But I still got myself quite a bit of paperwork to finish, a-and I'll need a written statement from both of you on—"

"Andrew. . ." Pierce's voice became stern, "Don't make me reassign you, again. How many times must we go through this? Pretty soon, we'll run out of places to send you. I'm certain you understand what that means, yes?"

"Ex-exile." Andrew said, a hint of sadness in his voice.

"And we wouldn't want that now, would we Andrew?"

Andrew shook his head, "N-n-no sir."

"Good. At least we understand what's at stake. Now, Andrew, please escort yourself from the premises. Here," tossing Andrew a small stack of ration tokens, "get yourself a late-night snack to calm yourself."

Andrew left, ration tokens in hand, still frightened at the thought of being exiled from the hospital; the door closing behind him slowly as his footsteps grew distant. "Fucking retards." Pierce said, "Another one of our fathers' *blunders.*"

"Why are you doing this?"

"Why? You seriously have to ask me why, old friend? Have you taken a moment to look around the hospital as you walk its halls? It's disgusting. Retards. Subjects. Schizophrenics. This place is overrun with worthless excuses for human existence—people our fathers welcomed with open arms, refusing to release them from their pathetic lives—and you have the nerve to ask me *why?*"

"So it wasn't just the one Subject you wanted dead; you wish to exterminate all of them?"

"They're a waste of time, Theodore. You and I both know that. We're never going to be able to wake *them all* up from their brain-dead states. In the end, it'll be better for us if we just lay them to rest. *Finally.*"

"But Cordelia. . ."

"Cordelia was a fluke and you know it. Her I'll allow the misfortune of continuing to live; she may prove herself useful in the future. As for the others, especially Subject No. 2990, it'll basically be a mercy killing. As for the others—*the retards and crazies*—they'll be sentenced to exile. They'll make a lovely meal for the creatures and savages out there in the desert."

"I won't allow this—this lunacy to occur, Pierce. It's inhumane!"

"And then there's you. . . I don't know if I'll ever feel *comfortable* again with you here, having experienced such a violent, and unwarranted, outburst from you. Perhaps you're beginning to experience the same misfortune your father met; a malignant brain tumor eating at your mind, causing you to have sudden flashes of paranoia, leading you to attack those around you while lost in an imaginary haze. I mean . . . it did happen to your father, who's to say it couldn't happen to us, as well? *It could run in the family for all we know.* And who are they going to believe—*a violent, deranged Negro?* or the Director with a fat bruise alongside his jaw? And with you out of the picture I'm certain the citizens of this hospital will come around to seeing things *my way.*"

Theodore refused to say anything else. Even if he ended up being exiled he knew the hospital's citizens wouldn't allow a genocide to occur within the building's walls. Those '*retards and crazies*' had family members—family members who cared for them and loved them unconditionally, despite their flaws. As for the Subjects, Theodore knew people like Elizabeth (especially Elizabeth, who would be able to sway Pierce into leaving the Subjects out of his purge; at least for a while) wouldn't allow their entire life's work be put to an end without a fight. *Go ahead and exile me,* he thought. *This doesn't spell out victory for you.*

• • •

THE LOS ANGELES LANDSCAPE had its own, undeniable charm. One that would usually go *unannounced* by anyone else who happened to come across it—only seeing the city as a place of depravity and hopelessness. She may not be what she was before the war raped her of her beauty, but what was left of Los Angeles' exterior (the all-but-rubble 'eco-friendly' homes, various shopping centers scattered across the landscape, large structural buildings [similar to the hospital's design] where—it is fabled—men and women of the 'upper-class' would spend their entire lives *pissing on those who were beneath them* in order to keep them submissive enough to work for *piss-poor* wages, and monumental structures where people used to go for scholarly pursuits; universities, they were called) was enough to still make Theodore gawk in astonishment—even at the wise age of forty-seven—at how civilization lived *before the bombs fell*.

Walking along a strip of old shopping establishments, Theodore Webb recalled a memory from his youth—the first time he ever walked into one of these buildings (a Costco, if his memory served him correctly) he couldn't understand why prewar society would *need* a place where produce and other household supplies were kept in bulk for everyone to come, periodically, to consume as desired when they had the ability to grow and harvest their own food on their own property, since the soil had yet to be soaked in radiation. It wouldn't be until years later when he entered a high school, assuming it was a place with medical supplies, where he would discover several educational texts, explaining the ways of the old world to him; the *Laws of Supply & Demand* restricting the amount of product available to the town's citizens (increasing the value of said item), creating a false sense of life or death should the ability to acquire the desired item become an impossibility for the less fortunate—Capitalism's 'humane' approach of establishing population control: if one cannot provide for themselves (and, by extension their family) they'll eventually waste away due to starvation, leaving only those who *can* to thrive; causing the demand of said product to decrease, lowering the price of said item—making it affordable for the families who didn't have access (and are now deceased) months prior. Theodore couldn't believe such a flawed economic principle would be allowed to continue as common practice for as long as it had. The hospital's system of running things had always been the complete opposite; that everyone should be *allowed to have the same opportunities and access* to food and medical supplies. Had he been alive before the war, Theodore would have propositioned to the American government that they jettison such an inhumane economic concept and, instead, establish the same principles he was raised with—and if there was ever a period when supplies were insufficient, he would implement another economic principle he had read: the bartering system. From what he had read, it seemed the most efficient. *It's basically what we were all doing up at the hospital. . .* he remarked as he continued his journey southbound on the war-torn streets of Los Angeles. *Why couldn't we, as a society, live like that before; leaving us to be overcome with greed to the point of damn-near extinction. . .* Capitalism. It didn't make sense to him.

It wasn't until the day's end, the pale sun having disappeared behind a wave of clouds as it sank behind the city's skyline, when the sight of the city limit sign appeared beyond the horizon, Theodore having spent most of the day scouring through every shopping center he happened to come across for whatever non-perishable food items he could find to take in order to last him until he reached his final destination; the city of San Pedro—to meet up with his wife and kids, *finally*; hopefully, if they were still there. If they made it there *at all*, actually. The fear of finding their decaying corpses along the way gently pecking at his brain as he continued; leaving the towering city of Los Angeles (and his old life) behind.

4

T CANNOT BE SAID with *any measure of certainty* whether or not the work we do for the Subjects will ever amount to anything but a waste of time and resources. At least this is what Pierce continues to tell me and the rest of us in the neurological field. Having convinced some of the others of Theodore's supposed crime (unable to sway myself and a scattered few of those among us—I having, unbeknownst to Pierce's knowledge, overheard his and Theodore's final conversation in the security wing before Theodore's exile a few days later), productivity in the Quiet Room became *practically non-existent*; leaving the obligation of finding the solution to myself and the assorted notes which were left behind upon Theodore's sudden departure. Because despite what Pierce continues to try and convince me every time we lie in bed together in the late hours of the night, that pulling the plug on *Project Arcadia* will only help push the hospital forward (being able to use the resources we've been using to keep the Subjects alive toward 'more productive means'; means which he refuses to share with me), I still believe the Subjects are the Key.

I hope this *destructive phase* Pierce finds himself in passes over him soon. If not, and he and I continue to fight over how to run things, I fear he may conspire against me in the same manner he was forced to do with poor, old Theodore. . .and unlike Theodore, I wouldn't last a day out in the arid wastes of Los Angeles.

I wonder how he's doing; how far he's made it these past few weeks; if I could manage to build an expedition crew—without Pierce catching wind of its existence—I would send them out to make sure my old friend was doing well. Unfortunately, Pierce has the hospital under heavy surveillance these days. . .so any hope of wandering out into the wilderness has been rendered an impossibility. . .for now.

- Elizabeth Hestler

• • •

HAVING NOT MADE IT as far as he would have liked, having spent a few weeks in the small settlement of Shrapnel (once known, in a previous life, as Huntington Park)—the citizens of the small makeshift town's hospitality having been welcoming enough to convince him to cancel his traveling plans for a while—if memory from previous journeys served him well enough, he calculated he was still seven hours away from his desired destination. He would never admit it to anyone back at the hospital, but part of him wouldn't have minded spending the rest of his life in a settlement like Shrapnel. It would've taken him a while to adjust to certain customs the town's residents practiced—weekly spiritual worship of 'the holy piece of shrapnel' at the northern section of the city (an old broadcasting satellite, FOX NEWS, which had plummeted to the Earth's surface roughly a decade after the Great War; the early citizens of Shrapnel having viewed it as *a sign from God*), the liberal use of any found drugs they happened to come across (as well as the creation of various cocktails), and the practice of only referring to oneself (as well as naming any future offspring) by only one name (very odd names as well, he noticed: Atom, Peregrine, Nat, Eldritch, Wendigo, and Kilgore being a few examples)—but other than that, Theodore Webb found the life of a 'Wastelander' to be a grand re-prieve from his life back at the hospital.

It didn't take long for Theodore to come across the familiar horrors of the outside world. Having come across a vast ocean of skeletons and fresh rotting corpses—the weathered bones welcoming the newly de-ceased to the world of slow decay—the ripe smell of mortality became a mainstay in Theodore's nostrils, even after the land below his feet had long been cleared of *bone and sinew*; the thought hadn't crossed his mind to question how the freshly made corpses came to find their way along the rubble-filled streets. For all he knew (hoped? yes, hoped sounds more appropriate), they had once found themselves in a similar position as he, himself, was in—having been cast out of their own homestead and were forced to seek shelter among the barren streets of old Los Angeles; casting judgment upon the departed as being "ill-equipped and far-too-fragile" for the *unknown dangers* of the California desert. The reality being unpleasant when compared to the censorious theory Theodore wished were the truth: that they were unfortunate enough to have crossed paths with barbaric drifters along their journey, the drifters, being unsatisfied with whatever they had on them as loot, shooting them down where they stood without thinking twice before carrying onward to the next settlement they wished to ransack. Such simple minded individuals.

As the hours pressed forward, the pale sun having arched itself over-head, beating down on the lonesome traveler, the distant sounds of gunfire and screaming echoing faintly throughout the Earth's barren landscape, Theodore finding solace in the chaotic nature the Califor-nia wilderness brought him (it being a wonderful change of rhythm when compared to the humdrum of the sleeping chambers), an unfa-miliar sound made itself known—just beyond the horizon. Growing nearer, the noise becoming a constant buzzing in his ears, Theodore paused to look around, scoping his surroundings as best he could; hop-ing to find whatever it was making the foreign disturbance. Nothing. Just dust and echoes. Whatever it was, it refused to make itself known to him. But the noise still continued. . .drowning out the distant screams and (now sporadic) gunfire.

Looking up, he saw what appeared to be a *rather large mechanical looking bird* soaring through the Earth's anemic blue sky. He had witnessed some colossal sized birds throughout the many expeditions he'd gone on with his father, their unnatural and ungodly proportions being the result of extended exposure to nuclear fallout. But the creature which soared overhead was unlike any aviary beast he had ever encountered; its body giving off a blinding metallic sheen, the sun's rays reflecting from its featherless torso. As it continued to pass over him it also appeared to be losing elevation, growing in size with each passing second, the buzzing sound becoming a deafening roar as it descended. Feeling the old *adventurous* desire to examine a wild creature, having been unable to go out on an expedition since he became a Director, Theodore rummaged through his rucksack to count the number of supplies he had—determining whether or not he would have enough to last him *until the next settlement* (which, having been gifted some essentials from the people of Shrapnel, he had more than he had accounted for)—and decided to backtrack (hopefully only a few miles) towards the descending beast; praying it would remain landed long enough for him to study it from afar, if not up close.

Sundown came and went, the final sliver of an amber colored moon having become his only source of light, as Theodore continued his laborious march toward the landing site of the metallic creature. *I hope it's still there when I arrive* he prayed, not wanting his haphazard decision to backtrack toward the city of Shrapnel—hoping to quell his curiosity—to be in vain.

The distant screams and gunfire which had consumed all hours of the daytime, it seemed, had ceased come nightfall. The sudden silence, having become a foreign presence, bringing with it a sense of horror to a now dimly lit landscape. The dying light of the distant moon only lighting the path enough for one to not trip over their own two feet.

When the silhouette of the creature finally came into view, Theodore could see plumes of pale white smoke rising to the stars; signs of a small, controlled fire. He cursed under his breath, *Son of a bitch. . .somebody beat me to it. . .*

As he edged closer, he could see it was only a lone traveler who had set up camp alongside the *mechanical beast.* Shouldn't be a problem, he thought. He'd dealt with strangers before on previous expeditions. Most people who found themselves out in the desert still had their sanity about them, asking any approaching stranger to identify themselves before coming any closer, hoping to avoid any unnecessary bloodshed; only on occasion would one come across a band of drifters who would soon enough kill you where you stood. But, contrary to popular belief, *most of them* were civil enough to keep you alive long enough to figure out if you were worth the trouble before deciding to *kill you or not*. You'd have to consider yourself lucky if they chose to go with the latter.

A single gunshot rang through the air. Before he could react, Theodore heard a brief whistle pass by his right ear; a lone bullet whizzing by—barely missing him. An annoying ring making itself home alongside his eardrum. Instinct kicking in, he fell to the floor. Hoping that feigning being hit by the stranger's gunshot would allow him enough cover to inch closer and overwhelm them—taking their weapon and demand why they shot at him without warning.

"Don't, not ev'n for a minute, think you fallin' to tha ground's gonna fool me, mister!" yelled the stranger. "That there wuz only a *warning shot*—'wuzn't even aiming fer yer skull. 'wuz just hoping to frighten yuh a bit, that's all. Going by yer cowardly response, I'mma guessin' it worked." They let out a short fit of laughter.

Theodore screamed, "You could've fucking said something before *shooting at me*," his voice creaked, still frightened. "I think you might've busted my right eardrum, for Christ's sake."

"Well *maybe* yuh shouldn' be wearin' a white long-coat, mister. It kinda gives you away—'specially at nighttime." Smart ass. Without his lab coat Theodore would've froze to death on the first night. An experienced traveler would know that. "Well don't be shy," the stranger called out, "come 'n join me by the fire. I sure could use the company, and *I'm betting* yuh could use the heat of a fire—looks like it's gonna be a cold one t'night."

Choosing to accept the generous offer to join the fellow traveler, more out of necessity than out of curiosity, having wasted the day away backtracking several miles to examine the enigmatic, metallic creature, acknowledging he too would have to set up camp soon (*why not take advantage of a free fire—and possibly some food, if the stranger offered*), Theodore Webb made his way off the paved road, toward the makeshift campsite.

"I must say," the traveler, who, upon closer inspection, was a young female—stark white hair, a bit on the short, hefty side (if Theodore had to make a guess, he'd say she was *just over* five feet tall), her porcelain skin pale enough to illuminate even the darkest of nights, "it's nice to know I won' hafta wait days, if not weeks, before a nearby search 'n rescue team decide ta come find me. Whatchu doin' out this late anyway, mister?"

Regrettably, Theodore responded, "I hate to say this, but I'm not a 'search and rescue' party of any kind. I was originally on my way down south before I saw the creature behind you crash land—"

"You mean my aeroplane?" the traveler, laughing, chimed in to correct him, "Shucks, mister, whadyou think it was, a giant-ass bird? Jeez, you don't get out much, do yuh? Well, if youse ain't my knight in shining armor, then who the heck are yuh?"

Theodore introduced himself and explained his situation to the young woman, explaining how he'd been cast out of his 'settlement' under false pretenses, having been betrayed by his oldest friend—set up to appear a monster to the rest of the 'town's' residents—and was currently on his way to the city of San Pedro to meet up with his wife and kids; unsure whether or not his family were still there, but remaining hopeful regardless.

"Dammit, Theo-dore, yuh gone'n started up my waterworks," a swift punch to Theodore's left shoulder, a sharp sting coursing through his torso before the arm itself went numb. "My name's Chevrolet, by the way," she acknowledged as she wiped away her tears, "Chevrolet Flieger, and this here's my trusty fly-bird—I call her *Charity*. My pride 'n joy. Took me lit'rally *years* t'find all them necessary parts I needed to get her keister up and flying again. Unfortunately, as you can see, I underestimated the amount of fuel she'd need to make it from Bomb City to them *Northern Mountains*."

Theodore turned to examine the grounded aeroplane known as *Charity*. He felt foolish believing it could've been a creature of biological design, that its metallic sheen was an organic occurrence; the dim light from the fire reflecting from the nose of the cockpit; its gleaming presence appearing to be mocking him as he continued to stare it down; losing (miserably) at a one-sided staring contest—with a machine for the love of God. . .Chevrolet continuing to share, in immense detail, what she had to go through "just to find the proper parts to build a decent tail-end"—eventually using any spare parts she could salvage from nearby vehicles and beached ships. A pain in her "backside" she'd claim.

An explosion in the distance, east of their current position, rose above the horizon—its blinding neon orange arms stretching out from the earth with a fevered intensity, desperately reaching for the moon and the stars; causing a brief pause in Chevrolet's long-winded anecdote. "Jesus. What do you think happened over there?" a curious Theodore asked, hoping to divert the conversation to *anything* other than the banal topic of aeronautics—a subject he knew very little about.

"Prolly just another town experiencing an unfortunate 'warm welcome' from a small gang of drifters. Normally they don't use explosions of such magnitude. Must've been an area where one of many E.R.Ws landed during the *war*."

"I'm sorry, I hate to ask, but what's an *E.R.W?*"

"Holy sweet mother of Francis, Theodore, you don't get out much do you?"

". . .is it that obvious?"

"Just a lil'bit," a fit of laughter left Chevrolet's stomach. "E.R.W. stands fer *explosive remnant o'war*. It simply means the damned thing didn't go *KABOOM!* when it hit ground. But that don't mean it won't go off without the proper . . . motivation—if yer gettin' me." She winked, hoping to get the old man to laugh at such a macabre situation with the subtle use of sexual innuendo—but only a continued look of confusion remained; not even an awkward smile could find its way to his face. "Thankfully," continuing on with reassurance, "it looks far away enough ta not be of immediate danger to us. And goin' by the size of that explosion, them drifters'll be fewer in numbers if they decide to come this way. Nothing me and my AMT Hardballer can't handle," another unnecessary (inappropriate) wink as she brandished her pistol—the same pistol she'd used to fire off a 'warning shot' which deafened Theodore's right ear. "It's getting late, though. I say you 'n' I take shifts. I got first watch, you just close them ebony eyelids of yers and dream yerself to sleep—promise I won't rummage through yer knapsack and leave you stranded here alongside ol'*Charity*; I kinda like keeping you around fer the company; yer kinda funny."

A cold chill running down his spine, the fire having died moments ago, pried Theodore's eyes open. With what was left of the moon having hidden itself behind a body of clouds, only the dim light from the sea of stars lit the surrounding area; Chevrolet's incessant snoring having carried through most of the night, making it hard for him to fall asleep, had stopped finally. Reaching for his rucksack, wishing to use the afghan comforter his wife had made him for their wedding so he could fall back asleep, his hand met the cold barren dirt. Turning around, believing to have forgotten where he'd laid down his belongings, Theodore's eyes met a set of worn steel-toed boots inches away from his face (the steel of the toes exposed, the top layer of leather having fallen away ages ago from excessive use); looking up to find a lanky looking character—he couldn't have been older than sixteen—staring down at him as he dumped Theodore's contents out of the rucksack, gravity throwing them onto the cold desert; a warped smile across his face, his gangrenous gums making his yellow-stained teeth (what little he had left, anyway) appear luminous in the pitch-black dark of night. He looked around to find two other drifters searching the surrounding area. Chevrolet was nowhere to be found. Her knapsack and weapons having disappeared with her. *My God*, he thought, *the others must've dragged her off somewhere, doing who-knows-what to her. . .*

"Well look what we 'ave 'ere, boys." escaped a tired, weathered voice —a voice too chilling (he thought) to have come from such a small framed individual. "We gots ourselves a dark-skinned fella. You don't see much of them these days, now do we?" the young man spoke as he continued to search the empty rucksack for contents worth stealing. Unsatisfied with his findings, the young drifter knelt down to Theodore's level. "Now what's an *old Negro like you* doing out 'ere in the wilderness, huh? I figured yer kind had died out decades ago when *Crazy Phoenix Lancaster* did them experiments wif people like you— tryin' ta see if you dark color'd folk could last longer when exposed to that *radioactif mumbo-jumbo* than yer typical light-skinned feller. 'ell I'll be honest wif'yih, I didn't mind the fucker testing out 'is crazy lil tests on random strangers, but when he started taking *my people* captive, that's when I 'ad to put me foot down." he pantomimed a gunshot to his left temple. The young drifter turned to face his fellow nomads, "You idiots find anything yet?"

"Sorry, Gauge," one of them—stoutly in appearance, twice the size of his 'supposed leader', with the voice of an underdeveloped child—replied, "it's just the old dark-skinned fella over there by you an' this *giant pile of warped metal*," he motioned toward the crashed aeroplane known as *Charity*. "It's looking like a bust, if you ask me, boss."

"Well no shit it's a bust, Kreg. I wasn't askin' yih ta state the fucking obvious, yih smart ass. I was askin' if ye'd found anything. How 'bout yih, Dremel—find anything?" The other lackey shook his head. "Yuh still unable to talk after the bullet to the throat?" A slow nod. "Well then start tearing that piece of shit apart, you two. I'm certain we can find *sumthin'* to salvage from it." The quiet one (Dremel?) and Kreg began to make their way to examine the crash site—wondering where they should start to begin tearing the aeroplane apart. "As fer you, my newfound friend" Gauge turned back to face Theodore—who had remained still this entire time, too scared to move—as he slowly pulled out a small caliber six-shooter pistol and aimed it at the frightened old man's head. "I'd say I'm gonna 'ate ending our brief encounter on such a sour note, but. . ." he cocked the hammer back, ". . .but I'd be lyin' if I did. So I guess this is so long—"

Theodore closed his eyes as Gauge's finger moved toward the trigger; accepting his fate. It felt odd. Facing death. He had always imagined either his life would flash before his eyes or he'd experience a last minute epiphany (much like he'd read about in old books he'd salvaged from abandoned bookstores and city libraries). Instead, he only felt anger. Anger toward himself. Toward the wasted life he'd spent away from his family—too absorbed in his work, trying desperately to find a solution for the countless Subjects (people he'd come to know *better than his own wife and kids*) who remained catatonic, and would probably remain that way forever now that Pierce would have *complete control* of the hospital's resources.

Three gunshots rang out in rapid succession. Silence fell shortly after. He waited for the moment when the pain would begin coursing through his body, his brain letting him know his body was dying; but nothing came. Instead, after the ringing had died down, he heard the sound of a two large objects fall hard to the ground. Opening his eyes to see what they could've been Theodore was met with a wounded Gauge falling on top of him. Theodore screamed—muffled and out of breath by the sudden weight of the bleeding drifter. As he continued to struggle for air, the sound of footsteps could be heard moving toward his position. Hoping the mysterious stranger would help him to his feet, old Theodore Webb pushed with what little strength he could muster with Gauge's dead weight becoming more cumbersome with each passing second. While he attempted to push the dying drifter off of him he could've swore he heard him mumble something incoherent —perhaps a last request—but before he could manage to decipher the young man's words the gun wielding stranger stopped beside the two limp bodies and let out a fourth shot into Gauge's skull; the close quarters blast deafening Theodore's left ear. "Oh c'mon!" he screamed, "The other ear? *Really?*"

"Oops, sorry, Theodore," Chevrolet's voice managed to pierce over the high-pitched ringing of his eardrums, "I figured you wuz de'd by the time I fired off the initial three shots. Sorry 'bout that." bending down to help lift the now mutilated Gauge off of Theodore. "You sure are a sound sleeper if three loud-mouthed drifters couldn't wake you. Consider yourself lucky, I guess." she laughed as she picked the old scientist up from the ground, " 'ell, I can't even sleep through a lite drizzle."

Comes with falling asleep in the loud atmosphere of the lower levels most nights. . . he thought, clearing off the dirt from his backside.

"Looks like the lil fucker got sum blood on you." examining Theodore's face and lab coat. "Makes you look more *refined*, if you ask me." She nudged him in the gut before bending back down to pick up Gauge's six-shooter. " 'ere, take this. You could use the protection. Besides, it's not like *he'll be needing it* anytime soon."

"If you thought I was already dead, why did you decide to shoot them?"

"Ain't nobody gon' touch my *Charity* without asking first. That's just principle," she rubbed the tail-end of her crashed aeroplane. "Well," walking over to Dremel's corpse, pushing it over to lay down her knapsack so she could lie down. "I don't know 'bout you, Theodore, but I'm goin' back down fer sum more shut-eye. You 'n' I've got an early mornin' ahead 'f us."

Theodore lie awake for the rest of the night watching the stars pass him by until the first rays of sunshine made their way over the mountains, unable to find rest due to the smell of copper which had permeated his surroundings; the ripe decay of Gauge's mutilated skull filling the air with a smell he'd never encountered before—a smell his nose couldn't shake—the smell of violent death. . .

. . .

SOMETHING FELT OFF ABOUT THIS PAST WEEK. More than usual, it would seem. From the moment he woke up, made breakfast from himself and the kids—Sarah having gone on one of those new 'trendy' diets (cutting out gluten and dairy products), and read the morning paper he could sense an unwanted alteration of the world around him. Colors he'd known his whole life felt off in a myriad of ways. The mint green walls of the dining room seemed drained of its subtle vibrant palate. His orange juice looked anemic. Even the newspaper's usual beige undertones appeared to have faded—leaving its pages pale and lifeless. The entire world, it seemed, had been bled of its natural high-def saturation—like a horrible 1960's sit-com had invaded the world outside of the TV; rendering it in its poorly expressed color palette. Thankfully, however, it was Friday, which meant the weekend would be arriving soon—he only had to get through the school day without incident. Lately, those days were few and far between for Tom Dolin.

Even the drive to work struck him as odd; the landscape of Santa Ana having become nothing but foreign to him. Where the Walmart once stood, a Montgomery Ward now resided—its parking lot packed full of vehicles which couldn't have predated the '50s. Other familiar scenes which he'd grown to detest over the years were now gone; replaced by open fields, fruit stands and dairy farms. By the time he had arrived at the school where he and Sarah taught he'd grown suspicious of his own sanity—questioning whether or not he was (once again!) experiencing another *warped nightmarish dream* where everything around him ceased to be how he remembered it, yet *everyone else* went along with it as if it had always been this way.

"Thomas, my boy! Happy Friday!" Putnam, in a rather good mood, happened to pass Tom on his way to the chem lab. He found it odd that Putnam (*Putnam! of all people*) would be in such a good mood—even if it were Friday; to him, a Friday at work was only a cruel reminder that he would have to return in two days to do it all over again for another set of five; with no sign of early retirement in sight. "Be sure to tell that wife of yours I said 'hello!', will yuh?" Putnam's voice faded as he turned the corner, refusing to slow down for more than a moment—wanting to get the day over with so he could end his day with a Cuban cigar while watching (and falling asleep to) a classic Humphrey Bogart film—*The Big Sleep* being one of his personal favorites, having been a wonderfully rendered film adaptation of the *highly acclaimed debut novel* of the same name by Raymond Chandler; leaving the viewer confused by the cryptic labyrinth which was the film's (and novel's) plot—a relic of the golden days of literature and cinema when film directors and novelists refused to hold your hand, explaining *every minute detail* of the narrative to their hopeful fan base.

The morning bell rang throughout the school. The students who occupied its immense hallways—from the nervous freshman to the experienced, jaded senior—broke from their aimless conversations and—like stoic faced zombies—headed for first period while Principal Dickerson did the morning announcements.

"Good morning, Wombats!" Dickerson's obnoxiously pep-filled voiced echoed from the speakers. "As this week comes to a close, I'd like to remind you all, despite the weekend coming up, to keep up the hard work and diligence as we near the end of our first quarter! As President Kennedy said, *'The goal of education is the advancement of knowledge and the dissemination of truth.'* I believe we can all agree on our President's words of wisdom and do our best to live by them. Also, I'd like to announce—"

Choosing to ignore Principal Dickerson, like everyone else—faculty *and* students—had chose to, since every morning announcement was the same regurgitated inspirational nonsense, Tom Dolin made his way to his classroom; past the seemingly endless maze of adolescent shadows (one moment every single one of them would be nose-deep in their smart phones, texting, tweeting, and updating their latest social media profiles to 'tell the world' that their *regular Friday educational indoctrination* was about to begin, emojis and shorthanded messages abound, while the next they'd be without their crippling technological devices; Tom's eyes never able to keep what they saw consistent, it seemed)—hoping to avoid any further *unusual encounters*.

Without failure, fate would deny him the simple luxury of going the rest of his day without incident. As he turned the corner to head down the hallway to his first class of the day Tom bumped into a student of his heading in the opposite direction, having forgotten to grab their required books from their locker before the bell rung.

It was Regina Wilson.

"Ah, Regina. Heading in the wrong direction, aren't we?"

"I'm so sorry, Mr. Dolin." her face still buried in a book (the same Don DeLillo novel from before), "I forgot to grab my literature and science books before school. Is it okay if I'm a few seconds late to class?"

"Only if you promise me to keep your nose out of that book of yours today. As fascinating as JFK's assassination might be, I assure you I can be *just as interesting*, I promise." he laughed.

A look of confusion met Regina's face. Without saying a word she nodded in response before turning to continue toward her locker, her pace slowing down every few steps to look back at her English teacher —still puzzled by something he said.

"Dolin, my man," Matthew Fritz, the school's tenth grade World History teacher and beatnik burnout who, throughout the school year (it didn't matter if it were hot or cold outside), would only wear black and white striped turtleneck sweaters, unwashed denim cut-offs, and what he referred to as his 'Jesus Boots', "Kennedy may not be who you voted for to be president, but it's not hep at all to even joke about something as serious as *assassination*. Not cool, my man. Not cool at all."

Fritz continued to carry on throughout the now desolate hallways, whistling the tune to Dee Dee Sharp's "Mashed Potato Time"—fading into the distance with each rambunctious step. *What a fucking loon*, Tom thought as he turned to continue toward his own ill-fated destination, his only scheduled lesson plan being this week's vocabulary test and the weekly 'philosophical' discussion. An idea Tom came up with during his third year of teaching to help the students feel less bombarded by the endless onslaught of tests and quizzes they would certainly face throughout their Friday. Instead of writing down topics of discussion which he thought were interesting, he would allow a student to suggest a thread which, if deemed appropriate, they would then spend the rest of the class period pontificating to their heart's content; ending the day with a reading assignment for the weekend to prepare for an open discussion on Monday.

After the vocabulary test, however, only two students raised their hands with suggestions for the classes quasi-philosophical subject matter: Brian Larson—the school's lead quarterback—and (participating in class for the first time? Quick, call the press!) Regina Wilson.

"Yes, Brian, go ahead."

Brian lowered his hand and, taking a moment to gather his thoughts (probably still recovering from last week's concussion from the homecoming game), said, "What if the outside world is just *one large hallway* separating us from the important places we have to be. . ." the other students stared at him in silence. Some refraining from laughter, others curious where this could possibly lead. "Like, imagine the school is just a room and outside. . .outside is an open corri-corridor? between us and the next room—for example, the grocery store. . . the meat market, or even our homes. . ."

"Sounds like someone needs to lay off the dope, am I right?" a student in the back snickered; a small fit of laughter following shortly.

"Now, now, you guys. Let's just calm down," Tom interrupted. "It's not *that off-kilter* to make such a 'bogus claim' that the world is nothing but a—as Brian put it—a *giant hallway?* interconnecting every piece of infrastructure on the planet. One could use the design of a shopping mall to help further clarify this theory—using the giant empty space as the 'outside hallway' and the individual shopping centers as the 'desired room' one wishes to move onto. Would anyone care to add to Brian's reasonable contribution?"

Nobody spoke. Instead, they all traded glances; taking turns staring at him and the clock—counting down the minutes, hoping no one else would speak, ending the rest of class in silence. The air in the room grew thick, the nervous energy between himself and his students making it impossible to breathe. As the silence grew a life of its own, creating a tension he had never felt before, Tom, not wanting to be consumed by it, began to look about the classroom to call upon another student to (hopefully!) fill the void with another 'hopeful' *philosophical discussion*—everyone's eyes piercing through him. Everyone except Regina's, who had buried her nose (again. . .) in the same book she'd been obsessed with since the first day of the school year. She must've been on her third read through of the damn thing. *Must be a good read.*

"Regina." The young girl, after placing her thumb as a temporary place-marker, looked up, remaining silent, her antagonizing gaze being enough of a response. "You always seem *enthralled* during our Friday discussions." A few students laugh at Mr. Dolin's sardonic observation. "I noticed you had your hand up earlier when I asked if anyone had any suggestions for a topic. Did you still have something to contribute or did my calling on Mr. Larson first dissuade you from sharing your thoughts—leading you to retreat, as always, to the hackneyed prose of Mr. DeLillo?"

Brian Larson (and a few others) muttered a rather harmonious "ooh" across the classroom. The sudden change of tone in Tom's voice having led them to believe Regina was about to be sent to Principal Dickerson's office; a place no student—especially females—wished to visit, considering the widespread rumors of Dickerson's (accidentally?) perverse mannerisms toward students.

"Ms. Wilson," his voice grew stern due to Regina's defiance, "I would like a response, please." The once silence-soaked room having been filled with contempt, Tom having grown impatient with Regina's refusal to speak.

Regina cleared her throat, removed her thumb from the pages of her book, placed it inside her backpack, gave Tom Dolin her undivided attention, and said, "What if everything you're experiencing is a lie; nothing more than a *fucked up dream*? What if we're all simply living inside our own heads while doctors pick and prod at our frail uncon-scious bodies—trying to figure us out like an *unsolvable mystery*? What if the world we think we know no longer exists and, in reality, was blown to hell centuries ago; only its ashes remaining. . . What if—"

Before she could continue rambling on (scaring her peers with her intensity) the school's intercom system screamed to life, high pitched feedback squealing from the speaker which hung above the room's blackboard. *What now?* Tom's inner-dialogue spoke annoyingly. *What could Archie possibly have to say this early in the morning?*

"Students and faculty of Central High. This is your principal, Mr. Dickerson. I find no pleasure in this morning's announcement, I'm afraid. It appears that, at 12:30pm, Central Standard Time, while visiting in Dallas, Texas, President John F. Kennedy was shot down and—"

The room went cold as Dickerson continued to ramble on over the intercom. He had to be hallucinating. There was no way the name he'd heard Dickerson speak was *John F. Kennedy's*. Without thinking twice, Tom searched his back pocket for his phone, hoping to lay the hallucinatory based confusion to rest. His phone, however, was nowhere to be found. Shit. Moving to his next resort he turned toward his desk to find only a stack of papers and various office supplies resided on the wooden surface. Tom looked around the entire classroom, hoping to see the same look of confusion on the faces of his students. What he saw, however, wasn't dumbstruck confusion, but dread weighing down the faces of his students—they'd just been told *the leader of their country had been assassinated.*

He had to sit down, gather his thoughts, still reeling from the fact he was experiencing one of the most horrific events in American history— the morning of November 22, 1963. Unwilling to deal with the anxiety-ridden paranoia of the '60s, Tom closed his eyes and, in *Wizard of Oz* fashion, prayed to return to 2028; a time he never thought he'd miss given the transgressive nature of the majority of the populace—countless riots breaking out on the streets, self-righteous political activists from both sides of the major political spectrum parading in a mindless sea of violence (the morally bankrupt left claiming 'crimes against humanity' were being committed by the Republican ruled White House and Congress, the ignorant conservatives—having grown tired of the 'politically correct' dribble being spewed by their Liberal counterparts —started showing up at the liberal's 'Freedom of Expression' rallies and provoking its attendees, convinced they wouldn't retaliate due to their *undying devotion for keeping things peaceful*, while the Libertarians and Centrists apathetically watched from the sidelines; the world continuing to crumble around them). Looking back, it seemed the *great nation of the United States of America* had spent most of its existence in a state of political turmoil—the 1960s being one of the most horrific, being dominated by the Vietnam War, Civil Rights Protests, and the assassinations of JFK, Martin Luther King Jr., and Robert Kennedy. *These kids have one hell of a decade to look forward to...*

Caught up in his thoughts, it had gone unnoticed that the entire classroom was staring up at him. All of them sitting in silence while they waited for him to speak, petrified by Dickerson's announcement. Regaining composure, Tom's attention turned to his students. Something was off. His eyes refused, no matter how hard he tried, to focus on his surroundings; the faces of everyone in the room being nothing but a blur. Calling out to the classroom, hoping someone would respond (and for the love of God, please, not Brian), Tom continued to ask if anyone else had anything to add to their Friday discussion; choosing to ignore recent developments, finding the thought of discussing the assassination of the President of the United States to be in poor taste. Let that be something in the private security of family and friends, not during school hours.

But nobody spoke.

In a flash the world had become a complete negative of itself. What was once stark white had become a blinding pitch black, the color of skin a haunting blue; making everyone and everything in the room feel alien to the eyes. Tom stared out the window to find the outside had suffered the same fate: the sky now a violent orange; the sun a black hole tearing at the edges of a weeping sky. A blink—hoping to correct the visual error, but the world chose to remain the same. Another blink, and another; still nothing. The world refused to return to its normal broadcast of primary colors. Giving up, he returned his focus back to the classroom. Everyone was still staring at him, awaiting further instruction. He wanted to leave the room, hoping the change in location would correct his vision, but he didn't want to start a panic—it would've proven itself unnecessary, given the circumstances. Instead he hoped the hindrance would correct itself on its own.

Only a fool would believe such a wish would come true...

As his vision worsened—the edges of his peripheral fading to black like an early 20th century film coming to a close—his eardrums began to pulsate, picking up conversations from adjacent classrooms. With the world becoming a cacophonous fading blur, it seemed the fragile veil of sanity was beginning to slip from Tom's mind. *This has to be another one of my nightmares*, he thought. *What else could it be?*

• • •

"ANOTHER SEIZURE? That's what, the fourth one this week just for *this one alone?*"

"It's not their fault. With Pierce diverting the building's power to other sections of the hospital the Subjects are becoming more unstable with each passing day—most of them having ventured so far from their primary tracking sequence it can take up to an hour, if not longer, just to re-sync *one of them.*"

"I can't even imagine what it must be like—to wake up in a sequence that's completely foreign to you, wondering what the hell is going on. Were it me in there, I'd probably go insane. Do you think they're even aware of what's going on while they're bouncing back and forth between sequences?"

"Even if we had full power to work with, it would be impossible to tell *exactly* what's going on inside a Subject's mind. Theodore had always assumed the Subjects passed the events of an improper sequence off as nothing more than a nightmare—waking up to their *appropriate sequencing* without second guessing what their brain had witnessed. But that was when we could resequence them *in a matter of minutes.* Given the amount of time it's taking us these days? for all we know, they could be experiencing a full-blown mental breakdown in there."

"..."

"What?" she asked.

"..."

"What is it?"

"..."

"What. Is. It?"

"..."

"Friedrich, I swear to God, I hate it when you decide to go silent on me when you've got something running through your mind you *know* has a high probability of pissing me off. It only infuriates me more when you choose to keep it within, so just fucking spit it out already, please!"

"How do we know, *really know*, given the increase in negative temporal activity, if there'll be anything left of them once we discover a way to wake them up?"

"Jesus, not this again. . ."

"No, Liz, could you just hear me out?"

". . .You have my *undivided* attention, Friedrich—go on."

"What if this has been Pierce's game plan all along, though; divert the building's power to other sections of the hospital, leaving the Subjects to fall into disrepair? It wouldn't be an ingenious plan, but it would create the perfect political narrative—claim their deaths as an 'unfortunate loss' for the *greater good of the hospital*. You have to admit, despite its obvious transparency, it's not a bad idea."

"It's downright absurd, his inane hatred for them. I've tried, God only knows how many times, to talk to him about it—try and sway his opinion about them—and, without effort, he diverts the conversation to topics of our current trading agreements with neighboring settlements and talks about cutting back on security, finding it unnecessary since we haven't been raided by drifters since his grandfather was Director; claims we could do away with everyone except Cordelia. He says it's due to her 'previous experience' as a soldier while synced to the *Arcadian Sequence* which makes her the perfect candidate to be the sole sentry for the hospital—keeping internal discrepancies at a minimum. I don't understand him, his elusive behavior or his—"

"Dammit, not again. . . He didn't even last an hour. . .Quick, do that intrusive hand stroke thing you always do. That tends to help—for *some reason*. Why do you care so much for this one, anyway? I'm going to have to agree with Pierce when it comes to *this one*—he's been nothing but a problem. . ."

"Just shut up and head over to his monitor, figure out what's wrong with him."

"He's off sequence. *Again*."

"Seizure?"

"No. As always, he's just being a stubborn asshole and jumping to different areas of the tracking sequence. It's never the same place either, which only makes it harder to find him and fix the issue. That's another thing! why do we even bother making sure their brains remain in sequence? Nothing—let me reiterate, nothing!—they're experiencing is real. Why should it matter if their brain wanders off to another part of the map? What if it's intentional? Who are we to disrupt a Subject's desire to experience time in a non-linear fashion? If you could go back—back to a simpler time, a time long before *the war*—wouldn't you? I know I would. I'll be honest with you, I've grown tired of waking up every day, every-god-damn-day, bouncing between here and the Quiet Room, and having nothing to show for it at the end of the day. If I could go back to, for example, let's say, 1893 to experience some of the world's technological wonders at their innocent, cerebral stages, I would hop on that train in a—hold on, I found him! This time the little twit made it as far back as. . .it looks like the 1960s; somehow, for some unexplained reason."

"Just put him back where he belongs—okay, Winsome? And watch him for the rest of the night. If he hiccups at all, call for me; I'm going up to the Quiet Room. I need some time alone to think."

5

FEELING THE BLOOD rush to his head, frustration beginning to take its toll on him, Pierce continued (desperately) to rummage through Elizabeth's drawers—hoping to find what he was looking for. *It has to be somewhere around here!* his mind screamed as he threw a small stack of papers to the floor, figuring them to be as unimportant as the previous stack. *I know you left your journal here for either Elizabeth or one of your other **loyal** followers to find. I'm not **that dense**, Theodore. . . You and I both know you were on the verge of a breakthrough before I managed to toss your ass out of here, and I know you wouldn't allow your progress to just disappear; by then you had grown suspicious of me and refused to leave your work on the blackboards overnight. Now, where the fuck is it?*

It was moments like this, moments when his kind, heartwarming facade had fallen to the wayside completely, he wished no one would ever bear witness to—to find a man clutching to the last bit of sanity he could hold onto while doing *everything he could* to secure a brighter future for the people of the hospital. This isn't a one-man job. He saw that now, having gone several months without Theodore's help. And without an heir to take Theodore's place (his family having left years ago), and having had no children of his own to take up the mantle of second Director, he was left to run the hospital by himself—unable to grant Elizabeth the title, the people having voted against the idea of allowing *anyone* outside of either the Needham or Webb bloodline to become a Director. *What will happen after I die, though?* he thought. *Will the entire place fall into disrepair? I cannot allow that to happen. I'll find a way to convince them to allow Elizabeth to be my Co-Director. I don't care what it takes, even if I have to coerce them into the idea. . .*

"Would you like some help, Director?"

"Honestly, Cordelia. . .please, *learn to knock* or something before you speak, will you? I swear, one of these days, you're going to give me—or someone else—a heart attack."

"Both you and ex-Director Webb have brought this to my attention *plenty of times.* While I feel *I've made progress* in this area of social conventions you still seem displeased whenever I make my presence known. I don't understand what I'm doing wrong."

Perhaps Theodore was right about her. . . the thought crossed his mind, the thought of agreeing with his old friend chilling him to the bone with each passing moment of silence which transpired between him and Cordelia—her vacant eyes staring him down, awaiting a response to her original question; Pierce having already forgotten she had asked him if he would like her assistance rummaging through Elizabeth's desk. Her eyes. He couldn't avert his gaze from them. Behind their vacancy Pierce felt he could sense a hostility lurking underneath them—the fate of everyone in the hospital held haphazardly in her hands, being the only one with formidable training with a firearm; if she ever decided to go postal one day. . .

"Director?"

Even the way she spoke unnerved him—the subtle (almost unnoticeable) pauses between each syllable creating a synthetic quality to her voice; any sign of humanity being lost to anyone who had the misfortune of coming into contact with her—no matter how brief. Had it not been for the weight of fear he felt around her (not knowing how she would respond, always assuming the worst) he would have given in to Theodore's suggestion and have her removed from the building. If anyone could handle themselves in the desolate wastelands of Southern California, it would be her.

"Director? *Are you okay?*"

"Yes, Cordelia. Sorry. In the middle of searching for some of Elizabeth's notes," he lied, creating a false narrative for his static-minded bodyguard. "I must've lost myself in my own thoughts. Was there something you needed, Cordelia?"

"I asked if you required my assistance. You seem, by the look of the mess, unable to find what you're looking for."

"No. But thank you, Cordelia. I am quite fine continuing my search on my own. You may go about your own business. Take the rest of the afternoon off, if you'd like." hoping to remove her from the room so he could go about his futile search in silence. "There is no need to be on patrol *all day, every day*. Please, for once, remove yourself from the idea of work—simply enjoy yourself." *Heed your own advice, Pierce. Who knows….it could save your life one day. . .*

Without speaking another word, and in the same manner she'd appeared, Cordelia turned about face and left Pierce alone in the room— among the strewn papers. A heavy sigh of relief left his lungs, returning to the task of finding Theodore's *lost journal* of mathematical equations. He found no pleasure from violating his partner's personal belongings, but Elizabeth—having been Theodore's main confidant— was proving herself a thorn in his side to his agenda of ridding the hospital of the burden of keeping the Subjects (worthless and debilitating) alive; allowing what resources went into keeping them in their lifeless state to better means: bringing life to levels of the hospital which hadn't seen a living soul since his grandfather, Alexandre Oliver Needham, was a child: one of them being a once operational secondary green room—allowing them to grow enough of their own vegetation; freeing them from the co-dependent relationships they had been forced to build with neighboring settlements for survival. Especially with a settlement like Shrapnel—a place filled with drug addled neanderthals who worshiped *the once destructive fragments of a nuclear missile*. He couldn't understand why Elizabeth continued to stand by the Subjects —doing all she could to rally what scientists she could persuade to keep *Project Arcadia* viable. It confused him. The amount of influence They had on her. It was unexplainable. Without words, They had somehow convinced her *They were worth her time*.

It wasn't here. Dammit. What a waste. The once organized contents of Elizabeth's desk now an ungodly mess on the floor. Theodore's journal was nowhere to be found. Where could she be keeping it? Despite being on opposite ends of the table when it came to the burden of the Subjects, he would never have assumed her trust in him had become nonexistent that she would go to the extent of hiding personal belongings from him anywhere that wasn't her desk. He wondered if anyone in her small circle of like-minded colleagues knew where she might be keeping it. Winsome, he thought. He's an impressionable fool. If I could get *anyone* to tell me the location of the journal, it'd be him.

The sound of wheels rolling across the tile floor of the hallway drew his attention to the open doorway of Elizabeth's office. Someone had—without him noticing—made their way to the eighth floor. He could feel his heart pounding at his chest as the high-pitched squeal edged closer to his location, pausing for a moment between advances. Paranoid he was about to be found out (again), Pierce dropped to the floor and began to collect the pile of papers which lay around the perimeter of Elizabeth's desk, hoping to clear as much of the mess as he could before the stranger came across the scene—the irregular stop-and-go of the wheels approach only adding tension to his already fast beating heart.

As he finished tidying up the area of his search (hoping Elizabeth wouldn't notice if a few things were out of place) the sound of the wheels came to an abrupt halt. He waited for a moment, wondering if they would start up again. Nothing came. Only the quiet back and forth of breathing in and out from his nose breaking the unpleasant silence which now filled both the office and outside corridor. Finding himself unable to endure the silence a second longer, Pierce called out into the æther—hoping for a response in return.

"Di-Di-Director Needham, is that you?" Andrew Goodman's stutter echoed throughout the empty corridor. Pierce remained silent, not wanting to trap himself in one of Andrew's endless, insipid conversations; especially when it took him longer than most to complete a goddamn sentence. "Who-who-whoever you are," young Andrew's voice rose in volume—hoping to come off intimidating to whoever decided to call out a moment ago. "I'm armed and fully c-c-c-capable to take you down."

"I'd hardly consider a mop and a bucket of dirty water an armed weapon, Andrew." Pierce finally spoke.

"Di-Director?" Andrew's silhouette moved closer, his head rearing around the left side corner of the doorway. "Wh-wh-what are you doing in Dr. Elizabeth's office?"

"Andrew. What did I tell you about asking questions which have no direct concern to your well-being?"

"Not t-to ask them?"

"That's correct. Now, please, continue about your duties. I wouldn't want you getting into trouble, this being your final reassignment before protocol dictates exile. We wouldn't want that now, would we?"

"N-no sir."

"Of course we wouldn't, Andrew. All of us at the hospital wouldn't want to lose another *valuable* member of our team." A lie. "As long as we're at a mutual understanding, you may carry on. I'll take care of Dr. Elizabeth's room for you; make your day go by a little faster. We can both agree that's quite a generous offer, can't we?"

Andrew nodded, disappeared beyond the corners of the doorway, and continued along his predetermined path—heading toward what used to be Theodore's office. Allowing himself to breathe with ease, Pierce waited for the unnerving sound of the mop bucket's wheels to come to a halt before deciding to leave Elizabeth's office. The item in question was nowhere to be found. Why waste another second in a room which held no significance to him with his search for Theodore's *missing journal. . .*

A distant voice inside his head asked him why he couldn't ask if Elizabeth was in possession of Theodore's journal and other miscellaneous academic scribblings. *Even if she did, what reason could I possibly give her, hoping to examine them?* It was well known throughout the halls of the hospital that their opinions on the fate of the Subjects differed. She'd suspect him of foul play before the words left his tongue.

Stepping into the compact space of the elevator, the dissonant voice having silenced itself (for now), Pierce's thoughts traveled to a place of regret. Despite furthering his own agenda, granting him complete oversight of the hospital and its citizens, he missed his old friend. *Why did you have to walk in on me during such an embarrassing indiscretion?* he asked the air around him. *Had your trajectory to the lower levels been interrupted, sparing me a few more seconds, I could've rid us of a burden; you being none the wiser. We could still be working together—to (eventu-*

ally) make the living situation for our residents — and their descendants — more accommodating. . . Politics is a game which is never kind to the fools who choose to practice it. The differing of opinions creating rifts among those who once considered themselves close friends — family, even. It is when one finds themselves on the opposite side of the political playing field of another, unable to come to a compromise of ideals, when instinct kicks in; where you will do whatever it takes to secure your voice's validity — even if it means discrediting the other in less than honorable measures. This was Pierce's fate, even if he didn't believe in the concept. From the womb of his mother, into the cold, calculated hands of his father, he was destined to play the unforgiving game of politics. *How did they refrain from killing each other?* he wondered, curious how the Directors before him and Theodore managed to keep a calm demeanor about them. *Did our predecessors find themselves in agreement on everything?* Impossible. No one, not even those with similar view points, could go without finding something to disagree upon. . .

An announcement echoed from the intercom speakers, stopping the elevator mid-floor — a courteous reminder for all residents to remember to take protection (and to "always have a *traveling companion!*") with them when deciding to leave the "security of our home"; an archaic ritual from when Pierce's grandfather was Director, to prevent anyone else from falling victim to any passing drifters they would come across while out in the Wastelands. Pierce laughed as the announcement came to an abrupt close, finding the thought of *having to remind* people of "the dangers the outside world held" to be rather trite after several decades of use. If one had to be told continuously to protect themselves from the horrors of the California desert, they probably shouldn't live to see the end of the day anyway, he thought as the elevator continued its slow descent. . .

•   •   •

APPREHENSION CURLED its way into a rather uncomfortable spot in Nikolai Sokolov's stomach as the elevator came to a screeching halt.

Until today he had never been allowed to venture beyond the second floor basement of the complex, having not had the proper security clearance. Where morbid curiosity had managed to find its way into the thoughts of others, an unrelenting sense of dread consumed Nikolai. Whatever it was they were hiding *that far below the surface* must've been kept down there for a reason—a secret better off left hidden in the depths of the cold, dying Earth. . .

"Feeling a bit anxious, are we?" The fellow occupant, a Senior Lieutenant Nikolai presumed upon closer examination of his insignia, laughed, blowing the last puff of smoke from his cigarette before putting it out above the elevator's control panel as the doors slowly opened. "Rest easy, мальчик. The lower levels of this base are nothing special. It's laughable, honestly—how secretive everyone is down here."

Too nervous to respond, Nikolai continued to look forward—following the Senior Lieutenant down a series of dimly lit cement hallways (every extending corridor blanketed with a myriad of doorways—all of them guarded by two well-armed military personnel) as he continued to ramble on about the USSR's unnecessary attempts to keep *everything a secret*. Yes, they were at the tail-end of a once seemingly endless Cold War with the Americans and their allies, Russia's economy having gone stagnant (no thanks to the recent downward slide in oil prices), their military arsenal surpassing that of the *patriotic United States*, but to keep Her own people in the dark (all while boasting their military prowess to the Western Bloc) felt inhumane to the Senior Lieutenant; who had served long enough to see the ugliness of *both sides* of this (rather pointless. . .) conflict.

"You don't speak much, do you?" the Senior Lieutenant turned right to salute the two guards standing in front of the doorway he desired to enter, saying, without skipping a beat, "**Вы должны бороться за свое право на вечеринку**," to both of them—while still saluting them. Remaining stoic, the two guards stepped aside to let him and Nikolai through. "It's okay. I was quiet a long time as well before I decided not to give a shit anymore. You'll get there, eventually; if you choose to make the military your career."

Nikolai chose to remain silent, perplexed at the concept of the Russian military choosing to use the title of a Beastie Boys song as a way of passage through a guarded doorway. "This is where you will be spending most of your days," the Senior Lieutenant spoke as he approached a broken down chair among a sea of filled seats. "I would suggest getting comfortable down here, Sokolov. Who knows the next time you'll get to see the sun—could be until the new millennium."

What struck Nikolai first was the smell of the place. It reminded him of the long, grueling months of basic training, when he and his fellow recruits had gone without a shower. Looking around, it felt like a dead end—a place where military careers faded into obscurity. A bunker. This was now his home; an underground bunker—safe from any nuclear blast, being six levels below the surface. It became clear to him that he (and everybody else who had been stationed here) would eventually become forgotten, much like whatever other secrets had been buried here during the decades which had been shrouded in the malevolent shadow of the Cold War. How many souls had found themselves lost down here throughout the years? before seeking early retirement—be it through the validation of receiving one's separation papers or the crisp, welcoming bite of a gunshot to the side of the head; relieving them from the disconnect that had found itself wedged between the poor soul and the outside world.

"It might seem bleak, at first," the man to Nikolai's left spoke, his gaze never leaving the computer screen in front of him. "But at least we're guaranteed a decent paycheck twice a month."

Nikolai let out a nervous chuckle; swiveling in his unstable chair, failing to find a comfortable balance. He knew he would have to make light of the dim situation he found himself in currently—somehow. At the moment, however, not even a stranger's thinly veiled attempt to ease the despondency of their shared predicament could cheer him up. This wasn't the military experience he had signed up for, being trapped behind a desk in front of a computer screen, filling out reports and filing them away in a cabinet—never to be seen or read; a never-ending loop of banality which, he was certain, would drive *anyone* to the brink of insanity. A bitterness which had grown to be a well-known visitor in Nikolai's thoughts, blaming Gromyko's (assumed?) senility and incompetence as a political figure for his misfortunes. The political world, itself, (not only in Russia, but at all corners of the Earth) had developed an ever-growing disconnect with its people; with the looming threat of war and the constant struggle for *nuclear superiority* taking the forefront of every politician's agenda, the needs of the people had fallen by the wayside—to be forgotten by *humanity's faulty design. . .*

. . .

—From the journal of Nathan Luckman

December 23, 1994

IF ONE MANAGED TO LOOK beyond the pale concrete, smog ridden skyline—its monochromatic, unfinished design throwing its oppressive weight onto anyone who caught themselves in between its infrastructure, suffocating them to sleep—they would find the once proud *City of Angels* weeping in the corner of California; saddened by its own decadence. Everything is surface these days. Instead of digging deeper to discover merit *worth our validation*, we base our opinions on that of image; one of *many* missteps of being a product of the *MTV generation*, according to the *boomers*. "All they care about is a product's name brand and how the item will make them appear superior among their colleagues! Fuck, you could sell them a sour lemon if you made it look nice and slapped an IKEA sticker on it; wouldn't matter if the damned thing was spoiled—they'd still buy it!" But what the boomers fail to acknowledge, however, is that *they* are the ones who decided how we spent our mild-mannered upbringing. *They* threw us in front of a television screen, having found the concept of *actually raising us* "too exhausting" for their mental health. I look around, my friends enjoying themselves to the sounds of Jawbreaker's *24 Hour Revenge Therapy*, and while, yes, we aren't the patriotic juggernauts like the citizens from the 1940s and '50s or find ourselves lost in the fires of the cultural revolution of the 1960s (can you blame us for not being patriotic? we had Reagan and Bush as a president during our adolescence), we did bear witness to the economic collapse—played off as a minor recession—of the early 1980s (which America had *quickly recovered* from, solidifying Reagan's re-election in '84) and *refused* to allow ourselves (and generations of the new millennium) to live in the moral squalor our parents felt comfortable in—having been conditioned to it throughout the years.

Tonight, the city looked peaceful as we (Katherine, Phillip, Danny, and myself) drove back from a punk show at the Jabberjaw; Danny still reeling hard from the ferocity of the bands that played. As I drove I'd occasionally glance over to find Katherine smiling as she sang along to Blake Schwarzenbach's lyrics. Her vacant eyes betraying her without knowing it. I wish she would talk to me. I may not be able to rid her from her agony *completely*, but at least she'd be talking to me about it; allowing me to feel included in the private world that resided inside her head. A desire for empathy—quite the contradiction for a generation presumed to be self-obsessed and concerned *only with the surface*.

"Do you ever wonder?"

"Wonder about what?" a confused Phillip's gaze drifted from the ceiling, meeting Katherine's; Danny half asleep in his arms.

"Just wonder, you know?" Katherine continued, refusing Nathan's attempt to hand off the bong, Phillip managing to slip from Danny's clutches enough to take his respected turn. "If the world will continue down its assumed projected path toward God knows what? If any of this will ever amount to anything? Will there even be a tomorrow to wake up to?"

"Okay, somebody's cut off for the night." Nathan managed to say through a mixed fit of laughter and choking from his last hit.

"I'm serious you guys. Sure, the Cold War is over, but the looming threat of nuclear annihilation is more present than it was in recent decades. We may have come to an agreement on the surface, but you can't deny the tension that still resides on both sides. Honestly, I believe the day will never come when the possibility of a World War 3 scenario fades from the minds of the world's populace; that ship sailed in 1945 when *we* dropped the bombs on Hiroshima and Nagasaki."

"Damn," Danny, stirred awake from his slumber, breathed, "You certainly have a way of harshing someone's mellow."

Everyone, even Katherine, laughed. You never knew where a late night of smoking would take them. Tonight, it seemed, they traveled down the rabbit hole of *nihilism and nuclear annihilation*. Once they all recovered from their bout of laughter, having lost all train of thought (their brains scrambled for the night), they decided to phone it in for now and cut the lights. Tomorrow, if it came, would be another day; another day of working themselves to the bone—ending the night with long-winded bong rip influenced conversations and stolen booze.

6

ARKNESS. IMPENETRABLE DARKNESS. Somehow, it had found him once again. Closing and opening his eyes continuously for what seemed like forever, he couldn't manage to wake himself up from the claustrophobic environment his mind *always managed* to conjure up. It didn't help matters much when the voices—the same, familiar voices; every time—came seeping back into the edges of his auditory perimeter; talking about him like a Subject on the brink of non-existence. Why did his mind continue to return to this doorway of subconscious thought? In the past, when he found himself returning to a dreamscape, he'd managed to close the door by writing about it in depth—a novel coming into existence because of it. With *Discord Avenue* and *In Flawless Strokes*, the dreams of a dystopic, drug-addled version of America had ceased to haunt him in his sleep. The perfect exorcism. Despite writing what would become *The Transmigration Trilogy*, this—this darkness—refused to let go of him; it remained relentless. He could still remember the fear he'd see in Sarah's eyes every night he spent writing the first draft of *Ascension*, having read a few passages which bled of depression and (to a large extent) well-detailed, irrational thoughts leaning on suicidal tendency—all of which would eventually be written out via a rather tiresome editing process; *never to be seen by the public.*

Man: [off in the distance; barely audible among the sound of alarms blaring] This is the worst one, yet. We can't keep doing this, Elizabeth; sooner or later, his brain is going to be fried due to a lack of oxygen, with how many seizures he has on a weekly basis.

Woman: [close enough to feel her breath as she speaks] Just keep me updated, Friedrich. Other than that, I don't want to hear another word out of you. [Her voice now a whisper] Stay with me, Thomas. We can't afford to lose another one. [her hand finds the Subjects; soothing him as she continues to speak to him]

Man: [moving closer] If he saw how *intimate* you are with the Subject, *you and I* both know Pierce would have him scheduled for "release" within the hour—regardless of the Subject's knack for being a burden. Why *are* you so close with *this one*? What makes him different from the others?

Woman: He's the reason I wanted to work down here. Seeing him as a child when it was *Take Your Child To Work Day* for my father's department, watching him experience one of his many gut wrenching seizures, which ignited my interest in the neurological sciences. . .I wanted to, one day, wake this poor soul from his torment; welcome him to a *better world*. . .

Man: [a brief fit of laughter ensues] Calling this place a "better world" is a bit of stretch, even for you. Sure, our small section of the city is faring better than other, more rural, settlements, but we are far from being *anywhere near* the fabled utopia this world once was centuries ago. And having spent a good portion of my adult life examining the *Arcadian Sequence* I'd say *he's* the one who is "better off"—if I'm going to be honest. In his world they managed to *avoid* world-wide atomic annihilation.

Woman: But he's living a goddamn lie! Oblivious to it, yes, but a fucking lie, nonetheless. Don't stand there and tell me you'd prefer to live your life in a well-constructed farce than to live in reality? not a perfect world—I'll admit that—but at least *our experience*s hold merit; his doesn't. . .

He took note that the dialogue was hardly ever the same twice. A frightening detail. One which would have gone unnoticed had it not been for the self-referential moments of the conversation of dreams *come and gone*. The names, however, remained the same—more or less. The soothing voice of a woman named Elizabeth, telling him to keep fighting, was the only one that felt like a friend. The others (predominately male) appeared indifferent to the situation, if not completely hostile in nature; talks of a man named Pierce wanting to release them from *the burden of taking care of brain dead vegetables. . .*

"It's okay, Tom. It's only a bad dream—just open your eyes."

Tom managed to open his eyes to find his wife hovering over him—her hair in curlers; wearing only a bra and skirt. He witnessed a smile make its way onto her lips to see her husband had woken from his tortured slumber before turning to head back into the bathroom to finish getting ready.

"He seems fine, now."

"Did you say something, babe?" he asked, lifting himself from his pillow.

Sarah's face appeared in the doorway, her toothbrush hanging from her mouth as she shook her head, attempting to mumble (through plastic and saliva) her response before disappearing into the white light of the bathroom—the high pitched drone of the faucet pouring water into the sink as she spat toothpaste residue out to meet its spiraling fate; creating an inconsistent rhythm in the drain's water flow.

"I'm going to keep an eye on him a bit longer—make sure he doesn't relapse for at least a few hours before leaving him alone."

*"Fine, just don't do anything that could get us into trouble. I don't care if you're his **pet**, even **you** aren't invincible to his unpredictable mood-swings."*

Shaking his head while rubbing his ears, hoping to rid himself of the voices which seemed to have followed him from his nightmare; into the real world—finding the act futile; the woman's voice having remained, whispering soft words of encouragement as if he were still there. . .lying motionless in a concealed case. Unable to drown out the mystery voice, Tom went to turn the radio on; hoping the annoyance of today's Top 40 would steal his focus away from the woman's voice which refused to leave him alone. Breakfast on the Boulevard droned on in the background—Tom Breneman interviewing a Hollywood big shot—forcing the unknown voice to the darker recesses of his brain. . .

"I'd start getting dressed if I were you," Sarah's voice came from the bathroom. "Ethel and James will be here soon to pick us up for movie night." She came out of the bathroom smiling, putting on her favorite pair of scarlet red Czech glass and crystal earrings. "Ethel kept complaining over the phone this afternoon about James' pick of film—*The Invisible Man Returns*. A poor man's attempt at a box office cash grab, if you ask me."

The Invisible Man Returns? a damned sequel? Tom thought. He knew Hollywood lacked originality (in today's world, what didn't?), but to try and continue onward with a story which met its tragic conclusion in the original production seven years ago felt downright lazy to him; the Invisible Man had died, after all. Unless they were planning on retconning his death, Tom couldn't think up a logical explanation the big wigs of Tinsel-town would use to explain the Invisible Man's "return"—(besides easy money like Sarah's friend, Ethel, had mentioned).

"I wonder how H.G. Wells felt about his work being bastardized by the film industry," Tom said as he grabbed a pair of gray slacks from his side of the closet. "I don't know what I would do if the greedy little schmucks down in Los Angeles decided to debase one of my own novels into a cheap form of entertainment."

"You'd drive down there and demand the, as you *eloquently put it*, 'greedy little schmucks' be ostracized; make damn sure they're unable to destroy another author's body of work ever again. *That's* what you would do, darling; This, I'm more than certain."

"*Burning the midnight oil again, I see.*"

"**Someone** *has to ensure this place remains functional. Otherwise, the whole Project would fall into disrepair.*"

"*Elizabeth. . .why must you* **continue** *to land on the other side of this petty argument? You and I both know, in the end, I'll have the final say whether or not this* **petty experiment** *remains a part of the hospital's way of life. Now, please, come to reason and let this damned pipe-dream die.*"

"*A 'pipe-dream' your father—and grandfather—refused to let fall by the wayside. Do you really hate them* **that much**; *to let countless, innocent lives go to waste just to spite them—their memory?*"

The voices had come back in full force, Tom could no longer focus on the outside world; the incessant chatter from the radio no longer a viable distraction; his wife's questions about whether or not to wear her hair in an up-do or to let her curls flow naturally for the night out on the town. Having grown impatient with him, Sarah came out into the bedroom to find her husband standing motionless—in the middle of tying his tie.

"Did we forget how to tie a tie all of a sudden?" she joked, hoping to coax a response out of him.

Nothing. Not even his usual, playful smirk.

"Thomas? Is everything okay?" she moved closer, swallowing what fear had begun to consume her—that her husband was experiencing the beginnings of a stroke.

Tom's head turned to meet Sarah's worried gaze—the two argumentative voices still screaming at the edges of his skull, making it feel swollen. He watched as his distressed wife's lips continued to move, but not a sound escaped her tongue. *Why can't I drown them out?* he thought as he made a futile attempt to suffocate their words by placing his hands over his ears and screaming for them to go away; unknowingly swatting Sarah's concerned hands away in the process.

After what felt like an eternity of cacophonous uproar, finally, there was absolute silence. Calm. Something he had lived without for so long, he had deemed the concept of achieving it again illusory. When he opened his eyes, however, he found himself met with a familiar horrific scene (a scene which had become a recurring motif throughout his body of work) of witnessing the world around him stuck on freeze-frame. Much like the characters in his novels, Tom, doing his best to remain calm, moved through the scene before him—each step echoing throughout. *This has got to be a dream*, he thought, keeping an eye on his wife as he made his way past her and headed for the door; hoping (knowing, however, his hopes would be in vain) to find an unaffected room within the house.

Upon opening the bedroom door a loud, deafening alarm began to scream incessantly through the hallway. *So much for the silence*, he scoffed as he continued down the empty corridor; toward Christie and Matilda's room. . .to see if they, too, had been affected by the sudden stopping of time.

"*What is it now? Don't tell me. . .your favorite **little pet** is having **another** nightmare. . .*"

—No. Not the voices again. I thought I'd rid myself of them.

"*Sequencing his mind is becoming more of a chore with each episode. It's almost as if he's becoming self-aware—that his surroundings are an artificial construct. Perhaps we should consider bringing him to soon?*"

"*Don't be so impulsive, Elizabeth. . .you and I both know it's damn near impossible to bring anyone out of the Sequence without **some form** of mental trauma; severe or benign. Just because one—one!—Subject came out unscathed from the process doesn't mean we can manage to recreate such a miracle.*"

"*Why must you always use 'the fear of failure' as a means to persuade those who wish to go against **your** agenda? It's pathetic. You look at these people and—*"

There was a brief moment of clarity that followed what sounded like a rather sharp slap to someone's face. Enough time passed for Tom to check in on his two little girls—finding them sound asleep in their beds; seemingly unaffected by the same affliction Sarah found herself met with.

"*Don't call them people, Elizabeth. That kind of term gives them a sense of credibility where they have none.*" the man's voice broke the silence, a sharp edge to his words. "*Eventually, the rest of this place will see things **my way** and your 'friends' will no longer be a burden to us. Remember that the next time you decide to call my actions pathetic.*"

Footsteps could be heard storming off into the distance as the young woman found herself sobbing; nursing the still warm sting, a sting which remained long after the initial strike had passed. . .

No matter how hard he tried, Tom couldn't seem to block out the sound of the woman's *pained sadness* from his mind—

• • •

THE SIGHT OF EARTH'S LANDSCAPE changed significantly the closer you approached the coast; flourishes of color springing from the dirt like a malignant tumor finding its place in the human body. It was a welcoming change of scenery to Theodore's travels as he and Chevrolet continued to head south, toward Bomb City—making a pit-stop at

San Pedro, hoping to persuade his wife and children to come with him now that he was no longer confined to the long, arduous hours of being one of the hospital's Co-Directors. They could be a family again, he thought—a cool breeze blowing from the west; perhaps find a new home along the Californian coastline and thrive from homegrown vegetation and trade from nearby settlements.

"Yer not one fer speaking much, are ya, Theodore?" Chevrolet chimed in. "Don' worry me none, I don't mind 'aving myself a few moments of introspection. Yer just the first companion I've had that ain't a damned jabberbox. I gotta admit, it's kinda nice."

Turning his gaze to meet Chevrolet's jubilant smile, remaining silent, having learned to not pay much attention to her incessant monologues (the apparent—undiagnosed—A.D.D. she suffered from preventing her from staying on topic for more than a couple of minutes; the aimless tangents having grown tiresome in the last hour, to put it kindly), Theodore clutched to the thoughts of his family being reunited after *years of separation*. Desperate, he looked ahead to see if he could find an upcoming sign—letting him know how far away he was from San Pedro, allowing him to leave Chevrolet to continue on her own (perhaps she'd come across another weary traveler to bother with her uncouth sensibilities). The only signs along the side of road, however, appeared to only show the distance from towns like Santa Ana, Irvine, and Chevrolet's infamous Bomb City (the original name of the city, ~~San Diego~~, having been crossed out with black spray paint; its *new name* written over it in white). *Are we even going the right way?* he thought as his companion continued to ramble on about the people of her home town. "An' don't get me started on—"

Attempting to distract himself, Theodore turned his attention (again) to the colorful scenery around him. It puzzled him. Los Angeles was a coastal city (close enough, anyway). Why hasn't *it* shared the same amount of growth in wild vegetation? only scattered weeds and patches of grass were commonplace. Out here, in unsettled territory, however, even trees had begun to breathe new life. His mind went back to his schoolhouse days, when they learned about *nuclear fallout*. Was this place barely hit by the War's radiation? If so, and his grandfather's tales of 'untouched cities' up north and to the east were true, then wouldn't *those places* bare the same—if not more pronounced—

greenness? *Why **did** we stay in that **godforsaken hospital**?* his mind asked. Such a worthless city. Even during it's (fabled) days, the stories which were passed down from generation to generation in the Webb family painted the city of Los Angeles in an ugly light—a divisive topic among the two families (Webb and Needham); the Needhams viewing the world of the past as a template for what the world could become, while the Webbs wished to avoid reliving the (potential horrors of) past; instead, seeing the mistakes of their ancestors and striving for something different altogether. There was a time, however, when Theodore felt Pierce would've strayed away from his grandfather's mindset—aligning himself with the ideals of his father—and set aside his nostalgia for *a world he never knew*; push forward, together, toward a better future for their citizens. A future which *didn't involve staying in a run-down building for the rest of their lives*. . .

"What about you, mister?" Chevrolet interjected, (finally) finished with telling Theodore—for the third time, today—about what her life was like back home. "What was yer life like back where you come from? Goin' by that spiffy white jacket o' yers, I'd say you was someone important."

"Do you have men of science where you're from, Chevrolet?" Theodore asked, hoping she'd give a negative response; ending the conversation before he had a chance to breathe.

"Yer one o' them science types?" her voice jumped an octave in excitement. "Shit, had I known you was a science-tist I'da had you help me inspect ol'*Charity*'s diagnostics alongside me. Could'a used me a second pair of eyes."

Theodore laughed. "I'm not that kind of scientist, I'm afraid. No, my area of expertise is of the mind. Back where I'm from, we tend to a group of people who were born with the inability to wake themselves. We've hooked them up to machines in order to keep them alive while the entire neurological research team work toward finding a solution to bringing them all to. So far. . .we've managed one success out of several decades worth of Subjects."

"Not gonna lie to ya, Theo, ya lost me at nermanological."

When they finally arrived at the city limits of ~~San Diego~~ Bomb City (he refused to say the city's name out loud, finding it to be juvenile and a little too *on the nose*), Theodore bore witness to Chevrolet's demeanor go from annoyingly chipper to unbearably ecstatic; her once gleeful, determined pace developing into a poorly paced gallop. Having not seen a single sign with San Pedro on it, he had assumed he still had a ways to travel before coming across anything worthwhile. He hoped, anyway. It would make the past couple of days seem worth the constant half-baked conversations he managed to push through with Chevrolet.

"Chevy? is dat you I see comin' down the road my way?" an older man's voice yelled from afar; barely audible. Looking around, Theodore couldn't make out where the stranger's voice had come from —he assumed from one of the crumbling buildings up ahead; unable to pinpoint which dilapidated structure. An unsettling feeling, had the stranger not been a friendly voice among the æther. It didn't take long for an ear-splitting gunshot to ring out from one of Chevrolet's pistols in response (something Theodore should've come to expect from her at this point).

"ARCO, ya old bastard," she cried. "Do they still have you on watch? Jeez, don't Lincoln know by now yer gettin' to a point where yous can't be climbing up all them stairs anymore?"

A bullet bounced off the dirt in front of them. Terrified, Theodore rushed behind Chevrolet for protection; not his proudest moment, he'd admit, but—being the seasoned wanderer that she was—hiding behind her tiny frame was far more comforting than staying out in the open.

"I don't wan' ta hear any comments on my age, ya hear?" the old man's voice echoed. "I may be pushing ninety-four, but I could still handle myself better than Lincoln can run all of Bomb City during drills."

"I swear," Chevrolet chuckled, "that man's gunna die complaining about sumthing; gun in his hand and all." She turned to Theodore, who was still hiding behind her for protection. "Well, here it is," she pointed with the barrel of her firearm, as they walked past the outer walls of the city. "Home sweet home." she continued, whistling an unfamiliar tune.

Observing the place, Theodore could see why the settlement which was once San Diego (in a previous life) had grown to be known as Bomb City after the war. In the center of the city, what was left of an atomic bomb rested several feet above the ground—held in place, midair, by shrine-like pillars made from the rubble of its surroundings; the bomb, itself, obviously pieced together by the town's citizens (pieces missing; either lost or no longer able to be welded back to its original, monolithic structure. Such an oddity, he thought, making what was once a tool of death and destruction into a monument; a centerpiece for anyone to gaze upon as they walked through the city. It was unnerving.

Beyond the reconstructed bomb, past the endless stretch of rubble-filled roads, lay the aqua blue of the Pacific Ocean; the sun edging its way toward the horizon—a fleet of half-sunken naval ships silhouetting the darkening skyline. Having never made it out west, the majestic silence of a coastal sunset felt like something out of a dream—a dream he'd never witnessed himself, but a marvel, nonetheless. It was in this brief moment, he had forgotten about San Pedro—about his family.

• • •

IN THE FINAL MOMENTS OF 1989, Nikolai's thoughts wandered to his family back home in Kaliningrad; to his mother, father, and two sisters. Did they miss him? Were they worried, having not received a letter from him in five years (had it really been *that long*?); taking his silence as an *unofficial declaration* of his death. "С Новым Годом," he whispered in silent defeat to a darkened computer monitor—the only company he had tonight. Everyone else had managed to escape from their post to celebrate the New Year appropriately. Sounds of celebration could be heard from up above, despite being as far below the surface as he found himself tonight. Alone, he pantomimed raising a cold pint of Zhigulevskoye to a non-existent crowd. "С Новым Годом," he repeated, taking a small 'sip' of his poorly-imagined pilsner.

Bored out of his mind, his eyes requesting a rest from mindlessly staring at a computer screen for hours, Nikolai searched Pyotr's mess of a desk—which was adjacent to his own—for a simple distraction. Among the havoc he found a novel. Thin, its spine worn beyond recognition. Reading the front cover, he sighed. Going by the title alone, *The Rules of Attraction* (a Bret Easton Ellis production—an American author; young, going by his photograph), it appeared his 'desk-mate' was into reading erotica. After reading the first couple of pages, a poorly written one, it seemed. He flipped through the book's pages, hoping it would get better (that the novel had a rough beginning). He found himself met with disappointment. *How does garbage like this get published?* he thought, tossing the poor excuse for a book back to Pyotr's desk. *The publishers in America must be getting desperate for material these days. . .*

Gunshots rang down from the surface. Unable to tell whether or not the shots were celebratory or filled with malicious intent, Nikolai continued his search for a distraction from the banality which was his New Year's; the fading echoes of gunfire still haunting him from his days in basic training. Giving up on finding a distraction worthy of his time, he went back to Pyotr's desk and picked up *The Rules of Attraction* once more—giving the poor excuse for a novel another shot at *entertaining* him. After all, he had nothing better to do. . .

By the time he finished reading Sean's second 'chapter', he found he was hooked, Ellis' caustic humor having caused him to experience a small fit of laughter. *This isn't that bad*, he thought, turning the page.

He couldn't remember the last time he'd laughed.

· · ·

THE NEW YEAR CAME AND WENT as they lived—lost in an alcohol and drug induced haze; like any other weekend. On the horizon, 1995 showed promise to be a far better year than 1994. But, as previous decades had dictated, the ugly truth was apparent. . .as the months of 1995 would continue to pass the world by, any signs of optimism would find themselves smothered by the well-oiled cynicism which was the cold honesty of time. He would never admit it to himself or anyone else, especially Katherine, but Nathan Luckman had hoped the night before would've been his last.

It wasn't until he heard Samuel L. Jackson scream *"English, mother-fucker, do you speak it?"* from the television's stereo (Daniel and Phillip watching *Pulp Fiction* for the *hundredth* time) that Nathan's faint bemusement—his mind still pounding away from last night's activities—trickled away; the scene around him laying out a vibrancy he'd never seen before. Not only were colors more lush, but sounds and vibrations had intensified, as well. To his left, behind him, Katherine's hushed snores shook the head of the mattress enough to massage the left side of his face—soothing him. On the floor Phillip and Daniel's naked bodies coalesced into one as *Pulp Fiction* continued to play quietly in the background; Phillip whispering sweet, incoherent nothings into Daniel's sleeping ear.

Outside the bedroom window two Blue Jays called back and forth, holding an argument over who deserved the morning worm. He couldn't tell if he had reached a new high of spiritual enlightenment or if he was still climbing from the ecstasy he took just before bed. Either way, the experience was enough to make Nathan Luckman forget about his hopes for death last night; if only for a moment.

The rest of the day would consist of the four of them driving around Los Angeles aimlessly until sundown (listening to *Siamese Dream*, *Yank Crime*—Phillip's favorite album of '94—and *Spiderland* on loop), when the nightlife of New Year's Day would come out to play; Daniel bringing up the idea (often, usually in-between album changes) of heading out to Pasadena—claiming he knew a guy who sold laced weed for cheap; every time Katherine would laugh, saying, "Laced weed? Why would someone go and ruin a good thing?"—Nathan, keeping his eyes on the road, would join Katherine in a fit of sarcastic laughter, leaving Daniel embarrassed enough to remain silent for another thirty to forty minutes. . .As the day grew into the evening, however, a cool January breeze passed through the city. Feeling a sudden chill wash over him, Nathan (reluctantly) rolled his window up.

"Getting cold, Luckman?" Phillip asked while playing the back of Nathan's headrest to the off-kilter drums to "Luau"—snark bleeding from his throat.

"*Getting cold, Luckman?*" Nathan mocked, turning the volume to the car's stereo down, hoping to ruin Phillip's 'drumming', "Shut up and put your lips to good use on Danny's dick."

Daniel's attention turned from staring out the window, curious how he and his penis became part of the conversation. "What about my dick?"

"Nathan wants a free show of you getting your balls drained by your boyfriend," Katherine replied.

"*Actually*, I changed my mind," Nathan said. "Danny, why don't *you* suck Phil's dick instead; keep you from bringing up buying 'cheap weed' from some wangsta motherfucker in Pasadena for a while longer. Hopefully, Phil will use your head as a drum set while you're down there—give my headrest a break from all the abuse."

Nathan felt five playful finger taps from Phillip before hearing the faint sound of a zipper being undone—followed (after a couple minutes of silence) by quiet moans of gratitude underneath the sloppy sounds of licking and gagging. Amused he turned to Katherine, who was watching the event take place; getting turned on by the homo-erotic turn of events in the backseat of the car—her hands finding their way to her crotch, to finger herself to live pornography; her gaze coming back up to the front to meet Nathan's—biting her lower lip as she fingered herself, mouthing how she wanted Nathan to take her later tonight once Philip and Daniel either went home or passed out for the night.

They ended up getting the cheap weed from Pasadena, the city of Los Angeles having been a dud for partying (who cares if it was a Sunday? When it's a *New Year*, you party until your heart stops). It wasn't *that bad* Katherine would admit later that night, tripping on a joint which had been laced with heroin.

New Year's Day (also) ended how they lived—*lost in an alcohol and drug induced haze*; Jawbox's "Cooling Card" playing on MTV as they all drifted off to sleep in one frame of mind or another, to find themselves waking up hungover and foggy from the night before—only to start the cycle over again. . .

7

HE HADN'T COME BACK YET. Six years had passed since his exile and Theodore Webb still hadn't come back, begging for his life to be let back in. Worried about his friend's well-being, Pierce sent Subject No. 2773 (Cordelia) out to search for him one more time. He thought he knew where to send her—where she could find him. San Pedro, where his wife, Gwenivere, and two children (he didn't bother to remember their names, not being a fan of little ones) had run off to when they left Theodore—feeling neglect on his part. Pierce was never fond of Gwenivere, either. He felt she did nothing but belittle his friend's devotion to his work. While he and Theodore may have not agreed on much, he did appreciate the dedication he put into what he believed in; even if he personally felt Theodore's efforts were a waste of the hospital's resources. But every time Cordelia came back from her travels, Theodore was not by her side.

Nine days had passed since Cordelia left for San Pedro. It felt nice —her absence. Had he been forced to endure another week of her obnoxious personality, he would have felt compelled to smother her in her sleep. Except she *never slept*, it seemed. Often, late at night, he could hear her footsteps (he could tell they were hers, how they made barely any noise—just enough to be paranoia inducing) as she passed by his bedroom door periodically throughout the night. It didn't help that he spent his nights alone, lately; Elizabeth having moved back to her own room a few months back after one fight too many about the Subjects and their *eventual fate*—their bodies used for emergency meat rations; their bones being ground into a fine powder to be traded with the people of Shrapnel as compost for their settlement's rooftop garden (a joke, obviously, but Elizabeth thought it *crossed a line*).

As he entered the elevator, making his rounds throughout the hospital—checking in with everyone, keeping up appearances—Pierce's mind wandered into the past; memories of him and Theodore exploring every inch of the building (even the 'restricted' *Quiet Room* and lower level where the Subjects resided) flooding the gates of nostalgia. It was an innocent time, back then—before the idea of conflicting ideologies and personal agendas became a mainstay in their adult lives. He often wondered, had their viewpoints been reversed, would his friend had done the same thing? cast him out into the barren Southern California desert.

Doing the math in his head, it wouldn't be for another week (or so) before Cordelia would come back with word of Theodore's well-being; hoping she'd be able to talk him into coming back to the hospital so they could make amends—that Theodore would forgive him for his *lapse in judgment*. His bout of nostalgia jumped to that night six years ago, when Theodore walked in on him attempting to release Subject No. 2990 from his lifelong torment—the inner lining of his left cheek scarred from the surprising blow Theodore delivered that night; the taste of blood still hung in the back of his throat in the early hours of the morning after waking up.

The elevator doors opened to Elizabeth standing patiently, waiting to be let on board the claustrophobic capsule. She didn't speak a word to Pierce, simply nodded, entered the elevator, and pressed the button to her desired floor: the lower level. Predictable, as always.

"Can we talk?" he mustered as the elevator doors closed and continued its descent. "No arguing. No making *ill-mannered* jokes at the Subjects' expense. Just you and me—talking."

Elizabeth turned her head—but only slightly—to bring Pierce's desperate gaze into her line of sight, "There's nothing for us to talk about,

Pierce," she said, cold and calculated. "Unless the next words to come out of your mouth are an apology.

"I'm sorr—"

"I don't want one if you're not going to *mean it*, Pierce," the elevator chimed, opening its doors to the seventh level of the building: cafeteria, recreational area, and daycare center. "I believe *this* is your exit," her gaze having not left the now open elevator doors.

Feeling defeated (yet again. . .), a sullen Pierce made his way past a cold, unmoving Elizabeth; continuing his daily routine of maintaining his image as the *caring Director*, which the residents had come to expect after his father's time as Co-Director—alongside Theodore's father. Watching as he disappeared into the hallway of people, the elevator doors closing to continue its descent to the lower levels, Elizabeth Hestler scolded herself for having allowed such a horrible lapse in judgment to occur; to consider becoming romantically involved with Pierce, a superior—the fucking Director, for Christ sake—a reasonable option. Not only did they disagree on all matters concerning the Subjects, he was a lousy companion—becoming clingy every time they had sex; talking about settling down and having a few kids. The man was forty-nine years old. His time for having children passed him by decades ago. And at thirty-six, the thought of getting pregnant repulsed her. . .maybe when she was at the young, naive age of twenty-three, but the idea of raising a family so close to her forties felt like a cry for help, if anything.

"You're late," a frantic Winsome welcomed her as the elevator came to a complete stop; the doors having malfunctioned, opening in-between the last two floors. "Meredith was a no show—morning sickness, again—I've had to deal with three code yellows *all by myself.*"

"My apologies, Friedrich," Elizabeth said, walking past Winsome to the monitors. "Next time, I'll use the stairs."

"Sarcasm? This early in the morning? Really?"

"Blame Pierce," her attention focused on this morning's logs. "I had the misfortune of sharing a brief elevator ride with him. Had I not been forced to make a pit-stop, I would've been here *on time.*"

Winsome rolled his eyes, joining Elizabeth so they could go over the logs together. "Still not on good terms with him, I take it?"

Elizabeth threw a sideways glare in Winsome's direction, not finding his question worthy of a verbal response. Continuing to scroll through the medical logs she skimmed to the bottom to see how Subject No. 2990 had been during the night, hoping to find he slept through her off-shift without issue. No demerits listed. Good, she thought. She didn't trust Winsome to act accordingly if anything were to have happened to him during her absence last night. While he was competent enough at his job to keep the Subjects alive and properly sequenced, he didn't know how to soothe 2990 naturally; without the use of medication. Relieved to see her friend had survived the night without her, Elizabeth eyed the lower right hand corner of the monitor; 6:34pm—only twenty-six minutes left to kill until Winsome would (finally. . .) relieve himself for the night, leaving her and Mason Dixon alone with the Subjects until 6:30am.

Tonight's the night, she thought as she finished reading what was required of her on the computer screen.

Tonight.

• • •

"WHAT THE HELL are we going to do on a *Tuesday night*?" an already cross-faded Daniel asked. "Nothing's going to be open this late except for fast-food chains, Denny's, and nightclubs which, and correct me if I'm not mistaken, aren't going to allow four nineteen year-old vagrants in without seeing our I.D.s first."

"Why do we have to be *doing something*?" Katherine yelled over the car's stereo, R.E.M.'s "It's the End of the World as We Know It (And I Feel Fine)" screaming from the radio, her feet hanging out the window while Nathan sped through downtown Los Angeles looking for the on-ramp for the Interstate; Phil attempting to sing along to Michael Stipe's fast-paced verses—failing miserably. Katherine turned to face Phillip, "We've never done anything *before*. . .why start *now*?"

Daniel rolled his eyes, turning his attention to the blurred scenery outside his window. He had never been fond of Katherine, to be honest. But she made Nathan happy, so he held his tongue whenever the two of them came to a disagreement, knowing Nathan would blindly take *her* side if it blew up into a full-fledged argument—despite the two of them being friends since first grade.

Staring out the window Daniel saw a lone helicopter looming in the distance, its searchlight roaming the barren streets below—with no real sense of urgency. He wondered what the world looked like from up in the sky. Would it appear peaceful? a silent, neon soaked utopia waiting for another sunrise to begin the cycle of life all over again? Or would the depravity of the city find itself echoing in the æther, becoming a cacophony of violent screams and gunshots; nothing more than a pornographic audio mosaic of civilization's suffering—

Daniel felt the car accelerate as Nathan made his way onto the freeway. Even this late at night, fear found its way into Daniel's chest as the car merged onto the Interstate; pounding away at him, making it harder to breathe. Hoping to calm his nerves he turned to face Phillip, who was singing (off key) to the final refrains of the song as it faded into the next song—Nine Inch Nails' "Head Like A Hole," from their 1989 release *Pretty Hate Machine*, Phillip turning his head to sing the first line in his direction, *"Got money? I'll do anything for you. . ."* while seductively moving his body in a grinding fashion against the car seat, *"Got money? nail me up against the wall. . ."*

He couldn't help but laugh at his boyfriend's descent into complete ridiculousness. Daniel had never said it out loud (or outside the context of sex), but he was in love with the dorky kid sitting on the other side of Katherine's beat-up Toyota Camry. *One day*, he thought, *when I'm able to, I'm going to be to marry that adorable little fuck.*

Out of nowhere, it seemed, Nathan swerved the vehicle into the passing lane for a brief moment, throwing Daniel's stomach; a faded blue Ford Mustang GT LX swerved back and forth for a moment as it disappeared into the background while Katherine yelled out her window, into the air, for the driver to either 'drive faster or piss off'. "Could you slow-the-fuck-down, please?" he cried. "It's not like we're *going anywhere!*"

Nathan lifted his right hand off the wheel to give Daniel the finger, increasing the car's speed in response to his friend's plea. Before he could reach up and grab Nathan's finger to mimic the notion of breaking it, a blinding flash of light consumed the sky and everything living underneath it. Silence found its way into the world—the radio now only playing static. The angst-ridden vocals of Trent Reznor had become nothing more than white noise. It didn't take long for the vehicle to come to a screeching halt.

"What the fuck just happened?" they all asked in confused unison; the once confident helicopter falling from the sky, down to an unforgiving earth in the distance; a small, rather anti-climactic explosion rising into the sky shortly after—unlike the monumental explosions he had seen in countless action films. In front of them, in slow motion, a towering mushroom cloud made its destructive presence known.

Frozen, Daniel fought every neural signal in his brain to scream for Nathan to turn the car around and begin speeding in the opposite direction. Nothing came out. Katherine, frightened beyond comprehension, managed to move her left arm to begin smacking Nathan violently across the shoulder—silently demanding the same sentiment. To his left, a hyperventilating Phillip found himself incapable of any other form of expression, be it physical or auditory; only the faint sounds of heavy breathing from disbelief escaped his lungs.

Finally able to move, Nathan put the car in reverse and, with little effort, turned the car around—pressing the pedal to the floor, hoping to outrun the heat wave which would inevitably find its way down the Interstate.

Despite being in an old, beat-up Toyota Camry, they found themselves flying down the freeway at 110mph in no time at all—pushing the car to its limits. They passed the blue Mustang again, which had also come to a complete stop due to the explosion, as they continued to drive southbound. "We're gonna make it. . .we're gonna make it. . ." a petrified Nathan mumbled nonstop as the streetlights sped past them in a pained fury. "We're gonna make it. . ."

A second flash of light—further out, beyond the horizon, but still noticeable to the four of them. "You've got to be fucking kidding me. . ." a defeated Nathan whispered as the sound of the engine died down, his foot no longer flooring the gas pedal.

· · ·

IT WAS 0924, 25 JANUARY 1995, when Russian satellites picked up a small blip. The entire base went into high alert. Still tired from last night's watch, Nikolai pulled himself out of his rack, got dressed, and headed toward the computer room to find out what was going on. When he arrived, the room was packed. Until today, he had never seen this many people in the computer room at once. He felt uncomfortable. *I should've stayed in my rack*, he thought while he awaited further instruction.

"What do you think this is about?" Pyotr's voice came from the left.

"I won't even bother to venture a guess," Nikolai replied. "This place has been rather boring ever since the Cold War ended in '91. It's probably just *another* drill—Kuznetsov can't have enough of them, it seems."

Holding the drills made no sense. If a fire were to start, everyone on a level *below the surface* would be dead within minutes—emergency protocol dictating emergency shutdown of the elevator and oxygen circulation; trapping them, essentially burying them in a multi-level, man-made coffin. Speaking his mind, it didn't make much sense to Nikolai to have all who were stationed here to remain four years after the end of a forty-six year long arms race. *I guess some habits are hard to break*, he concluded.

The room fell silent as Kuznetsov approached the podium standing at the front of the room. You could count the number of people who *actually* respected the man on one hand (and still have fingers to spare), but you couldn't deny the man's presence exuded authority. He stood tall and proud at the podium and waited for the silence to linger a moment longer—bordering on awkward.

"There are some battles—some wars. . ." he finally spoke, taking a short breath before he chose to continue. ". . .that cannot be won. Many a foolish man, most of them leaders of the world, would disagree with this statement. *Nuclear war* being one of these ill-fated pursuits—"

"Jesus, will he quit rambling and get to the fucking point?" a voice in the far back mumbled.

"— it is with great misfortune that, as of 0924, Russian satellites picked up what appeared to be a nuclear missile as it passed by our Olenegorsk early warning radar station in Murmansk Oblast; heading toward Moscow. In response, at 0930, President Boris Yeltsin, (apparently *still drunk* from last night), activated *the briefcase*, launching a retaliatory attack on the United States of America. Unfortunately, it was made known to us that the 'nuclear missile' was *actually* a Brant XII rocket launched from the coast of Norway to study the aurora borealis. By now, the President of the United States, Bill Clinton, will have been notified of our error in judgment and have sent his own retaliation. . ."

Silence. That was all that remained. Not even hushed whispers could find themselves floating among the crowd of people in the room. Nikolai looked around to see if he could read any sign of emotion fleeting from anyone's stoic gaze. Nothing. Only silence. He made a quick glance at his watch to see how much time they had left before the bombs fell upon them. Twenty minutes, if not less.

"Это конец света, как мы его знаем," he thought, certain he could hear the sound of explosions echoing from the surface — rippling downward, toward the lower levels; the rafters began to shake back and forth, the lights flickering on and off for a few moments before shutting off completely. "и я чувствую себя прекрасно."

Staring down from the heavens, overcome by the destructive nature of His children, God wept in the silence of His exile while pinpoints of violent bright light erupted from various parts of the planet He had spent so much time creating — perfecting for His most beloved of creatures. He reached out His hand to stop the destruction, to put a premature end to their misguided nature. But He could do nothing. Earth had severed its binds to Him long ago, when science invalidated His existence; rendering Him powerless.

The only thing He could do was sit and watch and listen — listen to the screams of a dying earth.

No matter how hard He tried, He could not bury the sound; He couldn't even bring Himself to look away.

. . .

AND IT WAS IN THIS MOMENT, he knew he had to be dreaming—the black leather-bound notebook sitting on his desk among an endless pile of papers being the giveaway to his subconscious state. As he edged toward his desk the *infamous notebook* opened, its pages aimlessly flipping back and forth until it found the desired page it wished for Tom to read:

> You will come to know me as a monster, a saint, and (quite possibly) the closest thing you'll ever get to when it comes to the idea of having a soul mate; for only I know you the way you truly are and not the way the world has come to perceive you. I know your darkest fears, your deepest desires, your hopes, and wildest dreams; but above all else, I know the sound you make when you can't stop screaming. It is only when your eyes go dead that you and I will cease to be *the perfect couple*. For now, though, let's have ourselves a night I know we'll both remember for the rest of our *selfish lives*.
>
> Taylor Swift's "Wildest Dreams" plays on your iPod in the background–setting the scene perfectly–as your eyes begin to open after the short nap you took when I hit you across the head with the butt of my firearm; your look of confusion complementing such delicate features. . .

The (rough) opening lines of *Modus Operandi* lay in front of him, begging to be read over and over again; their poetic, sadistic prose—painting a portrait for what was about to become of the Haiku Killer's first victim, Penelope Johnson—conning him into picking up the leather notebook to examine it closer; to make sure nothing was added or out of place. Squinting at the fine print which lived upon the page, finding his own handwriting difficult to read, Tom Dolin found the tips of his fingers developing a burning sensation from the edges of the notebook. It was in this moment time seemed to slow down to a standstill. *Not again*, he thought as the gutter of the notebook combusted; the paper turning black, the text lifting off the pages and into the smoke-filled æther. *Open your eyes, Thomas. C'mon, now—it is only a dream. None of this is **real**. Now, repeat after me: wake. . .the. . .fuck. . .up. . .*

Gasping for breath after waking up from the nightmare which found him at the beginning of *every* new writing venture (the words lifting themselves from the burning pages being—according to his friend Jared, a self-glorifying psychology major—the summation of *any* writer's fear: the thought of an idea going up in smoke; losing inspiration), Tom Dolin found himself in another familiar setting—confined to a small receptacle, the rest of the world shrouded in darkness, minus the blue light coming from a series of computer monitors in the background. He closed his eyes and, putting forth all of his mental focus, attempted to wake himself from the current dreamscape which was holding him captive.

Opening them he was met with disappointment to find he still remained trapped within a confined, cylindrical structure; a familiar, calming voice calling out to him, "Open your eyes, Thomas. C'mon, now—it is only a dream. . ." but he ignored it. Instead, his mind wandered to another probable means of escape—repeating an old, poetic phrase he'd written years ago and had (recently) been reacquainted to via one of his students:

> Sleeping, dreaming, but my eyes are still wide open
> While shadows in white talk among themselves, wrapped in unclear conversation
> *"Where am I?"* I ask, but the words won't leave my tongue
> Consolation finds my curious hand; a gentle caress of a thumb
> Echoes come and echoes fade, but the question still remains
> Why do I (finally) feel awake during these odd recurring dreams?

"This isn't a dream, Thomas," the voice broke through his failed attempt at meditation. "Now, for the love of god, *open your eyes!*" a drip of desperation flowing from her tongue, choking the words as they echoed throughout the room. He felt his eyes tighten as he continued to repeat the poem to himself until the words began to bleed into one another—becoming a scrambled mess, much like everything else had in his *previous dream world*. The woman's voice remained a constant, her pleas becoming more and more hopeless with each utterance of his name. "Thomas, I'm *begging* you, *please* wake up. . ."

Normally, the calming female voice would have metamorphosed into the familiar tone of his wife, Sarah, at this point of the dream—the weight of the words hanging in the æther carrying him into consciousness. But he could find no reprieve, not this time. No matter the effort, it seemed the thought of his wife's voice soothing his anxious ears became more and more a pipe-dream than a possible reality; a reality he refused to accept.

In this darkness, beyond the echoing words of a woman's desperate cries, beyond the dim blue lights emitting from the computer screens, Tom's psyche reached further into the recesses of his memory, back to the night which had inspired him to pursue a life of writing—a dark period of his life; the foundation of his stability crumbling beneath him, watching helplessly as his *nuclear family* became nothing but fragments of memory; photographs of a life long dream fading to white in a box forgotten by time. He prayed this was all just an extension of a dream he had had that night, a dream which would inspire the beginnings of his third novel (a novel which, through the insistent advice from both his agent and editor, would become the sprawling *Transmigration* trilogy), but his environment remained the same—a world shrouded in darkness, the confinement of his cylindrical prison mocking him as he continued, without success (digging deeper and deeper into the sea of memories. Hoping, if he dug deep enough, something would click), to wake himself; still, nothing. Not even a faint glimmer of hope found its way to his despairing thoughts.

"Open your eyes, Thomas," the voice continued, growing closer, it seemed, becoming a hushed whisper against the plane of glass which separated them. "Please. . .I'm begging you," she choked, the words getting caught in her throat. "For the love of God, *wake up*."

01001100	01101111	01110011	01110100
00100000	01101001	01101110	00100000
01100001	00100000	01101000	01100001
01111010	01100101	00101100	00100000
01110111	01101001	01110100	01101000
00100000	01101110	01101111	00100000
01000011	01101100	01100001	01110010

Part II: Ascension Dream

01101001	01101110	00100000	01110011
01101001	01100111	01101000	01110100
00101100	00100000	01110111	01100101
00100000	01100110	01101001	01101110
01100100	00100000	01101111	01110101
01110010	01110011	01100101	01101100
01110110	01100101	01110011	00100000
01110011	01100101	01100001	01110010
01100011	01101000	01101001	01101110
01100111	00100000	01100110	01101111
01110010	00100000	01110100	01110010
01110101	01110100	01101000	00100000
01101001	01101110	00100000	01110100
01101000	01100101	00100000	01100100
01100001	01110010	01101011	01100101
01110011	01110100	00100000	01101111
01100110	00100000	01110000	01101100
01100001	01100011	01100101	01110011

The past is only a dream, one which we look back upon with fond regret—hoping to fall asleep and relive it; making the false promise to ourselves that we'll never let the fleeting moment pass us by a second time.

8

THE CHOICES WE MAKE will define us in the end: a philosophical concept my late grandfather attempted to bestow upon me at a young age; *one I never believed held any merit.* I didn't *choose* to become Director when my father resigned, but it is what *defines* me to so many people (if not everyone) who live here. My grandfather may have been a wise man—far wiser than my piss-poor excuse of a father who, despite his legacy among the elder residents of the hospital, never (not once!) put forth the same effort to impart wisdom upon me; no matter how *flawed*—but his view of the world, and life itself, developed during a different time; a simpler time. How I wish I could have been the Director during *his era*: before the raids. Before the Subjects became a glaring issue, stripping various levels throughout the building from functioning at full capacity; causing power outages—one of *many* catastrophes my father left for me to attend to upon his resignation. . .

I *will* fix everything my father ruined during his time as Director. I *will* be better than him; if it's the only thing I achieve in my lifetime. The sins of my father *will not* follow me to the grave. . .

—Pierce Alexandre Needham

He couldn't sleep. No matter the method, from counting backwards from one hundred to succumbing to the use of sleep aides (which never had any *real* affect on him, but he thought he'd give them another chance), the notion of sleep escaped Pierce's tired mind. Finally giving up on the pursuit of finding some shut-eye, he turned to writing in his journal—something he hadn't been able to find the time to do in years. All he managed to write down was a continuation from his final entry—written years ago after his first week as Director:

. . .and even if I fail—fail to erase the errors of my father—I (thankfully) have no heir, no legacy, to leave my failures to rest upon their weary shoulders once I leave this world. I would not wish this burden, the burden of undoing all that ruined *this once great settlement* (knowing all their labors would be fruitless and in vain), on anyone. If I fail, which—with each passing year—it seems I will, this burden will die with me. The sins of my father will only follow *me* to the grave. . .

It is this, and only this, I am sure of anymore—the only statement which holds any truth to it.

He stopped. Laying the pen down he rested his face in the palms of his hands, attempting to wash away the exhaustion from his mind. It depressed him to see how little he'd come since taking on the mantle of Director. *I'm just like my father*, he thought, closing the journal with one hand, blindly placing it back in its drawer—*a failure; nothing more*. So much had gone wrong these past few years. He had lost a dear friend, having cast him out due to a petty assault charge, hoping to cover up his own transgression (the attempted murder of what some would call a *human being*). The woman he had loved for years having distanced herself from him due to their inability to agree on anything —*let alone trust one another*. . .It's rather bitter-sweet, actually, how we dedicate so much of our (limited) time *trying to justify ourselves* to the shadows of those who are long gone from this world—our efforts essentially going unnoticed; the task at hand now only pursued for *our own (self-absorbed) gratification*. And even if they were still here to witness all we've done in their name, would they acknowledge it; would they recall what they had said or done which had *compelled* us to spend the rest of our lives proving ourselves to their memory?

Looking out his window, the gray, desolate scenery of the night sky staring back at him, he often wondered if—

"Director?"

Startled, ripped from his (rather bleak) thoughts, Pierce turned to face the doorway to find Winsome, his fragile frame standing eagerly in the archway. "Yes?" he turned, asking, "What is it, Friedrich?" feeling the sudden aching sting of regret hit him in the pit of his stomach as the question left his tongue.

"We have ourselves a. . .situation."

"Clarify, please. I am not going to remove myself from the comfort of my room simply because *you* find yourself with a *situation*."

Winsome gulped, clearing his throat, hoping his situation was reason enough for the Director to follow him. "I have reason to suspect Elizabeth has awoken one of the Subjects."

He had his attention. "Which one?" he asked, already knowing the answer.

• • •

IT HURT TO OPEN HIS EYES. A once effortless task had become a chore, the weight of his eyelids having become unbearable. When he finally found the strength to separate them, however, he found himself blinded by a piercing white light—the source of light being brighter than anything he had ever encountered in his lifetime—his eyelids collapsed instantly, hoping to shut it out. The weight of his eyelids and the sensitivity to light weren't the only physical anomalies he found himself struggling with—the weight of his arms and legs, too, had appeared to increase. He could not move them, no matter the amount of determination and willpower he put into doing so. Not knowing where he was, he lay motionless; completely helpless to everything around him, whatever it may be. Before he could attempt any further in getting anything (even if it were only a finger or two) to move, his hopeless thoughts found themselves interrupted by a loud, ear-splitting echo of footsteps; growing louder as they honed in on his location. Was this what it felt like to be a newborn baby? he thought as the deafening echoes made their way to his left side, stopping only inches away, judging by the sudden warmth he felt against his torso. It wasn't until the appearance of an outside temperature that he realized he was freezing.

A warm, gentle hand took hold of his left arm, lifting it a few inches from the operating table (it had to be, he told himself, no average bed was *this cold and uncomfortable*) before laying it back down and jotting something down on a notepad—the sound of the ballpoint pen scraping against the clipboard, causing him to wince.

Was he dead? He demanded an answer. If death had (somehow?) happened upon him, he found himself suddenly filled with a nameless dread. *What if my soul failed to separate from my body?* his mind screamed, panic-stricken at the thought of being stuck in his own, soon-to-be decaying corpse for all eternity. *No. . .I'm not dead. . .* he concluded—a surge of pain having coursed its way from the tip of his brain stem, down his spine. *Death, I presume, wouldn't be this uncomfortable. There would've been some kind of relief, right?* "Rest easy, Thomas," a familiar voice arose from the darkness. "It'll all be over soon."

Days must've passed by (in the darkness it was impossible to tell how long it had *actually* been) before he could open his eyes—only to be met with a flash of white; his eyes unable to adjust to the lighting of the room. His ears, however, had found a balance between the silence and echoes—able to tell the distance between himself and everything around him. To his left, seven meters away (an estimation), he could hear the quiet sound of sporadic scribbling; the sound of someone jotting something down feverishly. They had poor penmanship, lacking the consistency which would've indicated the use of cursive, but too heavy-handed to be someone with legible handwriting.

"Do you think he can hear us?" an unfamiliar voice. Male.

"It's possible." Female. Familiar. "Why? Afraid to say anything that might insult him?"

"I'm just curious—wondering if he's figured it out yet; if the pieces of the puzzle have fallen into place."

"Even if he hasn't *figured it out yet*, and he still remains lost in a wash of confusion, his brain activity is significantly higher than any Subject that's come before him."

"But what if he strokes out upon awakening, like so many other Subjects have done in the past? Pierce will surely use this *potential failure* to get his way—shutting the Project down once and for all, without an ounce of hesitation; leaving us facing the possibility of exile, just like Theodore did six years ago. If a Director—*a Director, for Christ sake*—can find himself facing the humiliation of being cast out into the Wasteland, what's stopping him from doing the same *to us?*"

"Mason, that's enough. If I wanted to deal with unwarranted cynicism, I would've asked Winsome to have helped me with this process."

"Did you hear something?"

A twitch of the thumb and forefinger is all I can manage. Helpless, I continue to lay here while an aimless conversation between two shadows continues to fill the room. I find the paranoia of the one known as Mason entertaining—the dread in his voice at the mention of Pierce's name being drenched in an unmistakable wave of fear. Another twitch. This time more noticeable, I hope. A break in the conversation. I hear Mason ask, "Did you hear something?" and I find myself in an internal screaming fit—begging the tip of my tongue to allow the words "Somebody tell me what the fuck is going on!" to escape my uncooperative lips.

Although a twitch of the thumb and forefinger is (still) all I can manage, hearing the sound of footsteps coming toward me, I feel it's enough.

"Thomas, can you hear me?" Elizabeth's voice, he assumed; the faint, familiar caress against the back of his hand (similar to how Sarah would, especially during times of immense stress) sending a myriad of neurological signals to his brain—his increasing desire to manage more than the subtle twitch of his thumb and forefinger infuriating him to no end. "If you can, give us—me—a sign. . .anything. . ."

"This is hopeless," Mason sighed. "Besides the subtle twitches of two of his fingers, he's showing no signs of improvement. I'm calling out for the night. I haven't had a chance to see my wife and kids in three days. See you tomorrow?"

Another series of days pass. In those days I've managed to move my entire left arm off the edge of the platform I've been forced to call my home for god knows how long. I can hear the rushed scribbles of Mason taking note of my progress. I wonder if Elizabeth or anyone else can read his chicken scratch or if they're simply for his own amusement.

It isn't until days later when I can finally open my eyes and not be blinded by the piercing florescent lighting which hangs above me—my collected gaze being met with the apprehensive smile of a warm, female face.

"Good morning, Thomas," a calming whisper. "And let me be the first to welcome you to *the real world*."

Confusion—it was the only word to describe it. The dimmed lighting above him appeared to be spinning as his ears took the final three words in for interpretation. *What does she mean by* **the real world**? his thoughts raced for an answer; nothing, not even a half-baked solution coming to him. This couldn't be a dream, he concluded; the sharp pain of hunger which coursed through his entire body—a sensation which would have woken him by now had he been, in fact, dreaming—letting him know *this situation* was (indeed) happening.

"It's about damned time he decided to wake himself up," a frustrated Mason acknowledged. "I was beginning to think the bastard would be a vegetable and nothing more."

Lacking grace, smacking the corner of his face against the cold steel of the operating table, Tom turned his head to face the woman standing over him. She was young in the face, but her eyes betrayed the antiquity of her soul. He couldn't put his finger on it, but she looked familiar to him—a long, lost acquaintance, having forgotten where/when they first met, but familiar to him nonetheless. Her eyes, green, he noticed, upon further inspection, stared back at him; curiosity and childlike admiration filling them to the brim of their irises. *Where do I know you from?* his mind asked—the words, themselves, unable to leave his tongue. *I know you from somewhere. . .like a dream or something—*

"He looks confused," Mason continued, turning the page on his clipboard over to jot something else down. Tom attempted to say 'Fuck you, buddy,' but only the monosyllabic 'fuh' escaped his lips. "Why did you pick him again?"

Tom passed out before he could hear the woman's answer—the effort of keeping his eyes open and turning his head having exhausted him; his tired mind finding a dream along the way.

When I opened my eyes, what I saw terrified me. I was home (in Santa Ana) but the surrounding landscape had become something foreign to me; like a nightmare. The trees outside stood aflame, their burning leaves being blown by a strong, suffocating wind—the flames stretching westward. Looking up to meet the sky, I saw a mass of clouds dance in an arrhythmic fashion above my head. To my left, stretching on for miles upon miles of road (well into the horizon) abandoned vehicles lay hopelessly awaiting for their owners to return to them so they could continue their trek to wherever it was they were going. Am I in Hell? I asked myself, knowing I wouldn't get an answer.

Still finding myself curious, I began walking down a barren stretch of road. And as I made my way down N Broadway, past an abandoned, dilapidated Starbucks, I couldn't shake the odd sensation which pierced my skull with a nameless dread. It didn't help ease my mind knowing the strength of the wind would continue to grow stronger the further north I traveled—creating an ever increasing atmosphere of discomfort against my skin.

Before I knew it, I found myself on I-5; my trek of morbid curiosity having carried me onto the once lively Interstate. I stopped for a moment, taking in the world around me in one panoramic turn. Across the claustrophobic stretch of unoccupied automobiles, I watched as the world continued to burn all around me—all previously (well-known) boundaries having disappeared, it seemed, in the fiery orange filter which had swallowed the Earth. . .

Almost without warning (and without logic or reason), the arid wind changed direction, blowing the wave of debris east now instead of its original westward path—the world's deafening silence being replaced by something foreign; I couldn't quite make it out—just dust and echoes. The echoes soon turned into a cacophonous symphony of screams being played in reverse, the once free-floating debris finding their way back home to their corroded homes—to buildings and other various architecture scattered about the Interstate.

As I continued to stare upon a world set aflame, the once orange-tinged world began to develop its original color palette of blues and greens with scattered urban gray and brick thrown in; the trail of orange falling back to its point of origin. Dust recollected in small anthropomorphic clusters all around me while a mushroom cloud found itself being *swallowed into the city street off in the distance. I had witnessed this scene play itself in front of me plenty of times (in the opposite direction, of course). I will admit I find myself preferring the playback of destruction and death over its reversal—the absence of life being replaced by a sea of the living; despite the recreation of beauty it has to offer; knowing the destruction will only repeat itself once the unseen creator—if one found themselves believing in such a concept—decided to press play; overriding the rewinding sequence of events, swallowing the Earth (once more) in a wash of repugnant orange. . .*

• • •

STARING DOWN AT SUBJECT NO. 2990 (Thomas Dolin), Elizabeth Hestler sighed a breath of relief knowing she had, as far as she could tell, successfully *awoken* a Subject—unplugging their subconscious mind from the *Arcadian Sequence*; Theodore would've been proud. She watched as he continued to sleep, wondering if he was dreaming —if he knew how to dream, having lived his *entire life* trapped within one without knowing it.

"I'm not going to lie, Elizabeth. . .his waking up just to fall asleep again was kind of a buzzkill. Are they always this anticlimactic upon awakening?"

She couldn't answer him. She didn't know. The only *successful* awakening she had bore witness to was Cordelia's—not enough evidence to make a claim. What she could do, however, was read through the long list of failures throughout the decades. She stepped over to Theodore's old desk, opened the bottom drawer, pulled out a heavy file labeled "Project Homecoming," and opened it to find a long list of Subjects Theodore's father and grandfather had attempted to bring out of the *Arcadian Sequence*, but had been met with failure:

16 September 293 T.E.—Subject No. 1903 – *Eric Blair: Sensitivity to light. Relentless screams of anguish upon the slightest touch to his skin. Managed to break loose of his binds, kicking Alexandre in the face, breaking his nose. Resequenced until further notice.*

Garrison, who I had tasked with monitoring Subject No. 1903, notified me that today, **27 March 295 T.E.**, that 1903 had passed away due to respiratory complications beyond our comprehension. Must remain positive that a Subject can be unplugged from the sequence and allowed to live a normal life.

24 August 295 T.E. — Subject No. 1928 – *Phil Dick: Almost a success. Showed promise during the first week, but became violent toward Susan when she attempted to take a blood sample from him. Refused to call me and Alexandre by name; instead, he referred to us as 'Overlords of the State.'* Without consulting Alexandre, I resequenced Subject No. 1928 *(Phil). While Alexandre would've considered him a success, Phil's violent tendencies and paranoid delusions have raised enough concern for me to consider him another failure. Perhaps at a later date he will be ready for awakening.*

8 May 329 T.E. — *Despite my father's hopes for* Subject No. 1928 *to be a viable Subject for an awakening,* Subject No. 1928 *(AKA Phil Dick) passed away this morning due to a stroke five days prior* — *all brain activity having ceased, Matthew removed all life support systems. He was cremated two days later on* **10 May 329 T.E.** *Like my father before me, I shall remain vigilant that a Subject's brain can be fully realized and successfully unplugged from the* Arcadian Sequence; *Isaac, unfortunately, I feel, is beginning to lose faith in what we're doing.*

11 April 309 T.E. — Subject No. 1937 – *Thomas Pynchon: I don't know what it was that went wrong with* Subject No. 1937, *if Felicia and Garrison followed protocol to the letter or not, but I fear I may never forget the chain of events that followed. . .*

Alexandre and I were still in the elevator when we heard the shrill sound of Felicia's screams — *incoherent, at first. . .becoming clearer as the elevator doors opened:* "Oh my god, he's staring at me!" *she continued to say as she backed away from his sleeping chamber, Garrison frantically trying to find a sedative to put* Subject No. 1937 *back under until they could **properly** make an attempt to awaken him from the Arcadian Sequence. I feel this may be the last time we see Felicia in the lower levels. Such a shame, really. She brought a certain, feminine charm to the* *lower levels that was lacking. I guess, until then, it'll just be Alexandre, Garrison, and myself until we can find a replacement.*

8 May 309 T.E. *—it seems* Subject No. 1937 *is unable to be sequenced properly after our* **situation** *with him about a month ago. Garrison says his brain activity shows an increase in paranoia, as if he's become self aware of his artificial surroundings. I will keep this in my notes for emergencies. So far, he doesn't appear dangerous, unlike* Subject No. 1928. *who has begun to plant seeds of doubt in others via his literature; while works of fiction, they do question reality and whether or not the world they live in is the product of a computer program. If this continues, make plans to induce a chemical imbalance in his brain to either lobotomize him or cause cardiac arrest.*

29 April 337 T.E. — Subject No. 2990 – *Thomas Dolin: a baby was born today, his brain only half dormant—an anomaly we've never come across before; a mind not awake enough to function on its own or without activity entirely, but, instead, somewhere in the middle. Sequencing him proved difficult, the active portions of his brain unwilling to succumb to the rewiring process; refusing to accept the artificial reality we were all attempting to build for him. Hopefully, as the years press forward, we can see if* Subject No. 2990 *(little Tommy Dolin) will prove a viable candidate for any future awakening trials—though I would understand if Isaac were hesitant on this matter.*

21 July 337 T.E. . . . *I often find Isaac's son, Pierce (a troubled boy, I feel —emotionally unstable, to put it bluntly), leering at the young boy—as well as the other Subjects—often during his 'once a week' educational visits. I don't understand why Theodore likes hanging out with him (a younger boy, nonetheless) as much as he does; perhaps it has to do with me and Pierce's father being the hospital's Co-Directors. I'll have a talk with him—see what my son sees in Isaac's little boy. Maybe there's something I'm missing. . .?*

Jesus, she thought as she continued to flip through the pages which rested in Theodore's grandfather's file. There had been far too many failed attempts at awakening a Subject—she was surprised Isaac Oliver

Needham and Raymond Webb even bothered to continue their fathers' work, one of their attempts involving brothers (with a name she could not pronounce) sometime in the year 341 T.E.; another colossal failure.

With each defeat that followed it had become clear to her why Pierce hated the Subjects as much as he did; to watch your own father and grandfather give so much attention to a bunch of humans who had never experienced an *honest day on Earth* — instead living what he saw as an easygoing artificial life where (in his eyes) nothing negative could find its way into their lap. She turned, looking back at Thomas (Subject No. 2990, his designation number read) and — while still unable to agree with him on what should be done with Them — she understood the logic behind Pierce's loathsome attitude; especially towards Thomas.

When she looked at him, however, she was reminded of when she was a child, accompanying her father for *Take Your Child To Work Day*, how her five-year-old self stared at an unconscious boy two years older than her, sleeping peacefully while life support systems kept him alive — a tech monitoring his sequencing. Over the years, whenever her father was the tech monitoring the endless display of computers, she would come visit him — talk with him, despite the conversation being one-sided; updating him on current events happening around the hospital.

Now he lay before her, thirty-one years older, and she found her heart still skipped a beat whenever her gaze found him — a sensation she had never admitted to anyone. How stupid of me, she would tell herself, having found herself experiencing a series of biochemical precursors which, *anyone with even a limited* knowledge of biochemistry knew, would suggest the emotional response that was known as love; a man whose voice she had yet to hear utter a sentence, let alone a single word, and she was *infatuated by him.*

"Looks like someone's finally waking up from their little nap," Mason chimed from across the room. "Are you going to stay with us this time, buddy?"

Elizabeth rushed to the operating table where Thomas lay, his eyes now open enough to see his pale blue irises staring back at her; still lost in a subtle haze of confusion. She watched as he, with an extraneous amount of effort on his part, lifted his head to get a good look of his sur-roundings. After a couple rotations Thomas lowered his head back to the head of the operating table and, exhausted, asked, "Wh—" a short pause, the words getting caught in his throat. "Where am I?"

"You're home," was all she said, the small of her thumb finding its old familiar spot across the tops of his knuckles.

Tom looked up at the woman, confused. This can't be home, he thought as his eyes moved involuntarily—attempting to keep eye con-tact with her. She had to to be mistaken, his mind continued to speak. How is this, a dark, desolate operating room, home? It didn't make sense to him for a doctor, which he assumed she was, given the lab coat both she and her companion were wearing, to tell him he was home; the statement being a farce, even at face value.

"H-How did I get here?" he managed to say.

The woman turned away for a moment to consult with her male counterpart, unsure how to answer his question. The man shook his head worriedly, his gaze meeting Tom's for a second before turning back to meet hers. Tom, having grown impatient while he waited for a response, managed to turn his head so he could explore his surround-ings; hoping to find some information on his whereabouts. Beyond the bright overhead light which bathed him in ultraviolet radiation, there wasn't much to see—the rest of the room shrouded in darkness; only a blip of light from a computer monitor that had gone on standby. "How did I get here?" he repeated himself, this time with a crude immediacy in his voice which hadn't been there the first time—the awkward si-lence of the room having frustrated him.

It didn't help his attitude *knowing* he couldn't move his arms or legs.

"I know this may sound jarring," the woman finally spoke, "but you've been here *your whole life*, Thomas. What you've considered your reality your entire life was actually a simulated dream sequence. Having been born in a dormant state, you were hooked up to our building's life support systems until we either found a way to awaken the conscious part of your brain—thus unplugging you from the *Arca-dian Sequence*—or until you died."

"—And as you've probably already guessed, we were able to achieve the arduous process of *waking you up*." Mason chimed in. "Elizabeth and I will be expecting your *Thank You* card in a week or so, once you've relearned how to use your hands so you can write us one."

Tom closed his eyes in disbelief. Impossible, he told himself; the idea of living his *entire life* in a simulated dream was nauseating. It had to be a lie. Why would someone (anyone?!) hook up a comatose infant's *already fragile* mind up to a dream simulation (the *Arcadian Sequence?*) while hoping to find a cure or solution? how could they? Last he remembered, humanity didn't have *that kind of technology* in 2028. In a science fiction novel or film, perhaps, but not in the real world.

"Is this some kind of sick joke?" he asked.

Elizabeth, finding herself upset at Tom's immediate refusal to accept the truth, turned to look at Mason, who had disappeared into his notepad—unsure how to respond to Tom's doubt. "I understand this may seem like *a joke*, being told your entire existence was spent living a well-constructed lie, but it's not. Unfortunately, everything I've told you is the truth. I know it's asking a lot of you to give up any and all relationships you may have 'built' throughout your lifetime. I can't even begin to *fathom* what you are probably going through right now, internally..."

Tom Dolin's thoughts drifted to his family, to his wife, Sarah, and his three children (Christie, Matilda, and little Benjamin) and found himself saddened at the idea that their entire existence had been nothing more than a dream; a lie. He closed his eyes, still in denial, and found himself praying to wake up from this nightmare. But as the moments continued to pass, the weight of reality had grown heavy on his mind. There was no returning to his home in Santa Ana—to his family.

"But...it's just—" he began to say, the small beginnings of a tear collecting at the corner of his left eye. "I didn't get to say goodbye to them *before I left...*"

A wash of sadness found its way into Elizabeth's soul. Questioning her decision to awaken a Subject, essentially stripping them of their identity—taking away any semblance of familiarity. Was Pierce right after all? she asked herself, turning away from the sad, confused face of Subject No. 2990. No, she reassured herself. Pierce wanted to pull the plug on *Project Arcadia*, which was murder when one peeled back the thin layer of logistics he had applied to the concept. No, she had the right idea (awakening the Subjects from their slumber), even if it meant tearing them away from the lives they had made for themselves over the years—away from the ones they had grown to love and share a life with.

"Get some rest, Thomas," she said, choking on her words, still refusing to look at him. "Tomorrow's going to be a busy day for you. . ."

Elizabeth glanced at Mason, who only responded with a subtle lift of his eyebrows while he continued to write aimlessly into his notepad, as she headed toward the elevator. She, too, needed to rest. Tomorrow was going to be a busy day for her, as well.

You can't rebuild a human overnight.

• • •

YET ANOTHER ABOMINATION added to the maelstrom of responsibilities I will be forced to call my own, an ill-tempered Pierce stared down at Subject No. 2990 in disgust. Somehow, Elizabeth had managed to lift *another useless blunder* (a neurological fuck-up) from the confines of their subconscious prison; even without—he assumed—the use of Theodore's journal. He had underestimated her abilities. He knew she was brilliant, but had made the inaccurate assumption believing she had her limits. As he continued to stare down at Subject No. 2990, he contemplated making another attempt on his life. The thought of carrying out the action, however, was rendered moot as Pierce watched the Subject's eyes open.

"Who the fuck are you?" 2990 asked, lifting his body from the table.

"Now, now. There's no need for such *language*," he paused to examine the clipboard which hung at the Subject's feet. "Thomas. I'm Pierce, Pierce Alexandre Needham," he looked back up, feigning a polite smile. "And I am the Director of this *fine facility*."

"Where's Elizabeth or Mason?" the Subject asked, appearing uncomfortable.

"They've turned in for the night, I'm afraid. I was simply on my rounds of the place and, having heard a rumor of your *arrival*, I wanted to stop by and say 'hello'—welcoming you to our humble little abode," he lied, still holding the forced smile. *How much longer should I carry on with this already vapid conversation?* he asked himself. *Do I ask him if he's hungry or how his day is going? Jesus. . .* At least he didn't appear to be an empty husk like Cordelia—alive, but without a soul; a relief.

A silence fell upon them. The two men stared each other down, refusing to speak another word to each other—unsure where they could take the conversation from *what little verbal interaction they had shared*. Pierce examined 2990's frail frame from head to toe, his body hooked up to a myriad number of devices; their main functions being muscle stimulation and respiratory assistance. *Why did Elizabeth choose him—him?!—to unplug from Arcadia? one of the* **most difficult** *Subjects to ever show his face in this facility*, Pierce's mind asked, the silence which filled the room refusing to be broken. She could've picked anyone else, yet she chose *this one*. He had to hand it to her, though. She did manage to recreate a past success, despite his veiled attempts to thwart her and the rest of her loyal staff from achieving it. And that's when it hit him. She could—but would she?—use this success (this sad excuse for a human life) as a platform to convince the rest of the residents to press for the unplugging of the rest of the Subjects, claiming "even they are deserving of a *real* life; beyond their subconscious existence."

The thought of this terrified him. Without considering the "possible" addition of the Subjects as residents of the hospital, they were barely making it as they were—food was scarce, power outages were becoming an almost daily occurrence throughout the building, birthing season was approaching—available living quarters were going to be next to nothing in the coming months (and with those births, some of them risked being born catatonic, like the countless Subjects before them). If Elizabeth had figured out how to awaken a Subject from their neurological slumber—and could recreate that success—he wouldn't know which course of action he would be forced to take. He would either take his initial stance on the issue, ridding them from the premises (he didn't care what happened to them after, as long as they were gone), or, to appease Elizabeth, attempt to get back in her good graces, he could do his best to find a place for them, even if it meant he would have to assemble trading parties on a regular basis to better supply food for his citizens; forced to acknowledge and interact with the (uncivilized) neighboring settlements which rested a couple blocks away—stretching all along the horizon.

"Was it as we had feared, Director?"

Pierce turned to find Winsome standing behind his right shoulder, hovering like a hungry, impatient rodent waiting to be told he could feed—pathetic, he thought. "Don't ask a question, Friedrich, if the answer is staring you in the face."

"It's just. . .I can't believe she actually did it," the rodent (Winsome) continued. "She and I had spent *years* hoping to achieve such an impossible feat. I find it odd, honestly, that she was *finally* able to find success once her and I were working opposite shifts."

It was possible, Pierce speculated, Elizabeth had known how to successfully awaken a Subject for months, if not years; simply waiting for the opportune moment (a moment when her and Winsome, whom she had voiced her negative disposition towards to Pierce one night—he having recently moved Winsome to the morning shift, hoping Elizabeth would thank him for it; she hadn't) to use her concealed knowledge. Had this been her plan all along? to woo him into a malleable frame of mind; allowing her to suggest simple requests, knowing he would bend to her whims—without hesitation? No, he thought, clearing her name of malicious intent, immediately voiding his head of such a thought. Nobody, especially her (his dearest Elizabeth) could be capable of such an act. To falsely confess *mutual feelings of adoration*, only to use their significant other's blurred, bias opinion for their personal gain.

"What should we do with him?"

"Until the Subject is one hundred percent able there is nothing we can do *without* raising suspicion. I'm certain you're well aware of mine and Elizabeth's current. . .situation."

Winsome grew silent. He couldn't understand the magnetic pull Elizabeth had on Pierce—the way she could whittle him down from the unashamed voice of the people and turn him into a hesitant lapdog, patiently awaiting her command before doing anything; hoping to gain her approval. He could do better, he thought as he continued to gaze upon the sleeping Subject. Why does he waste his time, precious and limited—as time has proven itself to all of us throughout the years

—on *her?* He could have anyone (anyone, I say! be they male or female), yet he continues to torture himself with the idea of Elizabeth Hestler; a foul, stubborn, and obscenely pretentious woman. Still, despite her faults, the man known as Pierce Alexandre Needham, a man the young Friedrich Winsome had grown to admire, found himself lost in her. If the Subject—Subject No. 2990—were to disappear, without Pierce's knowledge (plausible deniability shall clear his name of any suspicion on Elizabeth's part), perhaps he would be free of her ghostly chains; free to pursue his efforts without the abject hope of seeking her groundless blessing.

You shall not be here much longer, his thoughts turned to the resting Subject. *Pierce will see his victory—I'll make sure of that.*

• • •

HAVING GROWN TIRED of the banality which had sewn its way into his daily routine in Bomb City—the paranoid rantings of ARCO, Chevrolet's incessant babbling of nothing even remotely interesting, Porsche's (a young, sexually ambiguous vixen of fifteen) failed attempts to lure him into bed; upon many others he wished not to mention—Theodore Webb left in the shadows of the night; without saying goodbye. He had spent enough time living in the comfort of *bedraggled luxury*. Returning to his original task, he set his sights Northwest—toward San Pedro, where his family was rumored to be staying. As he passed by the monument which the city took its name, Theodore told himself he would miss this place. Not the people in it, but the feeling of security which he never truly felt while in the hospital. *Perhaps I can convince Gwen to come back down here, once I've gathered her and the kids from up north,* he thought as he approached the front entrance of the city; a sleeping, snoring ARCO keeping any unwanted visitors from coming in.

"Yuh gon'n got tired of us *already*, Theo?" a familiar voice beckoned, turning Theodore around to find Chevrolet coming up behind him; her outburst awakening ARCO—the old man, bewildered, cursed under his breath at her inconsiderate outcry. People were trying to sleep, after all. "An' jus wen I thought we wuz havin' ar'selves a good thyme, too."

Theodore smiled. The people of Bomb City may not have been the most eloquent group he'd come across since being cast out from the sheltered confines of the hospital in old Los Angeles, but their undying, child-like disposition toward a humble, old traveler made them memorable.

"No," he replied, the smile still on his face, "I'm simply completing a personal task I set out for myself at the beginning of my travels." He witnessed the young woman's face fall with sadness. "But," he continued as he motioned with a flick of his left arm, "you're more than welcome to join me." He was being polite. "I'd imagine there isn't much else for you to do here besides work on fixing your aeroplane and bothering old ARCO."

Chevrolet's face beamed at the invitation. "I'll be right with ya, Theo!" her voice leapt with joy. "Jus let me go grab ma knapsack'n sum-o-my-guns and we'll git ta headin' north!" she finished, turning around, running toward her resting quarters.

It didn't take long for the sun to show itself from the east, lighting their way as the pushed themselves north—leaving the safety of Bomb City behind for the untold dangers of the California coastline. A reassuring notion by nature, thought Theodore as he attempted to find a distraction from Chevrolet's already wandering tongue. His thoughts had turned to Gwen and his two daughters, playing out a hopeful scene in his head of the moment their gazes would meet for the first time in years. He counted his fingers to figure the girls' ages, having missed several birthdays since their departure. His oldest (Dolores) would be seventeen in a month while his youngest (Jordyn) turned twelve nine weeks ago. So many years had passed him by, his appearance having shifted from a youthful face to one covered with wrinkles and gray hair. He wondered if his children would even recognize him.

"—an' ev'n though I may not agree widdit, I'm not one to tell Porsche how ta live 'er life; sleepin' around wit committed men and wut 'ave ya . . . I say, you've been awful quiet this morning, Theo. Gots anything on yer mind?"

Ignoring Chevrolet's question, tuning her out altogether, Theodore scanned the scenery which lay before them. Large, incongruous fragments of what had once been an overpass blocked their path up ahead. As they grew closer, still planning which direction they should turn to continue their trek north, the scene painted a picture of horror from centuries long since past. Several pieces of the asphalt had found their way on top of passing vehicles; their once lively owners forever trapped inside them, beneath the weight of the man-made road; green vegetation having worked its way among the wreckage, making the scene of death its home.

Pressing forward, having decided to move west, toward the ocean, Theodore's thoughts turned to his grandfather, Mitchell Emmett Webb. He wondered if traveling through the wastes was as unpredictable as he, himself, had witnessed—the constant fear of being ambushed by a group of drifters at any moment consuming him day and night, robbing him of a decent night's rest. Back then, it was safe to assume, there were fewer people on the planet, the planet's limited resources able to feed an entire settlement without hearing a word of complaint that someone got a larger serving.

By sundown they had approached the old city of Oceanside (a now empty and desolate ghost town; which Theodore found surprising—the remnants of a wooden pier would've been an ideal attraction for anyone; being able to walk out over the Pacific—fascinating, he thought), which was where they decided to call it a night.

9

HEAT. AN UNBEARABLE, RELENTLESS HEAT. It stretched on forever, it seemed. Everything that had once breathed *any form* of life now lay in complete ruin. Wanting (hoping?) to find any semblance of the world he once knew only days ago—the place he used to call home—Nathan Luckman walked the now *fiery streets of Los Angeles*; his search for something familiar continuing to show him nothing but disappointment. Towering buildings, once monuments of human accomplishment, appeared colossal and jagged—an unfinished game of Jenga from a long forgotten game night among friends. Plant life, what little had been left anyway, burned infamously. Scattered piles of bone (once human) lay strewn across the world while gusts of blackened ash blew about the atmosphere. The æther of a freshly scorched earth screamed, piercing the agonizing silence, claiming victory after centuries of torment. Humanity had (finally) lost all its relevance.

Similar to a tragic opening scene from an old film lost to the weight of time, Nathan trudged onward. He could've stayed in the car and awaited death to find him like it had with Katherine, Phillip, and Daniel (their short, pained screams still haunting him) when the heat blast consumed their vehicle, but death by starvation—since, apparently, he was immune to the effects of *nuclear fallout*—was a waiting game he had no patience to play. Instead, hoping to find refuge somewhere, away from the destructive palette which had consumed the world, he made his way south—away from the center of Los Angeles; all hope of living in the city (what little there had been, anyway) having been lost to a snapshot stripped from someone's (anyone's? everyone's?) nightmares; displayed for the whole world to gaze upon in abashed horror.

The entire scene was hopeless.

He wondered if there were others out there like him, someone else who found themselves trapped in a temporal standstill. Or was he alone? left to wander a desolate landscape until the end of his days. It was too soon to tell. Once the earth calmed down from its riotous uproar, perhaps a few fortunate souls (how fortunate would one feel? to come out from their safe havens to find the world they once knew a war-torn battleground—any illusion of their past life now a soon-to-be forgotten memory; lost to the unforgiving clutches of the Past?) would rise from the ashes to join him. All Nathan Luckman could do was wait; wait for a miracle to occur.

He had all the time in the world.

Decades passed. Still he roamed the County of Los Angeles, which continued to remain a vacant tomb; reminding him of a *better time*—a time when one could complain about humanity, wishing a majority of the population would disappear from the face of the Earth—be careful what you wish for—so the world would become less chaotic, less claustrophobic; not considering the isolation, the loneliness such a void would create—the pain which would eventually overcome oneself, dying for some form (*any form!*) of social interaction to occur. Without realizing it, we find ourselves lost in the words of others—so often, in fact, we have forgotten the sound of our own voice. When that voice (our voice) is all we have left, it becomes familiar to the point of irritation. Only in a world of nonexistence, a world of tortured silence (with only *our own thoughts* to keep us company), do we find ourselves desperate enough to pray for the clamoring noises we once found detestable; a sad moment when even the thought of this (a self-referential thought about one's own thoughts) couldn't satisfy Nathan's hopeless, selfish desire.

Nathan Luckman had all the time in the world, with *no proper way to spend it. . .*

Eventually, he found himself settling in the ruins of what used to be Huntington Park, finding himself a temporary home in the abandoned JCPenney south of the Community Hospital—the hospital's lights shining brightly in the distance; a trick of the eyes, he told himself—an hallucination. It had to be. There was no way a building's lights could still be functioning *decades after that fateful day*; a day which refused to leave his infallible memory anytime soon—

. . .

PAST A CANTED chain-linked fence wrapped in dying weeds and beaded with the unfortunate orange-brown oxidation iron often found itself covered with from the salted gusts of the misty California shoreline, one which found itself housing an old Southern California Edison building, a building which, unlike the majority of other pieces of architecture he had come across in his travels (which had seen better days), felt rather natural to gaze upon in its *haunted glory*; the rusted wire—with its now faded, tilted posts, one which read "DANGER: HIGH VOLTAGE"—now seemed more a symbol of plaintive withdrawal than a well-reserved warning. With the proper repairs and upkeep, something Theodore Webb could manage, had he the time to spare, the old city of Oceanside could (possibly) breathe new life. It pained him to see what *must've been a lively city* continue to rest in abandoned decay. So much could've been done with the world to rebuild it, transmute it back to its former glory, yet humanity chose to live in its benighted simplicity. If he ever found himself back here, in Oceanside—his family alongside him—he'd task it upon himself to liven up the place; call it home. It was a beautiful piece of land, he thought—with so much untapped potential waiting (nay, begging!) to be unearthed. And, even hours after they left the small coastal town, the idea of creating the ideal home for him and his family remained; a pleasant thought to occupy his mind—a distraction from the depressing sights which would lay before him as he continued to slowly (painfully) edge his way up to San Pedro. Just two more days of travel, he told himself; two more days.

Along the way, at about midday, having avoided many aimless conversations with Chevrolet (he couldn't understand her constant need for communication—what was wrong with traveling in silence?), moving along the lonesome Interstate, the occasional decoration of an automobile welcoming them as they passed by, Theodore's mind considered—only for a moment, mind you—turning back: return to Oceanside, work on restoring power to the town (postponing his trip to San Pedro a few weeks) so when he finally reunited with his family—convincing them to join him down south—he could surprise them with the luxury of a well-lighted place to call home.

Such a beautiful thought: to imagine waking up to the crashing waves of the Pacific in a town all to themselves; where one could walk the rickety timber of the Oceanside Pier and feel the Earth's raw, majestic atmosphere kiss their skin as a coastal wind blew itself inland— the morning sun beating against one's back as they took in the vast unknown along the horizon, wondering if civilized life lived beyond it.

Some day, he thought as he continued to traverse the landscape's lurid streets.

• • •

WHEN IT SEEMED the *triumph of success* would elevate her confidence to new heights, pushing her forward with the idea of awakening more Subjects (if not all of them) in the coming weeks, fatal weather found itself hanging over her head. Thoughts of regret rose from the depths of her subconscious, drowning her. Had she done the right thing? ripping a human being from their life—all they had ever known. . .*had it been worth all the trouble*; to watch a grown man be reduced to nothing in a matter of seconds? Why must I always, *always*, second guess myself, she asked herself in the quiet solitary confinement of her private quarters. For years she had struggled to achieve a goal which had been deemed impossible for decades by countless individuals who had made the same attempt, yet happiness alluded her. Not even the thought of using her success to deflate Pierce's ego could lift her spirits. Her mind a restless mess, failing to find sleep, Elizabeth Hestler rose from her cot, got dressed (only slipping on a pair of jeans and a t-shirt), and left the blackened security of her room, having decided to go for a late night stroll through the *almost vacant* hallways of the entire hospital—knowing her chances of running into Pierce would be next to none this time of night.

As the soft patter of her bare feet gently echoed throughout the building, her thoughts remained fixated, in one way or another, on the future of this place; what it would mean to have *new life* roaming the halls of the hospital. Would the integration of the Subjects among the established residents be a harmonious moment? or would tensions arise, causing a rift; a demand for segregation among the two to occur? There was no promise for either outcome, unfortunately. This thought saddened her; to think Thomas, along with the rest of the Subjects, may *never be one hundred percent accepted* by the rest of the community. It pained her to consider the thought of her childhood "friend" being considered *anything less than human* by the majority. Underneath the shallow questions about the Subjects' acceptance (or lack thereof) into the fold lay the glaring question which Elizabeth wished to avoid asking: what if this, all of this—this hopeless endeavor—had been a mistake, proving Pierce's cynical stance on the subject to be the logical conclusion to an *already wasted life.* This thought, the thought of potentially being on the wrong side of history, devastated her. But how could she be? all she wanted was to allow the Subjects a chance at living a life, and an honest one—not the falsity which had imprisoned them since their birth—give them a chance to breathe on their own.

Suffocating under the weight of self-doubt Elizabeth stopped midstep, turned about, and hurried toward the elevator to head down to the hospital's mortuary—where Subject No. 2990 (Thomas) still resided; hoping to quell the negative thoughts which had found themselves now coursing through her brain. As she made her descent the possibility of seeing Thomas up and about (curiosity consuming him, carrying him from one moment to the next) began to calm her troubled mind.

The moment she stepped through the doorway, into the mortuary, however, a newfound fear had found her, causing her heart rate to escalate. He was gone. Without explanation, Thomas' body had disappeared from the operating table; a passed out Mason snoozing, without shame, at his desk; his face buried in a soft pile of half-filled notepads. *This cannot be happening!* her mind screamed.

This had to be a nightmare, one she couldn't wake herself up from; it had to be. How could someone, especially a freshly awoken Subject (with no proper bearings of his surroundings), disappear without causing a scene? Someone on the skeleton crew would've taken notice of an unfamiliar face wandering about the empty corridors of the building, wouldn't they? Finding herself frozen in place, Elizabeth's eyes continued to take in the scene which lay before her—the unoccupied operating table laughing at her (now having *nothing* to show for her diligence) while Mason's snoring echoed off the cold, unassuming walls.

· · ·

THE SUBJECT WAS HEAVIER than he had anticipated. Having managed to remove him from the operating table, and onto a gurney, without waking him or Mason. Even with the 3mg of Eszopiclone and 80mg of Morphine he had given *both of them*, which had knocked them out cold, he still wasn't as graceful as he could've been in his execution. But still they slept through the clamor he couldn't refrain from creating. It wasn't until he left the confined quarters of the mortuary's walls that he found himself consumed with a nameless dread, the thought of running into either a wandering Pierce or Elizabeth while en route to ridding the building of Subject No. 2990 being enough to make him second guess himself as he continued toward the elevator. How would he explain his actions to either one of them, were they to discover him before the deed was done? Such toxic paranoia, how it poisoned his thoughts; tainting his *already diminished* confidence.

As he turned the corner, arriving at the elevator's closed doors, he heard the quiet, soft patter of footsteps creeping up behind him. Shit, he thought. I've been found out! When he turned, facing his stalker, preparing a thread of answers to weave about the possible questions which could arise during his ill-fated interrogation, he saw it was *only*

Andrew—the resident half-wit; recently downgraded to nothing more than a mindless drone, thanks to a mandated lobotomy; having proven himself only a nuisance to society in his previous condition. These days he mindlessly wandered the halls in complete silence, unable to do anything else; Winsome wondered if Andrew (the poor sap) could even acknowledge that there was somebody else occupying the hallway, if anything at all. His heart raced when Andrew opened his lips to speak, nervous at the thought of him experiencing a spark from his former life.

"D-D-Don't mind me, I'm just st-st-stretching my legs is all," a baseless response left the zombie's lips. Such a tragic affair, thought Winsome as the elevator doors finally pulled themselves open.

The anxiety-ridden waiting game began as the elevator trudged its way to ground level, the paranoid mindset of being found out having crept its way back into his skull. It wouldn't be until he found himself beyond the safety of the hospital's walls that he'd find himself wishing he had been discovered by either Pierce or Elizabeth, for the dangers of the California Wasteland had escaped his thoughts. He realized the notion of death was a *stark possibility* as he looked down at the unconscious Subject, still dreaming in his drug-induced sleep; his journey to the small settlement of Shrapnel (one which would take him an hour or two to complete until he found himself in the safety of his room) had only begun minutes ago.

It was cold. Even with the excessive amount of layers he had covered himself with (knowing the trek would be unbearable had he not done so), the crisp night air still stung Winsome's already shot nerves as he made his way south. As he passed the sullen streets of what used to be a rather *lively City of Los Angeles*, its towering streetlights—having become thoughtless decorations along the asphalt centuries ago—watching over him as he made his way past countless worn down automobiles, he found himself curious why no one had bothered to make an attempt at repairing one of the contraptions back into working order. If his understanding of them was correct, it would have certainly made traveling to other settlements less of a chore, he thought as he and the Subject continued onward on foot; the misshapen road—with its weed-patch filled pot holes, scattered with the litter of travelers long since passed—slowing him down.

Unknown, unnerving sounds crept all around him as he pressed forward toward Shrapnel, the obsessive rusty squeal of the gurney making it impossible to find solace; knowing the sound of the *vehicle's* joints, if they continued to clamor on, would attract anyone (or anything!) curious enough to wander in their direction—discovering the two of them and taking advantage of their vulnerability. What little inkling of survivalist instinct he held within him had kicked in, slowing his pace to a pathetic crawl.

This is going to take longer than I expected. . . he thought while the incessant squeal of the gurney continued to annoy him.

When he finally arrived at the tiny bookstore on the outskirts of Shrapnel only a lone female (young, going by her pale complexion) greeted him. He'd never met this one before. She must be new. But something about her felt out of place. Her all black attire appeared too clean–untouched by the atomic sands of time; not a whole or fraying thread could be found. Not wanting to leave the Subject unattended, he let her know the circumstances; his words falling on deaf ears as she continued to read her novel.

It wasn't until the early hours of the morning, as the warm amber glow of the rising sun's outstretched rays rose over the inanimate trees which rested on the horizon, that the weathered gray walls of the hospital welcomed a tired Winsome; the burden of Subject No. 2990 left behind, his well-being now the responsibility of the citizens of Shrapnel. Sluggish from his travels, he made his way back to his room—avoiding any interaction with any passersby. It was done. Elizabeth's ace in the hole, what she would use to manipulate Pierce, to bend him backwards to her selfish whims, was no longer a part of the equation. She would have to think of other ways (he was certain, from here on out, she would have none; it was safe to assume the success of awakening Subject No. 2990 had been nothing more than a fluke) to influence Pierce's decisions; after this, her talons would lose their poisonous grip on him. He would be a free man once more—free to do as he pleased.

10

HAVING BEEN FORGOTTEN BY THE COLD, dusty pages of time, several years having passed since that fateful day, Nikolai Sokolov had given up hope of a rescue party being sent to come find him. How much time had passed? Not even he could answer the question. After the first year, he'd lost interest in keeping tally of his days spent in isolation.

It didn't bother him, at first. For the first time in his life since he graduated from boot camp, the world had gone silent. Finally. There was no routine to follow, no orders from command to execute with feigned enthusiasm. There were only an overabundance of quiet moments of nuanced sensitivity. Every flicker of each passing second a monument to his newfound tragic sense of freedom.

He had learned to memorize the layout of every sub-floor available to him. This way, even as the lights dimmed and his world found itself consumed by a never-ending darkness, Nikolai found no issue getting around—his eyes adjusting to twilight's impenetrable permanence. The front cover of Pyotr's copy of *The Rules of Attraction* had fallen away after his tenth read through. He had grown to feel a strange sadness for the character Paul; any semblance of intimacy void from Sean's account of their relationship—their friendship essentially left in irreparable tatters by the end of the novel as Sean rode off into the night on his street bike; the novel ending mid-sentence. He even eventually took to recreating scenes of social interaction with the corpses of his former fellow soldiers, all of them having lost the will to live after a period of time and (one by one) ate the barrel of their own firearm; the haunting echo of each well-placed pull of the trigger laughing at him whenever his mind found itself without a preoccupied thought. Through the years, his favorite ornamental piece was the skull of his former lieutenant, which rested on the top shelf of his locker; barking orders at him in the earlier hours of what he assumed was morning.

There was nothing he could do to end his eternal boredom.

Something stirred him awake. A short scream of frustration caused the atmosphere to tremble. The scream sounded female, which only made every pained echo the more haunting to his solitary soul. He did his best to ignore it, assuming the noise was nothing more than his warped subconscious playing tricks on him. There was no one else alive down here except himself. Who could've possibly made such a noise? It probably wouldn't have bothered him, except one day—when he went to the second floor basement to acquire his morning MRE—he came across something impossible in nature: a group of still decaying corpses sat upright at a round table in the break room, staring him down with hollowed eyes; the phrase "Еще одна неудачная попытка спасти мир." etched into the wall behind them with what looked like dried bean juice from an expired can of pork and beans. *Another unsuccessful attempt to save the world?* It didn't make any sense. Had the world ended before that tragic morning in January?

The corner of his peripheral vision caught a swift movement, someone darting passed him, running down the darkened corridors. An intruder? How had they managed to find themselves down here? It wasn't possible. Access to the lower levels had been shut off when the bombs fell, crippling the elevator system; blocking anyone from getting in or out.

Having forgotten to grab an MRE, his focus no longer concerned with quelling his hunger, Nikolai made his way down the dark passageway. Even if he was hallucinating the suspicious movement from the corner of his eye and the agitated screams, he wanted to be sure he was alone; that no one else was down here with them. He had grown comfortable being alone, the rearranged corpses of his former comrades being the only company he desired. This bunker had become his home, and no living soul had the right to trespass the lonesome structure he'd claimed as his own. But after spending hours searching every inch of his humble abode, Nikolai returned to his barracks for a (midday?) nap.

When he returned to his living quarters, however, another disturbing message rested on the wall just above the area where he slept: "Добро поЖаловать в Аркадия."

He didn't know what the message could've meant. It didn't make any sense to him. Why was someone leaving him such cryptic messages? How did they manage to get inside, and this far down? But as he tried to examine it further, another piercing scream echoed throughout the complex–causing him to shudder.

He had never heard of a place called Arcadia.

• • •

THOMAS DOLIN FOUND HIMSELF back home in the safe arms of Santa Ana—the complementing smell of a freshly cut lawn greeting him as he stepped out of his car, the playful, clamoring screams of children playing in the cul-de-sac, the absurd music of nature's nonsensical symphony welcoming him back to a world of *old familiarity*; the forest green exterior of his family's household door begging him (*begging him, I tell you!*) to come inside to be welcomed by his wife and children. He looked around the neighborhood, taking in the pleasant scenery which presented itself before him, thanking a mystical being he had never had much faith in that he was no longer trapped in a hospital mortuary, lying on cold steel while a man and a woman took notes of his well-being—spouting off conspiracies of an artificial world known to them as Arcadia; the *real world* having ended centuries ago. Such nonsense, he told himself, laughing—the absurd details we find ourselves creating while the tired mind rests itself.

When Tom finally entered the house, however, he was met with a pained vacancy. The house appeared abandoned, like it hadn't been lived in for decades. The dust of age and soulless memories covered its lonesome walls. Desperate, he called out—hoping for a response from either Sarah or the kids, but only a silent echo answered back in response.

He was alone.

"What should we do with him?"

"I've not a clue, honestly. The kid left him here without saying much; just left him here and turned back toward that fucking building."

"I think he's kinda cute, for an older fella."

"Pipe down, Peregrine—there's no need for that kind of behavior in a situation such as this. Now, does anybody have any ideas or not?"

"Food?"

"No, Wendigo, you're not giving into the notion of cannibalism—not again."

"But I'm hungry. . .so hungry. . ."

"Ignore him, Nat. Now c'mon, people, let's concentrate on finding an actual, **reasonable** solution for this bloke."

"We could always pawn him off on to the drifters who live a few miles east of here. . ."

"Jesus, Eldritch, I'd rather Wendigo eat the guy than hand him over to a bunch of drifters; being a meal for us would be a far more merciful fate than being a plaything for a bunch of goddamn savages."

"I thought you decided **not** to succumb to cannibalism? Did you change your mind?"

"I'm just speaking my mind, for Christ's sake; not everything I say has to be taken **literally**."

"—I still think he's kinda cute."

Voices? No, please, not again, he demanded. He didn't know if he could handle being bombarded by another wave of formless dialogue floating around. Unlike the countless times before, however, these voices were unfamiliar to him. These people seemed confused by his presence—looking for a solution to get rid of him that didn't involve the practice of consuming human flesh or handing him off as, what the group had called, a "plaything" for another group of people which, according to the ancient sounding voice known as Nat, was a fate worse than being somebody's potential meal.

Attempting to push the voices to the back of his thoughts, their aimless conversation over his well-being going nowhere, Tom made his way through the interior of his house searching for any signs of life. First he tried the master bedroom, hoping to find Sarah and the kids asleep on the bed; the ending credits of a Pixar film playing quietly on the television's dimly-lit plasma screen. But there was nothing—only the cold void of an empty room lay open to greet him. Giving up on the bedroom, he moved to the backyard. A hopeless place to search because, had they been outside playing, the sounds of activity and delight would've been audible from the living room. Desperate, he searched anyway. Stepping outside, the backyard was unrecognizable from the last time he'd seen it—patches of weeds buried the playground he had installed for the kids a couple months ago (just before his last book tour). The sky itself appeared sick; its once vibrant blues now only a pale imitation.

When he entered his house again, he felt lost. The layout of the house had changed. What had been the dining room a moment earlier was now a long, derelict hallway; a lone elevator waiting for him patiently on the other side. Turning around he found the sliding glass door he had just walked through no longer led outside but to an empty observation room; a thick layer of dust and time covering its unused surroundings. Frightened by what all of this meant, Tom Dolin darted toward the open elevator—the walls trembling around him, plaster crumbling to the floor as the collapsing frame of his sanity found itself in shambles; the voices still haunting him.

"The guy who left him here obviously didn't want him. What makes you think he'd be of any use to us? I mean, look at him. The little fucker's beyond frail lookin'; probably never worked a day in his life."

"What's going on here?" a voice, vaguely familiar.

"Stay out of this, T., this don't concern you. Go back to attempting to fix the power-box and leave this matter to us."

"Shut up, Eldritch. He may not be a native here in Shrapnel, but T. has seen his fair share of the Wasteland. His opinion matters, as well—don't forget, he's helping us spruce up the place."

"Thank you for the kind words, Atom, but I don't—Jesus, is that who I think it is?"

"You know this man?"

"Know him? I spent years taking care of him."

"See? The poor sap can't even take care of himself—needs an old, washed up Negro to look after him."

"It's just—"

"Well c'mon now, T., don't be rude and leave us all hanging in suspense."

"—I can't believe they finally managed to do it. . ."

• • •

HE WAS ALMOST THERE. After days of travel, and countless reiterations of the same numbing conversation about (one day) flying over the endless stretch of wasteland, the city of San Pedro found itself only miles away from Theodore's grasp. He could feel the weight lift prematurely from his shoulders, knowing he'd soon be in the company of his family. He had seen so much in his travels (both wonders and nightmares), the stories he could tell his daughters seemed endless; the haunted beauty of Oceanside being at the forefront of his mind; the night he met Chevrolet (and witnessed her dispose a few curious drifters) a close second. But behind the wave of joy which occupied his thoughts, fear loomed in the distance—eating away at him slowly. What if Gwen and the girls wanted nothing to do with him? believing things would still be the same, even though the life he lived as Director of the hospital was behind him. The heartbreak would be unbearable. He hoped these thoughts were nothing more than nerves pouring baseless doubt into his soul; nothing more. But even as he and the young, white-haired woman continued north, he couldn't shake the thought from his mind.

"We shud be there by early sunup," Chevrolet's optimistic twang broke the early morning silence. "You excited?"

Theodore nodded. This early in the morning, it was the only response he could muster without coming off rude toward his companion. Looking down at his disheveled appearance he found himself laughing at the notion of Jordyn (his youngest) screaming in abashed horror at the sight of his blood-stained lab coat—not knowing the blood wasn't his but having belonged to an unfortunate drifter named Gauge.

"What're we gon' do once we find yer family in San Pedro, Theo?" a curious Chevrolet asked. "Yuh gon' try 'n convince 'em to join us down in Bomb City? Sure iza nice place fer a family ta grow up. I mean, I think I turned out purdy good, don' you?"

Avoiding answering her directly, Theodore chuckled while he shook his head, knowing Chevrolet wouldn't find the response offensive. While Bomb City was a quiet, peaceful town, he wouldn't want to spend the rest of his life there. It was hard enough listening to only Chevrolet speak the way she did, and only in small doses. If he had to listen to an entire city talk that way, he'd eventually go insane. Forcing his family to live with such a lack of conversational eloquence was out of the question.

The morning sun made its way into the sky, bringing light to their way—the vague landscape of San Pedro making itself known to the two weary travelers. Elation consumed Theodore's well-being. Soon, he told himself. Soon he would be in the arms of the women he loved; refusing to let them fall from his sight ever again. They approached the first building of San Pedro as the shining sun finished painting the world in color. Something was off. Unlike other populated cities, there was no one to greet them with flaccid hostility—threatening them with a firearm, demanding to state their business before allowing them to continue further into town. It was quiet; unnervingly quiet, like a ghost town being discovered after years of dormancy—its lost souls long since crossed over to the afterlife, with no unfinished business keeping them held prisoner on this cold, dead, earthly plane. As they moved into the interior of the city, bodies slowly began to pile up; the remnants of a slaughter, its corpses painting a tragic picture—a macabre memorial left to decay.

"Holy 'ell. . ." a dumbstruck Chevrolet managed. "Looks like drifters made their way thru 'ere an' 'ad their way wif ev'ryone. . ." She turned to find Theodore focused on the series of bodies, looking for something. "I wunder if anyone managed ta get out alive. . ."

Wherever he looked, destruction and death found Theodore's eyes. He had never witnessed such a grim sight, the wake of dead bodies causing his stomach to turn. Silently, he prayed for the sea of death to end soon; he didn't know how much more he could take. None of it made sense to him—the depravity which society outside of the hospital's walls chose to live in. How could somebody find such a horrific act such as murder (and on such a massive scale) an act they could commit with ease? leaving the bodies frozen in their final moments of life; some face down while others lay twisted—seeming to suggest a final act of horror and supplication. Only a deranged mind could accomplish such a task as this and still manage to find sleep at night. . .

Unable to hold back his nausea any longer, Theodore attempted to turn away from the horrific scene (a futile effort since *everywhere he looked* death found him) and unleashed the contents of his stomach along the pavement—barely missing the corpse of a young girl (she couldn't have been older than age seven, judging by her small frame) who appeared to have been running toward her mother, who lie several yards ahead of her; her outstretched arms still begging for the safety of her mother's embrace—an embrace which would go on forever being unfulfilled.

A couple meters away from where he stood Chevrolet had managed to pull out one of her assault rifles and found herself griping it with a vigor he had never witnessed before. Whatever it was that had made this town a graveyard had awoken the carnal instincts which resided within the white-haired woman from Bomb City; something Theodore prayed to never find himself on the receiving end of. He had witnessed how precise she was with a firearm. She only missed when her aim was to intimidate the opposing force. Their gazes having met briefly, Chevrolet's head nodded toward her knapsack, asking if Theodore would like a weapon of his own. He declined. Were they to find themselves in a conflict, he knew he would be too overwhelmed to be of *any real use* during a gunfight.

Beyond Chevrolet's bold physique—her weapon still at the ready position—lying on the ground for any curious passerby to find, among the nightmare filled streets of wasted massacre, there among the rubble, lie a familiar shadow of life. It took him a moment before the curtain of disbelief lifted itself and the weight of loss found its way to his knees. Lying helpless in front of him was the fading memory of his Gwenivere; alone, pale, and cold. He attempted to call out to her, but the words refused to leave his throat—the very words choking him as he continued to stare at the corpse of his beloved. Unnoticed, Chevrolet had made her way to Theodore's side to comfort him, knowing the agony he was going through.

"I'm sorry fer yer loss, Theo," she managed to say, gently caressing his shoulder. "I, too've experienced the loss'ofa luved one; my lil kid brother, Shell, to a band'a drifters when I wuz only fourteen—him only eight. . .If you'd like ta'ave a moment to yerself, I'll be just up ahead," she smiled with grief.

Still on his knees, Theodore crawled toward the fragile monument of his departed loved one. Even in death, Gwenivere's beauty persevered; a task not many corpses could manage. As he gathered his wife's limp body into his arms the dreams he had imagined living out with her and the children flooded his thoughts. Their secluded home in Oceanside, living off the land until the end of their days; a man-made paradise lost along the shoreline. Traveling to nearby settlements to trade vegetation for other supplies, Dolores and Jordyn carelessly flirting with the local young men of each town they visited, annoying their father—the overabundance of testosterone fueling the young gentlemen to fawn over his daughters (them being mixed: a rarity among social circles) being an afterthought to their actions. While he continued to hold his wife's lifeless body, a bout of tears found themselves falling down his face—the dream of Oceanside dimmed; becoming nothing more than the wishful thinking of an aging man. Now? he found he was left with only the memories which they had shared together for the first nineteen years of their twenty-one year long marriage. And beyond the abandoned architecture which made up San Pedro, violent, incoherent screams and gunfire could be heard in the distance; screams which had become familiar to him during his exhaustive travels.

"We'd bedder move soon," Chevrolet motioned with the barrel of her rifle. "Sumtimes drifters like ta come back ta prior locales, mop up any stragglers who happen ta come across their *handiwork*. I wudn't want ta be here when they dew."

Theodore, still holding Gwenivere in his arms, lay his thoughts aside to look up at the white-haired Chevrolet and shake his head no to her suggestion. Confused, Chevrolet figured he had misheard her somehow, she repeated herself, hoping the words would sink in—that he'd lay aside the fading memory of his wife and join her in leaving the city. But that didn't happen. Still he remained knelt on the ground, his gaze drifting back to the face of his departed loved one.

Minutes later (the time having drawn itself out to feel like hours) Theodore finally lay his lifeless spouse down to rest in the streets of San Pedro; the once cacophonous screams of the approaching drifters having grown closer (more coherent, actual words being made out among the echoes) in the passing moments.

Chevrolet stood over Theodore's mourning silhouette as she heard a small group of drifters closing in on their location. She didn't bother to mention the dire situation they would soon find themselves in a third time to the old man. It seemed he had given up on life, his gaze still fixated on the limp corpse of his deceased wife. Refusing to remain a sitting duck—allowing the approaching drifters to pick them off with ease, which, considering how poor they all seemed to be with their marksmanship, would have been an embarrassing way to die—Chevrolet left a still grief-stricken Theodore alone in the center of the city, hoping to find a well-hidden place to hide and eliminate the on-coming threat; using Theodore as bait.

From the third story of a building which used to be a corporate bank, Chevrolet lie horizontal on her stomach peering down the scope of her rifle as she waited for the drifters to move closer, allowing her to pick them off; one bullet each, not wanting to waste her ammunition if she didn't have to—wishing she could've found a spot closer.

When the three drifters finally came within shooting distance, however, they refrained from opening fire on the still target which was Theodore. Instead they approached him and attempted making conversation with him. Given the distance, Chevrolet couldn't make out what they were saying, but what happened next would continue to amaze her for days to come.

The main drifter, a towering fellow, wielding a blood-stained cricket bat decorated with nails, left the comfort of his small posse to approach a non-responsive Theodore, pulling at his shoulder to turn him around —probably while saying *"Imma talkin' to yih, ya filthy Negro. Look at me when I is talkin' to yih."* He found himself met with a swift elbow to the crotch, keeling over in pain, dropping his weapon to better soothe the unpleasant sensation coursing from his groin.

Taking advantage of the moment, Theodore picked up the bat and, without remorse, started swinging away at the distracted drifter's skull; the mongrel collapsed to the floor, blood pouring from the open wound, onto the asphalt as the drifter's cronies watched in baffled horror their leader being crippled and slain. It didn't take long for the violent spell to pull Theodore's crazed frame in a magnetic, frantic run toward the other two men, the smallest of the two running away—not wanting to join the sea of corpses he had been a part of laying to waste; dropping his firearm in the process.

Continuing to view the scene through the scope of her own weapon, Chevrolet watched as Theodore crippled the second fellow at the knees before hacking away at the poor bastard's torso until all movement had stopped. Robotic, Theodore found the dropped firearm, picked it up with his free hand and aimed blindly toward the staggering third and emptied the chamber into the æther; three out of the eight shots finding their target, causing the small speck to fall to the floor. In a dead silence Theodore walked toward the fallen drifter. After what felt like forever, Chevrolet watched as the old, grief-stricken scientist had his way with the wounded drifter's head with the now *well used cricket bat.*

Minutes passed between the final blow and Theodore's decision to continue walking, heading southbound instead of north—bloody cricket bat still in hand, dragging it through the dirt. Chevrolet didn't know his intentions for turning back (returning from which he came, perhaps?), but she did not protest—did not bellow (or even mutter) a word in his direction. *The poor fella just lost his ol'lady. He could use some time alone.*

The freshly spilled blood had yet to settle among the old—a hint of copper still hanging in the air.

• • •

Panic and anger filled Elizabeth's thoughts—anger toward Mason for having fallen asleep while she was away from Thomas for a few hours to find a well-earned rest; the panic arising from the mysterious circumstances which surrounded Thomas' sudden disappearance. Years of planning and hard work had dissipated into thin air in the short amount of time she was away. Her mind now dominated by anger, she stormed out of the morgue, back toward the elevator, and awaited for the lift to take her to the twelfth floor. Only one person, she thought, would have the audacity to snuff out *any sort of progress* she had made with awakening a Subject: Pierce Alexandre Needham. *I mean, who else could it have been?* she thought.

By the time she arrived to the twelfth floor of the building her anger had managed to transmute itself into a fit of rage. She wanted answers; why, at every step (every *goddamn* turn), he felt the obsessive impulse to sabotage her work? If this were an attempt to get back at her for ending things with him, she would see to it that he was put on trial and exiled from the hospital for his actions—if not simply demoted from his prestigious title of Director. If she could only pry two answers from him it would be the whereabouts of Thomas' body and whether or not he was still alive. In a fury she glided (still barefoot) toward the door which led into Pierce's living quarters, only to find the room empty upon opening the door; his desk and other scarce trinkets from an all-but-forgotten history greeting her in an awkward silence. Still livid from his betrayal Elizabeth scoured through his belongings, hoping to find evidence (of any kind) to prove her accusation true. There was nothing— only an aging leather-bound journal having found its way into her hands, with several years in between its most recent entry and its last. She flipped through its tired pages looking for any entries which carried her name among them, looking for malicious intent on his part, but found nothing; only the desperate longings of a heartbroken individual—among the earlier, positive, disgustingly romantic passages which would follow a morning after her spending the night at his place. It was obvious he was (still) obsessed with her.

Unable to find anything to help justify her anger toward him (the morning rays of the rising sun now pouring through the window, indicating how long she had been in Pierce's room without interruption), Elizabeth closed the journal, took one last look around his living quarters, her eyes meeting the solemn gaze of the old wooden relic from a world she never knew. A *baseball bat?* if she remembered the name of it correctly. Pierce was a fool with a soft spot for the past, she concluded upon further inspection of the room—its haunting memorabilia piercing her thoughts with unwelcome false memories of a life she never lived; would never live—the world having been stuck in time since that dreadful day (or night, it was unclear when the massacre of humanity occurred), when hell rose from the depths of the planet, from underwater transports and other ungodly inventions of man, as it reached with outstretched fingers toward its apex before falling back to a doomed defenseless earth, which cried a song of sorrow as death swallowed it whole in a slow moving wash of fire and buried, tortured screams. These memories, memories which once belonged to the ashes of long deceased ancestors, echoed different screams—screams of pleasure, of drunken cheer and delectation, the violent scream as a fly ball soared through the air, having been hit by a determined batter (perhaps by the same baseball bat which now lay on Pierce's desk— pleading to the æther to be returned to its former days), into an overjoyous crowd of devoted, intoxicated fans.

Finding herself desperate for the relief of a quiet mind Elizabeth left the nostalgia-ridden confines of Pierce's room—trading it for the claustrophobic walls of the elevator; the imagined tormented outcries of the past chasing after her as the doors closed them off from haunting her any further.

When the doors of the elevator chimed to indicate the success of her escape, its doors opening to reveal the third floor of the hospital—her tired gaze finding the door which led to the *Quiet Room*; a room which had been a safe haven for years as she worked alongside Theodore, Winsome, and many others (including Pierce) who chose to abandon the real world for hours (if not days) at a time, attempting to come to a *humane solution* for their 'Subject issue.' Upon entering Elizabeth witnessed a familiar scene: Winsome sleeping, slouched over. His tired head rested on an unsuspecting desk. She found it funny, the difference in response to seeing Winsome dozing opposed to how she felt when she came upon Mason doing the same act. With Mason, whose company she enjoyed, she felt contempt—having fallen asleep during his watch; leading to their current, unfortunate circumstance. Now, as she continued to stare down at Winsome's dormant state (a man she could no longer stand being in the same room with), she felt all negativity fall away from her; leaving her in a calm state of mind.

"It's funny, isn't it? the places we go to find sleep when it decides to elude us in our usual place of comfort. Ironic that *he* found it in the *Quiet Room*, of all places. I take it you are unable to find sleep as well, tonight?"

"Originally I had planned on getting some rest, but regret found its way into my thoughts; leading me back to the mortuary where I came across your *handiwork*. Well played, Pierce. I'll admit that much."

A pause.

"What 'handiwork' are you referring to? I'm confused."

Annoyed with Pierce's false-ignorance, Elizabeth turned and slapped the man who was thirteen years her senior across the face. "Don't act innocent with me, Pierce," she snarled, pointing in the direction of the hospital's morgue. "Who else would have the nerve to remove a Subject, especially one you've shown unconcealed disdain toward *for years* from the hospital?"

"Wait. The Subject has gone *missing*?"

Another momentary pause—this one a couple beats longer than the one before.

"Are you trying to make me believe this is *news to you*—that the disappearance of Subject No. 2990 was not your doing?"

Pierce took a step back, finding himself at a loss for words upon hearing such an accusation. Elizabeth simply kept staring, waiting for a response.

"Why would you jump to such an obscene assumption, Elizabeth; accusing me of tampering with your work to the extent of removing a Subject's body from the hospital."

"Honestly, Pierce? Who else would steep to such a *low* level? to go out of your way to spite someone who, in your *warped view of the world*, had wronged you in someway. You did it to Theodore years ago when he happened to stumble upon you attempting to murder Thomas one night. So please, tell me, humor me if you will, what could *possibly stop you* from doing something as sinister as sabotaging my work?"

The truth was simple. A series of words which, if Pierce could build the nerve to speak them, would end their current argument—ridding Elizabeth of her falsely placed frustrations. He hadn't the faintest clue what had happened to Subject No. 2990 (Thomas—god he hated hearing *his name*). But instead of repeating an already well-worn confession for the nth time, Pierce Alexandre Needham chose to take the verbal abuse Elizabeth (his dearest Elizabeth) continued to spew in his direction; like a disappointed mother would to their child.

"—and if I even *feel* you making another attempt at fucking me over, Pierce, I swear to all that I am, you'll find yourself out in the desert wastes before the next sunset," she finished as she turned away, finding herself still livid.

Pierce watched her turn into the hallway, heading to the elevator to return to either the morgue—where it had been decided by his grandfather they would house awoken Subjects (possibly to mourn the death of their *previous life?*—or the lower levels; to begin making preparations to start the process all over again on another unfortunate soul. Not knowing what to do, still processing the conversation which transpired a moment ago, he turned toward his desk and gripped the head of the baseball bat which still rested at the top-end of his desk. He lifted the relic and held it in his hands how he imagined the fabled athletes from the past had held it a thousand times before him. As he gripped the old wooden instrument, its cold polished feel becoming familiar to his hands, a lost anger brew at the center of his chest. He wanted to know who had done the deed which had caused Elizabeth to storm into his room and accuse him without considering anyone else. Why would she jump to such a baseless conclusion?

His frustrations finally striking an exposed nerve, Pierce turned away from his desk, still holding the bat, and started swinging relentlessly at the wall ahead of him. With each hit reverberating off the surface (leaving a tennis ball shaped dent behind after each resentful ping) he felt the wall's retaliation bounce back with equal force; only causing the fire of his wrath to grow. It wasn't until he heard the sound of shattering glass did he take a breather and notice he had pulverized the glass frame of his city portrait of old Los Angeles. Blinking away the violence which consumed him he stared down at the floor, the scattered remnants of glass littering his surroundings. His gaze returned to the photograph—which now barely hung from his wall—for a brief moment before bouncing back and forth from it to the baseball bat; analyzing his actions with silent disdain. In a bout of blinding frustration his actions had brought about the destruction of one of his most cherished reminders of the past; recreating the horrific destruction to a once quiet city, a city which had done nothing to deserve such punishment.

· · ·

EVERYONE SWARMED the still sleeping newcomer. It wasn't every day a lone resident from the towering building from the north traveled in the quiet hours of the night, abandoning one of their own before turning back toward the safety of their homestead, without breathing a word to anyone. But why would one leave the other stranded in the first place? They certainly were an odd bunch, that much was obvious, Atom thought while the others continued to converse about what to do with the Stranger. Unable to focus on any particular aspect of the incestuous uproar between his fellow citizens (although Peregrine's lust-filled thoughts were the dominant driving force among them—the rest of the crowd choosing to ignore her in silent protest), Atom fixated on the curious, strikingly familiar approach—similar to a lukewarm reception one would receive from old friends and family after years of separation —T., their latest addition to the city known as Shrapnel, a wizard with ancient electrical equipment, knelt beside the comatose individual in awe. He kept repeating to himself, *"I still can't believe it, after all these years. . ."*—the words themselves holding their own private meaning to T. and T. alone.

Moving his gaze from the weathered traveler over to his unconscious counterpart Atom noticed how frail he *actually* seemed. Were there others like him? malnourished; barely holding onto the threads of life. A worried look found its way to his face as his eyes shifted to the towering building to the north. *What the hell have they been doing up there all these years? to allow someone to grow this weak. . .*

"He should come to in a day or two, at most," T.'s gravelly, soft spoken voice managed to rise above the clamor. "For now, however, we best find a place for him to keep warm. His body won't be able to handle the frigid temperatures of the outside world just yet."

"He could sleep with me," an overzealous Peregrine voiced, the rest of the crowd staring her down, damning her intentions. "*I'd* make sure his body temperature was kept up during the night."

"Sure you would," spoke the well-aged Nat. "As long as it meant exploring every facet of his being in the process, right?"

Peregrine's youthful face now found itself wearing an unpleasant scowl. "Don't be getting jealous, old-timer, just because there ain't no one around for miles who would fancy a roll with you any time soon." she barked as she pushed the elderly man away from her, making her way back to her small set up; leaving the small group to continue on without her. And while the others carried on in aimless succession, Atom made his way to T.'s side, hoping to coax the old man out of his dumbstruck stupor. If anyone would know what to do with the unwelcome visitor, having come from the towering behemoth which was the hospital from up north, it would be him—he being the only resident of Shrapnel to know of T.'s unwanted connection to the place.

"Why does he look like this?" he whispered, not wanting the others to hear his question. "Why does he appear so delicate?"

It was a while before T. responded, an unpleasant silence replacing the chaos of conversation moments earlier; the same tired expression which never seemed to leave T.'s face greeting him as the traveler's worn gaze met his desperate and inquisitive one.

"Boy," the aged man spoke. "In my long fifty-three years of life I've seen many people like him." He pointed down at his quiescent acquaintance. "And they all have been *this* thin, if not more so. They manage to bulk up—if you manage to wake them up, of course. But that's proven itself an almost impossible task—with enough failures to compile an entire notebook's worth, I'm sad to admit."

Confused by the man's response Atom changed gears. Instead of pursuing his previous question any further he decided to (hopefully) bring light to something he had mentioned earlier, upon the discovery of the sleeping individual's presence.

"What did you mean when you said you couldn't believe they managed to finally do it?" he asked. "Do what, exactly?"

11

TOM'S MIND COULDN'T BEGIN to fathom the concept of a human life being encapsulated behind a plate of glass. Their thoughts, their heartbeat, *every aspect of their inanimate existence* being monitored by machines beyond his limited comprehension until they were either, as T. put it, *awoken* or they died of old age—if not a foreign medical complication. He had experienced a similar phenomenon growing up in a small town without a name a day or two's travel west of Shrapnel—the unfortunate occurrence of a new born coming into the world without the proper mental functionality to live long after entering this world. Unlike those who found themselves *lucky enough* to be born inside the hospital, however, the young ones who were born in the violent hands of the California Wastes were considered a loss and later consumed for nourishment; a decent meal being few and far between. How far humanity had come since then (in certain areas, others still finding themselves forced to succumb to such a desperate formality) was a healthy far cry from their animalistic tendencies of the past.

"But why put forth so much effort into keeping someone, especially someone whose quality of life is next to non-existent, alive? As Eldritch pointed out earlier, it's been made clear to us by *this one's* frail physical state, what good could come from, as you put it, *awakening* them?"

Theodore, known to the people of Shrapnel simply as *T.* (his full name considered a relic of a lifetime long since past) confessed the apparent futility which lie on the surface of such a project, admitting his failures throughout the decades having dulled his desires to see the *Arcadian Project* come to a definite close; that during his time alone, before settling in the small settlement which rest miles away from his childhood home, he'd managed to develop the same cynicism his lifelong friend, Pierce, had had since adolescence. But seeing Subject No. 2990—a Subject known to be a burden—here, *awoken and abandoned* in the cloaked darkness of the night, renewed his forgotten faith in the work they were hoping achieve. If Elizabeth (safely assuming it was *she who managed to do the impossible*) could find success with Subject No. 2990, he projected the rest of the Subjects would soon find themselves relieved from their slumber.

"So he's not the first *subject* you've 'awoken' from dormancy?"

"No, we've had one other. While the other Subject's awakening showed promise, her *lack of humanity* was off-putting."

"Do they always look this frail?"

"At first, yes. Normally, we like to spend about a month's time putting their body through intense physical therapy to help rebuild their muscle tissue to what they *believed* it was while they were sequenced."

Atom sat amazed at how different T.'s world was compared to his— looking up at the towering monolith which loomed in the distance, finding himself more curious than he had ever been during his brief time in Shrapnel.

"With what I imagine must've been an overbearing amount of stress, was that why you left?"

Theodore's stoic gaze lowered to the sleeping Subject. The memory of the fateful night he and Pierce had shared flooding his thoughts with a toxic speed. "You know something, kid," he paused, turning to face the inquisitive nineteen-year-old. "I think that's a story for another time."

"Quit towering over the poor sap, will ya?" Nat's crackling voice bellowed in the distance. His pale silhouette towered from one of the second floor windows of the bookstore they called home. "Don't think I forgot about the mess you made in my corner of the apartment complex a couple days ago, Atom. Now get your scrawny ass up and away from our *sleeping friend over there* and get back to finishing your daily chore-set."

. . .

OLD MAN NAT WASN'T SURE how he felt about the latest addition to his home. The old ruins of one of Huntington Park's shopping centers having housed him well-enough for almost four hundred years. Could he manage to let another lost soul live alongside him? Sure. Did he want to? On the surface he would complain about the logistics of taking on *yet another* vagrant, reminding every single one of them that 'this wasn't a permanent living situation'—that he would soon demand they all leave his property. But underneath his cold exterior? he was glad nobody had taken him seriously enough to obey his shallow threats. Despite their peculiar personalities, as he watched Atom lift himself away from the sleeping Arcadian with pained reluctance, Nat could feel the beginnings of a smile make its way across his aged face. It reminded him of centuries long since past, when he was the young boy's age— the naive year of nineteen, eager to take on the world which lay ahead of him; Her seemingly endless boundaries calling out to him, creating a restless fever within him. Unlike Nat's unfortunate self, his chance for a hopeful future filled with adventure having been ripped from him in the late hours of January 24, 1995—the horrific screams of his friends being turned to dust still haunting his dreams on the anniversary of that fateful night—Atom's world remained in a constant state of disarray; *the laws of entropy no longer applied to the cold dead earth.*

Remembering his past, how long he'd gone without the social interaction of another living person (311 years, if recollection served him properly) when a man named Alexandre Oliver Needham stumbled into his humble abode—an old used bookstore which housed a small apartment complex on the second floor above it—asking if he knew where he might find medical supplies.

He was still going by Nathan at the time.

Months would pass in between Alexandre's visits, eventually tagging his son, Isaac, along for short-lived expeditions (trading small crops—vegetation which Nathan had thought were extinct—for random scraps of metal and coil, as well as loaning volumes of literature whenever they asked). Alexandre would always offer him a place in the hospital, claiming there was *plenty of room* for an old-timer. And Nathan would politely refuse the offer every time, afraid the moment would come when questions would arise about his past: why he never seemed to age appropriately—everyone else slowly dying around him while he remained healthy. Why he never seemed to eat with the rest of the group, not wanting to explain the fact he was an empty shell; his insides having turned to dust long before their grandparents were a thought in *their* parents' minds.

Soon Alexandre and Isaac quit making their friendly pit-stops to his bookshop on the corner, Nathan having refused to acknowledge them when they knocked at his door—one time even going to the extreme of hiding in another shop when he saw their humble silhouettes coming his way—and he found himself alone once more. It would take another thirty years before the rascals known as Atom, Eldritch, Wendigo, and Peregrine would find themselves passing through and deciding to call the little town of Shrapnel home (the name change having been a running gag for passing nomads who had stumbled across an old Ace Hardware Store which still housed an aisle of spray paint, renaming any small town they happened to come across). Nathan, having slowly slipped into the horrifying slope of madness brought on by cabin fever during the preceding decades, hid for weeks in the walls of the apartment complex—pretending to be a ghost from *the old world*; a gag which scared a then thirteen-year-old Peregrine enough to warrant forcing the rest of the group (having been males of varying ages) to search for the disembodied spirit and attempt to drive it out. When he finally revealed himself to them he couldn't help but keep from laughing at how furious the young girl was to discover her phantom had been the musings of a senile old man hiding in the interior of her bedroom.

Reflecting on his time after *nuclear detonation*, Nathan found himself wondering why, in his immortality, he didn't venture out into the world, embark on life of uninterrupted travel—seeing sights he could only daydream of seeing in his youth. He would blame it on the city of

Los Angeles, her decadent beauty having a firm grip on his soul. The reality, however, buried deep down in his often untapped subconscious, was that he refused to leave the burial town of his friends Philip and Daniel, along with his love, Katherine.

The furthest he ever strayed from his hidden fortress of unread literature and abandoned rooms was when he visited his elementary school. It was odd, to see an eternal monument of childhood innocence lost to a world of *nuclear vacancy*; the seemingly untouched spider web playground welcoming him to the memories of a time lost to him long before the first bomb dropped on American soil; everything else lay in ruin. The cadence of the once live blacktop (where he and his closest classmates would play foursquare without pause) now felt off-beat, its once flawless landscape having become pockmarked with disrepair. Iron poles which once housed ball and string for tether-ball stood lonesome, without purpose. The world he used to drift through uncomplainingly was now a cruel joke of its former self.

It was after that day, a day he wish he could forget (but could not), Nathan Luckman refused to find a reason to leave the safe walls of his makeshift home.

"What were you two blabbering on about?" he acknowledged an approaching Atom.

"I wanted to learn more about the stranger's backstory, why he looks the way he does and what-have-you. From what T. told me, that building is a place of nightmares; hundreds, if not thousands, of still births encased in sleeping chambers while being monitored by machines — their inactive brains aroused enough to dream. The machines they've hooked these *Subjects* up to having the capability to manipulate their brainwaves to believe they're living in a world which wasn't ravaged by a raging fire which fell from the sky *so many years ago*. . .How people like *him* have spent decades making fruitless attempts to *awaken* these people, to allow them to live a life which isn't, as T. put it, *a well-constructed lie carried out by the baseless impulses of a soulless machine*. I'm not sure I understand most of it, honestly, but were *I* in T.'s shoes? I would've left that place ages ago."

Despite his tepid reservations toward the sleeping castaway, if what Atom were relaying back to him was accurate, Nat(than Luckman) found himself curious — curious to know what it must've felt like to have lived a life where hell didn't fall from the sky in the shape of an atomic bomb, destroying everything in its lifeless path. *Wake up soon, you scrawny little bastard*, he muttered under his breath, hoping Atom wouldn't assume he was talking to him, *because I've got some questions.*

· · ·

EVERYTHING WAS BACK *to how it used to be for Tom Dolin*. The savage nightmare which had consumed his fragile, subconscious thoughts—refusing to let him go, despite his relentless protest—had withered away, retiring to the darker recesses of his mind. Pleasant forest greens and vibrant baby blues replaced the barren fields and gray skies which seemed to be commonplace in the *land of rubble and death*. A family of birds could be seen flying high among the clouds, migrating south for the winter months to come—flying together as one infrangible unit; soaring in perfect lines. At ground level miles of unkempt road stretched out in front of him, waiting to be to explored for the Nth time of its immortal existence.

He found himself driving alone in his wife's car, their faithful dark blue 2017 Ford Escape. A comfortable vehicle—well-constructed (requiring minimal upkeep; an oil change here and there), easy to handle, with decent enough gas mileage to keep an *experienced* driver from complaining. Henry Ford would have been proud if he could manage to look past the modern manufacturing process: an automated system of faceless machinery working tirelessly, each function finely tuned and back-referenced to such ungodly precision; the art of its once *miraculous construction* having been paired down to a mathematical sequence which would continue on forever—long after the species which had originally programmed its nuanced function had faded from the face of reality—the machine's immaculate creations, which would forever sit in silence, awaiting approval, going unseen by their creators; their faithful robotic diligence to the task becoming nothing more than *a waste of ones and zeroes.*

Tom Dolin lived in a world of binary.

As he continued his lonesome drive, his final destination unknown, only the weightless freedom of the act keeping him from floating adrift into a network of aimless daydreams, Tom gathered in the wealth of information which was (had always been) the untouched beauty of the California fields which lie just off the side of the Interstate—where untamed horses would chase one another in playful competition while a family of cows watched with an unimpressed stare. From there his eyes focused on the invisible force of the wind blowing the weeds back and forth, creating a silent, well-choreographed dance for any solemn passerby to enjoy.

Ahead of him a sea of billboards floated past him as he continued to sail down an ocean of asphalt; an endless wave of advertisement crashing in on him left and right, telling him the number of miles before he could enjoy the "FINGER LICKING GOOD" contents of KFC's famous 'big box meal' or the juicy selection of Arby's—the world was his oyster for unhealthy dietary consumption. Not in the mood for anything, finding himself not hungry, he chose to ignore them as best he could.

Hours passed with no sign of progress, not a town had found its way to him nor an off-ramp to leave the main road so he could find his bearings. Looking around, finding the road unoccupied by any other signs of human life, without pulling over to the side of the road, Tom lulled his vehicle to a complete stop.

Stepping out of his car, the engine still running, the faint droning of KCUF's talk radio pouring from the vehicle's speakers, Tom scanned the landscape in a slow, panoramic swoop; not another vehicle could be seen coming in either direction, only the sea of birds flying farther away from him—*a nonsensical series of Morse code becoming obscured by the pale horizon which would soon swallow them whole*—while the beginnings of a dust devil arose from the still sleeping earth. The solitude of being the only human along the Interstate was hauntingly calming to him, having spent what *felt like weeks* lost in a horrific dreamscape where the world he knew was nothing more than another series of *ones and zeroes* haphazardly carrying him along while his real body slept behind a plate of glass.

A bout of clarity striking him suddenly, Tom began to question the credibility of his memory. Unable to recall how he managed to find himself traveling down the interstate, everything before this moment being a non-existent blur, he felt his heart begin to race; the unpleasant feeling of not knowing causing a panic attack. Hoping to quell his fears, Tom searched for something tangible to focus on. His eager eyes found a billboard facing the opposite direction he was traversing, he took in every astute detail. The artwork harked back to the optimistic simplicity of the 1950s—a blonde female with green eyes and rosy cheeks sharing her company with a young male with brown hair and a perfect smile; the two of them laughing at nothing (an inside joke which remained unknown to its audience), a dialogue bubble floating above the man's head, only giving us the half-baked punchline: "THE WORLD ENDED ON JANUARY 25, 1995. EVERYTHING YOU KNOW HAS BEEN A LIE. WELCOME TO ARCADIA, YOUR NEW HOME!"

It was only after reading these chilling words on the billboard—the mention of Arcadia and the end of the world—did Tom's eyes notice an intricacy of horrid detail which tarnished every minutiae of his surroundings; a detail which had gone unnoticed before the billboard's revealing message. Everything, even the tiny fragments of dust which found themselves being carried away in the cool breeze, was composed of *ones and zeroes*—in a seemingly random sequence. He couldn't escape them. Everywhere he looked the ones and zeroes surrounded him. They were even in the air his lungs continued to breathe in and expel. Ones and zeroes, ones and zeroes. It was like being forced to stare at a sick joke inspired by Gottfried Leibniz's ancient mathematical creation—a physical manifestation of *Ones & Zeroes*.

Even with his eyes closed tightly he couldn't seem to block the constant barrage of numeric imagery from seeping past his eyelids, imprinting themselves upon his retinas; becoming his (unwanted) primary focus.

Tom Dolin found himself living in a world of binary, with no logical way (one which he found desirable, anyway) to escape it. The world as he knew it began to collapse around him. The stable frame of reality he used to call home had been replaced by an ugly truth, one which refused to loosen its grip. Not even the attempt of closing his eyes could block out the image of the billboard screaming at him that everything he had known as truth had been a well-constructed lie.

Welcome to Arcadia, your new home!

• • •

HE COULD STILL REMEMBER the soft smell of her rose-tinted hair, how it would glisten under the sun's welcomed rays whenever she and the children—along with other wives and daughters of the building—would make their way to the roof of the hospital to pick fresh fruits and vegetables for the bi-monthly harvest, trading their surplus with the local settlements for fresh-killed meat and fish, along with any other necessities they required. Even among the odors of ancient decay, the salty winds of the Pacific having had their caustic way with the architecture of Oceanside for well over three centuries, the scent of Gwenivere's hair remained an imprint in the memory banks of his olfactory glands. Days would turn to weeks, and weeks would (sometimes) become ageless months, as Theodore made slow progress at restoring power to a small section of Oceanside's power-grid—an impossible task had the power plant's storage room been above ground, instead of being an underground basement; its contents having remained untouched by the withering weathers of time. Had anyone known his story they would have presumed insanity had claimed his fragile mind: reestablishing the foundation to an uninhabitable ghost town, making it a place one could call home—his original motivation for wanting to take on the hopeless task having been taken away from him by a group of ruthless barbarians. Still, it was the smell of his wife's hair which propelled him to continue on with the project.

As he worked tirelessly through the pains of restoring power to the humble town, the pauses in his progress becoming an art form of its own (having to leave his electrical canvas to find the appropriate set of wires and tools), Theodore's thoughts of what the town would look like once he was finished—despite its original intent being nothing more than a hopeless daydream—made the long days and merciless nights of ill-placed diligence seem worth the effort.

It wasn't until the constant hum of the generator breathed its first breath that Theodore Webb would shed a set of tears for his dearly departed Gwenivere and the unknown whereabouts of his daughters Jordyn and Dolores (he assumed they, too, were dead and gone from this world—why would the savages who desecrated the town of San Pedro take two young girls captive?). He found himself embarrassed, despite not having an audience to witness his sad state; not being one to wear his emotions on his sleeve. With the city now breathing new life his next move was to pick a house which he could've pictured his family of four living in until the girls found significant others and moved elsewhere—be it at another house within the city of Oceanside or another settlement altogether; making the (sometimes false) promise to visit him and their mother. He wondered if families of the past functioned the same way, that his thoughts were a cerebral hereditary instinct passed on through humanity's DNA—a fragment of residual memory which (somehow?) found itself carried through the *atomic frays* of time and space; basic programming hardwired into the acumen of human existence. . .

It took him several months to decide which house he wanted to dedicate his time to, creating *the perfect home for his family*. He decided on a sea foam colored beach house along the shoreline—its front yard being only a small stretch of grass covered sand before finding itself met by a symphony of crashing waves; the noonday tide ebbing into the distance, granting him a lovely scene to gaze upon as he walked barefoot into the still wet, loosened soil. Why would anyone think sea foam green would be a suitable color to paint a house? he thought as he pushed the leftovers of a couch from one end of the room to the next, hoping to find an equilibrium to the weighted contours of the faded living room.

There were days (some colliding with the others, creating a timeless loop) when it seemed Gwenivere and the girls were standing elsewhere in the room, judging his haphazard selections on where to place the furniture.

"You shouldn't have the couch so close to the recliner."

"But daddy, how do you expect me to sleep with the love seat so close to the picture window?"

"Do you really expect me to read with such poor lighting?"

"Theodore, listen to your children."

"Yeah, dad, listen to us."

It was rampant dialogue such as this which kept him busy as he made his way toward the finishing touches to the small home, distracting him from the grim world which would face him the moment he was finished. The hallucinations of an unsatisfied family kept him sane a while longer—rationality leaving him at the foot of the door, awaiting his rapid descent into the hard-hitting truth of reality.

From room to faithless room small flashes of false memory skirted across his line of sight, visual hallucinations of his girls lying on their separate beds in their room while talking gossip with their friends through the cordless phone, the smell of Gwen's cooking drifting down the hallway, letting everyone in the house know dinner would soon be ready, while Theodore would be sitting in his private office reading the newspaper which was delivered earlier that day by the paperboy. This was what he thought life was like before the war—simple and comfortable in its quiet predictability.

Once he finished perfecting the house—making it a home even a wife and two daughters would be proud to call their own—was when the voices would cease their pleasant haunting upon his hopeful ears; their ghosts fading into the destitute walls. Hours would pass, not a complaint to be heard about the placement of this-or-that, with anticipation as he sat in the recliner, taking a well-deserved rest after countless weeks of hard work; not an utterance could be heard among the æther.

This was it. He had accomplished what he had set out to do in the town of Oceanside, California: restored a home to the best of his ability for his family to live in until the end of their days. And as the ghosts of his departed loved ones left him for the placid walls of the home's infrastructure, so did his desire to remain here until the cold hand of Death welcomed him to the afterlife. Without giving it a second thought, Theodore lifted himself up out of the recliner, headed to the old 76 gas station, gathered what he thought was enough fuel, and returned to the sea foam exterior of his beach-side home and poured a trail of gasoline from the doorway, up into the family room and other sections of the house before striking two rocks together to create a spark.

From a safe distance, as the haze of the setting sun set the evening sky ablaze with the bleeding colors of twilight, Theodore Webb watched with stoic apathy as his dream home burned and collapsed into a pile of ash and rubble. Among the roaring flames, he thought he saw the silhouette of a woman sitting where Dolores' reading chair had been. She appeared to be reading, the flames not bothering her as they consumed her. Theodore didn't bother to give the shadowed projection a second thought, assuming the outline was a trick of the eyes—nothing more. Any hope of saving the house having faded into the atmosphere in a puff of smoke, along with his wife and children's kindred spirits.

As the flames died down, the foundation of the house now glowing embers, Theodore turned his attention to the nighttime sky; a dotted sea of stars and war torn constellations staring back at him in silent wonder. He could follow the north star back to Shrapnel or trail behind the moon as it traveled south toward Bomb City; both options offered a place to call home among people who would welcome him with open arms.

His gaze turned north and stayed there. While Bomb City boasted better security from intruders, he desired to be closer to a place he had once called home; a place which held memories of better days.

· · ·

FOREWORD

Everything thou has read so far has been nothing more than a lie. Through the millennia, through countless translations, with passages—important ones at that—having been omitted, passages being rewritten to suit a hierarchy's personal agenda, and some having been fabricated out of thin air. This shall be an attempt at a reparation of the errors which My children have created—all records prior to this new addition shall be rendered nontruth.

CHAPTER I

It began with a *selfish act of rebellion*, according to My father; choosing to favor the humans over My own kind—the angels. I must admit, My admiration for the humans came with numerous warnings —that I shouldn't consider the savage beasts known as man to be of higher importance than My winged brothers and sisters.

2. Finding Myself unable to heed My father's countless warnings, I found Myself eventually cast out from My nebulous home (the Kingdom of Paradise); sentenced to a life of exile until I could come to terms with the truth —that the humans were nothing in comparison to My own species. Unimportant and designed entirely for our own amusement, nothing more.

3. After several millennia had passed (which accounted to nothing more than a fortnight for Me) that it was in My solitude, brought on by My aforementioned exile from the Greater Kingdom of Paradise, that I thought I could create something beautiful. I started small, bringing light to the dark place which *My own father* had banished Me to. What I saw lay before Me was something I couldn't begin to fathom as to why the Elders would have kept it shrouded in darkness. It was a place of endless possibility.

I

CHAPTER II

After several days of tireless creation, I considered it to be perfection; an achievement not even My father could attest to, his Kingdom of Paradise having been passed down to him by his own father and his father before him. My little Garden of Eden.

2. However, the world I had created still felt incomplete. But what could be missing, I asked Myself.

3. And that's when it hit Me—here, the planet Terra, the monument of My exile, was where I could attempt to recreate My most beloved creature: humans; give it a place where it could be appreciated instead of ridiculed and forced to entertain angels until the end of their days.

4. I started off small, creating a male from the rich soil of Terra; a man which I had felt inspiration to call Adam—in memory of My dearest brother from back home. We would walk the vibrant lands of My creation and talk for what seemed only hours but had *actually* been close to 210 years time to that of man (thankfully, unlike My father, I eradicated the cruel confines of mortality upon my beloved Adam.

5. Soon, however, My dearest Adam sought companionship. He desired that I create him an equal—even *My* version of humanity (sadly) could distinguish the difference between the two of us; stating his humanity's inferiority to a being of My godliness: a term which caused My skin to cringe at first, not liking the comparison to My father.

6. After several failed attempts to recreate the miracle of life which I had managed to bring Adam into this world, I found Myself becoming frustrated for the first time since My exile.

7. It was in My anger that I attacked Adam, tackling him to the ground, clawing at every inch of his frail self.

CHAPTER III

He lay there terrified at the violence which continued to pour from My being, begging Me to stop—promising to give up his soul if it meant I would cease hurting him. But by the time I finally heard his cries, it was already too late.

2. With the broken-end of a rib, I stood above him, still furious at My (countless) failures at granting Adam his companion. I looked down and saw the horror on Adam's face. His eyes never left the blood-drenched bone which rested in My closed hand. Not wanting to watch My greatest creation die in front of Me, I laid My open hand upon his bleeding chest and (successfully, this time) wished the wound away.

3. Adam's rib still resting in My tired hand I dropped it to the dirt, finding Myself embarrassed by My inability to abstain from such a transgression.

4. The green land of Eden began to shake violently, having absorbed the still fresh blood from Adam's rib. What happened that day, along with how, remains a mystery to this day, even to Myself.

5. Out from the earth rose a hand (female) weak and grasping for life. This terrified Adam and—I'll admit this now, after having lived in blatant denial for several millennia—Me; we both stood there confused, not knowing how to respond to the horror which continued to play itself out in front of us.

CHAPTER IV

She said her name was Eve, which struck Me something peculiar in nature. Unlike her male predecessor the woman who stood before us named *herself*, without the guided assistance of her Creator.

2. Adam and I took to her quickly. Within her lie a wit I had yet to see in a human, including the humans I knew from My *many years* spent in Paradise. She seemed to be omniscient, knowing of things not even I, Myself, could know as we walked the land of Eden. We would pass a small group of animals and she would name each one: "That one's a flamingo. And that, a lion and his lioness." She amazed me with her endless capacity of knowledge, to know so much after having lived such a short life on this (still freshly de-

signed) landscape I had created.

3. Eve soon developed a liking —a strong one, at that—for Adam, finding him to be far more stimulating than Myself. Soon My days were spent in search of where the two had run off to; waking up early to roam the earth to find anything they had yet to find a name for, leaving me to become the third wheel in a barren landscape. You'd have to paint Me a fool if I were to ever admit jealousy found its way into My heart (I'll supply the brush, no worries) due to this natural development.

4. It didn't take long for My jealousy to evoke malevolent thoughts toward *My own* creations. For I had grown envious of Eve's (unexplained) vast knowledge of Eden. So, in order to obtain the upperhand, I devised a white lie to tell them once they returned back to our resting ground for the evening.

5. I told them of the "Tree of Life" as well as the "Tree of Knowledge of Good and Evil" and how, if they wished to stay in the land of Eden, they should *never* partake of the fruit which grew from its branches. Given how 'insightful' Eve found herself I figured she would challenge Me, partaking of the Forbidden Fruit. But I was wrong, she instead chose to heed My warning and advised Adam to do the same.

6. I had to be craftier than I originally thought. It would be another series of weeks (4,000 years in human time) before a brilliant idea would strike Me.

7. One day Adam and Eve asked why I was the only angel residing within Eden, their curiosity of My loneliness becoming the linchpin to what would be a clever deception. I told them the "History of Paradise" and the War which took place due to *one of My sons' treasonous acts of rebellion.* I twisted the tale of My own fall from grace into a tale of heartbreak, having to cast one of My own children to the depths of Hell (a horrible place of torment and suffering)—a place where even the rays of the brightest star failed to reach; sound familiar?

8. Adam and Eve stared back at me with looks of abashed horror—

shall never understand where I went wrong. . .

CHAPTER XXIII

And it shall be known that I was patient and forgiving of My children, despite their foolish ways—a Father who would forgive even a *mortal sinner*, as long as they sought redemption in My name. *But how quickly One's disposition can change in time.*
2. Even One such as *Myself.*
3. As I continued to watch My children fight senseless battle after senseless battle—with no sign of peace in sight—I began to lose faith in Them. It seems My children were doomed to fail, even with the promise of *Eternal Salvation* at their fingertips.
4. Finally, after what had only amounted to a little over a decade, I had grown tired of their petty squabbles and decided to take matters into My own hands.
5. Choosing to play on the still ripe paranoia of the Cold War era (a dispute I believe I shall never *truly* understand), I redirected the course of a rocket which was designed to study the Aurora Borealis—a doodle of a wave of light I was fond of in My infancy and hadn't the heart to rid it from the Earth's atmosphere before abandoning it due to My having grown tired of humanity's destructive, explatory nature—to fly mindlessly over paranoid Russian airspace. Humanity, being an impulsive species, lit up the planet with their soulless creations.
6. The monument to My failure didn't end there, I'm afraid. Unfortunately, like the countless plagues I had used before (hoping to wipe out such vermin), humans began to rise from the ashes of the scorched earth like the Phoenix.
7. Time, however, granted Me a favor with the *birth* of a new Apostle; one who could help Me finish lay to waste the fragments of a memory which haunted Me for 4,000,000,000 Earth years.
8. Even now, as My only remaining Apostle scribbles My will into Eternal Testament (to be read by no one, should he succeed in carrying about My task for him), My heart aches to be left alone in My Everlasting exile. Forgive me, fa-

ther, for I now understand why it was foolish to favor the humans over angels—they are a selfish and foolish species which should never be granted the same gift of free agency which the Elders had bestowed upon us.

9. I am ready to come back home, father. I have learned My lesson...

THE END

* * *

STILL PICKING AT THE SCAR which rested above his left eyebrow, a scar he had received from a short-tempered drifter named Gauge—a constant reminder of his previous life when he was lost, without the wisdom of *the Holy God*—Phoenix Lancaster rose from his bed. He couldn't sleep. The voice inside his head, a voice he had deduced was the *disembodied voice of God* (after skimming through the beat-up pages of a prewar Bible), wouldn't allow him the luxury of rest until His work was finished. It was the curse of being blessed as an Apostle of God—one must give up their sanity in order to keep Him at their side. Were he to ever cross paths with Gauge in the near future he would feel obligated to thank him; that despite the constant headaches from the lack of sleep—brought on by the bullet which still remained in the backside of his skull—he was given a new purpose in life: to carry through God's tired desire to eradicate humanity from the face of the earth. And after thanking the young Gauge for the small part he played in his salvation, Phoenix would then kill him where he stood, along with any fellow drifters who found themselves accompanying him that day (only after offering them the choice to join him in his *holy crusade* first, of course—he wasn't an unreasonable man after all).

Years ago Phoenix Lancaster would've been content living the rest of his days finding *unknowing volunteers* for his countless experiments with barrels of radioactive waste he happened to stumble across while taking an early morning piss along the outskirts of Bomb City, his childhood home. He was foolish. To waste one's life away with such a ludicrous hobby, he couldn't help but laugh at himself. Now? he had *the voice of an impatient god* whispering prophecy into his ears 24/7.

Mankind is a plague—one which continues to breathe a burning decay into the silent corners of the rotting earth, the disembodied voice spoke as Phoenix stared out the window of his restless abode. The calmness of the ocean (not a single wave crashing along the beach) being a humble contrast to his bitter thoughts. *Even back then, in what humanity* claimed to be **Their finest hours**, I could feel the strain of relentless hatred bleed from every stone, tree, and flower — begging for any form of reprieve from Their heartless domination over them; the greed of the humans' selfish consumption causing extinction to become a pandemic across the globe.

He agreed with the silent voice's every word. *Mankind was a plague;* one which needed to be eradicated from the planet in order for it to thrive once more. Humanity's momentary throne — a throne which found itself formed from the ashes of their failure — would soon be no more.

The land of God's exile would soon return to its peaceful, silent origins.

From the depths of his building (an abandoned lighthouse overlooking Cabrillo Beach on the outskirts of San Pedro), coming from the basement level, Phoenix Lancaster could hear the welcoming screams of his latest conquest, telling him good morning.

He made his way downstairs, grabbing his favorite riding crop, its · tongue being split from excessive use in recent years — desiring a short visit with his recent additions to his living situation: two young females; mixed complexion (*light chocolate lovelies* he liked to call them) with rose-tinted hair which flowed effortlessly to their supple waistlines. He'd always had an affinity for the darker-skin; their exotic mysticism somehow captivating his carnal desires in ways the fair-skins couldn't, despite being a fair-skin himself. And as he approached the door leading into the basement the old familiar combination of smells of blood, urine, and fecal matter leapt into his nostrils, reminding him of visitors who had long since passed. He stood there, outside the door, for a brief moment — taking in the warm aroma he would soon find himself swallowed in upon entering the room.

"Gu'mornin', my lovelies," he said with a child's grin on his face. "I hope we both slept well last night." He stepped up to the youngest of the two. A soft whimper escaped her tired throat. The fresh smell of copper still lingered at the base of her warm cunt — unsure whether or not the cause of the bleeding was from last night's activities or if she had finally been welcomed to the world of being a woman.

The oldest of the two managed a swift kick into the air, an attempt to ward off a playful Phoenix's advances toward her baby sister.

"Now, now, little one," his attention turning toward the elder for a moment. "You'll get your turn soon enough. There's no need fer jealousy among sisters."

His childish smile lingered a moment longer before turning sinister in the shadows.

The cold sweat of fear was a welcoming sensation as he lay his body atop each of them, the moist chill against his skin a pleasant reminder of his childhood when his mother would bathe him with the irradiated waters of the ocean, the salty taste collecting on his tongue as he licked the younger one's neck while the steady motions of his pelvis pushed into hers—the grip of her cunt tightening around him, making the experience unbearably enjoyable.

· · ·

DOLORES WEBB CLOSED HER EYES as tightly as she could, finding herself unable to watch as the old man continued to edge toward her baby sister (his steps resembling a playful skip) to continue where he left off with his twisted fantasies. She was left with the tortured pleas—mixed with the animalistic grunts of a satisfied monster—to pierce her restless ears, knowing the aging beast would turn his attention to her next. This was how it went. He would have his way with Jordyn first, taking a short break to whip himself on the back with his own riding crop (punishing himself for his own sexual perversion?); his pained screams being the prelude to her moment of violation.

When it was finally her turn, Dolores' senses kicked into overdrive. But no amount of distraction could deaden her focus on what was happening around her. She found his smell putrid; ripe with decay. A smell so foul, she swore she could taste the stink emanating from his being. The dead weight of his aging skin against hers would cause the nerves under her skin to crawl in disgust. And in the darkness, somewhere, the sound of Jordyn's cries reverberated off the walls. Her sister's cries were the product of a nightmare having become grim reality; something she could not escape.

But what terrified her most about the whole ordeal was when he would lean in close, usually as he approached his repulsive climax, and whisper what she assumed was an avant-garde poem—"For my Father who art beside me, hallowed be thy name. Thy kingdom come. Thy will be done, *on this dying earth as it once was in Heaven.* Grant me the ability to carry Your will through to fruition (to its bitter end) and, please, forgive me of my transgressions, for I am still but a creature of habit."—into her captive ears. His words would echo long after the pain within her lower extremities had passed, haunting her until his next visit. It was during these quiet moments when Dolores would attempt to comfort Jordyn—ease her pain with simple distraction.

"Do you remember the morning when father burst through the door excited—excited beyond the point of proper description—about the progress he and Pierce had *finally* made with the Subjects down in the lower levels of the hospital, having woken the one known as Cordelia?"

A brief sniffle arose from the shadows, her sister having to clear away the phlegm from her nose before being able to respond.

"A little bit, yeah."

"Yeah, you were only eight when it happened. I'm betting most of your memories from that age are nothing more than a blur."

". . .Yeah."

"Anyway," she continued. "I still remember the look on his face. He was so proud of himself, having figured out—by accident, I'm sure—how to bring a Subject out of their dormant state. I miss moments like that." she said, the memory bringing about a sense of longing to the head of her focus.

She often wondered why their mother, a woman of science as well (having given up the life of equations and endless hours of second-guessing one's work so she could tackle the duties which came with motherhood without distraction), decided to leave the security of living at the hospital. It was safe to assume it had something to do with their father's diminishing appearance among the family unit, having devoted most of his time either in the lower levels of the hospital—among the Subjects—or in the Quiet Room to write endless along the wall of chalkboard, falling asleep until the next bout of inspiration struck him over the head. Why? Why did mother find such dedication offensive? Had she been offered a choice, Dolores would've stayed with her father. She understood the importance of her father's work, understanding very little of the pure mathematics behind it all. But she understood the magnetic pull such work had on him. She had found the same spark in the old literature which was housed in old-man Nat's homestead down in Shrapnel when she joined her grandfather during a trading expedition.

"*I really do miss moments like that,*" she repeated as the small makings of a tear fell to her chin.

"Do you think we'll die this way?" said a faint Jordyn.

"I wouldn't let such a negative thought linger. It'll only eat you from the inside out."

"Why didn't he kill us back in San Pedro like he did mom?"

A choking silence befell her. The question lay unanswered between them—an acrid sting hung over her sister's words.

"While it's happening, while he's *violating* me, I imagine him towering over us, the both of us crying over mom's body, his rifle in hand, his aim bouncing back and forth between the two of us, reveling in our mix of loss and desperation before pulling the trigger; reuniting us with our mother."

"Jordyn. . .I—"

"And after it's all done and over with, after he's returned to the surface, I can't help but pray the next time he comes down it's to finish us off, like he should've weeks ago."

Another tear fell to Dolores' chin. And another. And another. She couldn't regain her composure to reassure her sister that this wasn't the end of the road for them. They would get away from the crazy old man who was holding them captive. They *would* find their way back home, to the hospital where they had been born—to rejoin their father in the security of family. They wouldn't be the same as they once were, their psyche's covered in scars from their shared experiences of watching their mother die in front of them and being defiled by an ancient drifter with a religious agenda of death driving his motives, but they would find their way back home; even if it meant having to endure being used as living, breathing sex toys for a while longer. They would find their way home. . .

"Do *you* think we'll die this way?" she asked, her sister's question from earlier now eating at *her own fragile state of mind*.

". . ."

"Jordyn?"

". . ."

"Are you still there?"

"Sometimes, Dolly, I like to think we're *already dead*."

12

I T DIDN'T MATTER HOW MUCH TIME HAD PASSED since her awakening, in the eyes of Subject No. 2773 (Cordelia Dashkov), the endless landscape of California would always remain untouched, left unscathed (perfect, despite its many flaws) from the unforgiving clutches of *nuclear holocaust*. She refused to believe humanity had lost the skyline, their ghosts trapped within the ashes of downtown; swallowed up by the passing storm. Standing atop an old Macy's building a couple miles south of the hospital, Cordelia Dashkov scanned the horizon for any sign of her fellow Subject: Subject No. 2990; the sky moving sideways without her as her search proved itself fruitless from her current vantage point.

She found herself feeling conflicted knowing there was someone else in this world *just like her*—an alien to the world she was forced to call her reality. A never-ending sense of disconnect had attached itself to her being; a feeling she had felt during her time in Arcadia as well. But the thought of no longer being *alone in this world* (that another Subject found themselves lost in a world which had stepped off the map of time centuries ago) gave her both a feeling of comfort and bitter resentment. Her unexplained hostility toward Subject No. 2990 being the realization she was no longer a novelty in such a backwards world. Out there, among the endless waves of sand and rubble, was someone whose importance trumped her own. Had she never returned from San Diego—which was now called Bomb City (how she hated referring to her hometown as such)—Pierce and company would've never sent out a search party for her had she managed to disappear from the hospital unannounced; she knew this.

But the truth? buried underneath her cold stoicism (appearing robotic to everyone she came into contact with), Cordelia had yet to admit that *this*—the harsh reality: the world having been scorched by humanity's unholiest of creations—was now her life. She believed this all to be a dream. She convinced herself *this place was all a **lucid dream***, the *true* Arcadia which Director Webb had explained to her many years ago as being nothing more than a sequence of ones and zeroes dictating her digitally projected existence—a simulated reality. She believed this post-apocalyptic landscape was the fabrication; a man-made construction; the true monument of her exile. A complete farce; a lie. There had to be a way to return to her home, to the place where the birds would chirp in the distance while hidden in the trees, people silently despised one another (yet refrained from killing each other—some of them, anyway), war had been reduced to proxy battles among the world's leading superpowers (in her day—*her version of the world*—the United States, the EU, Russia, and China), while nuclear annihilation still hung in the air as a distant, looming threat—the world's leaders teasing humanity with the idea of setting the world ablaze but never living up to their empty declarations of violence.

She despised the Directors for what they had done to her; tearing her away from a life where she had purpose, where causality was a living, breathing entity. Here, in the *real world*, the days felt pointless—without meaning or structure—a fictitious counterfeit of her life from before her awakening.

There had to be a way to go back home, she thought, turning toward the rooftop entrance of the building so she could return to ground level, continuing her search for Subject No. 2990; leaving the sheet-metal skyline behind. There just had to be. . .

Memory conspires against the ever-changing winds of time, its one-sided frailty muting its cries for a worldwide standstill in the name of selfish reminiscence before they can even leave its desperate lips—whatever claim to immortality it had being reduced to yet another forgotten photograph of times come and gone; buried among an endless pile of other worthless mnemonic trinkets held close to the chest for comfort. Why does memory betray us this way? leaving us an empty shell, with nothing to latch onto as we pass from one vicious cycle of life to the next; only our brain's tired attempts to carry bitter fragments of memory along with us keeping our feeble bodies pressing forward in a cruel world designed to rip us to shreds and spit us back into the æther as just dust and echoes; a pale reflection of our former selves.

She hadn't the slightest idea where to look for Subject No. 2990, walking along the weed-patched streets of Shrapnel. He couldn't have gotten far—a safe assumption. To be honest, she wasn't giving the search her full attention. She only agreed to look for the Subject as a favor to Director Needham, he having displayed a generosity toward her early on in her post-Arcadian development; allowing her to travel south to ~~San Diego~~ Bomb City (hoping to help her come to terms with the harsh reality of the well-established surroundings which would claim her). Had it not been for Director Needham's early act of kindness Cordelia would've risked being cast out, telling the Director no. But despite her disconnect from everything and everyone in *this world*, the desperate look on Needham's face while he pled for her compliance convinced her to take on the fruitless task of searching for a human who found themselves lost in the seemingly endless landscape of the Californian Wastes.

This thought brought her attention to an aspect of the *post-apocalyptic future* which she loathed with every fiber of her being: the lack of vehicular transport; a thorn in the side of anyone who wished to travel a great distance—an hour long trip being stretched into an unnecessarily excruciating four day expedition. Had no one's curiosity pushed them to attempt at making repairs to a relic (one which would've proven its use time and time again) from the *old world?*

She left the city of Shrapnel. There was nothing of worth there to hold her interest—just a small band of misfits (and an old loon claiming to have been alive before hell was unleashed on the planet) who happened to call a small section of the place their home; a second story apartment complex on top of a once family-owned bookshop. Following the faded street signs, she made her way southbound toward Bomb City, the desire to feel at home calling her in a desperate way; like the tortured cries of a newborn child screaming for the warm blanket of security of its mother's womb. She would find no solace in the vacant streets of ~~San Diego~~ Bomb City, its dead streets holding only the memories of a life which had been claimed by others to have been only a work of fiction. It was her metaphorical womb—a place which she could not return to. And like the newborn child, she refused to accept such a grim fate as her reality.

Traveling south, using the Pacific coastline as her guide, apprehension gathered itself inside her being. She had heard plenty of rumors of drifters who were settled along the shoreline but had yet to run across an encampment. While having gone through extensive combat training during her previous life, she would be no match for an entire camp of drifters; their violence-obsessed minds making them monsters with an insatiable thirst for blood from *anyone* outside their close-knit ilk they happened to come across. To help soothe her fears, Cordelia stroked the barrel of her rifle—occasionally pulling the magazine from its chamber so she could thumb her limited ammunition. Once, during one of her endless loops of boredom in the hospital, she etched names into the bottoms of each cartridge: Francis, William, Nicholas, and Hamilton. Names from another life—a life where memory was welcomed with open arms and not a haunting nightmare of man-made fabrication.

As she continued along the shoreline, staring out at the dead calm waters of the Pacific, a wave of memories flooded her with an intensity she hadn't felt since her awakening: the sense of abandonment she'd experienced her entire life, her father having left her and her mother moments after her birth; her four older brothers toughening her up throughout childhood, not wanting to have to worry about their baby sister once they all left the house for either college or a life in the military. The sadness she felt when she received a text message from Hamilton telling her their mother had passed after a long battle with Hodgkin's lymphoma. All these memories passed through her and dove into the dark blue waters of the ocean, where they would remain fragments of a long forgotten song from a time now lost to her; lost forever, for an ocean has no memory.

Hours and miles passed when she found herself in the middle of a drifter encampment. What she saw wasn't what her imagination had conjured up. Instead of violent screams and gunfire swallowing her in a cacophonous uproar, she found herself standing among a sea of corpses—a majority of them still sound asleep in their beds; the rest struggling to rise to their feet. What the hell happened? her mind raced as she examined the deceased, a good number of them being unidentifiable due to their faces having been turned to a gelatinous blob of skin and blood. Perhaps a rival faction? she assumed. Rivalries still existed, right? The concept of irreconcilable disagreement among thugs hadn't succumbed to extinction with the falling of the atom bomb. Wherever humanity existed, the opportunity for dissension would forever linger in the background; waiting for its moment to arrive so it can rise to the surface.

Choosing not to linger on the violent scenery (even barbarians deserved a silent respect when it came to the rules of death), Cordelia continued her steady pace toward the town of Bomb City.

But even as the sun sank into the ocean and nightfall peered its head over the mountains to the east, she couldn't seem to shake the image of slaughtered drifters from her mind—their deaths being an enigma she couldn't solve, no matter which angle she chose to look at it. One thing was certain, however: she would not return to Pierce empty-handed. Even if it took her months, she would return to the hospital with Subject No. 2990.

• • •

HE TOOK HIS TIME while traveling northbound, going out of his way to look for signs of a settlement where a band of drifters might be located: a cloud of smoke trailing down to earth, the sound of gunshots being wasted into the æther, screams of violent delectation echoing across the barren landscape, hoping to find a listening ear—to evoke fear upon anyone who happened to hear them. Theodore, however, took these *warning signs* as welcoming, edging closer instead of changing course like so many before him had done; the ancestral desire to live to see tomorrow pushing themselves away from the unknown chaos. But Theodore's mental wiring—his fight or flight response—had been altered after that day in San Pedro, when he happened across the devastating scene of his wife lying lifeless in the streets among the other unfortunate souls who lost their lives that day. He ventured toward the city of Shrapnel with a death wish hanging around his neck, going out of his way to cross paths with any drifters he could stumble upon, letting his presence provoke an attack on the drifter's part.

The claim to his life wouldn't be without a fight. He knew his wife Gwenivere wouldn't approve of him giving up on life without standing his ground. What he came to realize, after many a drifter had fallen by his hand, was that a drifter couldn't handle themselves well in a situation where their intended victim fought back with the taste of bloodshed lingering at the tip of their tongue. With each fallen drifter, Theodore's desire to have his own pain put to an end dwindled to nothing; only a violent, inextinguishable rage remained, a rage which would stay with him until his dying breath, for it didn't matter how many he lay to waste with the cricket bat he'd kept as a sordid reminder of that tragic day. Nothing he did would bring back his family.

It's a curious thing, the singular driving force behind humanity. An often selfish species, looking only to secure a life of well-being for themselves, will allow others to come into their life—strangers turned friends turned to lovers—eventually creating new life (*the next generation of selfish beings*) and lay such foolishness aside to ensure the survival of their offspring—willing to die for them, if needed. It's amazing to watch them deteriorate into violent, hopeless monsters (developing such animalistic qualities) when everything they hold dear is torn from their possession. A selfish fool who had yet to experience the joy of bringing new life into such a cold dark place—that new life shining light into the darkest corners of their lives—would deny being capable of falling into such madness; the selfishness of their youth blinding them to the reality of parenthood, a two-sided coin: with joy resting on one side and fear and paranoia on the other; both coming together to wash away the selfish nature humanity is born with in a fleeting moment of agonizing pain and screams. Theodore and Gwenivere considered it a blessing to have managed to experience this phenomenon twice in their lifetime. . .

Nightfall came in like a singing bullet, the open pale moonlight making it easier for him to look for nearby settlements to head toward for a night's rest.

Ahead of him, on the edge of the horizon, the flickering light of a burning flame could be seen breathing a cloud of smoke into the air. He knew it could mean one of two things: either a small settlement of cordial Wastelanders or a rowdy band of drifters celebrating their day's pillage with the meat of their freshest fallen victims. And he didn't care which it happened to be. Either way, he was going to find a warm place to sleep.

It didn't take long for the flickering light of signaling flames to die down, leaving only a plume of smoke hanging in the æther. Doing quick math in his head, from where he was standing when the fire disappeared into the ground, he calculated he still had an hour before he would reach his desired destination.

His thoughts drifted to Bomb City, wondering if Chevrolet made it back okay, having abandoned her in San Pedro for Oceanside. While the majority of the time he found her presence bothersome, there were moments when her naivete reminded him of his daughters; a less educated, mechanically inclined version of them, but glimmers of Dolores and Jordyn's personalities peaked through every now and then—Jordyn's curiousness and Dolores' ambition for adventure. He considered turning back and heading there instead of Shrapnel, but he was more than halfway through with his current trek. If he were to ever return to the humble town of Bomb City, he would rather prepare accordingly before venturing out for several days.

Perhaps during his next visit he could convince ARCO, the old loon, to educate him in the proper ways to use a firearm; his experience firing one in San Pedro being an embarrassment. With how scarce ammunition had become in recent years, thanks to the drifters' liberal use, if he were to ever acquire a weapon of his own, he would like to know how to properly aim and shoot his desired target.

A devilish grin found its way to Theodore's face as he approached the campsite. Rows of scattered drifters lay sleeping across the cold soil of the earth, ready for the slaughter. Years ago, during his time as Co-Director at the hospital, he would've condemned the killing of anyone (including an enemy) while they slept. They posed zero threat to you while in such a state. There was no need for unnecessary bloodshed. But the passing of a loved one, a tragic end brought about by savages of the same ilk as the ones who lay sleeping at his feet, can change a person's outlook on such things.

He scoped the bodies and their nearby surroundings. If he was going to take them all out without any trouble he was going to need a weapon besides his cricket bat—one which didn't require multiple blows before rendering his victim lifeless. He spotted one with a hand-made blade—having welded several hand saws together. Too many issues could arise; the myriad of blades could get caught between flesh, bone, and sinew after a while. A few bodies down he saw another with a semi-automatic rifle (a 44 Magnum rifle)—too much noise. The entire camp would be alarmed to his presence the moment the first shot rang out. Moving on he scoped further out and saw—

Jackpot.

Close to the dying embers of the once lively fire lie a drifter holding a handgun (a first generation Glock 17, a firearm he was mildly familiar with, Subject No. 2773—Cordelia—having brought one back to the hospital after her first visit to Bomb City) tight to his chest; a suppressor attached to the end of its barrel. That could work, he thought.

Now came the trying part of the task: walking past the sea of sleeping bodies to obtain the weapon. Using what light he could gather from the moon Theodore tip-toed his way toward his destination, past each dormant drifter, using their obnoxious snores of dreaming as white noise to cover the soft crunch of hard dirt underneath his feet. He could feel a small cluster of sweat beginning to collect at the edge of his brow. One misstep and it would all be over in a matter of seconds. Each step felt it took a lifetime to make, but he could tell progress (no matter how slow) was being made.

When he finally arrived, standing over the sleeping drifter—still holding the Glock 17 tight to his chest, like a child would a stuffed animal for comfort—Theodore froze, collecting himself. He thought of his wife and children, how they were taken from him by someone of similar nature. Pushing past his old naive philosophy of refraining from killing a foe without giving them a fighting chance he lifted his cricket bat above his head and let it hang there for a moment, preparing himself for the amount of momentum he would need to crack the mongrel's skull with one well-placed swing.

There was a moment, hidden somewhere in the seconds which passed between the swing and impact, where Theodore swore he witnessed the drifter's eyes open—a look of confusion forming across his tired face; the tight grip on his of his firearm unable to save him from such a grim fate. There was no way to know if this is what actually happened, but Theodore liked to think the bastard's last moments alive were spent in a mix of confusion and fear.

It only took one swing to (*crack!*) silence him. Had it only been the one drifter he had to worry about, he would've put in a few more good swings; allow the flesh to split, letting chips of skull fragments and scrambled brain matter flow out onto the earth. Instead, he recollected himself and gathered the Glock from the drifter's dead (but still warm) clutches, checked the magazine to count how many shots he would have at his disposal—he had eight—and glanced over the rest of the still sleeping bodies; wondering which unlucky soul would be next to find death in their dreams.

Thinking methodically, he went for the one sleeping next to the 44 Magnum Rifle; best to silence the greatest threat within his current surroundings. The rest would become child's play after that, he imagined.

He pondered breaking the silence with the rifle-toting drifter, not knowing how much ammunition he'd have with the rifle, blowing his brains out with the Glock. But there were ten drifters verses his eight bullets, which would mean two would be left standing to charge toward him once he ran out of; the slick taste of willow wood and linseed oil awaiting them.

He welcomed the challenge.

Under the light of the moon and the stars Theodore twisted the suppressor from the barrel of the firearm (cricket bat resting underneath the pit of his arm), held the cylindrical object over Magnum's forehead, whistled gently—hoping the noise would wake him—and let it go; letting gravity do the rest.

Time seemed to move in slow motion once the suppressor left his nimble fingertips. He watched as the earth's magnetic pull dragged the item down toward the drifter's face, its trajectory leading to the inevitable impact between his brow. Waiting for the satisfying moment of object meeting flesh, Theodore's eyes made one last glance across the moonlit landscape; his (future) victims all still lost in a dreamless sleep.

It happened in a matter of seconds. From the moment the suppressor made contact a quick burst of adrenaline began to course through his veins. There had been no time to react for the first three drifters, the reflex of Theodore repositioning his aim and trigger finger catching them before realizing what horror was falling down upon them. The rest of the ten, however, became fair sport for him. He missed the fourth as he rose from his slumber, the wasted bullet digging a home in the dirt which had been the bastard's pillow only second's ago; the fifth finding its place, sending the now lifeless coward back to the ground to enjoy an eternal sleep. Five, Six, and Seven were easier targets, their inability to understand the dire circumstance they found themselves in leading to their scrambled demise.

Finished with the Glock he chucked the now worthless weapon at Eight's torso, clipping his left shoulder, causing a brief stumble in his lethargic advance. Nine and Ten managed to take control of the situation, Theodore's focus on Eight having sidetracked him for a moment longer than he would have liked. Nine wrapped his arms around him, holding his arms down. "Gotcha, yih fuckin' negro," Nine whispered into his ear as Ten approached, clenched fists waiting to land a few punches.

The pain of a quick one-two-three to his torso knocked the air from his lungs, all momentum of rage the adrenaline in his bloodstream had built having come to an unexpected halt. Ten's punches kept landing one after another, Theodore's thoughts drifting to his wife and children. Perhaps tonight's the night? his mind spoke between blows. *I'll finally get to see them once again.*

On reflex to the sensation of pain, Theodore's legs lifted from the dirt and kicked outward toward Ten's gut, knocking him back; the force of pushing Ten back sending Nine into a backward motion, stumbling over himself, his grip over Theodore's torso loosening—granting him the freedom to gain control of the situation if he wanted to. If the will to live outweighed the desire to see his family.

Regathering his footing, Theodore tightened his grip to the base of the cricket bat, turned, and swung up and down with a fervor he felt every time the bloodstained wood met with the fragile crack of bone underneath Ten's bearded flesh—a feeling he first experienced a little over a year ago in San Pedro when a band of drifters made the unfortunate decision to turn back to finish off any survivors among their original onslaught.

It was during each violent outburst, with every skull which found itself under the cold weight of willow wood coming down upon them, the image of Gwenivere's fragile, lifeless body would flash before his eyes; in that moment, the rest of the world faded into the backdrop, becoming secondary to his mind's eyes. Nothing else mattered. Subconsciously he hoped if he fractured enough skulls the world would rewind itself, give him a second chance at a life with his wife and kids. A life where they could live in dysfunctional harmony within the confines of a small suburban home by the shore in a ghost town once known to the world as Oceanside.

When the wave of reality came crashing in around him—Eight, Nine and Ten now lifeless rag dolls on the cold desert sand; off-beat drips of curdling blood falling from the tip of his cricket bat—his wife and children were nowhere to be found, just the horrific scene which he had painted with heavy-handed strokes and a couple of bullets.

He made his way back to the once Glock-wielding drifter, dragged his corpse a couple yards away from his original sleeping grounds, a second Glock slipping from his waistline, which Theodore collected for future encounters. Theodore retired, removing his lab coat to fold it and laid it over the pool of blood, which had yet to soak into the cold earth for a pillow. He then settled down next to the dying embers of the fire to await the moment sleep would find his untired eyes.

●　●　●

SLEEP REFUSED TO FIND ITS WAY to his tired mind, shutting it off from the world for a few precious hours. It would only grant him subconscious solitude for a few brief minutes before jolting him awake, his heart racing; a layer of sweat beading at the edge of his nervous brow. An unappeasable surge of fear and paranoia had taken hold on him these past few weeks, ever since he abducted Subject No. 2990 from the mortuary (from underneath a sleeping Mason's nose, thanks to the *tried and true miracles of ancient science*) and left him outside the door of a bookshop—to be taken care of by the residents of Shrapnel. He couldn't shake the peculiar feeling of a nameless dread which hung over his head, pounding at the wall of his skull relentlessly, driving him to a sleep deprived madness. Even when he managed to drift off for a moment, Friedrich Winsome's subconscious would betray him, replaying flash images of the deed he had done—a deed he thought would've put Pierce's mind at ease—while auditory remarks of guilt drowned him to the point of waking up in a cold sweat, unable to breathe without using every ounce of his concentration to avoid hyperventilating due to the recurring nightmare. He wished he could turn it off, turn off the section of his brain which continued to implant the seed of doubt into his thoughts. *Why should I feel this guilty?* he thought, wiping his brow dry, the cool breeze against his forehead unable to calm him. *I haven't done anything wrong.*

Still, he couldn't shake the nightmares, nightmares of either Pierce or Elizabeth arriving at his doorstep, their faces wearing the look of dissatisfaction. He could handle Elizabeth's imagined cold gaze, their tumultuous relationship being nothing new to world. It came to no surprise when her apparition wrapped her hands around his neck to squeeze the life out of him. She must've had this thought a dozen times a day, if not more. Pierce, however, caused him to quiver at the thought. He had always done his best to appear satisfactory while in the Director's presence, hiding his admiration for him as best he could without making it obvious. This version of the nightmare usually ended with a stoic, seemingly forgivable Pierce losing his temper, edging themselves closer to the window and being pushed out to fall seven stories to the desert floor. The sensation of falling to his untimely demise stirring him awake; screaming in a sweating panic.

A knock at the door. Startled by the late night visitor, knowing the chance to find sleep had left him (again. . .), Winsome stumbled out of bed. Catching his balance as gracelessly as he lived his life, he managed to move his tired legs toward the door, hoping to find the midnight disturbance was nothing more than a hallucinatory auditory experience brought on by his lack of sleep.

It was Andrew.

"Christ, Andrew. What are you doing up so late?"

He knew this was a useless question to ask, his visitor's limited mental capacity restricting the types of questions you could ask him and find yourself getting a competent response in return.

"I-I-I—"

They could reduce him to a roaming, droning zombie but they couldn't rid him of his annoying stutter?

"—kn-kn-know what you did."

Dread filled Friedrich Winsome's soul to hear Andrew stutter such a sentence. Andrew somehow managed to retain a memory, despite his damaged brain. Whether or not this was a fleeting moment of clarity or the foundation of other untold recollected memories remained a mystery.

His secret felt threatened—the only witness to his dark deed having come forward while on one of his late night strolls through the hospital's silent, slumbering halls. He welcomed Andrew into his room, hoping he could manage some more information out of ne'er-do-well's stuttering mouth; needing to know if Andrew's stumbling to his sleeping doorway and murmuring the aggressive phrase was *indeed a threat* or a mere flicker of lucidity in his limited neurological programming.

"What is it, Andrew? What is it you *know* I did?"

"I-I kn-know what you did, D-D-Doctor Win. . .some."

"Yes . . . we've already established that part," he rubbed his face with impatient vigor. "But you haven't told me what it *is you know I did*, Andrew. *Now what is it?*"

He hoped repeating his name several times within a short series of sentences would con him into breaking his loop cycle of repeating "I know what you did" in classic stuttering fashion. Tiredness aside, Winsome's patience had always been thin with Andrew. He could never understand why the Directors (old and current) allowed such a useless excuse for a human being develop into adulthood, only to be reduced to a walking, talking vegetable.

"I-I-I saw you. . ."

This is what happens when you allow outsiders to come into this place (. . .) you get half-wit fuck ups like Andrew who can't even manage a sentence from their tongue without tripping over themselves left and right.

"I saw you t-t-take that Subject from the ho-hospital, Fr-Friedrich."

Again, the nameless dread had found its way into Winsome's psyche, pounding at the center of his chest—like something alien lie underneath the thin bone of his sternum dying to escape. If Andrew was capable of remembering the night they had exchanged words outside the elevator—Subject No. 2990 sleeping underneath a sheet on a gurney—almost a week after its occurrence, what's stopping him from spilling this information to Elizabeth or Pierce *accidentally* during casual conversation?

He couldn't take such a risk.

Without appearing suspicious (an easy task for him to achieve, given the individual), Friedrich Winsome moved the conversation toward his window; keeping the line of dialogue alive by attempting to pull more information out of Andrew. The wheels of plotting set themselves into an eager sense of motion when he placed his arm across Andrew's malleable shoulder, leading him where he wanted him to be when the moment arrived.

"You can keep a secret, can't you, Andrew?"

"B-B-But what you did wasn't r-r-right."

"And I agree with you. But it *had* to be done. Do you understand?"

"Y-Y-You should be repor. . .ted."

A cold nervous sweat.

"This has to remain between us, Andrew. Do. You. Understand?"

Andrew didn't have the chance to respond. One moment he was standing in Friedrich Winsome's dimly lit room, the next he found himself caught in the fatal dance with gravity as he plummeted toward the moonlit earth. The shock to his nervous system preventing him from letting out a final (stuttering) cry for help.

Winsome watched as Andrew (the simpleton) Goodman's body distanced itself, falling seven stories down. It only took seconds for Andrew's silhouette to make impact, but time appears to slow down to a crawl during moments such as this; a rush of adrenaline coursing through your veins, creating an altered sense of time to the affected. If two seconds appeared to take a minute to transpire for him he wondered how long the fall must've felt for Andrew.

He stared down at the body, limp and lifeless—it was a sad sight to witness, regardless of the circumstances; the weight of guilt was no stranger to Winsome's gut, having felt a similar knot form in his stomach during his journey back from Shrapnel after abandoning Subject No. 2990. As he continued to examine the freshly made crime scene seven stories below him Winsome blinked twice, finding the next series of events unbelievable.

Coming out from nowhere, materializing before his eyes, the same mysterious girl from Shrapnel appeared at Andrew's recently deceased corpse. She looked up, her vacant gaze meeting Winsome's. He found himself frozen in place, unable to look away from what was happening below.

Suddenly, against the laws of physics, gravity reversed itself—Andrew's rag doll remains fell up toward Winsome's open window. Had his guilt somehow managed to manifest a reversal in the space-time continuum, allowing him to undo his impulsive misconduct? The look of stupefaction leaving Andrew's face, being replaced by a look of rage and contempt.

Before he could react to the fantastical events happening around him time switched back to its forward motion, a vindictive Andrew grabbing Winsome by the shoulders and forcing him out the same window he had pushed him out only moments earlier. And as he found himself falling to his untimely demise Friedrich Winsome attempted to let out a dying scream, but the desperate vibrations refused to leave his panic-stricken vocal chords. He watched as the stone gray concrete outer walls of the hospital flew past him, the desert sands coming up to meet him with a vicious, conclusive hello.

Winsome's eyes opened in a panic, the nightmare of falling to his death still haunting him; his subconscious continuing to betray him, including a new element of dread to his already anxious brain: an unlikely moment of clarity in Andrew's brain leading to the revelation of his morally bankrupt wrongdoing.

Another night of no sleep, it seemed. Another night of restlessness awaited him. The morning sun could be seen coming up over the eastern hills to mock him.

There was a knock at his door. Simple at first, but it soon grew into a series of violent raps, followed one after another in quick succession. That familiar nameless dread which remained in the darker recesses of his mind kept him frozen in his bed—finding himself more than reluctant to leave the warm security of his covers. He knew the unknown knocker was only Andrew making his rounds throughout the hospital, double-checking the integrity of the building's doors; another loop of his he'd developed after his lobotomy. The knocking continued, refusing to cease—only growing louder as the seconds passed. Just another annoyance to add to one more sleep deprived night.

· · ·

A CHANGE IN FOCUS helped to distract Elizabeth's mind from the fact a year's worth of her life was no longer a beacon of hope to a world which had none, but a tragedy lost to an unsolvable mystery. She didn't know if she believed Pierce completely, having had nothing to do with Thomas' sudden disappearance from the hospital. To keep herself from losing sleep over the unexpected misfortune, she chose to explore different avenues which she could work with the Subjects; the idea of awakening another boring her for the time being. Instead, she found herself in the medical library, drifting from bookshelf to bookshelf, looking for something to (hopefully) spark her interest. Endless rows of texts stared back at her, the higher shelves looming over her, mocking her and her temporary inability to grab them by the spine and absorb the words written within them.

She remembered many warm summer nights as a child when her father would come home late from a long day in the lower levels, a small stack of medical journals underneath his arm, a complacent smile on his face, having checked them out without going through the proper channels (he felt one shouldn't have to be held accountable for wanting to further their knowledge). He would lift young Elizabeth up with his free hand, give her an "I'm home, little Lizzy!" kiss on the cheek, carry her to their bedroom, and would sit his inquisitive daughter on his tired lap so he could read her to sleep as he skimmed through various topics of archaic medical and surgical practices; *most of them they had yet to try themselves on a willing participant.*

As she got older their nightly readings became more frequent and invaluable, her mind now able to retain the information her eyes took in from each journal's musky dog-eared pages. She often found herself returning to an essay on the neurobiology of catatonia. The weight of such curiosity having been ignited after her visit to her father's work space, in the lower levels, during the hospital's annual *Take Your Child To Work Day*—seeing a young quiescent Thomas behind a thick layer of glass experience what she would later find out was one of his *infamous seizures*. It was this memory which continued to push her forward as the years passed. She liked to think her father would've been proud to see how far she had come in her thirty-six years of life; the smile he would wear to hear she had successfully awoken a Subject.

Her affinity for catatonia had waned after the success of awakening Thomas from his thirty-eight year slumber, her end-goal having been achieved. She now found herself curious about a procedure which, according to various texts, had been deemed "inhumane" by those in the medical field *before the War.* Upon further reading she would agree it was an archaic surgical procedure with a rather uncivilized technique —the use of an orbitoclast (essentially a glorified ice pick), which was used to access the brain through a patient's eye socket—under the eyelid—via several light taps with a mallet until it was five centimeters into the frontal lobe, pivoting the ice pick forty degrees, so the instrument pointed inward (toward the nose) before returning it back to the neutral position to be hammered two centimeters further into the brain, before being pivoted back and forth twenty-eight degrees, doing its job with the patient still conscious. She concluded it must've been a relatively painless procedure.

Despite its taboo status after the prewar date of 1967 A.D., the process seemed promising to a curious Elizabeth, wondering if she could adapt the procedure to help a Subject transition from the simulated landscape of Arcadia and into the real world. With only two successes (Cordelia and Thomas, respectively) and enough Subjects left to experiment a couple lobotomies on, she figured it was worth the risk— potentially destroying a Subject's mind for the sake of securing any future success for herself and her colleagues.

"Still no word on the Subject's whereabouts?"

Elizabeth continued to thumb through the pages of the medical journal, ignoring the question, examining the black and white photographs detailing the procedure known as the *transorbital lobotomy*.

"I'm going to assume you're still not speaking to me." Mason said, already feeling the cloud of defeat edge itself between them after the first bout of silence.

But, stubborn as he always was, Mason remained standing in the doorway, staring down Elizabeth's backside until the quiet tension between them became unbearable; forcing her to turn and face him, even if it was to tell him to leave. Regret weighed down on him, having lost Subject No. 2990 while he was on watch. The whole thing still confused him. It wasn't like the Subject's condition allowed him to walk out of the mortuary of his own volition. And despite Elizabeth's allegations against Pierce, he couldn't imagine the Director surrendering to such petty malfeasance. Not that he wasn't capable of steeping to low heights in decorum. It had been under speculation for years that it had been *him* behind the lack of progress with the Subjects—having sabotaged everyone's work during the quiet hours of the night during his rounds throughout the hospital.

But despite Pierce's *assumed efforts*, Elizabeth had managed to awaken a Subject from their lifelong dormant state.

"If you felt you had the ability to create a better future for humanity, one which shared a likeness to the fabled world of the past, where humans lived in discordant harmony—instead of under an eternal cloud of unknowing—would you act upon such knowledge, even if it meant running the risk of losing everything in the process?" Elizabeth turned to face her visitor.

Mason stood confused, Elizabeth's non-sequitur leaving him speechless. Would he act? Sure. The thought of living in a world reminiscent of the past was a mental image anyone living today (had they the luxury of knowing what used to be) found themselves daydreaming about during life's many quiet moments. But if the past were as harmonious as everyone made it seem, why did the world end up the way it had—a vacant, soulless landscape; humanity's dying legacy fading away with each passing decade.

Did Elizabeth's question call for a response? He didn't know. Had he known their conversation was going to stretch its legs beyond him running through his pathetic laundry list of ice breakers, especially with such an enigmatic question, he would have prepared himself more, mentally. If he allowed himself to be honest with the world, he found Elizabeth's intellect to be intimidating. There were moments when he felt she was the most intelligent resident in the hospital, wondering why she had held such a low status among her colleagues for as long as she had—before Pierce's blind faith allowed her to climb the scientific ranks with little to no effort.

"I would only act if I knew success were a sure thing."

"And that's why you remain nothing more than an assistant. You lack the drive to work outside your comfort zone."

Elizabeth's barefaced insult stung, but he appreciated such honesty. Yes, it was known among everyone who worked in the lower levels—scientist and assistant alike—Mason preferred to play it safe when it came to his work; a human's life (and their sanity) was in his hands, after all. Daring to be unconventional with one's methods was unsound. It was rumored she was difficult to work with, Winsome having removed himself from working with her ever again. But even with her abrasive nature, she had proven herself time after time to be efficient when it came to her work.

"Why did you choose this line of work?"

"Excuse me?"

"Being a lab assistant. Why did you choose this line of work if you admit a distaste for taking risks?"

"My mother. She was Isaac Needham's assistant during the first half of his tenure as Co-Director and lead neuro-technician. Even after her unexpected resignation, when I was only two years of age, all she had were fond memories to tell—working alongside him and the other technicians, tending to the Subjects and recording Director Needham's personal notes. I had always looked up to her; her undying passion being an admirable trait which I hoped to inherit."

"I can accept that. Did she ever state why she was forced to resign?"

"No. It remained a secret, one which she took with her when she killed herself—having thrown herself from the rooftop. But I remember the arguments her and my father would have when she would find herself smiling her way through memory lane, especially whenever Director Needham's name was mentioned. The animosity which carried itself between them making it unbearable to be in the same room during such heated moments. I can still remember, almost as clear as day, the bipolar weight of our complex when Isaac Needham finally passed —my mother having locked herself in the bathroom crying, stuttering hysterics, a silent smirk wearing itself proudly on my father's face; being beyond proud to hear the poor bastard had finally bit the dust."

Elizabeth found Mason's confession sentimental. His motive for pursuing a career in the science field sounded familiar, relatable. It seemed everyone currently in the lower levels had found themselves there because of a parental figure—Mason to follow in his mother's footsteps, feeling closer to her in an unusual sense; Pierce to bury his father's legacy, replacing it with his own; Theodore to pick up where his left off; and herself? she wanted to make the memory of her father proud, to know his *little Lizzy* had achieved what many neuro-technicans had failed to accomplish for decades, deeming the task impossible; bringing a Subject out of catatonia, into the real world—free of the artificial lie known as Arcadia.

13

CEREBRAL DARKNESS. IT WAS a feeling which was familiar for him to experience, having spent most of his life in an unknowing state of neural inaction. He wanted to make sense of it, understand it. He was tired of the confusion. His short time spent stranded along a California freeway—the vacant world which surrounded him deconstructing itself into a barrage of ones and zeroes, a 1950s pop-art stylized billboard mocking his entire existence from a safe distance—having been the final straw to his *already well-tested patience*.

An occasional heaviness found itself weighing down on him, a mix of biological reactions taking place against his will. His heart rate accelerated. His breathing grew shallow. An unwelcomed warmth, wet in its execution, made itself known, grinding across the top of his groin in an aggressive manner. He felt a pulsating pressure against his chest, the weight of someone's palms pushing up and down. The easing tension being the counterbalance to the weight against his hips.

He wanted to wake up. At this point, he didn't care what he woke up to, even the orange-soaked imagery of a world ravaged by a ruthless nuclear detonation would've been deemed pleasant. Tom Dolin was tired of the endless cycle of false starts, waking up to a different time period, the rest of the world carrying on without notice—as if it were all they had ever known, the previous temporal framework of their lives having been erased from the mind's existence.

The motion was arhythmic but pleasant. He let his thoughts melt away for a moment, letting the sensation take over him. The opposing aesthetics of a subdued calm and violent exhilaration affecting his breathing, changing it from its previous shallow gasps of breath to deep, heavy intakes of oxygen. He could hear the sound of quiet moans of delectation coming from above him; female, innocent sounding by the pitch of her voice—the syncopated grinding motion against his crotch becoming more aggressive in nature with each subsequent thrust.

He aimed his focus on remembering things (little things, really; nothing too important) from his life, reaching as far back as his early childhood, hoping something would stick. Only a mess of fragmented memories greeted him in a non-linear fashion. A faint image of his wife, Sarah, came first, her blurry silhouette calling out to him, begging for him to come back home. But this instance passed without allowing him a moment's rest. It raced past a series of memories, making a pit stop to when he was nine years old, he and his elementary school friends obsessing over their latest additions to their Pokémon trading card collection during recess and lunch—jumping to his first high school dance freshman year, the isolation he had felt while leaning against the gymnasium wall closest to the exit doorway, being the only one in his grade without a *proper date.* And as soon as the memories entered his brain, they faded away into the pitch black æther; eventually fizzling out, like the bulb of a well-used nightlight—unable to find their way back to the nostalgia factory part of his brain.

He was having sex. This was the conclusion he'd come to, given the minutiae of his surroundings. The awkward silence of it all reminded him of his first time—his senior year of high school. Jasmine Cooper. He remembered the quiver of her lips as she lay defenseless across the queen-sized motel bed, half drunk from downing several miniature bottles of Cognac she'd plucked from the room's mini-fridge. (*"But Tom, it says they're complimentary!"* she would say before and after each bottle's consumption, her speech eventually becoming a slurred mess.)

The feel of her soft porcelain skin under the clumsy weight of his body was an experience he deemed, at the time, to be angelic. Behind the nervous sweat from the hands which currently found themselves against his torso shared the same smooth quality of Jasmine Cooper's.

He recalled telling Jasmine he loved her that night. An innocent lie which had carried itself from his tongue, out into the sweat stink-filled air during a moment of passion. A moment which signified the death of his childhood innocence and the birth of adolescent decadence. This was one of the only memories of his life before Sarah which he didn't mind carrying with him. It was the only time he'd experienced a nervousness emanating from another human being, an experience which was beyond his limited comprehension at the time; the subtle quiver of her lips pulling him toward her in a magnetic frenzy of un-knowing consequence.

"Sa-Sarah. . . ?" the name managed to escape his lips.

When he opened his eyes the view that met him wasn't the soothing image of his loving wife. No. Instead, the silhouette of a young, tender skinned redhead filled his limited perception of the world. *Where am I?* his mind raced, his tired eyes moving from left to right in a panic-stricken fever, taking in whatever scraps of detail he could gather. She couldn't have been older than fifteen or sixteen, the youthful cadence which she carried herself with, even as she continued to execute such a deed with an amount of skill only a professional would have, giving away her biological innocence.

All his memories, both cherished and despised, had faded into a fog of obscurity—the floating image of his wife and children being the only remaining, unconsumed fragment of a once lively portfolio of mental recollection; any residual flake of memory leaving in a hurried fashion. There was no farewell. There was no bittersweet moment, watching all the accounts of his life (a seemingly endless cast of charac-ters, friends and family, mostly. . .but it even included those he didn't care much for; nameless, one-off individuals with little to no signifi-cance to his narrative) walking away, into the horizon, in slow motion while the end credits crept out from the bottom of the screen, an ambi-ent instrumental playing them off as the scene faded to black. Only a pained emptiness welcomed him while the mystery girl continued to ride him with such carnal vigor.

"Wha. . .what's going on?"

"Shh. . .you're ruining the moment."

She placed two fingers over his lips for a second or two, hoping to shush him. She was almost at the point of climax, where she could let herself go in a fit of ecstasy. It had been several months since her last encounter; she wanted to make this one count.

"I don't—"

"Please, don't speak."

"But who are you? And why are you doing this to me?"

The girl let out a sigh of sexual defeat, Tom's sudden breath of consciousness and obsessive series of questions diminishing her drive to keep going; whatever buildup she had managed to collect having dissipated into bitter disappointment. Another wasted moment, she thought as she lifted herself from her unwilling *horizontal partner.*

"I told you, attempting to get one in with our *visitor* was going to wake him. I don't know why you refused to listen to me," said an undisturbed Eldritch, his eyes still closed, not wanting to wake up.

"Shut up, Eldritch. You can't blame a girl for trying."

"Just don't let T. find out what you did just now, okay? He considers him an invaluable asset, for some unknown reason."

"Please, like that old negro could do anything to seriously harm me. Everybody here knows he's *originally from that damned tower*. Them science types are nothing but a bunch of spineless prigs. Hell, the chickenshit who dropped this guy off was spooked away by Nat's obnoxious snores; fucking snores, Eldritch. T.? he can do what he wants with me, I'm not scared of him. Hell, who knows, I might even enjoy it."

Tom could sense the thick layer of tension in the room. His presence was considered sacred by a character who identified himself with only a single letter, an opinion which was not shared by the one in the room known as Eldritch. He wanted to speak, to interact with the others in the room, but what little energy he had earlier was sapped. All he could do was acknowledge his unwanted erection finally subsiding. There were questions he wanted answers to, to bring a sense of clarity to his uninformed situation. *Where am I? Why do I feel* **this** *weak? And what is that god awful smell?*

"I wouldn't understate T.'s ability to inflict pain, Peregrine. You've heard the stories. Even you can't deny the brutality of it all doesn't frighten you. Now please, put some pants on. Sure, you may be the only female in this camp, but that doesn't mean we all want to see your naked ass all-damn-day. Also, pull up our *friend's* pants as well; don't leave a mess of evidence for anyone to find when they come in. It's bad enough I had to be here to witness it."

A sliver of anemic light poured itself into the room, the morning sun having moved into the small square view of the room's east side window, the shallow sound of a newcomer's footsteps following the subtle creak of a door being opened.

"Did we finally manage to wake ourselves up?"

This man's voice was familiar. Its scratchy, comforting inflection carrying a definite weight to it, every word that left his tongue presenting itself as calculated—refined with a mathematical precision, suiting the flow of any conversation. Managing to twist his lethargic gaze in the voice's direction, Tom saw a swarthy colored face, patches of gray wisps of hair surrounding his chin, staring down at him; a warm smile welcoming him to the conscious world.

"To be honest with you, I thought this day would never *actually* come to fruition," he said, kneeling down to meet Tom at ground level. "But here you are: awake, unplugged, and, without a doubt, I'm assuming, confused."

"Where do I kn—"

"Don't try to speak. Not yet, anyway. You haven't had the time to build your strength. I'm certain you have a lot of questions."

Tom managed a subtle nod.

"For now, however, I'm going to have to ask you to just lie here and listen. I don't know the details of how you ended up here in Shrapnel, but I *can* answer questions I found myself being asked by someone else who found themselves in your situation several years prior."

There was so much to digest. Wave after wave of information fell onto his half-attentive ears. To have his worst fears realized, to be told his entire life was a digital construct, a lie; monitored day and night by devoted neuro-technicans. The countless seizures which would throw a Subject's sequencing out of sync explaining his *jumps through time* — being led to believe they were nothing but a well-composed picturesque dream/nightmare when they woke up in their proper sequence. But what stung most was being told his family was only a part of his lucid dream's predetermined structure; the emotional connection he'd felt being a monitored response of biochemistry, nothing more.

He didn't want to believe it, to accept everything Theodore had told him as an irrefutable truth would prove itself a monument of heartbreak. To ask him to let go of every memory he had of his wife and children, even if they were fabricated and false in nature, was a road he refused to cross. *It couldn't be true*, he thought, averting his eyes from the towering shadow in a blood-stained lab coat. *The connection I felt with Sarah and the kids was the only true thing I've experienced; that part **had** to be real. It had to be. . .*

"It may take a while to accept," Theodore's voice floated down to Tom's unprotected ears. "But everything I've told you is the truth, son; there's no way around that."

Theodore's gaze moved from the floor to the other side of the room, finally acknowledging the other two people in the room.

"Eldritch, let Nat and Atom know our friend is awake. I'm going to need all the help I can get if I'm ever going to get Thomas into any semblance of functioning order."

"T., I don't think there's a need to bring my brother and the old man in here. Peregrine and I are mor—"

"That wasn't a suggestion, son. Now get your ass downstairs and collect Atom and Nat like I told you to. I don't need any of your lip this early in the morning."

A *post-nuclear sunrise* in early August was like any other during the year; basic and uninspired, the atmosphere's ability to paint the sky with the subtle shades of pink and violet (before settling on its familiar indigo hue) no longer a natural occurring phenomenon. The warm, welcoming sounds of birds chirping in the distance, their melodious songs greeting the rising sun, replaced by the scattered echoes of gun-shots caught in a vacant breeze. The rumbling charge of the morning train transporting lumber and limestone along the Pacific coast having fallen silent centuries ago—nothing of the modern age being able to replace its early morning roar. Whatever audience the sun could manage to acquire never knowing the majesty it once held as it peaked over California's mountainous eastern horizon. To those living today, the sun had become nothing more than a bookend to the day, leading them silently into the next. In a strange way, stranger to admit it to himself, Nathan envied post-war humanity's ignorance to the past; not knowing what hidden treasures the earth used to carry with her.

When he heard the news of the Arcadian's awakening it came as a pleasant surprise to Nat's ears. After three days of inactivity he'd assumed the poor sap was going to remain a vegetable, doomed to a rather short existence outside his lifelong, digitized dormancy. But when Eldritch came downstairs claiming T. requested his and Atom's assistance he swore he felt the nervous sensation of his heartbeat accelerating (a sensation which was impossible for him to experience, considering his *post-nuclear* condition). For the first time in centuries, there was going to be someone on this bleak planet who shared a similar loss—having their familiar world torn from them; everything they held dear now a fading impression stored in a cache somewhere in the corners of his brain, haunting his dreams every time he closed his eyes. He wanted to know what it was like living in a world where humanity hadn't lost itself to its bomb-crazed lunacy.

He wondered if the Arcadian got to witness the same colorful sunrises of his own past within the digital land of Arcadia—the lush strokes of lavender and raspberry flowing across the binary representation which was his skyline; a "place" which T. attempted to explain to everyone. (And judging by the vacant stares he had received, only he, Atom, and silent Kilgore managed to grasp the concept.) It sounded like science fiction to him, a fantastical plot device which would've fit well in one of Philip K. Dick's lesser known, poorly written sci-fi novels from the 1960s. A long forgotten novel he had feverishly penned during one of his *countless* amphetamine binges during that decade but never desired to see it through to publication.

"So tell me, Nat. What do you think T.'s plans are for our visitor?" a snide Eldritch asked, leading the old man and his brother upstairs to his and Peregrine's room. "I mean, honestly, why go to all this trouble just to keep *one person* alive? It doesn't make sense to me."

Old man Nat chose to remain silent as the three of them continued their way upstairs. If he had to pick a least favorite of the other six (not including the newcomer) living with him, Eldritch, without a breath of doubt, would be the name he uttered, should anyone ever ask him such a blatant question. How two brothers could turn out as different as Atom and Eldritch, having survived the same circumstances before happening across the quiet town of Shrapnel, was a puzzle which he couldn't solve. Unlike his brother, Atom's outlook on life was without cynicism, despite the horrific events which stained his past. He was compassionate, willing to sacrifice everything to help a stranger — Eldritch had closed himself off from everyone; his only concern was self-preservation.

Nat found it sad to find he preferred Wendigo's off-beat, simplistic company — a struggling, recovering cannibal whose occasional hunger-filled stare could unnerve anyone within seconds — over an outspoken twenty-three year old man-child; frightened he would snap one day, the animosity he had come to feel for everyone in the complex brewing to its inevitable breaking point and killing them all in their sleep. He could tell by the weight of Eldritch's footsteps as they climbed the rickety staircase that *that* moment might come sooner than he originally imagined. The kid needed an escape from the banality he found himself drowning in living in such a boring excuse for a town. *Maybe I'll ask if T. will take the kid out of town for a while — help clear his head...*

"Do you think he'll stay awake this time?" Atom asked, breaking the silence as they reached the top of the stairs.

"After what Peregrine did to him earlier this morning? I don't see how *anyone* could manage to find sleep anytime soon after that."

Nathan didn't bother asking what Eldritch was implying. He knew (far too well) about Peregrine's inclination to make an attempt at fucking anyone within breathing distance, having spent five years of her life on the bitter end of countless drifter's sexual releases before escaping in the darkness of a new moon, stumbling into Atom and Eldritch along the way and, eventually, ending up here; scraping away what little was left of Nathan's sanity, he would often joke.

"Keep your distance, everybody," T. warned, his hands stretched out, hoping to keep everyone else at bay. "We don't want him feeling claustrophobic on his first day of recovery."

"A little late for that, ain't it," Eldritch whispered into his brother's ear, elbowing him in corner of his gut, winking at a still sexually perturbed Peregrine while T. continued with his examination of the Arcadian's vitals.

He felt he was witnessing the cold welcome a newborn would experience half a millennia ago, behind a hospital's sacred walls. All things considered, the comparison wasn't too far-fetched; the Arcadian's torpid existence behind a plate of glass being his man-made womb—the disarray his thoughts must have found themselves lost in, wondering where he was and why he felt so weak, physically. He couldn't even begin, nor did he want to, to fathom the turmoil he was going through; the memories he had been imprinted with while sequenced colliding with the hollow nothingness this world had waiting for him.

"You told us you've dealt with waking *one of them* up before, right," a concerned Atom spoke up. "That wasn't a conversation I made up?"

Without removing his gaze from the Subject, Theodore nodded in response.

"Do his eyes have to remain open like that?" Eldritch said. "It's fucking creepy, how they just stare up at the ceiling like that."

"You—you know I can hear you, right?"

"Did it. . .did it just speak?"

It would be days before Tom could manage to lift himself from the floor's magnetic hold it had on his body. Until then, he was stuck listening to everyone around him carry on with their lives. The one who went by T. would stop by every few hours to check on his progress; appearing dissatisfied with his results every time. His nights were spent on high-alert, refusing to allow the young redhead (Peregrine, was that her name?) another chance to sneak up on him for another casual go-around. It was during these long days and tortuous nights most his time was spent in his own head, the pieces beginning to take shape, forming a picture for him to examine.

The room he was in felt unkempt. The smell of urine and what he assumed was dried sexual discharge filled the air. If there was any motivation to reacquire his motor skills it would be to escape the repulsive array of smells which consumed his current living conditions.

Lost in his thoughts, the weight of his brain pulling at the back of his skull—like hefty sandbags left to collect dust somewhere along the shoreline—Tom managed a subtle twitch of his thumb and forefinger; a sensation which brought a small sense of reassurance to his fractured psyche; building his confidence, a small window of hope telling him this vegetative state wasn't permanent. He could feel the warm flow of his blood coursing through him, reaching the tips of his toes, as he tapped the floorboards which claimed his body. It wasn't much, but it was progress, nonetheless.

"T. says you're a man without a past."

Tom's eyes opened to find a patchy haired face staring down at him. It was the one who went by the name of Atom, if memory served him right; the young boy's eyes troubled with questions.

"Downstairs, among the endless rows of books, I remember reading a passage which said, 'a man without a past has no future.' Is it true, then? Are you without a past?"

He couldn't answer him. Because despite the random shards of recollection which had fled to the inaccessible sections of his brain, he could still manage to access minute flashes of memory and relive them with abundant clarity. But were these memories? *Actual memories*? Or were they as T. had claimed; digital imprints of false consciousness—a series of artificial daydreams, which found themselves fleeing at the sight of cognizance.

"Nat claims the past is only a dream. A dream where we often find ourselves looking back with a fond sense of regret—hoping we will fall asleep in order to relive it; making the false promise to ourselves that we'll never let such a fleeting moment pass us by a second time. Then again, he's *beyond ancient*. His view of the world is clouded by the weight of nostalgia."

Tom liked to think he had a past, that the life he knew wasn't what T. claimed it was—that everything he'd be told was a lie; a sick joke. He wanted the memories of Sarah and the kids to be real, to be more than *digital imprints* designed to keep him preoccupied during his dormancy. It all felt so real, he thought as Atom continued to drone. It had to be real. It had to be.

"Eldritch told me Peregrine managed to give you *quite the warm welcome*."

Tom let out a soft chuckle. "That's one way to put it, I guess."

"Even if what T. says is true, that you're a man without a past, I'll look past it and be the first to *properly* welcome you to Shrapnel."

• • •

IT WAS SUNRISE WHEN A LONE GUNMAN could be seen making their slow approach to the outer border of Bomb City. After ARCO passed away a week ago Chevrolet had been stuck sitting watch day and night with a young Roosevelt; ARCO's bloated decaying corpse in his favorite corner, still holding his rifle, a scowl across his face. Roosevelt's nerves were getting the better of him, having never encountered an intruder approaching the borders of his home.

"Wut do we do, Chev?" the young kid asked.

"Th'only thing we can do," Chevrolet said, her eyes focused down the scope of her rifle. "Sit and wait."

But waiting would prove fruitless, the gunman turning back to disappear into the sunlit horizon.

"Ya think they changed der mind?"

Not wanting to spook the kid, Chevrolet remained silent as she continued looking down the scope of her rifle. She had hoped the stranger coming their way was Theodore, but the stoic face of Cordelia found itself staring her down as she marched toward their location. A welcoming sigh of relief filled and left her lungs when she saw Cordelia turn about face and begin her early departure from her line of sight. After her last visit, surpassing her humble town for the settlement behind Bomb City (comprised of old prewar Naval ships, called Fleet Street by its inhabitants: individuals who thought themselves a part of a militia because they came across a stockpile of old Navy uniforms), Chevrolet prayed it would be her last.

"You think we ev'r gon remove ARCO's body from 'ere? He's startin' ta stink up da place."

"Ain't nobody wanna get close enuff to 'im," she replied. "Hell, I don't even think Phoenix, were he still a part'o our society, would be able to manage da courage to get up close."

"It fuckin' stinks, Chev. I dunno if I can . . . take it fer much . . . longer."

As Roosevelt left the room in disgust her thoughts returned to Theodore, wondering how the old geezer was doing ever since their last moment together as traveling companions; the awful scene they witnessed that afternoon in San Pedro awakening a violent side of him she would've never thought existed. She wondered if he had found peace somewhere among the chaos which was the world they lived in. He deserved that much, having lost everything he knew to a massacre.

The lost streets of ~~San Diego~~ Bomb City held the keys to Cordelia Dashkov's heart—every avenue and city block retaining a memory from her childhood, despite the surrounding architecture which towered over her being nothing like she remembered. Its once labyrinthine monster concrete expressways had become a series of empty monuments along a skyline of burnt-out buildings filled with unclaimed souls. A complimenting scene designed by a god with a macabre sense of humor. She thought the lingering feelings of loss had left her after her initial visit, but the vacancy of her hometown still tormented her as she made her slow approach toward the scattered civilization which had claimed it as their own; the inarticulate post-war rednecks who couldn't string a coherent sentence together if their lives depended on it. It depressed her, to witness a city fall to such squalor. San Diego used to be a central hub for an ever-growing community of native and transplant; coming together in one cacophonous harmony which played day and night. In this reality, it was as silent as an abandoned cemetery. Not even the haunting whispers of the dead could break the unwanted silence which consumed the city.

A glimmer of light reflected off a sniper's scope from one of the buildings; either ARCO or Chevrolet zoning in on her as she edged closer to their city's border. The early morning sun's rays betraying their position. She could've, if she wanted to, lifted her own weapon in their direction and let out a single shot and managed to hit her mark with ease. But one doesn't waste ammunition on those who pose little to no threat.

It was pointless, coming back here, she thought. Only misery could be found in the cold, gray remains of San Diego.

Cordelia changed directions, heading back north instead of continuing south, giving up on finding any solace in the antiquated town which had been the inspiration for the place she once called home. Such a convoluted concept, she thought, the crunch of each step along the concrete pushing herself away, the idea of home. Ever since Director Webb woke her from dormancy the only remaining fragment she had left was the deconstructed phantom of a town; *a series of incomprehensible binary coding playing on an endless loop inside her mind*; she held onto it with every mental fiber she could manage to coerce into concentrating on such a hopeless task. But ever since her first breath after waking up from her lifelong coma, she found herself lost in a world unrecognizable to her, the security blanket of knowing what home was no longer there to comfort her.

It would be days until the gray outline of the hospital's concrete walls slipped into view. The trip from San Diego to Los Angeles, on foot, taking as long as it did, one's thoughts had time to wander. But Cordelia could only think of one thing. She wanted to go back, back to that digital world *known as Arcadia*. She would do anything to see her brothers again; to be a part of a family—something this world lacked. The people who called this world their home were soulless creatures, living their banal lives day to day without consequence; nothing weighing them down. Just hollow avatars waiting to die.

All she had was time, time to continue drowning in her thoughts, only her knapsack and firearm to keep her company. She rubbed the magazine of her rifle, feeling nostalgic. She wondered how her brothers were faring without her. Did they even notice she was gone? It had been several years since her awakening, the days and weeks bleeding into one another after the first year. Out of all of them, she missed Francis, the youngest, the most. They were only three years apart in age, their relationship being more intimate than her other three brothers. She released the bolt of her rifle, ejecting the brass shell casing she had named after her youngest brother, catching it before it had a chance to escape her, and kissed the bottom, tasting its copper-base alloy against her lips. *I miss you, brother* she whispered to the inanimate representation of her loved one before placing it back into the chamber and continuing onward toward the rural remains of Los Angeles. The hope of saying hello to her family once more still very much alive; only buried under the thin layer of stoic cynicism which she wore well around everyone—both stranger and well-known acquaintance.

Cordelia looked back at San Diego one last time, its dour skyline a fading portrait in the distance, the grim atmosphere it emanated picturesque enough to one day (if civilization ever decided to rebuild itself) be immortalized on a postcard: GREETINGS FROM ~~SAN DIEGO~~ BOMB CITY, CALIFORNIA!, the historic snapshot taken from a boat out on the ocean, the towers of rubble lined up along the horizon, staring out at their unknown cameraman; welcoming anyone willing to enter its boundaries with open arms.

. . .

NO MATTER THE AMOUNT of river water she was given, the burn of irradiation couldn't replace the aftertaste of burnt flesh which sat at the back of Dolores' throat. The old man's tactics had changed several months ago, his proclivity for expressing sexual dominance over her and Jordyn having ceased—being replaced with a repulsive sense of tenderness. During scheduled intervals of the day the door would open, letting in a blinding stream of light, and he would trudge down the stairs, dragging a fresh corpse behind him; a warm, demented smile on his face. "I hope you're hungry, my lovelies!" he would exclaim as he reached the final steps, bypassing the two of them so he could begin prepping their lunch; singing a song she wish she could unhear.

> First, let's start with the phalanges
> Fingers, thumbs, and toes.
> We'll serve them up like sausages
> 'Cept with cartilage & bones.
> Next'll come the lips, the tongue
> The ears, and both the eyes.
> Don't let the smell turn you away
> The taste is sure to satisfy.

"I can't. . .I can't take it anymore."

"Try not to think about it as bits and pieces of another person," Dolores said. "If you imagine it as something else, it helps keep the urge to vomit from climbing up your throat."

"*Because tonight's the night we'll eat like kings and queens of ole.*"

"Please—"

"*With our taste buds happy and our stomachs full.*"

"—not another bite. I don't think I can take anymore."

"We have to eat. Not just for us, but for the babies as well."

"It makes me sick, the taste alone."

"We have to."

"Eat up, my lovelies. We've got to keep our strength up if we're going to go full term."

He left their flame roasted meals on old glass plates; ceramic relics which he managed to lift from an old shopping center several miles northeast from the lighthouse a few summer's back while looking for paper to continue writing his exegesis. The appetite of his youngest lovely showing no sign of improving—kicking the plate of food away, tossing the gourmet meal across the dirt ridden floor—Phoenix Lancaster removed himself. It disappointed him to watch good food go to waste. He stared down at her. The bump of her belly kept his spirits up, knowing a life was growing inside of her. The future of the Lancaster bloodline; disciples to continue the work he started, and would fail to see to fruition.

The older one, despite her initial frostiness toward him, having taken longer to impregnate than the little one, consumed the meat from a finger in a matter of seconds; moving to the next part of the course before swallowing her current mouthful. She was hungry and it showed.

He knelt down to speak face to face with the twelve year old.

"I promise you," he entangled his middle and forefinger in a lock of her hair. "You'll manage to find the will to push past the disgust of eating something that was once human. When that happens, my lovely, I hope you'll realize I'm not trying to punish you. I'm trying to help you —help you survive."

No response left Jordyn's lips. Only silent discontent met the old man's ears.

"Help you and *the little miracle of life* that is growing inside of you." He looked over at Dolores, who was finishing the last of her portion of the tongue. "Both of you."

. . .

SHE STORMED INTO HIS OFFICE without announcing herself beforehand, a social custom which bothered him whenever it was broken; Pierce was victim to being a creature of habit. The anger which held dominion over Elizabeth at the moment, having discovered his futile attempts to help her find her missing Subject, bypassed common courtesy in search of much desired answers.

"I don't understand the sudden turn your disposition toward Thomas has taken, Pierce," her voice carried as his door slammed behind her. "For your entire life you've done nothing but show violent contempt toward him. But now that he's missing I find—from Andrew, of all people—you're exhausting every avenue, every goddamn resource at your fingertips, hoping to find an answer to his whereabouts. Why the sudden change of heart? It's not like you. And if you think this will get you back into my good graces, that you and I will *ever* get back together, then your feelings have mislead you."

He remained silent, attempting to look past her social discrepancy. Failing. He could feel the subtle twitch of his right eyelid begin its nervous spasm as her voice continued to echo with anger. What could he tell her? The truth? The unbelievable truth, a truth he had kept hidden for decades, behind his lifelong disdain toward Subject No. 2990, was a history he felt her mind would not believe; seen as nothing more than a tall-tale to lead her astray from the *actual reason* behind his hatred—which she assumed was simple and baseless. A petty bout of unwarranted emotions toward an inanimate being who had done nothing (could do nothing) to have wronged him.

Pierce's feelings toward Subject No. 2990 (Thomas Dolin) were personal. Thomas Dolin was, had always been, a constant reminder of his father's one-time indiscretion with his assistant, Camille Dolin (a gentle woman who would, a few years later, marry the insufferable Norman Dixon and give birth to Elizabeth's assistant, Mason). It would be her first born son, born catatonic, who would become known to the neuro-technicians throughout the years as Subject No. 2990.

"And yet here I am, again, having taken the elevator twelve floors up here, airing my grievances without objection, and you're just going to remain silent."

"Elizabeth—"

"Or, as you occasionally do, you will attempt to dig yourself out of a decent sized hole by giving me a poorly fabricated lie or excuse to explain yourself."

"He's my brother."

"I honestly don't know why I contin—Wait. Who is your brother?"

"The only reason you and I seem to keep in contact. *Him*."

"Pierce, you know I hate it when you attempt to be cryptic with me."

"Thomas."

"Yes, what about him?"

"He's my half-brother."

The truth was finally out. He despised Subject No. 2990 because he was a biological stain on his father's legacy; a momentary lapse in judgment, giving in to one's carnal desires. A sin which sent his mother to an early grave from the heartache of discovering her husband's infidelity.

Thomas Dolin was a stain he grew up wanting to erase without anyone but Theodore knowing the ugly truth—wiping the slate clean of its lifelong contamination.

14

THE OCCUPANTS OF the old bookstore in Huntington Park (known these days as Shrapnel) were a queer cast of characters. Atypical in every sense. The odd amalgam of their personalities would've been a hotbed for conflict had they met in any other situation. Misfits, every single one of them. And out of the entire group, Tom found Theodore and Nathan the most tolerable. But that didn't deter the others from attempting to connect with the newest addition to their makeshift family.

Atom was the most curious of the bunch, wanting to know what it was like to live a life where the world was functional—witnessing the beauty he only got to read in books, to hear the sound of prewar birds chirping as they traveled through the sky. And what it felt like to wake up and realize it was all a *fictitious landscape*; a dream.

He answered his questions without protest, allowing a young, optimistic Atom to catch a vicarious glimpse of what the world used to be like—before mankind unleashed the fury of the heavens upon it.

"It all sounds too good to be true."

"And it was, apparently," Tom said.

"Sorry."

"Don't be."

"You're probably still digesting the ugly truth," Atom frowned. "That the world hasn't seen such beauty in centuries."

A silence grew between them as Tom glanced out the window of the bookstore. The view he saw wasn't as horrific as his dreams had painted the world. In a bizarre way it reminded him of the scene outside the picture window of his childhood home, the gentle rustle of the wind creating a silent dance among the trees and patches of green in the distance. All that was missing from completing the nostalgia trip were the disjointed voices of news correspondents playing in the background from the television screen while his father slept in his recliner—snoring a rolling thunder storm as he dreamed of memories long since past.

"It must be hard," Atom said. "Telling yourself to let go of something that felt so real."

Tom looked at him, taking in the statement, his mind still focused on repainting the scene from his childhood. He could remember the vague smell of peanut butter cookies baking in the oven, his mother singing along to Pat Benatar's "Hell Is For Children" into a wooden spoon while the unpleasant cadence of Rush Limbaugh's voice carried from the living room, through the rest of the house.

"Would probably drive me mad, honestly," Atom continued. "To have to re-educate my brain to accept the truth that everything, *everything*, I knew was false; a world of fiction. It must feel like you've woken up from a dream, the life you knew simplified to the point of nausea—like reading your life's story from the dusty pages of a novel left unfinished; ending mid-sentence at the moment you woke up to find yourself here, an ugly reality when compared to what you had from before."

He was tired of the pity. Yes, he had come to to find himself in a grim world where society had lost itself to nuclear annihilation. But that didn't mean he wanted everyone who knew his *tragic backstory* to feel sadness for him. He wanted to deal with it on his own terms; without the constant reassurance that everything was going to be okay once he got used to his new surroundings.

After three weeks of physical therapy with Theodore (his tactics bordering on psychotic, forcing him to pick himself up and begin again with little to no time to rest in between each attempt), Tom's body managed to allow itself to be functional enough to get up and walk around—to leave his limited, four-walled prison and breathe in air which didn't hold the trapped essence of six other people.

"Look who finally dragged himself out of bed," the old man's voice could be heard acknowledging Tom's presence to the rest of the group.

The glimmer of the noonday sun blinded Tom. Seconds passed before he attempted to open them again, only to be met with the same discomfort he had felt the moment he stepped outside. Remember Tom, you've technically never been outside in the sun before; the first time your eyes are constricting to a change in lighting. It's going to take some time before your eyes adapt to this extent of sunlight.

"You'll get used to sun, kid. It's going to hurt like a bitch for the first few days, but it gets less annoying over time, I promise."

"It'll be just another day in paradise," Eldritch said with derision.

"I'm certain you still have questions, questions T. probably refused to answer thinking you couldn't handle the load of information."

"Could anyone tell me where I am—or, to be more accurate, when I am, exactly? Theodore, or T., or whatever you guys call him, kept giving me the answer 375 T.E. I was wondering if any of you could give me an approximation in Common Era years."

"Don't even think of it, old-timer. I don't know if I can handle another session of listening to your bullshit."

"Having—"

"Old man, I'm warning you."

"You couldn't hurt me if you tried, Eldritch," the old man called his bluff. "An inability to feel the neurological response of pain comes with the territory of being the walking dead, son."

"Don't tempt him, Nat. Asshole's just peeved he's had to share what little space we have with someone else," Peregrine attempted to diffuse the situation.

"Could someone please answer the question?"

Tom managed a squint, the four silhouettes of Nat, Eldritch, Peregrine, and Kilgore (he assumed, given the silence) staring him down—his question going unanswered. He waited a moment longer, hoping someone would break the silence.

"Anyone?"

When it finally came out he didn't want to believe the answer. It sent him reeling to think it was possible he found himself living in the 24th century; the face of Los Angeles reduced to a lifeless echo of what he remembered it looking like in his other life. Eldritch would argue the validity of Nat's estimation, claiming he couldn't know the exact number, considering his age. There was no way he could be over the age of seventy-five, he would debate the old man's words.

"Kid, I'm going to be four hundred this fall, don't—"

"You'd be dead if you were that old!"

"—think my age won't keep me from coming over there and clocking you upside the head. And it's called overexposure to atomic radiation. Shit does some pretty weird shit to you, should you find yourself immune to the violent and agonizing death which usually comes with the situation."

"But here you go, spewing the tall-tale that you were there the night it all happened; that the world ended on—"

"January 25, 1995," Tom interjected, the words finding themselves sharing the same airspace as Eldritch's fell from his own tongue.

"How—how did you know I was going to say that?"

"Honestly, if I told you the truth it would probably sound like a horrible, thinly veiled piece of exposition coming straight out of a trashy, poorly written science fiction novel."

Nat let out a short chuckle. "You and me both, kid."

The sound of another person's laughter arrived. Its gruff origins could be heard approaching from behind him in the distance. "It's good to hear you have a sense of humor about all of this, Thomas. Cordelia sure as hell didn't."

Theodore Webb stared at the man who, until recently, had gone by designation Subject No. 2990. He could still remember the day his father introduced him to Tom's file; the dark secrets its pages held; the decades he kept such a secret from his childhood friend, not knowing he had figured it out while they were still in school—the truth of Pierce's pain releasing itself out into the æther during a long night of wine and benzodiazepines. The ex-Director couldn't help but see Pierce's father, Isaac, in Tom's features. Had it been *his own father* who had had a love child born out of an affair with his assistant and the child grew up to be a genetic twin of his old man (a constant reminder of his father's indiscretion), he would probably hate him as well.

But the sins of the father shouldn't weigh down on the shoulders of a son who was never given the chance to refuse the embarrassment of being born under such scarlet shame.

Tom's eyes were still closed shut, still finding themselves unable to adjust to natural sunlight. He had so many questions. And if Nat(than)'s claim was the truth, the world having ended 380 years ago, he did the math in his head during his moment of blindness and concluded he found himself trapped in the year 2375; three and a half centuries away from the life he knew—*and it never existed in the first place.*

• • •

THE AGONIZING SCREAMS of childbirth echoed across the room, waking Dolores from a rather pleasant dream. Jordyn's contractions were getting worse. She cried for the pain to stop. They were relentless, the pain being unlike anything else she had felt. She wanted the abomination inside of her out. A year of her life had been stolen from her; nine of those months spent pregnant with the child of a monster—a delusional monster who murdered her mother, taking them in as his own in his own twisted way; and all in the name of a God he claimed had chosen him to carry out Their grotesque design for what was left of humanity.

"It's almost time, little one; time to welcome the first of my progeny into this world."

She dreamed she was somewhere else. Not here but not home either. In the dream she could fly, up into the atmosphere and view the world from the heavens old man Phoenix talked about so much. It was humbling, to see the world as it truly was and not from the limited perspective of humanity. Quiet. Peaceful. The act of distancing one's self from the harsh realities of her current situation on planet Earth had calmed her mind. It allowed her a moment to breathe without thinking today could be her last day, should Phoenix find himself unable to procure a meal for dinner.

"Keep pushing, darlin', he's almost out."

The silence of the earth found itself almost haunting after a while, the inability to interact with another human being creating a loneliness Dolores had yet to experience for herself. Down below, hidden behind the salt eroded walls of a lighthouse, she could still hear the cries of her sister as she continued to push a baby into the world.

"That's it, just a few more pushes and it'll all be over with."

"Gah, I just want this fucking thing out of me! I want it to be over!"

The old man loomed over her sister as she continued to cry in pain, a look of anticipation and premature satisfaction wearing itself well on his wrinkled face. A miracle of life was about to take place in front of his eyes—one the world didn't ask for, but was getting nonetheless.

"Here he comes!" Phoenix said, ecstatic, as the child fell into his arms. "My immortality."

There was a moment of nothing, not even the sound of the ocean's waves crashing along the shoreline. A moment of serenity in a world shaped by chaos; it was peaceful.

And then came the incessant cries of innocence—the cries of a newborn child. The scene, had it been anything other than an old man taking his newborn child in his arms as it left the womb of its thirteen year old mother, would've been beautiful—worthy of remembrance years after.

"No, no, no," the old man's voice could be heard among the child's cries. "This is all wrong. You're supposed to be a boy."

Jordyn's face went from being consumed by immense relief from hours worth of pain to one of absolute admiration. "I had a baby girl?" her voice was soft and timid, the fact of it being a child born of sexual perversion having washed away from her thoughts.

"You were supposed to give me a son, you stupid cunt," the old man yelled; the baby's screams intensifying due to her father's dissatisfaction with her gender. "What the fuck would allow you to think it would be okay for you to give me a goddamn daughter!"

It's not like she had a choice, asshole! Dolores thought, too afraid to actually speak her mind while Phoenix found himself in an outrage.

The baby looked malnourished in his arms, her twig-like arms and legs flailing about, grasping for the unknown with an untamed fever. Jordyn remained awestruck by the visage of her daughter's infantile face as it continued to weep for the warmth and comfort of her mother's breast.

"I mean honestly, what the hell am I supposed to do with this?" Phoenix shouted as he threw the still crying infant into the wall closest to him.

The weeping stopped shortly after, followed by another bout of silence—an unrecoverable silence. Dolores stared in discomposed horror as the baby's arms continued to twitch for a moment before going still indefinitely; its small, delicate head crushed in from the sudden impact against cold concrete. Violent cries of torment escaped Jordyn's lungs—eventually choking on her panic-stricken voice, any resemblance of sound finding itself trapped in her throat—but nothing could remove her eyes from the tiny dead corpse of her niece.

"*Oh my god, what did you just do?*" Dolores, a hysterical mess, asked the old man; her voice fraught with mixed emotions. She fought to get up from the floor, to attack the sociopath whose instinctual response was to throw an unknowing child (his own child, at that) headfirst to its death because he found its sexual organs unsatisfactory, but the chains which held her steadfast to the floor refused to grant her any slack.

A smell had permeated the small atmosphere of the room. It was the rancid smell of copper. Pushing away the silence of the basement, Dolores' eyes scanned the entirety of her surroundings, hoping to find the origin of the metallic odor which had dominated her sensitive olfactory glands.

Her thoughts froze at first glance. Trailing from the child's umbilical cord, across the dimly lit floor, lying inches away from a faint Jordyn lay minced remains of what looked like uncooked pork roast which had been butchered; unappetizing and unsalvageable for human consumption. Trying hard to remember what she had learned during early childhood development with Mrs. Hodiak she concluded what lay in pieces had to be the placenta, followed by a growing puddle of blood and expelled embryonic fluids. Moving her gaze Dolores analyzed her sister's unmoving frame. Only the subtle expansion of her chest cavity

—letting in slow, labored breaths—let her know her sister was still alive; barely holding on, but still alive.

"We've gone and made a mess of ourselves, haven't we?" Phoenix knelt down beside Jordyn, twirling his fingers in the puddle of crimson red and translucence. "Pity. I was rather fond of your snatch."

And in one swift motion, Phoenix Lancaster placed his weathered hands on both sides of Jordyn's head and shifted it ninety degrees to the right, the sound of bones and cartilage cracking from the momentum.

Dolores couldn't breathe. In a short matter of minutes she had witnessed her sister's newborn child get tossed across the room, into the cold, gray concrete of the lighthouse wall, trailed the mess of afterbirth back to its maternal origins, and watched as the father of the child knelt down beside its dying mother (hemorrhaging from the abrupt abuse her uterus had been put through, having had the placenta ripped out of her prematurely during the commotion) so he could snap her neck—eliminating the final trace of his disappointment. Even if words could escape her, nothing could voice what she was feeling internally.

"Don't worry, lovely," the old man turned his attention over to her. "In a few more months it'll be your turn to experience such a beautiful event. Hopefully you display *better results*. I'd hate to lose two lovelies in the span of a year."

Going silent, unable to think of anything else to say, Phoenix picked himself and his recently departed lovely up off the floor and carried themselves toward the stairs. But before beginning the slow climb, he kicked the pint-sized corpse of his daughter in Dolores' direction. "Eat up," he said. "Dinner won't be for another couple of hours, and I figure you must be hungry."

Wanting to find an escape from the current scene which surrounded her, the abused remains of what would've been her niece staring up at her, Dolores' thoughts returned to the sun scorched heavens —watching the earth continue to spin in complete silence as death washed itself over her life once more, claiming another piece of her already diminished soul. First her mother in the town of San Pedro and now her thirteen year old sister.

She felt completely alone in the world. All at the hands of a man claiming to be an apostle of God; continuing His work in the glory of His name.

If where her mind found itself was truly heaven then she would have some disappointing news for the old man: there was no God—only the view of a quiet Earth among a static backdrop of stars and distant planets; continuing along their predestined orbital paths around a dying sun.

Hours passed without her knowing, having fallen asleep while soaring through a rather pleasant daydream. It wasn't until the door leading upstairs creaked open that her attention was brought hurtling back to reality. The room still smelled of afterbirth and aged copper, the infant's purple corpse having remained untouched—the caved in remains of its face still staring up at her. At the top of the stairs stood the silhouette of the old man, carrying a silver tray topped with another one of his *gourmet meals*.

"I hope you're hungry, darlin," he said with a smile, "because tonight you and I will be eating like the king and queen we are."

He hurried down the stairs, excited to dig into tonight's meal. When he came across the small remains of his disappointment he kicked it to the other side of the basement and sat in its place—staring Dolores dead in the eyes; smiling, waiting for her to commence tonight's feast.

But she didn't move. Instead, she drifted off to the farthest corner from where she sat, ignoring the old man, hoping to lose herself in her thoughts.

"Now, now," Phoenix nudged the platter closer toward her. "There's no need to be rude. I slaved for hours to make us this meal. I know you're hungry. You didn't even touch the small snack I left for you." His cold gaze shifted to the darkened corner where his deceased daughter lay. "Now eat up, dammit. I'm not going to take no for an answer." He picked up a charbroiled forearm and took three generous bites before offering her some.

Dolores tilted her gaze toward the slab of meat being displayed for her fancy, disinterested in partaking in its consumption. Her eyes widened, however—the item now holding her full attention—when she noticed a familiar birthmark resting on the inside of what used to be the limb's wrist; the hand having been removed and set aside for a later date. She grew up knowing that birthmark like it was her own. Horror settled into her nerves as she watched the old man rescind his offer and took a couple more bites of charred flesh from the severed body part.

15

UNBEKNOWNST TO HIMSELF, Phoenix Lancaster sealed his fate that night. After he finished feasting on the flesh of his dearly departed lovely, without speaking a word to Dolores, who had refused to take a bite throughout their meal together, Phoenix went upstairs to retire for the night; he left the devoured remains of her sister in front of her—scattered along the floor. And with his mind clouded with the satisfaction of a fulfilling meal, his sense dulled, he failed to hear the subtle clink of his keys slipping from his backside pocket.

It was a small detail Dolores caught.

She remained silent, watching him carry himself upstairs, not wanting to bring attention to her captor's oversight. *This is my chance*, she thought as she continued to eye the set of keys.

An hour passed before Dolores made her move toward the keys. She felt her heart race, her tired fingers finding a firm enough grip on the metal ring. Weakened by the exertion of energy, Dolores sat a while, hoping to regain some of her strength. The idea of freedom being within her grasp was a liberating feeling to experience; the weight of captivity lifting itself from her well-worn shoulders. She wouldn't have to share the same unfortunate fate of her sister.

The sound of her restraints releasing themselves from her wrists and ankles echoed reprieve throughout her previously constrained joints. It was a feeling she had all but forgotten this past year. A sharp kick to her stomach brought her back to the ugly circumstance of her condition. "Don't worry, little one," she whispered, hoping to soothe the unborn child resting inside her. "We're getting out of here."

Surrounded by a sea of darkness, Dolores stumbled her way across the cobblestone floor; only a small sliver of moonlight coming from the upstairs levels kept her from making an unfortunate misstep. Staring down at the floor she could manage to make out a thin outline of her legs and feet. Applying extreme caution with each step, not wanting to accidentally step on any of Jordyn's discarded bones (further desecrating her memory), she would feel the floor with a gentle caress of her big toe before planting her foot with each succeeding step.

When she finally arrived at the top of the stairs and opened the door Dolores looked down at the grim scene which had been her home for longer than she cared for. "I'll come back for you," she said to the inanimate bones of her sister. "I won't let this place be your final resting ground."

She entered the ground level, finding the door leading outside — to her freedom — wide open. It would've been easy, she thought, to walk back down, gather her sister's remains, and walk out without giving this place a second thought. But the distant, haunting echo of the old man's snores compelled her to take a different route.

Using what little light she had, attempting to make as little noise as she could, Dolores searched the room for something sharp; something the old man used while he would prepare his meals. On the surface level there appeared to be nothing of use to her. It wasn't until she opened one of the drawers of an aged mantle-piece that she found something she could use — an old, rusty set of lopping shears; the wooden handles splintering throughout.

The old man's snores led her upstairs two more levels. Shears now in hand, she took each step with determination. As she made her way to his room the snores grew obnoxious; reminding her of the countless nights when Director Pierce Needham would find himself passed out on the couch of their complex—sleep-talking himself into an agitated state.

He appeared to be dreaming, a smug smile wearing itself proudly on his face. We'll see how long that smile lasts when I'm done with you, Dolores thought as she opened the shears, prepping them for the deed she had climbed two flights of stairs to accomplish.

The blades hovered over Phoenix's neck, shaking—her nerves beginning to feel the preemptive weight of ending someone's life. Why couldn't she bring herself to go through with it? The old man had killed a lot of people. A *lot of people*. But staring down at him, watching him sleep, any traces of his villainous personality had been replaced by a child-like innocence. She knew the truth, however—that behind that look of naivete lie the makings of a monster; a monster who kills and eats people.

He had to be put down.

Closing the shears she steadied herself, gaining back her composure. With her renewed sense of purpose, Dolores lifted the cutting tool—still closed—above her head. She froze in that position when she saw the old man's eyes open. His smile widened, still in a euphoric state, he assumed he was still dreaming.

"Lovely, is that yo—"

On reflex, Dolores lowered her arms in one swift motion. The dull tips of the closed blades pierced his flesh in a violent manner. Blood fell all around the old man, a few quick sputters escaping his mouth; his central nervous system going into shock from the sudden surge of pain. And before he could attempt to utter another word through his blood-soaked teeth, Dolores pried the shears' blades open; only unintelligible sounds escaped his dying tongue.

Exhausted from the deed, Dolores made her way back downstairs. A new weight had entered her mind. Despite it being the heinous being known as Phoenix Lancaster, the reality of killing someone had stolen something from her; a piece of her she knew she would never see again.

Pushing the thought aside, refusing to let the old man continue to have a grip on her—even in death—she searched for something big enough to help her carry her sister's bones with her.

She came across a decent sized army green rucksack. "Here we go," she mumbled, picking it up. Heading downstairs to collect her sister's remains Dolores found herself met with a wave of relief. This place would soon be a distant memory which she would hopefully soon forget. "Come, Jordyn," she said to the gnawed-on bones as she placed them in the canvas sack. "We're getting out of here."

As Dolores stepped out into the crisp night air, with her sister slung across her shoulder, all she could see was the dark blue Pacific staring back at her; the moon's patient glow reflecting from its dead calm surface. She didn't know which way to go; no discernible landmark to direct her. The fetal growth residing in her belly kicked laboriously, attempting to find any form of comfort for the night's rest. With the adrenaline thinning in her bloodstream, it struck her that she was still pregnant. I'm not going to get far, she realized—her physical limitations putting a damper in her escape plan.

I guess I'll wait until daybreak before heading off, she thought, turning back to head inside the lighthouse one last time.

· · ·

TRAVELING ALONG THE PACIFIC coastline comforted Theodore as he traveled north toward the town of Shrapnel. Its reclusive nature held no weight on him as it paced back and forth, collapsing in on itself with each stumbling wave. He had grown tired of roaming the vast Southern California desert in search of drifter campsites, waiting until the final moments of a dwindling afterglow signaled him to begin his violent ambush. But through it all, the only constant which remained in his life was the continual ebb and flow of the Pacific—never faltering, always crashing and recollecting itself for another failed approach; wishing to soothe him, bury his recent tragedies with the false pretense of a calming surf; pulling him under with the rolling tide, relieving him of his suffering while still appearing gentle on the surface.

He felt he and the ocean had that in common—unsuspecting on the surface, but violent intent rumbled underneath such a shallow facade.

A tortured sigh left Theodore's lungs when he saw a familiar sight peek its head over the northern horizon. The forlorn remnants of San Pedro greeted him with a jagged smile. Months had passed since his last visit, but the memory of coming upon Gwenivere's lifeless shell still haunted him.

He turned his attention eastward, attempting to calculate a possible detour, hoping to avoid the pained reunion altogether. But the evening sun behind him was showing signs of waning, the faint sliver of a crescent moon taking its place as ruler of the sky. He knew he'd have to find shelter soon, before the nightmares of the earth's darkened landscape took temporary claim over its twilit terrain.

West of the ghostly remains of San Pedro stood a lighthouse, separated from the rest of the town. The monument's lonesome personality reminded him of a story he read as a child. A solitary island fortress, surrounded by the unforgiving waters of the Atlantic, which housed prisoners and traitors. It was an ancient tale of revenge, something he never thought he'd relate to in his lifetime.

When he arrived at the lighthouse's wooden door he banged on its petrified veneer three times, unsure if it was truly abandoned or not, allowing a breath before each set of labored knocks.

No one answered.

Still, he entered with caution. Drifters were known to take shelter if the opportunity presented itself.

The building's interior atmosphere felt clammy to the touch, a cold caress fondling his exposed skin, making him feel unwelcomed. A chilling silence lingered throughout. As he edged toward the opposite end of the lighthouse's circular structure he could hear the sound of the ocean while it played its twilight song. But between each responding rumble of the sea's percussive composition, he thought he could hear the faint sound of someone weeping. The noise appeared to be coming from underneath the wooden floorboards.

Nervous, he reached for the Glock he had kept from his last encounter and, with a firm grip, steadied it toward the cellar door as he lifted it; the stranger's faint whimpers now echoing upward through the small opening he had created.

"Is somebody down there?" he asked, the gun's nozzle pointed into the abyss. He could hear an incoherent dialogue in the distance. It sounded female. Young, given its frailty. "I don't want to alarm you, but I'm coming down."

As he stepped closer toward the delicate voice's location he could make out some of what the poor girl was saying.

"I'm sorry. I'm so sorry. I had to, baby. I needed to do it. It had to be this way."

"Is there someone else down here? Who are you talking to?"

A faint stream of amber light from the night's crescent moon pour through an upstairs window, through the opening of the cellar door, and shone upon the unknown figure.

Theodore froze when he realized who it was. Sitting before him on the cold, damp stone paved basement floor, was a traumatized Dolores.

She appeared thinner than he remembered, it having been close to several years since he saw her last. He wanted to rush toward her, take her up into his arms and tell her it was okay—her father was here. Nothing could hurt her. Except the sliver of moonlight had shown him more than just her worn down physique.

The skirt of her dress was stained crimson. He couldn't tell if the blood was her own or if it had belonged to someone else. Next to her, an army green knapsack rested. When she finally noticed him standing there she instinctively pulled it closer, protecting its mysterious contents from leaving her possession.

"Please don't take her away from me. She's all I have left." she cried.

The entire scene was a confusing mess. He didn't blame her for not recognizing her own father, his own appearance being a far cry from what her last memory of him would recall. But she hadn't made (could not make) the connection to the cadence of his voice. It was a voice she had heard since she was a baby, but he still remained a stranger to her.

She saw the Glock in his hands, pointed down toward the floor.

"Have you come to kill me?"

"Dolores," he said, edging closer. "It's me. It's your father."

"Da—daddy?"

"It's me, pumpkin. Everything's going to be fine."

Dolores stumbled to her feet and rushed into her father's arms and broke down crying. With his daughter in his arms, the stench of aged copper ravaged Theodore's nose. He pulled her away to get a better look at his eldest child and saw the same, blood-red hue smeared across her lips.

"How long have you been down here? Where's your sister?"

"I—I. . . I'm so sorry."

"Dolores." Worry had found its way to his throat. "Where's Jordyn?"

"He—he killed her. He killed her baby. He—he—he took her upstairs and he—he. . ." Her frightened gaze traveled down to the green knapsack.

Theodore stared down at the knapsack as well. Still holding Dolores close, he moved them both toward the bag. He wanted to know why his daughter referred to the cloth sack as *Her*. Why she looked down at it with a look of horror, cutting her words short before she could finish telling him her sister's fate. But part of him already knew the truth. If he opened the knapsack he would find the remains of his little girl.

Beyond the lump of army green, Theodore saw the makings of a silhouette lying on the floor. There were pieces missing, chunks of flesh gnawed away in a random fashion up and down his ancient corpse.

He noticed the man's head was missing.

"I'm so sorry," Dolores repeated. "So, so sorry."

"It's okay, baby girl," he said, pushing her away so he could look her in her eyes—eyes which reminded him of his Gwenivere. "Nothing can hurt you anymore."

"I—I can't. It had to be done. I had to eat him. He was so young. I can still hear him crying."

He didn't know what to do. She had become hysterical. Nothing he said calmed her down. She just kept saying how sorry she was.

"All he wanted was for his mother to feed him, to show him love; that there was still beauty in this ugly world. But I'm no better than his father—"

Amid Dolores' disjointed cries, among the grim scene which displayed itself in alarming fashion, he hadn't noticed his daughter's left hand creeping down his right arm. And in one swift motion, she clutched his hand, which was still gripping the stolen Glock, forced it against the base where her neck met her lower jaw, and violently pulled the trigger.

It was over before he knew how to react.

16

WHEN HIS EYES FINALLY PRIED themselves open he was met by the silhouette of a looming tower in the distance, the noonday sun shining brightly overhead. It still stung like hell, as Nathan had promised, but Tom managed to push past the initial pain and gain back his sense of sight. Upon his first fully realized view of the city, a wave of dismay echoed throughout Tom's body. The city of Los Angeles, a city he would often visit in his younger years of writing, wasting away the long months leading up to *Discord Avenue's* publication date—drinking until the early hours of the morning with his literary agent—barely resembled itself; the City of Angels reduced to a ghost town, his memories filling in the blanks. While a lot of the city's infrastructure remained standing, the weight of time had run what was left into disrepair. Where buildings which once functioned as shelter to people and businesses alike, only their skeletal framework remained.

The clearing of someone's throat reverted Tom's focus from the distant horizon and back to his nearby surroundings. He found himself met by the entire cast of Shrapnel staring him down, each with their own blend of curiosity.

The young redhead who had aroused him out of unconsciousness smiled, an eastbound wind blowing strands of her wavy locks across her olive-toned skin. While he found the young girl attractive in this new light he still quivered at the gesture, remembering the fluidity of her motions when she attempted to steal a raw sexual encounter from him in his anesthetized state.

"Not as tall as I would've figured, but still cute." She winked, pulling her hair back and curving it behind her ear.

Averting his gaze from Peregrine's subtle advances, Tom's attention turned to the one known as Wendigo—who, along with Atom, had joined the small gathering outside. Taller than everyone else, Wendigo appeared the most threatening, but the glaze around his eyes proved otherwise; he was a harmless half-wit—a puppy stuck in the body of a giant; a terrifying concept to consider since the man was prone to indulge in cannibalistic tendencies. Unsure if his ears were functioning correctly during his dormant state, but if his auditory nerves hadn't betrayed him (and memory served him right), Tom thought he recalled Wendigo making the suggestion to the others they consider him for a meal, were he to never arise from his quiescent condition. Funny, he thought, that the man's name happened to be Wendigo. He wondered if anyone else among the small social circle he found himself a part of was aware of the irony.

"Lay off of him, Peri," laughed Eldritch. "I'm certain he's had enough of your *warm personality*."

Peregrine curled her lip at Eldritch's comment, spitting an insult in his direction; the two of them going back and forth for another round of verbal vilification—a nervous Atom attempting to break it up before getting out of hand. A starving Wendigo continued to stare at Tom with curious eyes, not saying a word—subtly licking his lips, his eyes moving up and down as he examined him; making Tom feel more uncomfortable by the second.

"You look just like your old man," Theodore's voice broke among the clamor. He laughed, "Pierce would kill me if he heard me say that."

"Pierce?" a confused Tom asked.

"Your asshole of a brother. Well, half-brother, really—his and your father wasn't the most honorable man when it came to the concept of fidelity. He had a fling with his assistant, your mother, while married to his wife of fourteen years at the time. Tragic, what ended up happening to both of them. Your mother would've cried tears of joy if she could see you up and walking. We all thought you, like so many Subjects before you, were a lost cause."

The names flooded his memory banks. They were names which had become a mainstay throughout the years, one by one.

*"That's quite the kid you got there, Isaac. Shame he's got to live his life this way. His vitals are strong though, which is a good thing. Most Subjects' numbers don't even read half of his on a **good day**."*

". . ."

"What's bothering you, old friend?"

"It's such a surreal experience. I've watched over countless Subjects before him, but when it's your own flesh and blood it. . .it makes coming down here every day a chore. It hurts to see him. He may seem at peace, relaxed, but—"

*"We'll figure it out, Isaac. We've had our ups and downs, sure, but we **will** figure it out. It's just going to take time."*

"Time I'm afraid we don't have, Raymond."

He could remember hearing the man who Theodore claimed was his father's voice as a child, taking the conversation as the first of what would be a lifelong stream of vivid dreams—dreams which would help inspire the setting of his greatest work as an author. A short laugh escaped Tom's lungs. To think, what he originally presumed to be blips of creativity brought on by a recurring dream were actually tiny fragments of reality slipping through the veil of his simulated reality. It saddened him, to have never met the man whose voice had haunted his ears for decades—having spent as much time as he had looking over him. He couldn't imagine what it must've felt like, to spend days and nights watching over a child, your child (your own flesh and blood), waste away, year by year, behind a layer of glass—

His mind jumped to more recent names, names like Pierce and Elizabeth. In recent years it had been their voices (along with Theodore's and a few others) which drowned his ears with aimless conversation. He could recall hearing, feeling, the sincere concern in Elizabeth's voice whenever she was near—defending him and the other Subjects from Pierce's tone of negativity and prejudice.

"*Elizabeth. . .why must you **continue** to land on the other side of this petty argument? You and I both know, in the end, I'll have the final say whether or not this **petty experiment** remains a part of the hospital's way of life. Now, please, come to reason and let this damned pipe-dream die.*"

"*A 'pipe-dream' your father—and grandfather—refused to let fall by the wayside. Do you really hate them **that much**; to let countless, innocent lives go to waste just to spite them—their memory?*"

He had to admire Elizabeth for her inability to be swayed like other voices he had heard throughout recent years—Pierce's cynicism infecting their confidence in the Project, causing them to doubt the nature of their work.

"*Why must you always use 'the fear of failure' as a means to persuade those who wish to go against **your** agenda? It's pathetic. You look at these people and—*"

"*Don't call them people, Elizabeth. That kind of term gives them a sense of credibility where they have none.*"

Tom also remembered the poison he felt coursing through his veins when he would wake up from his dreams, hating Pierce—wanting his voice silenced from his memory. At first he couldn't understand his brother's disdain for him. But it all made sense when everything was put into the correct context. Their father had spent all his waking hours trying to find a solution to Tom's condition, hoping to wake his catatonic son from what he assumed to be a cerebral nightmare; a young, growing Pierce left unattended to, dying for his father's attention—a silent hatred for the motionless child Subject growing in his heart.

A mnemonic shard of warmth enveloped the tops of Tom's fingers, soothing him, washing away the toxic emotions he had been feeling moments earlier. *Elizabeth?* his mind echoed her name. *Was that you all along?* The warm aesthetic, a welcomed sensation, which still lingered across the back of his hand, reminded him of Sarah—waking up to find her caressing the tops of his knuckles, a well-versed exploration which she would often do to express her admiration for the weight of innocence Tom's unconscious self expelled with each relaxed breath.

"But now that you're finally awake, Thomas," Theodore's voice shook Tom from his thoughts, bringing him back to the present. "You and I should talk. I'm certain you have your own questions to ask, as I have mine."

"We've all got questions for the boy, T.," Nat interjected. He turned his head to the rest of the group, only Atom nodding his head in concurrence with the old man.

"And I'm sure they'll get answered eventually, but right now Tom and I, having both come from the hospital up north, have more *private* matters to attend to. Tom, follow me."

Wrapping his arm around Tom's shoulder, Theodore led him away from the claustrophobic social circle which had gathered outside the bookstore, heading northbound through the shopping center—toward the building they both used to call home. Theodore was curious, wanting to know what thoughts were traveling around in Thomas' head upon seeing the world as it was and not how the *Arcadian Sequence* had mapped it out for him.

His curiosity of Arcadia, much like another technician of the hospital, had reached a critical point; considering medically inducing themselves into a coma and witnessing the Sequence firsthand. But such a risk was not allowed, not after the tragic death of a fellow technician decades before them—having become obsessed with the simulation which was the *Arcadian Sequence*; finding the real world plain and bleak by comparison. It was all he saw every time he closed his eyes—a perfect world where the bombs never dropped. He eventually couldn't take it anymore, waking up from his dreams to find himself still trapped inside the truth—that his world was still one where society found itself slowly withering away as time continued. One night, while everyone was either asleep or on night-watch, he snuck into the hospital's armory, took a firearm from the gun safe, climbed up to the building's roof, placed the barrel of the weapon into his mouth as he stared off into the dark blue horizon—the dead cityscape filled skyline mocking him one last time—and gently pulled the trigger.

"How're you adjusting to everything?"

"Aside from the local Starbucks being closed indefinitely and the absence of a lunchtime traffic jam, it's not that different."

Theodore stopped, halting Tom mid-step. "Seriously?"

"I mean, we are in Los Angeles after all. The only place worse than here would be most of Shasta County, up north from here. Now had we been in Santa Ana or Bakersfield? sure, I'd require an adjustment period, but—"

The dry crackle of Theodore's laughter interrupted Tom's depreciative remarks. He appreciated his instinct to immediately respond to a serious question with sarcasm—wit, it was something the other Subject, Cordelia, lacked.

"Though I find it tragic you found yourself dumped out here in the Wastes, I'm glad they dropped you off at Nat's doorstep. The old man may have a sense of humor, but your caustic delivery sure is a breath of fresh air."

A silence stood between the two men, both essentially strangers to one another, as they continued their walk away from Shrapnel and toward the looming tower which was the hospital. Tom had a myriad of questions he had wanted to ask Theodore. But finding himself conscious and able to get around on his own—no longer a vegetable trapped on Eldritch's and Peregrine's bedroom floor—the words escaped him.

"How could something so artificial feel so real?" Tom whispered as he continued to take in his surroundings.

"When all you've ever known is artificial, your frame of reference knows nothing else. For you, I'm certain *all of this* feels like a dream— some twisted version of a nightmare you're dying to wake up from."

"But my wife . . . and my children," he paused, reflecting on the final coherent memory he had of them. "If they were only physical manifestations of data imprinted on my subconscious mind, then why do I find myself missing them as much as I do?"

"Only the children were digital imprints," Theodore answered casually.

"What do you mean by that—*only the children were digital imprints.*"

"That was one of the many things which was *unique* about your file," Theodore continued. "Unlike every Subject before you, you somehow managed to make a neural connection with another Subject.

I remember both our fathers spending countless hours trying to figure out how such a phenomenon could occur. But, then again, you've never been one to follow the well-established protocol." He couldn't refrain from laughing at the small bout of nostalgia their conversation was beginning to stir.

"Sarah's. . .real?" A layer of disbelief saturated Tom's voice. "She's alive?"

"Being real and being alive don't always go hand in hand."

Tom turned his head in Theodore's direction, confused. "What do you mean?"

"Does Sarah, your wife in Arcadia, exist in the real world—flesh and blood? Yes, though we all know her as Subject No. 2996. But yes, Sarah is *real*. Alive, however? *That* is a topic which is still up for debate among the best of us back at the hospital—that while her neural network may be hooked up to the Sequence, this doesn't count her as a living person; her otherwise *inanimate existence* considered less than human."

"And where do you stand on the matter?" Tom asked, still consuming everything Theodore was explaining.

"Had it not been for my interference several years back—an act which resulted in my exile—your brother would've suffocated you in your sleeping chamber. Does that answer your question?"

Tom grew silent, finding Theodore's answer satisfactory enough to drop that particular line of questioning. He examined the once honored Director of the hospital, his disheveled appearance (wild, nappy hair, overgrown, yet patchy, facial hair, and a once pristine white lab coat now a mix of faded brown and blotched carmine—were those blood stains?) showed no signs of once living a posh existence; something Eldritch couldn't refrain from bringing up whenever he would enter the room while Tom was relearning how to hold himself up well enough to walk.

"Would—would she remember me?" he asked.

"You remember her, don't you?"

"Well, yeah, but—"

"Memories don't fade away in an instant—if only that's how they worked. . ." Theodore paused for a moment, swallowing an unpleasant memory of his own. "No, only after time has passed, and the mind has had a chance to create new memories, will the old ones—in this case, her memories from Arcadia—begin to fade into nothing."

"Just like old photographs." Tom sighed.

"I'm actually surprised you still have such a firm grasp on your false memories from the Arcadian Sequence. Our other Subject, Cordelia, quit showing interest in her past life after a couple of weeks. She may have kept her thoughts to herself, of course; an oddity, she was. I'm curious. Why, after all this time disconnected from the Sequence, do you still find yourself preoccupied with your *former life*—with Sarah?"

"Because she's all I've ever known. . ."

Tom looked up at the towering building which was the hospital—the place which housed his lifeless self for close to four decades; its daunting presence stealing his breath as he continued to take in the outer layer of its mystery. Inside its concrete walls, buried in the belly of its lower levels, lay his comatose wife. He wanted to see her. He wanted to know she was okay, that the people looking over her while she slept were doing a well-enough job at keeping her mind intact. And if it were at all possible, awaken her from her dormant state so he would have someone from his old life carried over into this one; to have someone help him accept the nightmare which was reality.

But the odds weren't in her favor. Like Theodore said, he was only the *second case* of a successful awakening. And if waking her up wasn't an option, then he would want to be put back under—resequenced to the simulated life he knew so well; where he had memories to fall back onto. A place to call home and a bed to fall into and rest his tired mind at the end of the day.

I have to find a way to make it back there, he thought. Someone has to be willing to reconnect me back to Arcadia—I don't care if my life was a simulated dreamworld. I didn't ask to be waken up, to be thrust into this unrelenting reality; claimed by a world awash in monochrome.

As he continued to eye the hospital resting on the horizon, thinking of home, Tom's attention was drawn toward the top of the building. Unable to focus clearly, he witnessed what he assumed to be the faint silhouette of a person—only appearing as a dot among the concrete backdrop. He continued to watch as the small black dot of human existence took a step away from the rooftop; its faint outline falling in slow motion as it plummeted toward the sunburnt dirt; a small plume of dust arising from the earth upon impact.

• • •

IN A STRANGE WAY, it all made sense. The warped sense of loathing implicated by Pierce's actions toward Thomas all these years had been nothing more than a one-sided sibling rivalry—fighting for their father's attention. It was a jealousy which, six years ago, had led him to contemplate and attempt to snuff the life out of his own brother's unconscious lungs. Pathetic, half of her thought as she stared at the man she once shared a bed with—the other half actually feeling sorry for him, unable to understand how it must have felt to be shrouded in the shadow of someone whose entire existence was spent inactive behind a layer of glass; his life reduced to vitals and endless waves of numerical data on a computer screen.

Jesus, Elizabeth thought. *I must have a thing for the Needham bloodline.* She couldn't help but laugh at herself as the revelation of Thomas being Pierce's half-brother sank in. But why the mystery? Why would Pierce have kept this information a secret from her until now? the question arose in her mind. Was he *that ashamed* of his father's indiscretion; he couldn't tell anyone about it?

"I know this doesn't excuse my past behavior," a regretful Pierce continued. "But I know how much the Subject, along with the success of his awakening, means to you. It is because of this fact, I am trying my best to put my feelings for him aside; asking anyone who might know of his whereabouts."

Watching the mask of distance slip from Pierce's cold exterior, Elizabeth felt a small knot of pity beginning to develop in her chest. She didn't know what she could say to comfort him—let him know he wasn't a *complete ass.* But if he didn't have anything to do with Thomas' disappearance, there was no way he could help her. Even if by some off-hand drop of luck Thomas were to return, she had moved on from the soul sucking preoccupation of awakening Subjects from their eternal slumber.

"I appreciate the effort you've put forward, Pierce, but it isn't necessary. Now if you'll excuse me, I'm currently on-shift downstairs and this visit was not validated as an official break."

Leaving the same way she entered, Elizabeth stepped out into the hallway; empty, as it always seemed to be these days. It hadn't always been this way. The hospital used to be teeming with life. Growing up, she remembered the hallways (no matter which floor you happened to find yourself on) being a hub for civilization—scattered conversation bouncing off every wall until each word found their proper ear. What happened? Nowadays, everyone stayed indoors; satisfied with living in privacy—only leaving their living quarters for work or supper. People no longer found comfort in each other, but in solitude; their attention consumed by either a computer screen or the execution of a mundane task performed from sun up until sun down.

You could hear a pin drop in these sullen halls, she thought, the dull click of her feet among the ancient linoleum echoing throughout the entire floor. Sad how such a lively place could now feel so abandoned. It didn't help that numerous families had chosen to leave the asylum of the hospital's walls over the years once rumor caught wind of settlements up north which weren't as affected by the destructive winds of the past. Sad, it seemed these hallway walls would never experience such life ever again.

The succinct ding of the elevator stopping at the twelfth floor reverberated down the hallway, its dysfunctional doors sliding apart unevenly to show a solitary Winsome exiting the claustrophobic compartment. He didn't seem himself. A usually upkept individual, Winsome appeared disheveled—his face having not seen a razor for several weeks, his hair unkempt, the left hem of his shirt untucked and wrinkled. She nodded as they crossed each other's paths; the small gesture of civility going unnoticed. *I wonder what kind of complaint he's going to bother Pierce with this time*, she thought as she made her way to the still open elevator doors.

Before the elevator doors finished closing Elizabeth kept her gaze on Friedrich Winsome; even facing in the other direction, she could still tell how disorganized he was feeling. Instead of turning in at Pierce's doorway, however, Winsome kept pushing forward—toward the staircase which led to the rooftop entrance. Upon the silent hiss of the elevator doors closing, the image of Winsome disappearing from sight, the 5'8"x8'0" steel trap beginning its slow descent, Elizabeth didn't bother to give the oddity of her former colleague's trip toward the rooftop a second thought.

The back of Mason's head greeted Elizabeth when she reached the lower levels; his attention lost in the wealth of data traveling across a Subject's monitor.

"How is the Subject recovering?" she asked, startling him.

"I'm still not sure whether or not I agree with you, adding this theoretical preemptive measure to the awakening process. So far we've only seen failure after failure with it."

Elizabeth walked over to the sleeping Subject, a female this time; her seventh attempt at molding an archaic medical procedure to better suit her needs. After analyzing Raymond and Isaac's notes to the point of insanity, Elizabeth concluded the reason there were so many failed trials at attempting to bring a Subject out of their quiescent state was due to their minds having been too connected—too attached—to the Arcadian Sequence; their dependency to a life which *did not* exist. She hoped her spin on the transorbital lobotomy would prove a success. But, so far, the results of six dead Subjects lay jotted down in her journal. She prayed their sacrifice would push her in the right direction.

The Subject looked peaceful, still sedated from the surgery. For the moment, time was Elizabeth's enemy. She would have to wait until the drugs were out of the Subject's system before she could begin the first step of the awakening process. Growing impatient, she turned to Mason, only to find his face still glued to the monitor.

"May I ask why you wish to accomplish such a task—to erase a Subject's imprinted memories before awakening them? Why even bother giving them memories to begin with if you're going to force them to forget everything?"

"A simple error in judgment on our predecessors' behalf," she replied. "One which I intend to fix via this *new* course of action."

"Making them a clean slate, essentially."

"An eloquent way to—"

Something above them hit the ground, hard enough to send a shock-wave through several layers of dirt—reverberating the fortified ceiling to the lower levels; a suffocated thud echoing from its point of origin.

"—put it, Dixon. What the hell was that?"

"Probably just a small group of kids dropping pieces of garbage off the rooftop; any way to help pass the time once class is out. You remember what it was like when we were kids."

Elizabeth's attention returned to the Subject, choosing to ignore the mysterious thump from above. It was time. Without speaking, she motioned for Mason to begin the awakening process. Hesitant, his fingers hovered over the Ctrl, Alt, and f3 keys. Elizabeth could tell he was still unsure with her new methods of operation—six dead Subjects weighing down on his still young conscience.

The lights flickered and dimmed, electricity draining its focus from other parts of the floor to direct itself to the task Mason initiated upon Elizabeth's silent request. An anxious sweat began to bead at the top of Mason's brow, unsure if he could handle the possibility of another failure painting its ugly mark upon this seventh attempt. His monitor went blank. Despite this being the seventh time through this procedure, the thought of not knowing the results until the end sent him into an undeserved panic.

Having nothing to do until the end, Mason turned his attention to Elizabeth, watching her tend to the Subject—making small adjustments here and there whenever needed. It was a marvel watching her work. A small part of him wondered if his mother had ever had the pleasure of watching Isaac Needham execute the same process; if she felt the same sensation of one's heart skipping a beat in anticipation to whether or not success would find its way to the surface.

"Quit staring," Elizabeth snapped, still focusing on the Subject. "If you're curious, Dixon, don't remain so aloof. Come up and get a better look for yourself."

"My being up there won't disrupt your focus?" he asked.

"Should I rescind my offer—help you make up your mind?"

Despite the feeling of apprehension in his stomach telling him not to appear at his superior's side while she worked, curiosity won Mason's mind over. Not wanting to leave the comfort of his chair, however, he wheeled himself over to the operating table. The Subject still looked peaceful upon first glance; her expressionless features in an unbreakable state of ataraxia he had never witnessed on a non-Subject's face. It reminded him of his mother on the day of her funeral, before the hospital's mortician drove her inanimate body into the crematorium's flames to be reduced to ashes.

Peering over Elizabeth's shoulder, Mason read what notes she had managed to jot down while she waited for the final results of today's trial:

16 August 375 T.E. — Subject No. 2996 – *Sarah Baker: My latest specimen, Subject No. 2996, so far has shown zero signs of flat-lining. A promising start, I must say—perhaps due to her connection to Subject No. 2990? If her awakening proves successful we can only hope the lobotomy works as well as I've hypothesized; that she'll remember* **nothing** *from her time synced to the Arcadian Sequence. While it'll pain me to wash away Sarah's memories of her life with another Subject, I'm running out of opt—*

A full body tremor took hold of the Subject, possessing her, forcing her unconscious self to convulse. Not again, Mason thought. I can *not* take another fatality—to watch another human life unknowingly rob itself of any potential it had of experiencing sentience. Panic stricken, refusing to sit and watch the poor woman die, Mason pushed away from the operating table, sailing toward his computer monitor—the screen still blank—to unplug everything; hoping to derail the entire process before the Subject's vitals hit critical.

"Don't you dare touch a damn thing!" Elizabeth's voice beckoned.

Mason turned in his chair, obeying his superior's direct order. He watched as she worked effortlessly to stabilize the Subject's vitals. A natural, he thought as he witnessed her application of Midazolam via an injection along the outer muscle tissue of Subject No. 2996's left bicep; its effects taking affect two minutes later.

"There we go," she said, placing the used needle in its proper casing. "Just a mild seizure to help push us forward to the end." She turned and smiled at a still anxious Mason; his face agleam from a thin layer of panic-induced sweat.

He didn't know what to think. Was this a success? It couldn't be. He had witnessed success before, while short-lived, with Thomas. In this moment, the Subject still lie motionless on the operating table. A failure, perhaps? Only a failure which had yet to claim its tragic victory as it had before—the relentless droning of her vitals flat-lining. He had hoped this time would be differ—

A small, sudden tilt of the Subject's head startled both him and Elizabeth. After that, nothing; a delayed reaction of the Subject's neck muscles loosening after her brief seizure. Her vitals still read green. It seemed death, for the moment, would not claim victory on this Subject today.

Between the quick, arhythmic bursts of illumination coming from the still flickering lights Mason swore he witnessed the Subject's eyes open to a subtle squint. He felt his body jump an inch in his chair when her left hand rose to meet her face, attempting to rub the cloud of nausea from her brain.

"Wh—where am I?" the Subject asked. A typical question to ask Mason thought; anyone would want to know their whereabouts upon waking from a lifelong dream. The confusion must be overwhelming. One minute you're living a well-established life, the next you're lying on a cold operating table—not a memory to fall back on; lost in every sense of the word. "Where am I?" she repeated, having gone unanswered.

"Do you know who you are?" Elizabeth asked.

"What kind of question is that?"

"Protocol. When a patient has been catatonic for a long period of time amnesia is a possibility. So it's mandatory to ask. Now, I'll ask again. *Do you know who you are?*"

She did not.

Minutes passed, attempting in vain to remember something from her life before this moment, but nothing came. An obnoxious weight of shame buried itself in the pit of her stomach, the two strangers continuing to stare at her. She did not want to admit it, but the words stumbled from her lips—acknowledging defeat.

After hearing the success of her work on Subject No. 2996's brain, wiping her of the memories of her Arcadian life, Elizabeth reached for another syringe—this one a tranquilizer—and inserted the fresh needle into her patient's bicep; letting the medication lull her back into her original unconscious state.

"What are you doing?" a confused Mason asked. "You wake her up, only to put her back under?"

"Phase One has proven itself a success," she said, pulling the needle out and discarding it. "We shall now move to Phase Two of this Project. Once your computer is up and running again find me Subject No. 2773's digital memory file. And be sure to highlight her years spent in military—focus on her combat training. It'll prove itself useful for what I have in-store for the future."

• • •

WINSOME'S EYES OPENED TO FIND himself still living in the guilt-ridden nightmare which had become his life. He closed his eyes and grunted. It didn't matter his original intentions, everything he had done in hopes of making life within the hospital peaceful had been met with chaos. Word had gotten out about Subject No. 2990's awakening and sudden disappearance. The divisive opinions of the residents bubbling to the surface for the first time in decades; some praising Elizabeth's work, others making the argument whether or not it should be left up to the technicians (or the Director) to decide the fate of the Subjects— making the case it should be left up to the families of said Subjects whether or not to attempt an awakening or to pull the plug and let them whither away. This is not what I wanted to happen, he thought; hating himself.

With what little energy he had left in him, having gone *another* night without much sleep, Friedrich Winsome lifted himself out of bed. He wanted to undo his mistake. Enough turmoil had been allowed to fester due to his error in judgment. It was time to confess his sins. He only hoped Pierce would forgive him for his actions.

Leaving his complex, Winsome headed toward the elevator. Stepping inside the cramped steel box he punched the number twelve and watched the doors close, the beginning of his journey toward redemption.

When the elevator doors opened he found himself met with an approaching Elizabeth. He froze for a brief second. He could feel the contempt she felt for him radiating from her being, her stern eyes penetrating him as he started his way down the corridor. She nodded in his direction, he averted his gaze toward the window; the noonday sun shining through, illuminating the hallway. Did she know? he asked himself. Did she know it was I who had taken the Subject from the morgue and removed him from the building? She must know, his paranoid mind concluded. And instead of confronting me head-on with the matter she's gone to Pierce — has convinced him to change his views, guilt-tripping him into wasting all his time trying to find out what happened.

Upon arriving at Pierce's doorway Friedrich Winsome looked inside to find the Director, a man he had admired since he was a teenager, hoping to one day work underneath him; a look of defeat pulling at his face. It's too late, he thought. The damage has been done. If I were to tell him now it wouldn't change anything. All hope of making things right is lost.

Winsome turned his gaze forward and found himself being pulled toward the stairway which led to the rooftop. The thought of stepping outside for some fresh air soothed his troubled brain. He made his way up the flight of stairs, opened the door which brought him into the greenhouse where they grew their vegetables. Bypassing the urge to nibble on a carrot, he continued outside. There he was met with the backside of Cordelia, who had returned a week ago from her futile search for the Subject. Her attention was focused on readjusting the sights of her scope; a common practice for her whenever she found herself bored, which was often. He turned in the opposite direction and walked until he found himself near the edge of the rooftop. It was calm up here, not a sound but the whistling wind blowing a subtle breeze across the landscape. Looking down he saw the cold dead earth staring up at him, underneath it the lower levels dwelt in undisturbed silence. It'll be easy, he told himself as he stepped up onto the ledge; his sense of balance growing uneasy.

He took a small step off the ledge.

All I have to do is let gravity do its thing.

And as he fell toward the earth's cold, unforgiving surface, Winsome could've swore he saw the familiar face of the young visitor from Shrapnel watching him as he plummeted to his demise—her vacant gaze following his doomed trajectory; *such a haunting set of eyes*, he thought as his body made impact.

17

WHAT A GODDAMN MESS, Pierce thought as he rummaged through what little there was of Winsome's belongings, hoping to find something that would bring any semblance of light to his out-of-the-blue suicide. But there was nothing—only an endless pile of journals filled with daily notes; some academic, others personal accounts of his day/week. Regardless of their contents, Pierce skimmed through them. Perhaps something will strike me odd, he thought.

Flipping from cover-to-cover through his third journal a minor detail caught his eye. There were several mentions of a specific Subject: Subject No. 2990; his brother, Thomas.

28 June 375 T.E. - *There's a rumor spreading. One which claims Elizabeth has finally managed to awaken a Subject—her pet project: Subject No. 2990. If this turns out to be more than mere hearsay I fear trouble will find its way to Pierce's table. Something has to be done. And as much as I hate to admit it, putting my own job security at risk, it's time to put the Arcadian Project to rest. While we may have experienced some success with Subject No. 2773—a fluke, I've concluded—until recent de-*

velopments, it appeared we had hit a dead-end with the idea of saving lives from the hell of living behind a plate of glass.

2 July 375 T.E. *- The Subject was heavier than I had expected. Due to this miscalculation I didn't make it back to the hospital until the early hours of the morning. But it is done. Any evidence of Elizabeth's potential success has been erased.*

That son of a bitch, Pierce thought as he continued to flip through the pages of a dead man's thoughts. He had spent well over a month stressing over the disappearance of his half-brother, surreptitiously interviewing everyone he came across, and the perpetrator had been standing by his side all this time. Why did I not see it? he asked, finding himself at the final journal entry.

13 August 375 T.E. *- My plan did not pan out how I had anticipated. Elizabeth still controls the lower levels—my interference essentially helping her efforts instead of obstructing them. Now sleep eludes me. When I manage to find the strength to close my eyes for a moment or two, however, I find myself met with guilt-ridden nightmares where everyone knows of my deed. Even during my waking hours, I can see it in their eyes. They know. If I should go down for my loyalty to my Director's desires it shall be a punishment I take with pride.*

But, unfortunately, Director Needham seems to have lost his edge— Elizabeth still having some kind of hold on him.

It's hopeless, utterly hopeless. I'm beginning to doubt my decision to leave the unconscious Subject on Shrapnel's doorstep all those nights ago. . .

It's hopeless. I think I need to lie down and attempt to get some rest.

Shrapnel. Thomas, his brother, was in Shrapnel.

Throwing the journal to the floor Pierce hurried out into the hallway, bumping into a content Andrew (counting the leaves growing on a nearby tree outside the hallway window). "Wi-Wi-Win-Winsome did a bad thing," the stuttering fool would repeat as Pierce continued down the hallway, toward the elevator. *I hope I can find her*, his mind raced as he arrived to the closed steel doors. *We have little time to waste. Thomas is out there, and he* **needs** *to be found.* He could feel his legs shaking with nervous tension. Please be on the rooftop, he begged, the elevator doors opening after what felt like an eternity of waiting.

During the elevator's slow rise to the twelfth level, Pierce's mind found itself attempting to understand the mindset Friedrich Winsome was in during his final moments. What was he thinking? Had it been the thought of killing himself that had carried him to the rooftop that day? Or did he have an original agenda; one which found itself abandoned upon the opening of the elevator's steel doors? By the end of the day none of it really mattered. This would only end as another pile of paperwork he would have to add to his filing cabinet.

The dying ding of the elevator announcing its arrival to the twelfth floor awoke a memory in Pierce's brain; a memory he had all but forgotten. As he walked the soundless hallway, heading toward the flight of stairs which led to the hospital's rooftop, his mind manipulated a temporal time loop to play in front of his eyes. Pierce saw himself— young, at the age of twenty-five—walking up to the rooftop; anger and determination riding the smooth contours of his face. He knew he would find her alone, picking fruits and vegetables before the sun broke over the horizon. Camille Dixon, though her maiden name still clung to his memory as the woman his father had become infatuated with, giving birth to a comatose bastard fourteen years prior to this day.

He hated her.

On the rooftop she stood, humming a song he did not recognize as she gently placed each piece of harvest into a hand-sewn sack.

"*Pierce,*" she said, shocked to find herself no longer alone. "*You're up rather early. Come to enjoy a sunrise in private?*"

But he did not speak. Instead, he edged toward her—the rage he still felt in his heart from discovering his father's secret had preoccupied his thoughts. All he heard was silence. Only the sight of her lips moving had indicated she was asking him a question.

"*How's your father doing?*" Camille had attempted (once again) to get a response from the boy. "*It's been years since he and I have been able to—*"

No longer in control of his actions, Pierce found his left hand wrapped around Camille's throat. Whatever it was she had to say, it didn't mean anything to him. Forty-nine year old Pierce watched in nostalgic horror as his younger-self pushed a frightened Camille toward the ledge. The older version of himself wanted to reach out, to stop his younger counterpart from committing such a heinous act. But the moment had long-since past; only the dream-like memory playing before him remained.

"It's all your fault," were the only words to leave the twenty-five year old's mouth before he pushed Camille out into the æther, letting gravity play its well-practiced role.

"Director?" Cordelia's voice echoed through the daydream. "Director Needham, are you okay?"

He felt her cold, distant hands collect upon his shoulders. Even after years of being out of the frigid temperatures of her sleeping chamber, Cordelia still felt *unnaturally cold to the touch*—not from this world. His distracted gaze left the hallucination behind, meeting the concerned look which consumed her honey brown eyes. It was the first time he saw any semblance of emotion take over Cordelia's usual stoic stare.

"Director?"

"I'm fine," Pierce managed a response. He scanned their surroundings, wondering what it was about staring out at a sea of dilapidated buildings Cordelia found appealing; but he could think of nothing. "I'm not interrupting anything, am I?"

"Not at all," she replied, the concerned look leaving her eyes, returning to their unemotional nature. "I was about to head downstairs, actually—head to the mess hall to grab a bite to eat. Did you need something?"

"I know you just got back not too long ago," he paused, his attention turning toward the city of Shrapnel. "But I need you to head south, back down to Shrapnel. I have reason to believe you'll find Subject No. 2990 there."

Without acknowledging the Director's request, Cordelia turned to gather her things from the north-side of the building, looked back at Pierce (who wore a despairing look on his face), and nodded in compliance. Anything to escape the relentless banality of this place, she thought, opening the door which led downstairs—leaving the despondent Director alone in the summer breeze; the sharp echo of the door slamming behind her being her unofficial farewell.

• • •

A DARK BLUE-ISH GLOW hummed across the room as Mason waited for the process to finish—the implantation of Cordelia's memories of military training into the empty shell of Subject No. 2996's brain. This was all new territory for him, supplanting selected memories from one Subject and sending them into another; filling the void due to the recent erasure of original memory—reducing the human mind to the disposability of a worn computer's hard drive. At what point does Subject No. 2996 (Sarah Baker) cease to exist, leaving only a mental replica of Cordelia in its place? When it came in regards to the Subjects, did it even matter?

"Almost done, I see," Elizabeth's voice rang with renewed confidence. There was a gleam in her eye Mason hadn't seen since the day they had *successfully* pulled Subject No. 2990's brain from the Arcadian Sequence. "Soon we'll be able to move forward with the rest of the viable Subjects."

"Why are we doing this?" Mason asked. He wanted to understand her motives behind the insane idea of stripping a human being of their identity and replacing it with minimal structural detail. "What purpose will it serve us to create mindless drones; their only *remembered* frame of cognizance being how to use a firearm?"

"I believe it's time for us to quit moving in place." she said, the warm gleam in her eye disappearing. "For centuries we've remained stagnant while the world continued to spin—allowing decadence to stretch its foul fingers across the land. If we refuse to change our projection, make an effort to build a better future for ourselves and the generations to come, I fear it won't be long before *we* eventually fade from the face of the earth; any mark of civility becoming lost in the process. It is with this idea, reprogramming the rest of the Subjects with

Cordelia's military training, I believe we can wipe out the infection *before it consumes us."*

Mason remained silent. Elizabeth's explanation frightened him. It appeared, to him, she had gone insane with the delusion she (and she alone) could make a difference in the world; using a brainwashed legion of Subjects as a disposable means to an end. There was nothing he could do at this point. Even if he chose to resign from this experimental Project of hers, Elizabeth now had a *reprogrammed* killing machine by her side; and he was the one who helped her achieve the unthinkable goal.

In the end it wouldn't matter if he resigned or not, the guilt of helping to create an army of unthinking, unflinching weapons would remain with him until his dying day. Is this what it felt like for the unfortunate souls who were also lured under false pretenses to help bring about the creation of the first atomic bomb? he thought, staring down at the still unconscious Subject; creating something—or someone—with annihilation being the core focus of its existence.

The lights dimmed for a moment before returning to their original amber hue, indicating the end of the programming sequence. There was a brief pause which clung to every fiber of the room; both Mason and Elizabeth's glances bouncing back and forth between themselves and the Subject.

Elizabeth smiled. "Now only one question remains unanswered," she said in an inauspicious breath. "Did any of our hard work stick?"

They both leaned in closer to examine their quiescent patient, the steady beep of the monitor keeping their curiosity at a slow, even pace. "How long do you think it'll take before she wa—"

Before Mason could finish his question he found himself on the receiving end of a confused Subject's firm grip on his neck. He could barely breathe. For someone who was just beginning to come out of anesthesia, he thought, the world around him going dim, she certainly has complete control of her faculties.

"Where the hell am I?" the familiar question flew from Sarah Baker's trembling lips. Her grip tightened on Mason's neck among the confusion. She felt her static eyes wander to the countless wires and patches covering her pale skin; the fear of unknowing sending her into a frenzy. "Who am I? And what the fuck did you people do to me?"

"I understand this must all seem confusing for you," Elizabeth said, holding up her arms in surrender, eyeing the situation. "But you have to remain calm. I can explain *everything*. The only thing I ask is that you let go of Mr. Dixon."

Sarah Baker remained steadfast with her grip on Mason's neck, the look of strained fear shimmering from her focused eyes. "Answers first. If I find myself satisfied, then I'll let go of your friend here."

Elizabeth told her nothing but lies. She moved closer with each far-fetched sentence, making Sarah believe she, along with the other (still sleeping) Subjects, were all soldiers who had suffered terrible, near fatal wounds from an encounter with a band of drifters—wounds which left a large number of them in catatonic states.

"But why don't I remember anything? Not the encounter which you speak of, or anything, to be honest. My mind is a blank. And if I try to concentrate on remembering, I see only murk."

"We noticed you, and quite a few others, suffered head trauma. A brain injury can cause bouts of amnesia. Your memories might come back to you. Just give it time."

There was a new look in Sarah's eyes; a look of trust. Seeing this, Elizabeth eased up on her advancement toward her and Mason. Sarah's eyes flickered for a moment, processing the wealth of information which had been laid upon her, her grip on Mason's throat lessening—believing Elizabeth's words to be the truth.

"I know you just woke up from your coma, but I'm going to have to ask you to lie back down so Mr. Dixon and I can finish mending any areas left unattended to due to your sudden awakening."

Without protest, Sarah lay herself flat on the operating table and calmly awaited for the two strangers to continue where they left off. Keeping an eye on her, Elizabeth felt for a prepared anesthetic and gently inserted the needle into Sarah's neck and pressed down. "When you come to again, you'll be good as new. I promise." And as Sarah's eyes dimmed and the lights fell to their dark blue-ish glow once again, an exhausted Elizabeth turned to face a still shaking Mason, "Dixon, find a way to nullify future Subjects from experiencing such confusion. I don't believe I can handle *this* every time."

. . .

IT DIDN'T MATTER HOW HARD HE TRIED, or that an hour had passed since witnessing such a terrible sight, Tom couldn't shake the awful image of a man plummeting to his death. It was an image he had seen many times growing up via media coverage, his first memory of such a horrific scene being that of a desperate Colorado high school student crawling to assumed safety through a shattered window—falling several feet into a sea of untrimmed bushes; away from the two shooters who were still on their unholy rampage. His second exposure to such macabre imagery was when he was eleven, eyeing the image of *The Falling Man* as his father read the news article about the attacks on September 11, 2001. Throughout his life Tom had witnessed countless acts of violence portrayed on media outlets; he had become desensitized to it all. Why, then, did he find himself in such a state of shock? Considering none of his past experiences had actually occurred—every detail of his life having been an eternal lucid dream—he realized this was actually *his first time witnessing such a horrific act take place*; and here there was no filter—no lens, no line of division—separating him from the moment. He had not viewed it from the safety of a television screen or the firm disconnect of seeing it on the printed page. It was all live. And in the real world his mind had no previous experience to pull from to help him compartmentalize such raw emotions—hiding them from the world.

"How do you manage to retain such a calm demeanor, having witnessed such a tragedy?" he asked Theodore as they turned to make their way back to the bookstore.

"Unfortunately, the hospital has had the misfortune of having to deal with several suicides a year since the beginning of the Arcadian Project almost one-hundred years ago." Theodore pulled a still shaking Tom closer to help comfort him. "I'd like to say it gets easier to deal with, but it only gets easier to conceal the tortured unease such a sight manages to ignite in your gut. Sometimes it makes you think, What's keeping me here? How am I any different? I too have a series of failures under my bel—"

"I see you two finally decided to rejoin us," Eldritch called out, interrupting their conversation. "While you two were gone having a good time the rest of us discussed logistics of taking on another body to feed."

Nat stepped forward. "Unfortunately, with our new friend Thomas joining us, we won't have enough supplies to last us until the next full moon." Tom could sense the weight of dread on Nat's shoulders as he spoke. "This means we're going to have to make an unexpected visit to our surrounding settlements and ask for an early restock on food and medicine; letting them know the situation on our hands, hoping they'll be willing to part with some of their provisions ahead of schedule."

"Personally, I suggested giving the newbie back over to the hospital," Eldritch eyed Tom with a sour look on his face. "Save us the hassle of having to beg for next month's rations a couple week's early. Hell, I'd even let Wendigo have him for a few meals and kill two birds with one stone."

"Neither of those suggestions would ever live past a vote."

"Well shit, Atom, we didn't ask for him to be dropped on our doorstep. Why should we have to carry his weight when those pious assholes up at the hospital didn't even want him?"

"That's enough," Nat commanded. "I don't want to hear another word out of you two. This isn't up for a debate. We are going to swallow what little pride we have and split off into pairs of two and head our separate ways to each settlement and ask, with tact," he eyed Eldritch, "hoping they'll lend us what we need to survive."

"Fine," Eldritch sighed in deflated defeat. He took a step closer to his brother. "Atom and I will head west to the old airport, see what they have growing; it being a more coastal town, their crops should be doing pretty well."

Wendigo walked slowly toward Peregrine, patting her on the shoulder. "Me and Red will try the abandoned strip malls down south. See if any drugs remain untouched from scavengers."

Peregrine looked over at Tom. "As much as I'd love to spend some time with our new friend, I'd rather have the guaranteed protection of our jolly giant." She hopped on Wendigo's back, wrapping her arms and legs around his thick build. "Maybe next time," she finished with a sly wink.

"I guess that leaves me and you, kid." Theodore nudged Tom in the side. "Since it's safe to assume Nat and Kilgore will stay here and make sure nobody comes to steal *what little we do have* while we're gone."

"Where are we heading?" Tom asked, fearing he already knew the answer.

Theodore turned his head north, his eyes glazed over. Tom could see a look of nostalgic regret wearing itself heavy on his face. He had left the hospital on sour terms. Even after six years of exile, the emotions never died down. His gaze returned to Tom. "We're heading home, kid."

"But won't they recognize you? You were a high member of society in that place; a Director, for Christ's sake. Will they even let us in?"

A warm laugh soared from Theodore's belly. "Back in those days I didn't have a full beard or unruly hair like I do now—not to mention a lab coat covered in dirt and blood. I think my identity will remain a secret; just as long as nobody scrutinizes my appearance for too long. Now c'mon. It's already the afternoon and I'd prefer if we were getting back here before nightf—"

```
01010111  01101000  01100001  01110100
00100000  01101100  01101001  01100101
00100000  01100001  01101000  01100101
01100001  01100100  00100000  01101111
01100110  00100000  01010100  01101000
01101111  01101101  01100001  01110011
00100000  01110111  01100001  01110011
00100000  01110001  00100000  01101100
01101111  01101111  01101101  01101001
01101110  01100111  00100000  01110100
01101111  01110111  01100101  01110010
00111011  00100000  01110100  01101000
01100101  00100000  01110000  01101100
01100001  01100011  01100101  00100000
01101000  01101001  01110011  00100000
01100010  01101111  01100100  01111001
00100000  01101000  01100001  01100100
00100000  01100011  01100001  01101100
01101100  01100101  01100100  00100000
01101000  01101111  01101101  01100101
00100000  01100110  01101111  01110010
00100000  01100100  01100101  01100011
01100001  01100100  01100101  01110011
00101110  00100000  01010111  01100101
01101100  01100011  01101111  01101101
01100101  00100000  01101000  00100001
```

Part III: Happy Returns

Intention is partial. What one might view to be for the betterment of mankind, another could see as inhumane—nothing but a destructive means to a horrifying conclusion. There are no villains in actuality, only opposition of thought and execution.

18

THE SOUND OF SILENCE—it was something Cordelia Dashkov didn't think she would have to fight for in a reality where the constant, cacophonous static of white noise had been subdued for the rest of eternity by the long-since-passed crackle of the atomic bomb. It was one of the reasons why she would spend most of her time on the rooftop of the hospital, to escape the endless clicking of people coming and going along the linoleum floor, heading from one level of the building to the next; the mindless chatter among residents as they continued to go about their uneventful lives; the screaming of children; even the subtle hum of the lights shining above her would bring her to grind her teeth in agitation.

This place was unlike home, she thought as she made her way to the ground floor. Back home (back in Arcadia) she didn't feel the need to escape the world she lived in—every shade of sound which invaded her ears was welcomed. Here, in this ungodly building, the only escape she had from such dissonance was inside her own head.

A delayed thought flew by as she waited for the elevator to take her to the ground floor. I should've bargained with Pierce before leaving to find his precious Subject, she cursed herself with a hollow grimace— have him promise to return me to my cerebral paradise, where I could lose myself in the company of my brothers once more. She considered turning back, to state her terms upon the Subject's safe return, but knew the moment for negotiations had passed. There was little room for alterations once an agreement with Pierce had been made.

Cordelia braced herself, having felt the subtle nudge of the elevator coming to a stop at the appropriate floor. Schooling would be coming to a close this time of day, which meant she would be met with a sea of children pushing toward the staircase to climb their way back home for the rest of the afternoon. She didn't care for the children of this world. Holding her breath, she made her way through the half-sized waves of youthful souls eager to return to their families—toward the exit.

"Leaving again so soon?" a familiar voice asked as she approached the steel door. "What ridiculous errand has Pierce forced upon you this time?"

It was Elizabeth Hestler, one of the only people in this place who treated her as an equal—not some second class citizen who either didn't belong or whose only purpose was serving as the Director's pet. Considering her romantic history with Pierce, why Elizabeth hadn't been promoted to the title of Co-Director upon Theodore Webb's sudden removal was baffling to her. Perhaps one day, she thought, Needham will find *himself* removed from the hospital and she'll take on the role of Director by her own volition.

"The Subject," she replied. "Through some nameless source, he's convinced I'll find him in Shrapnel with the misfits living in the bookstore."

Elizabeth sighed. "I told him—only hours ago, mind you—he should quit worrying about the whereabouts of Thomas. But he never listens. Yet I find myself still surprised by his antics." She shook her head in shallow disappointment. "As much as I'd like to know Thomas is safe, too much time has passed for him to be of any use to me."

A brief pause lingered between them. "Just be safe out there, okay? We've suffered enough losses to the harsh conditions of the Wasteland. The world doesn't need to add another," she said, staring into Cordelia's hardened gaze.

It was with Elizabeth's words of concern Cordelia nodded with the small makings of a smile at her lips and, without uttering another word, turned back to leave the hospital.

Upon stepping outside her nostrils were immediately met with the fresh aroma of Winsome's sun-soaked corpse—ripe with the subtle beginnings of decay. Overhead she saw the slow growing silhouette of a wake of buzzards circling their afternoon meal. It was a sight one saw so often in the untamed desert, anyone who came across it would shrug it off like a passing cloud. She never took a second to reflect—to realize this world was no longer the humans' domain; wild creatures (what few had survived the atomic winds) were its new masters. We've become nothing more than a living, breeding food source for the untamed beast. She stopped to look back at Winsome's lonesome remains. She wondered if she would suffer the same fate as him once she passed—left outside to be claimed cruelly by nature—or if they'd grant her the honor of being cremated and tossed off into the wind; to be carried away like so many lost souls had centuries ago.

As the settlement of Shrapnel grew closer Cordelia found herself once again surrounded by the derelict infrastructure of what used to be Huntington Park. She knew she wouldn't be able to approach the people of Shrapnel, them being a paranoid bunch when it came to travelers—especially ones who carried a weapon with them. Knowing this, she turned left from Pacific Boulevard onto Zoe Avenue before making her way down an alleyway. Making her way to Saturn Avenue, she found the tallest remaining building and entered.

She found herself in a music store. In front of her rows of CDs and cassette tapes rested, like tombstones of a long forgotten era. On the walls posters of bands and upcoming events turned brown and faded with time clung with what little life they had left in them. Using the barrel of her rifle, she thumbed through a rack of cassettes. It was such a haunting experience, to see a world on the brink of unimaginable technological potential brought to a standstill before it could truly hit the ground running. Would humanity have followed the same trajectory she had witnessed in her previous life, had the world been given the chance to continue without its harsh interruption? No one would ever know. Instead, the world would remain a museum of worthless trinkets—slowly decaying until all that's left of humanity's legacy are plastic bottles, radio waves and reruns of *Star Trek: The Next Generation*.

Having wasted enough time floating through memory lane, Cordelia found the door which led into the manager's office; where she would find the stairs leading to the second story—where the owner of the shop would retire at the end of the day.

When she stepped through the doorway leading into the apartment her ears were met with the sound of conversation coming through the paneless windows. It sounded like the old man talking, his ancient vocal chords forcing the words from his throat.

"—joining us, we won't have enough supplies to last us until the next full moon."

It appeared the people of Shrapnel were having issues keeping their rations portioned well enough to last until next month's scheduled visit for replenishment. A consequence of taking on a new inhabitant, perhaps? Hunched to her knees, Cordelia moved closer to the edge of the living room wall. With her back against the torn, dust covered wallpaper she listened; listened until she knew the Subject was among them.

"Personally, I suggested giving the newbie back over to the hospital, save us the hassle of having to beg for next month's rations a couple week's early. Hell, I'd even let Wendigo have him for a few meals and kill two birds with one stone."

A cold smirk curled at the edge of Cordelia's right cheek. She knew she liked Eldritch. Even though he had given her a similar treatment each time she passed through town, at least he was consistent—letting outsiders feel his contempt for their simple intrusion. And with the mention of handing someone back over to the hospital, she now had reason enough to inspect the scene below her. Given their predicament, she figured she could easily talk them into handing him over; save them from the embarrassment of having to beg for supplies. But she wanted to make sure the newbie Eldritch had mentioned was actually her intended target. There was no need to go down and spook them if she went down offering to remove someone who was of no interest to her.

Aiming her rifle down at them she saw the usual group had gathered just outside their humble abode. The old man stood scolding the two brothers before they could jump down each other's throats like an old family ritual. Behind them, standing in the afternoon shade, stood the bumbling giant idiot, the insatiable redhead, and the mute; not contributing to the conversation, as always. To the old man's left, however, were two individuals who caught her eye.

First was her *person of interest*, the reason she found herself traveling in the relentless summer heat—Subject No. 2990, Thomas Dolin. He looked weak, barely able to hold up the weight of his own body. But that was to be expected, having not been able to go through the hospital's physical therapy; plus, having lived a sterile life behind a sheet of glass, only to be thrown out into the *still lightly irradiated air of the Wasteland wasn't helping his situation*. She found herself still bemused by Pierce's (and, at a time, Elizabeth's) interest in him. What was it about *him* that made him such a special case?

It wasn't until she let out a sigh of indignation when the second individual slipped into the edge of her scope. Had it not been for his body language, she wouldn't have recognized him—his hair no longer kept short, but grown into an unruly Afro, his facial hair grown past its usual five o'clock shadow (now full and encrusted with dirt), and his once white lab coat stained beyond the point of recognition. But it was the distinct way he used his hands to speak, applying meaning to such arbitrary gestures, which gave him away. Theodore Webb. Ex-Director and the man she held responsible for taking everything she once held dear away from her—ripping her from a life she still considered home. Seeing him reminded her of her brothers, how she would never get to see them again because of him; the only physical quasi-connection she had left of them were the four bullets housed in the magazine of her rifle—their names etched into the casings so even *after* she had spent each round, *they would always be with her.*

Anger now filled her lungs completely. All these years, since his exile, she had assumed he had met a well-deserved death. But there he stood, still breathing. Still lying through his teeth. She felt her blood begin to boil as she watched him interact with the Subject.

"I guess that leaves me and you, kid." she saw Theodore nudge Tom in the side. "Since it's safe to assume Nat and Kilgore will stay here and make sure nobody comes to steal *what little we do have* while we're gone."

"Where are we heading?"

Cordelia moved her focus back to Theodore and stayed as he turned his head north, a glaze washing over his eyes. He looked back at the Subject and answered, "We're heading home, kid." *No*, she thought, feeling her right hand lift on impulse, leaving the trigger and pulling the bolt action back and forth to load one into the chamber. *I refuse to let you step foot in that place ever again.* In one swift motion her hand returned to the trigger and, without holding her breath to help steady the shot, pulled the trigger. . .

"So long, old man."

THE STORY OF FRANCIS THE BULLET

ORIGINALLY MANUFACTURED in Madison, North Carolina, Francis and his box of brothers didn't take too kindly to the dry summer heat of Los Angeles. The winters were pleasant enough though, which made up for it. It was at a family owned gun and ammo shop they would call home for a long time. In darkness they waited, hoping to be purchased by either a well-to-do hobbyist—eager to get out to an outside shooting range to spend an entire case on paper targets—or a bloodthirsty, big game hunter looking for the right amount of firepower to take down his desired prize. But customer after customer passed them over for a lower caliber. This was Los Angeles, after all. The only use these Southern Californian Liberals had for ammunition was for protection; small firearms, *nothing designed with annihilation in mind*. Still, he and his brothers remained hopeful, hopeful to the idea of a level-headed conservative walking through the gun shop's doors and purchasing them.

Depression set in as the days turned to weeks turned to months, watching countless humans purchase *everything but them*—no sign of being purchased in sight. They began to wonder if there were other gun shops where high caliber ammunition sat in downcast silence while the .22s, .38s, and 9mms were whisked away hour by hour. Their high pitched squeals of joy had become an annoyance for even the row of 12 gauge shells who, while still purchased in bulk during certain seasons, found themselves also waiting a while before getting to move on to the next step of their journey.

After a while, however, people quit coming in altogether. It was as if the use (the obsession) for purchasing and collecting weaponry and ammunition had diminished overnight. There had been no warning or discussion to justify such a change, except the quiet rumble rising from the earth one night while they all slept soundly in their cardboard boxes. Decades—if not centuries—would pass before a small group of wandering souls found themselves stepping through the open doorway of the once popular gun and ammo shop. Francis could feel the entire store stiffen with anticipation, each round hoping one of the wanderers would snatch them up, taking them away from this place, which had grown to feel like a prison in recent years.

"Looks like we 'it da jackpot," one of them spoke as he thumbed through various shelves. "Whaddya say, Gauge?"

"I'd h'afta agree wit yih, Kreg," the other spoke, leading their third, silent companion through the store while they looked. "Jus be sure ta keep it under 38, okay? Anyfing else carries too much kick for me, yih here? Dremel, yih mind snatchin' me that piece restin' jus above yer 'ead?"

Even after years of silence, Francis and his brothers still found themselves cast aside for the lower caliber ammunition.

The travelers took what they wanted and left, leaving the untouched munitions feeling down on themselves for having been cast as such; we didn't choose to be made this way. *Fate's cruel hand decided that for us long ago.* And unlike the gift bestowed upon most sentient life, we can not evolve, adapt. We are stuck as we were originally designed.

It wouldn't be until years later a young, silent female traveler would happen across them. Her weathered appearance screamed dedication to the craft of marksmanship—her undying grip on her Barrett M90 was a sight Francis (or any other bullet or shell in the store) hadn't had the pleasure of witnessing in a long time. It was refreshing. For a moment, he and his band of brothers had forgotten the rifle she carried used their caliber. It wasn't until she picked them up, along with what little remained of the 9mm ammo, they realized they were finally leaving the gun shop for good.

The feeling of being removed from the confining space of the cardboard box and placed into a steel box magazine felt similar to being born again. A renewed sense of purpose coursed through Francis' lead core, warming his metal jacket exterior and copper casing. It was the closest he felt he could come to feeling the sensation of being fired without prematurely sparking the primer; igniting the powder which comprised his lower internal organs.

Francis and his brothers saw the world together, carried safely in the hands of their new owner, Cordelia. At every stop she made to rest for the night she would take them out of their steel home and speak to them until she fell asleep. One night, out of boredom, she etched their names into their copper skin; an honor. It was after that night she always placed Francis at the top of the magazine. He felt content knowing he was her favorite.

But as the years set in, he and his three brothers had grown tired of being kept locked away in the darkness, only to be let out during the late hours of the night; nothing but the distant light of an ever-shifting moon keeping their entire world from being shrouded in a blanket of black. They wanted to be fired, used as they were created to be. Instead, they felt like relics being housed in a museum; where objects from the past sat to be admired but never touched—never to be used to their fullest potential. This angered him. He could feel the itch of his primer begging to be set of, to combust the power in a fiery blaze, sending him off into the æther until gravity no longer held him down to Earth; forever soaring. He had seen enough of the California desert pass him by at such a slow pace.

He wanted to explore new territories; at the speed he was designed to travel.

"Do you think Cordelia will *ever fire us?*" a muffled Nicholas spoke from the bottom of the magazine.

"If she does, we'll probably be wasted as target practice on an already deceased drifter; keeping us without purpose," Hamilton remarked caustically. His booming voice reverberated off Francis' exterior, causing a deep echo to bounce off the walls for a solid minute.

"Don't listen to him, Nick," William's soft voice managed to break through. "If Cordelia wanted to use us as simple target practice, she would've done so by now on something less than a drifter. No, I believe she has something *special* planned for us."

The grinding sound of the bolt action being moved back rang down from above. And as its sliding mechanism disappeared, its fabled noise and disappearance being something Francis and his brothers had only heard and seen in their dreams, a sharp stream of light came pouring down on their cold bodies.

This was the moment—what he had been anticipating his entire life. It happened with such a swift ferocity, he hadn't the chance to say farewell to his brothers; telling them he would see them on the other side. Before he could take a breath to calm his nerves, he found himself locked in place inside the barrel, awaiting the split second when the firing pin would kick him into overdrive.

All he could see from inside the claustrophobic cylindrical structure of the barrel was the weak pinpoint of light looking down on him from the other end. The muffled cheers from below (his brothers proud to see at least one of them meet their long-awaited fate) were soon drowned out by a human conversation. He couldn't make out everything they were saying, but he focused as best he could to strengthen his eyesight; curious to know the target Cordelia wished to fire him at.

"But won't they recognize you?" out of frame of his limited view, a young man's voice traveled down to his steel ear. "You were a high member of society in that place; a Director, for Christ's sake. Will they even let us in?"

Finally able to get a decent look at his owner's target, Francis saw an older gentleman, darker in skin tone. He let out an infectious chuckle—seemingly mocking the younger male for asking such a question. If he's the desired target, what's taking her so long? he asked, growing impatient now that he was within seconds of being transcended.

"So long, old man," Cordelia's voice echoed on his left side, and before Francis could react he felt an overwhelming amount of pressure against the butt of his casing.

He found himself screaming through the long, spiraled trail of the gun's barrel, And in no time at all, he was soaring through the air. His moment had finally come.

The world was brighter than he imagined, having only the hours of the night as a point of reference. As he spun he looked up at the sun, its majesty pouring down on him while the distance between him and his endpoint shrank considerably. The world is such a beautiful place, he thought. And our time to soak in its wonder is so short. Humans take this place for granted. They complain about *this-and-that*—they've forgotten to appreciate the little things in life.

"Now c'mon. It's already the afternoon and I'd prefer if we were getting back here before nightf—"

The dark-skinned man's words were cut short as Francis' steel dome pierced through flesh and bone. He had left the world of light and reentered a world of darkness. This one was naturally warm, at least. It was here his trajectory changed course by a small degree, and also slowed down. He hadn't a clue where he was anatomically speaking when it came to a human being, but he marveled as a surge of energy traveled in every direction, sending cryptic messages to the rest of the body as a last ditch effort before it was completely destroyed by Francis' fleeting presence. They painted a picture of techni-colored light around him. An image of a pale-skinned woman, her hair a delicate tint of rose, flashed for a brief moment before everything went dark.

. . .And before she could lift her gaze from the scope, Theodore Webb's body no longer stood where it had a moment earlier. Instead of the ex-Director's mendacious grin, a quick smear of dark red along the building behind the small group caught itself in her line of view. She continued to watch from the window as shock took over the remaining cast members of Shrapnel. One of them, the young redhead, finally let out an ear-splitting scream, still dangling from the giant's back. The two brother's darted inside for assumed cover—goddamn cowards. But it was the Subject's response which stunned her. He was looking up at her. Can he see me? she wondered as she turned the rifle on its side, extracting the casing from the barrel, ejecting it into the air, and catching it before its gravitational arc began its descent. There's no way he can see me, she concluded. Had he actually seen me, he would have—

And he was gone; disappeared through the front entrance of the music shop below. Shit, she thought, lowering her rifle to the floor and pulling her sidearm from its holster. *The fucker is going to try and avenge the asshole's death.* Let's hope Thomas is smart enough to stop dead in his tracks at the sight of a firearm pointing at his chest.

• • •

OVERCOME WITH FACELESS RAGE, Tom Dolin darted through the interior of the building where he had seen a slim figure standing, holding a rifle; the rifle which was used to send the top of Theodore's skull flying in a multitude of directions. He found the only flight of stairs leading to the upper levels. Unless the killer braved jumping from the second story, there was no other form of escape. Whoever did this is going to pay, his mind screamed as he started his way up the steps.

He stumbled a few times. His legs were still unstable, having had no time to practice moving at such a hurried pace. Determined, he continued on—the fire inside him continuing to push him upward. But when he finally arrived at the top of the stairs he was greeted by a gentle voice.

"Thomas, now don't be an idiot, thinking you can storm in here and take me head on. Unlike you, I've had the proper therapy, so my faculties are functioning without fault. Also, if my memory is serving me correctly, you are without military training—*just an English teacher with a penchant for the written word.*"

Insulted, Tom continued forward at a hearty pace. "What the hell did Theodore ever do—"

"But like you, I am also a stranger to this world," Cordelia's voice managed to remain calm as Tom appeared from around the corner. "You and I, we've been ripped from a life we thought to be truth, only to be told by the authority here it was all a lie. Now, please, I beg of you, don't take another step." She let out a warning shot, the spent bullet making a home in the drywall just to the left of Thomas' frail-looking frame.

There was a moment between the two of them where neither one spoke. They simply stared each other down, examining one another; Cordelia's aim unwavering from the center of Tom's chest. He was older than she had pictured in her mind. She assumed he would've been around her age, if not a year or two in either direction. But in front of her stood a man pushing forty, about the same age as Elizabeth Hestler. On his end, he saw a young female (between the ages of twenty-five and twenty-eight) holding him at gunpoint. Two Subjects from Arcadia attempting to figure each other out without speaking a word.

"Why did you kill Theodore?" Tom spoke, the question no longer being able to remain locked inside his stomach.

"Call it violent impulse," she smirked. "A six-year-old desire to get even with the person I felt was responsible for taking everything away from me; *everything I used to know.*"

Another pause in the conversation. Here, Tom reflected on how the woman must've felt when she was told (by Theodore, it was safe to assume) her entire life up to this point had been nothing but a work of fiction; the hatred she had to have felt—and harbored all these years since then—for the man she held accountable. Poor Theodore, he thought. All he wanted was to give her life, a life he deemed worth living. But all she wanted (and could ever want) was now nothing more than information on a computer screen.

"We can stand here until nightfall, when the drifters like to scavenge these parts, or we can find a solution which ends with the two of us heading back to the hospital; preferably with both of us alive. You're wanted alive, so you're no good to me dead."

"Let's start with you lowering your weapon, then." Tom suggested.

Cordelia looked Thomas up and down one last time before considering it safe enough to allow herself to go completely unarmed. Were he to try anything, she was confident she would be able to take control of the situation with ease. Child's play. She let the 9mm go limp in her hands. With her eyes still focused on Subject No. 2990, she bent her knees at a slow pace so she could gently place the firearm on the floor.

"Y'know," she started, the heavy thump of her trustworthy Glock 17 meeting the carpeted floor. "I think, had life gone down a different path, you and I would've hit it off, being the only Subjects to successfully be awoken from their lifelong slumber."

"Instead, our first encounter is marred with the murder of a man you and I both knew; the only person who knew our story—who could fill in the blanks with answers."

"And you believed he was being honest with you; telling you the truth?" A sharp laugh escaped Cordelia's lungs. "Please. *Lies were the only thing that man was capable of speaking.* You haven't had the opportunity, the same misfortune, of living *outside the sequence* long enough to notice the absurdity, the inconsistency of this place. I've seen enough of this war-torn world to know the Directors, and everyone else at that hospital, are withholding the truth from our naive ears."

Conflicted, Tom remained motionless. His mind didn't know who to trust anymore. Was the woman telling him the truth? Had Theodore been lying to him this entire time? The lines had been blurred beyond recognition. He could no longer tell the difference between fact and falsity. Who was telling him the truth and who was feeding him lies. Theodore's words felt genuine when they spoke; there were no signs of deception. What little he could remember of his time with Elizabeth also appeared sincere—her eyes filled with regret at the thought of stealing him from his world, even if it had been nothing but a simulation. The woman's, however, dripped with self-preservation. She knew he had come up here with revenge on his mind and, having the upper hand (being armed with a firearm) was confident she could talk him out of the idea.

But Theodore had mentioned Sarah, had let him know that, out of everything, she was the one thing from his previous life which had crossed over into the real world. She was real. And if that—and that alone—was the only truth to find itself coming out of Theodore's words, then that was enough.

"You want to go back. I can tell. It's in your eyes," Cordelia's tone transitioned from one of venomous spite to that of shallow comfort. "You could, you know," she continued as she straightened her knees, her hands held out in surrender. "They'll probably tell you it's impossible, but I've read their journal entries; their written documentation of countless failures before us where a Subject was brought out of stasis, only to be put back under days later indicating otherwise. We could work together, you and I—*coerce them to put us back under; take us back to the place they call Arcadia; back to a world of reason.*"

It was here Tom made his move; catch the bitch off guard during a monologue, he thought. He had thought out as best he could, given the small opening she had granted him with her incessant rambling. First, he would tackle her to the ground, collecting the momentum to thrust the both of them to the ground. From there, the woman temporarily stunned by the shift in gravity, he would reach for her recently discarded firearm and press the weapon against her left temple—his free arm pressing down on her windpipe.

Tom's takedown fantasy was cut short, however. He only managed to wrap his arms around the lower half of her torso when the sharp sting of an elbow met his spine.

She was fast. He should've expect this. Advantage was not in his favor, she having had years of adjustment to this world on her side. With his arms still clasped around her waistline, his intention of knocking her to the ground proved fruitless.

"Unwise," she managed as they stood interlocked with one another. "You're still recovering from a lifetime of an inanimate existence. It can take months to relearn the simple task of raising a spoon to your lips, let alone attempt to take down another human being."

Reevaluating his position, Tom brought his left leg up and forced it behind her right, bringing it out from beneath her; succeeding at finally getting her to the floor. There was a moment of nothing, the air being knocked out of both of them from the impact. Both sets of arms flailed to find structure among the chaos. Had the act of violent survival been erased from the scene, you'd assume they were lovers tragically attempting to rediscover each other's forgotten bodies.

A set of knuckles found their way to his lower jaw. His eyes blinked while he recovered from the blow, his arms blindly searching for her own, to keep her from swinging. He didn't know if he could handle another hit. Among the confusion his fingers met what felt like long, slender, cold steel. He felt around, hoping to find a firm grip on the object.

Another blow—this one met his lower ribs. He swore he heard a subtle crack. The actions felt muddled after this. Pain coursed throughout his body as she continued to land each hit. There was no way of telling who had the upper hand. He could only feel his weight grow heavier upon her while blow after blow met their intended target. During this endless cycle his left hand continued to search for a hold on the weapon which lay within his reach. He felt something, a small curvature along the bottom; a place for one of his fingers to wrap around and cling to. Triumph coursed through his aching blood as he manged to close his thumb around the steel curve, giving it a sudden yank to pull it—

Bang!

Silence befell the room. Tom no longer felt the constant barrage of the woman's fists against his body. It didn't take long for the smell of copper to find his nostrils. He knew he'd regret looking up, to see why the woman's well-aimed strikes had ceased so suddenly, but curious instinct took over—rearing his head up to find everything from the neck up no longer recognizable.

The smell of copper only grew stronger by the second.

19

RANCID COPPER STILL MOLESTING the hairs of his nostrils, Tom trudged downstairs to meet the rest of Shrapnel's surviving citizens; to join them in hushed solemnity as they mourned their recently fallen friend. It was an odd affair. While it appeared death was a common occurrence in this world, the act of honoring the departed by means of a proper burial appeared to have died at the cruel hands of the mushroom cloud.

"You look like you just got done having a fun time," Eldritch said, a hunting rifle resting in his arms. "What happened?"

Wendigo answered. "New guy went upstairs across the street, then silence for a long time. After a while there was a loud bang. Bang similar to bang which killed T. New guy come back down not long after; bruised and beaten."

The giant, still carrying tiny Peregrine on his back, turned to stare at Theodore's mutilated corpse. You could tell the sight of blood, bone, and brain tissue was beginning to get to him; feed his animalistic cravings. He refrained, though. A struggle. Peregrine whispered something into his ear; the small makings of a doleful nod before returning his attention to the rest of the group.

Alternating between staring down at Theodore and the second-story window, where the woman from the hospital had met a similar fate, Tom couldn't help but feel cheated. He still had so many questions, and they would go unanswered; having lost the one person who would've happily answered everything eating at his insatiable curiosity by a stranger who claimed his words spoke nothing but falsehood.

"Must've not been much of a challenge if the newbie was able to handle it without any trouble."

Peregrine hopped off Wendigo's backside. "Are you fucking kidding me right now? Look at him—he's been beaten senseless!" She rushed over to shove Eldritch for the comment. "He's probably lucky to have made it out of there alive." The young girl turned to gaze at Tom with a look of honest concern.

A part of him did feel lucky. He didn't know how many more blows to the side of the chest he could've taken before the woman managed to thrust him off of her. But the woman's death had done more harm than good. With Theodore gone the only other person around who could've enlightened him further on his background now lay essentially headless along the carpeted floor of an apartment's living room.

"We could look at the silver lining of the situation," Eldritch said, recovering from Peregrine's push against his sternum. "We no longer have to drag ourselves to nearby settlements for an advancement on supplies."

"He does have a point," Atom agreed.

"I'd still like to go to the hospital."

"Kid, you barely made it out of the music store alive. Why would you want to go to a place where they want to kill you?"

"The shooter said I was wanted alive. Apparently, someone at the hospital wanted her to retrieve me and bring me back."

"You're not going alone," Nat said. "I'll have Wendigo or Atom go with you; ensure you make it there and back safely."

"No. I have to go alone. The woman said they wanted *me* alive. There would be no guarantee harm wouldn't befall any of you, should someone accompany me." Tom's head turned north toward the building his body had unknowingly called home for thirty-eight years. After a brief moment his gaze returned to Nat and the rest of the group. "I'm going alone. I have to, and that's final."

Having convinced them this was his journey and his alone, Tom left Shrapnel. But even as distance began to separate them he could still hear Nat's voice reverberating off the surrounding buildings, its volume losing itself down the city's restless alleyways; offering someone to come along with him.

· · ·

PROGRESS PROVED ITSELF a possibility as Elizabeth read over her notes on Sarah's reprogramming. Originally, the idea struck her, she figured, if she could attain success (let alone replicate the results) with her experiments, she would be able to further her efforts on any of the other Subjects she deemed worthy to experiment on, she hoped she could succeed in creating something this hospital had always needed but—thanks to generations of gutless Directors—had never been deemed necessary enough to pursue; a militia to help defend the hospital's citizens from invasion. But why stop at civil protection? she eventually thought. If one found themselves with the ability to fend off unwanted hostility from outsiders, why should they feel limited to only using this gift as a final stand at the building's doors? Why not venture beyond the security of one's own walls and stop such an attack at its source?

"Are you sure you want to attempt another awakening?" Mason asked. "So soon after our last success?"

"Yes. Time is sensitive."

"We've been working non-stop for days. You don't want to take a few hours to recharge?"

"We can allow ourselves time to rest when we've finished what we started," she said, taking the instruments away from her subordinate, assuming control of the process.

"I'm just tired, don't mind me. Once I hit my third wind my complaints will cease."

"Done. Hook him up to the mainframe and begin the reprogramming procedure."

"If I ever hit my third wind. . ."

Once more Elizabeth's fingers sped across the keyboard in a well-choreographed dance, causing the lights to dim to their familiar dark shade of blue; the process indicating the beginning of its slow crawl toward completion.

Just a couple dozen more to sort through, Elizabeth's thoughts breathed gently; *just a couple dozen more and you'll be done with this mess.*

While the two of them waited in reverence, Elizabeth's thoughts wandered to two people who now belonged solely to her past. Staring down at the unconscious Subject as Cordelia's military training replaced everything else, her thoughts first traveled to her father. She had come a long way from being his little Lizzy. Would he have been proud of her efforts? The work she was doing was something nobody had ever considered an avenue of exploration. Their minds were limited to answering the question of bringing a catatonic mind out of their cerebral prison. Abruptly, her mind shifted to Director Webb. Would he approve of this—the destruction of a human being's identity in pursuit of making the world a better place? She didn't see anything wrong with her progressive methods of indoctrination. *People from the past had their own versions of it; albeit far less messier processes.* Given the cruelty which was inherent throughout humanity's blighted existence, she felt her actions were justified.

Just a couple dozen more, she reminded herself. That's all.

20

MEMORY (ONCE MORE) MADE an attempt to fill in the blanks as Tom traversed north through the streets of Los Angeles. It felt like a dream. Landmarks of both familiarity and novelty juxtaposed themselves against one another, refusing to allow any sense of tranquility to find him with each passing step. To think, had the simulated reality of Arcadia been unable to divert itself from such a tragic event, the world would've ended (again) when he was only four years old. But the sequence had spared them that fate, allowed them to live to see the possibilities this world had been denied — the technological advances which helped to connect the globe.

It certainly wasn't perfect. The threat of nuclear annihilation had never truly gone away, even after the end of the Cold War; it would never fully dissipate, despite humanity's efforts to disarm themselves. Their existence was a double-edged sword. Nuclear weapons had become too significant of an advantage in avoiding conventional warfare between countries whose relationships were less than amicable. And when he looked around at the surviving architecture of this version of Los Angeles—of the world—he considered *this version of humanity lucky*. At the cost of living in a world of order, the unending dread of living in a world of nuclear unknowing had become a distant memory.

Already feeling winded, the endurance of his lungs not what he had grown accustomed to while in Arcadia, Tom looked back. A sigh of defeat left him when he observed he had only managed to make it three blocks away from the bookstore. And judging by the slow shift of the shadows cast upon the earth, Tom calculated he wouldn't make it to the hospital until nightf—

He couldn't bring himself to say nightfall, it having been the word which had been cut short due to Theodore's untimely death. He had only known the man a little under a month's time, but he had been the closest thing to a friend since waking up to find himself in such an unfamiliar world. Irrational regret poisoned his thoughts looking back on the memory, now only fragmented snapshots of recollection. *If only we'd moved the conversation inside—perhaps if I had been standing in front of him, refusing the woman a clear shot—maybe he'd still be alive; I wouldn't have to make this journey alone. I wouldn't have to be alone.*

Rusted remnants of automobiles lined both sides of the street as he continued down the center of the road, still lost in his dispirited thoughts. Wild patches of harmless weeds struggled through the sun baked cracks in the asphalt to greet him as he passed; their attempts going in vain as he trampled them without a shred of acknowledgment.

Ahead, in the distance, the hospital's looming presence taunted him; the surrounding buildings, long since dead and empty, their sense of purpose abandoned to the weight of time, cheered him on in haunted silence. I'm coming for you, Tom breathed, refusing to let the inanimate object win, to talk him out of walking through its doors hoping to find answers; an inkling of Cordelia's words had stuck with him —perhaps he could talk the people who had once worked alongside Theodore into hooking him back up to the Arcadian Sequence. Even if he spent the rest of his life knowing he was living in a simulation, if it meant getting to be with his wife and children, that's all that mattered.

The sun had tucked itself nicely behind the warm blanket of the ocean-filled horizon by the time he stepped foot in the hospital's parking lot; empty except for the lifeless shape just outside the front entrance. Intimidation formed in the pit of his stomach. Although his time inside the hospital's walls had been spent in an unconscious state, the hold it held on Tom's psyche was unavoidable. The doors leading inside had a permanence to them. He knew, once he stepped through their steel threshold, they wouldn't allow him to leave again. They would welcome him back home with a sense of finality in their voice as they slowly closed behind him.

An empty lobby greeted him. It was odd. He had expected to walk in to find the building a claustrophobic's worst nightmare. That's how Theodore made this place seem, anyway; a busy sea of people going about their predictive lives. It was the end of the day, however—everyone was winding down for the evening before turning in for the night. Letting himself feel welcome, Tom headed for the elevator; hoping to find it in functioning order.

When the elevator doors opened a lone male pushing a cleaning cart made his way out, mumbling the same phrase over and over—tripping over himself with the occasional stutter; Tom's presence having gone unnoticed. "Wi-Wi-Winsome did a bad thing."

Paying no attention to the stranger, Tom stepped into the enclosed space. He found himself greeted by a silent woman leaning against the front corner of the elevator. She appeared to be guarding the control panel. There was a look in her eye. He couldn't place it, but it made him feel uncomfortable nonetheless.

"Going up?" she asked.

"Ye-yeah. Next floor, please."

She felt familiar, like something out of a dream. Nothing about her appearance struck him, her blonde hair and green eyes only reminding him of the billboard he saw in the revelatory dream dominated by an endless bombardment of *ones & zeroes*. She was wearing a white lab coat, however. He wondered if she had ever worked with Theodore. She was young. About his age, he concluded. The chances of the two of them having worked together were slim. But still, he wondered.

The elevator dinged, the doors opened. "Looks like this is where you get off," the woman spoke.

Tom nodded. Still feeling her sharp gaze, he stepped out of the lift.

Like the lobby downstairs, this floor appeared abandoned. He turned to find the elevator doors closing slowly.

"Hold the door," he beckoned, not wanting to have to wait for the elevator to make its drawn-out return after taking the woman to her desired destination. The small tips of the woman's fingers wrapped around one end, forcing the doors to disappear into their side panels, allowing him to come aboard once more.

"Lost?"

"You could say that," he responded.

"Need help finding what you're looking for?" The woman smiled. "Perhaps I could be of some assistance."

Her voice. There was something about it. He couldn't place it, but Tom felt he knew it, had heard it before this moment. There was a soothing warmness to it—motherly. Maybe in a dream?

"Could you tell me where I might find the person in charge of this place?"

The woman told him the most likely place he could find the person in charge. Pierce. His brother. During his walk here he had failed to make such a connection. The person running this place was his own flesh and blood. That alone sent another series of questions tapping at his already curious skull. All he had to go on were the cold words of critique from Theodore's tongue; a man who had been scorned by him years ago. That, and his unproven assumptions, were all he could go on. And while there was probably some truth to Theodore's words, he wanted to hear Pierce's justification for his less than admirable behavior from the man, himself.

"It looks like this is where I get off," the woman said. The elevator having come to a brief stop. "Once you find yourself on the twelfth floor just remember, the last door to your right will be his. It's usually open, so feel free to walk in unannounced."

Tom thanked the woman as she made her way out, still unable to place the feeling of familiarity which he still felt toward her as the doors to the lift closed—separating them completely. He looked up at the analog display as it counted up toward his final destination. The twelfth floor. He felt himself growing nervous, a knot forming within his stomach. This would be the first time he and his brother would stand face-to-face, talking to one another as sentient equals; not the one-sided conversations which he was certain had to have transpired throughout their lives.

He held his breath as the doors opened, revealing a lonesome corridor. The last door on the right standing wide open, just as the woman from the elevator had said.

$$\bullet \quad \bullet \quad \bullet$$

HE HADN'T RECOGNIZED HER. They rode several floors in an enclosed compartment, staring each other down as they spoke, and Thomas continued on without acknowledging any form of familiarity. Elizabeth couldn't tell if she should be offended by this fact or not, considering the only moments they shared together were either during one of her shifts as she watched over him or in his early stages of consciousness. Anything he would have witnessed during that time would've been cast off as a confusing dream sequence and nothing else. Still, the thought that *not even her voice* had managed to trigger a small denotation of suppressed recollection within him ate at her.

She needed to rest. It was a marvel she was still able to stand, having gone days without a second's worth of shut-eye. Her work had kept her occupied. It had become an obsession these past few days, scraping away at each new Subject's frontal lobe, the erasure of their memories, and reprogramming having finally taken its toll on her. Confident that Mason had a handle on things, she decided to head up to her quarters to take a nap and recharge. But she hadn't planned on running into Thomas along the way. The unexpected reunion, the rush of serotonin and dopamine, had overwhelmed her brain. She could hardly contain herself.

It didn't feel right when she stepped into her living quarters. Something felt off. Which didn't make sense, since everything was where it had been when she last saw it—untouched, as it should be—yet there was this unknown feeling tugging at her insides, eating at her brain.

Fuck, her brain screamed. In the mix of her tired, elated state, having seen someone she'd considered lost for the first time in three weeks, Elizabeth had told Thomas where he could find Pierce—his half brother. *The person in charge of this place.* Despite Pierce's apparent change of heart, the uncertainty of what would transpire when the two came face-to-face frightened her. Behind the mask of sincerity, Elizabeth could still detect the animosity Pierce had carried with him toward Thomas his entire life. There was no promise Pierce would be able to restrain himself from acting out violently like he had years before.

Worried sick for Thomas' well-being, a determined, revitalized Elizabeth rushed to her medicine cabinet. Behind the mirror she kept an assortment of narcotics—primarily tranquilizers and opiates, for when she found herself on a restless streak—and grabbed a couple readied syringes; in case she had to nullify one of them before things got out of hand.

Leaving her living quarters Elizabeth hurried down the empty hallway, toward the elevator she'd only left moments earlier. As she reached the end of the corridor the knot in her stomach only tightened as she watched the needle climb to the number twelve before coming to a complete stop. Desperate and running out of time, she went for the staircase. With one foot in the stairwell, the mocking ding of the elevator pulled her back to the steel contraption.

She hoped her paranoid concern wasn't as last minute as it felt with each passing step—with each passing second.

God, please don't let it be too late.

• • •

LATELY, SUNSETS HAD GROWN to feel like an omen—a harbinger of unspeakable dread. As the dwindling light shifted into unending darkness Pierce couldn't help but fear the worst for Cordelia and his half-brother. Sure, Cordelia could handle herself well during the daytime. Drifters weren't an issue. They were child's play in her eyes. No, it was the nocturnal creatures which claimed the deserted lands as their home that worried him. It shouldn't be taking her this long to walk down to Shrapnel, find Thomas, and bring him back here.

The wilderness—such a well-composed portrait of chaos. Only the sadistic mind of a careless creator could've created something with such a macabre outlook as their color palette.

It fascinated him, how the world worked; with little to no regard to its remaining inhabitants. Through its plaintive ugliness, brought on by people like himself, it somehow managed to keep going. Among the dying weeds, wild vegetation sprouted from the earth. Nothing special, only the occasional flower here and there. But after centuries of being barren, the world was beginning to show signs of life. Humanity did not share this trait. It was apparent. At the height of adversity we crumble under the pressure, accepting extinction without the faintest argument against the violent notion. Soon (a century more, if not less) the blight known as humankind would be gone from this planet, allowing the flora and fauna a chance to thrive like it once had; before man had developed its misguided superiority complex.

The brain wanders to dark places once the sun disappears under the horizon; perhaps to match the current scenery, only the delicate glimmer of the moon's pale glow being the silver lining to each passing thought. Yet there still remained those who continued to bleed optimism, despite the insurmountable odds which refused to let up. *They think they're going to save the world.* It was a fool's errand, even before this bleak era was born. Environmentalists thought they could heal the Earth, reverse the adverse effects humanity had inflicted upon it. The planet's trajectory toward collapse was something the human race could not correct. You can't be the malady for centuries, only to attempt at becoming the cure once you realize the harm you've caused to your generous host will affect your well-being.

"Excuse me," an unfamiliar voice spoke. "I hate to bother you at such a late hour, but would you happen to be Director Pierce?"

21

S LOWLY, PIERCE TURNED to find a familiar face staring him down from the edge of the doorway. Subject No. 2990. Thomas Dolin. His brother. It was weird, seeing him standing at the other end of the room. Every interaction between the two of them had Thomas lying behind a thick sheet of glass. The change in perspective was chilling.

From what Pierce could tell (the lighting being poor at night), it appeared the wilderness had not been kind to his brother; the left side of Tom's face covered with the beginnings of bruises. He was surprised to see him standing there alone, no sign of an escort. Had he found his way up here on his own accord? Surely he had to have had help of some kind in order to make it up to the twelfth floor, looking for him specifically.

"I take it Cordelia showed you the way before letting you roam free through the building's halls."

"Is she the woman in the lab coat or the one you sent to Shrapnel armed with a rifle?"

The woman in the lab coat? He must've meant Elizabeth. No one else in the neurological department would've been wandering the halls this late, sacrificing what little time they were granted to catch a few hours of rest. What was she up to now? And why hadn't she taken advantage of her favored Subject's return? For years she had obsessed over him. Her actions didn't sit right with him.

"Cordelia's the one with rifle," Pierce replied. The 'woman in the lab coat' held no relevance to the situation. "Normally she sees an errand through to the end. Did she turn in early for the night?"

"She didn't make it back."

Fear developed at the base of Pierce's throat. What did he mean, 'she didn't make it back.' How had he managed to make it from Shrapnel to here on his own? There was no way he had traversed the long walk, malnourished and beaten, without assistance of some kind. Yet here he was, alone. Remarkable, he thought. "That's unlike her," he spoke finally. "She's made trips to Bomb City and back," not that Tom would know where Bomb City was. "You're telling me something became of her while she was trying to retrieve you?" Of all places, in Shrapnel? Had old man Nat and his gang of misfits finally dove off the deep end and attacked an outsider, instead of retreating to their hole in the wall for safety?

Tom only nodded in response.

"What happened to her?"

Tom, stepping further into the room (stopping at the corner of Pierce's desk), went on to tell everything that had transpired hours earlier. He told him about Theodore's death. *So that's where the bastard ended up settling—must've given up on traveling to San Pedro, but couldn't bring himself to return back home.* He knew of Cordelia's derision toward his friend, the ex-Director, but would've never pegged her as someone who would choose to execute such hatred in a physical, aggressive manner. The next part of Tom's story felt unbelievable. Despite his poor physical condition, he had managed to overtake a military trained individual. By the sound of things, however, it seemed her death was an accident; a sensitive trigger pull during a moment of disoriented conflict.

"Well, so it goes," Pierce whispered, accepting both Theodore's and Cordelia's deaths in one long defeated sigh. "What brings you up here to my office? Clearly something had to have motivated you to make the long walk from Shrapnel all the way here, up twelve stories to see me. I assume your mind is probably swarming with questions."

"Is it possible—can you hook me back up to Arcadia; let me return to my original life?"

"What is your obsession with that place? Cordelia longed to go back as well. It baffles me. You both were given the gift of consciousness, *to live in the real world*, and all you want to do is go back—back to a land of fantasy."

"Answer the question."

"Yes, it's possible. But not without consequence."

"Explain."

"Having been disconnected for as long as you have, and having seen the world as it really is, even if we resequenced you you'd never feel the same. Basic interactions from before would seem pointless. The ability to derive pleasure in your daily life would be an impossibility. Also, your mind would be scarred from your time outside the sequence. The veil of digital illusion would slip periodically, overlapping fragmented images of the real world with the false one you call home. Is that what you want? *Would you risk insanity just to feel at home once more?*"

"If it means getting to be with my family again, then yes. I believe it's worth the risk."

Pierce scoffed. "Did you ever think it a possibility you could have family here? Perhaps a mother and a father who would love to see you awake finally."

"I know my mother and *our* father have already passed."

"So Theodore told you about us being . . . brothers."

"Yes. He also managed to fill me in on your animosity toward me."

"Y'know, you look just like him; our father. It's kind of eerie, I must admit."

"How did he die?"

"An undiagnosed brain aneurysm. We didn't know until the building's coroner performed the autopsy."

"And my mother?"

Pierce fell silent. His jaw tensed under the weight of the question. He didn't know how much information Theodore had told him. While it was never proven, Theodore had always suspected foul play with

Camille's death. Having analyzed several suicides which involved jumping from the rooftop, he saw through the act. Her body was too far out to have been a suicide. And the only person who would've had the incentive to push her off the rooftop, he concluded, was the only other man (besides himself) who had carried the secret of Isaac Needham's infidelity with him since grade school.

Had he shared this theory with Thomas? If he attempted to lie there was the small chance Thomas would call him out on it. There was no use lying to him. There was nothing he could do. It was in the past.

"She was murdered." he said hesitantly. He moved toward his desk, hoping to bridge the gap between the two of them; appearing sympathetic. "But you have to understand, I was young and full of hatred back then."

"What are you saying?"

"If I could go back I would undo the horrible act. I would undo a lot of things."

Tom never knew the real Camille (Dolin) Dixon—never knew the sound of her voice, what she looked like, or the kind of life she lived. But he did know the love he felt from his mother in Arcadia. An odd-ball but always putting her son's needs before her own, he liked to think the digital projection he called 'mom' would've been a reflection of what his actual mother was like. But he would never know. He would never know because the man standing in front of him had stolen the chance to meet her.

"How old was she when she—when she died?"

"About her early forties."

"And I?"

"I was twenty-five, so you would've been fourteen."

Fourteen. That was around the time his mother, the digital imprint he called his mother, fell into a depression. It could've been a coincidence, but he had witnessed too many instances during his lifetime where the outside world had influence on what he experienced in his subconscious state. His own brother (half-brother, he reminded himself) killed his mother; and through that action, forever changed the sequence of ones and zeroes that called herself his mother in Arcadia.

Hatred bubbled to the surface, taking control. Tom felt his hands ball into fists, his right arm rearing back, gaining momentum, before asserting itself dead center across Pierce's face.

He thought he heard the sound of bones breaking. He wasn't sure if they were the bones in Pierce's nose or the eight small bones in his wrist. Either way, he watched as his brother stumbled back in shock, clutching his nose in horror—blood gushing from the sides of his cupped hand.

"Okay. I deserved tha—"

Still livid, Tom turned his attention toward Pierce's desk to find a classic baseball bat resting on a shrine. Unable to stop himself, he picked up the wooden instrument, gripped it tightly, returned his gaze back to his now disfigured brother, and (without reservation) started swinging.

Every hit sent shivers throughout his body. The impact of wood against flesh-covered bone was a sensation akin to chopping down a tree, except he couldn't refrain from swinging, even once *the tree* had fallen to the floor—its screams of agony reduced to mild whimpers before fading into silence. He kept swinging, only the sound of cracking bones and muscle tissue being tenderized indicating he was still hitting his desired target.

Something stopped him mid-swing. He felt the bat being ripped from his hands, the tightening grip of someone's arm around his neck, and the cold steel prick of a needle puncturing through skin, finding a vein, and sending a foreign substance into his bloodstream. Seconds later, he collapsed to the floor.

The last thing he saw were the unrecognizable remnants of the man who used to be Pierce Alexandre Needham.

• • •

THE ELEVATOR DOORS TOOK FOREVER to open; their uncommon malfunction continuing to mock her. Still determined to prevent Pierce from doing the unthinkable, Elizabeth Hestler scurried into the small steel box and pressed the number twelve; tranquilizers in hand.

I should've stopped him—convinced him to join me instead of telling him where he could find Pierce, she thought as the lift carried her upward. I could've told him who I am. Certainly he would've recognized my name and followed me without question. Stupid. Fucking stupid.

Too impatient to wait for the doors to open themselves, Elizabeth pried them ajar, almost tripping over herself as she stepped out into the hallway.

She stopped several feet outside the office, horrified. Inside Pierce's quarters she could hear the muffled sound of something being hit with extreme force. There were no wounded pleas, so it couldn't be what she feared would happen, right? Perhaps Thomas had gotten lost along the way and what she was hearing was another one of Pierce's violent outbursts; adding more dents and holes to his walls and floor.

Breathing in, calming her nerves, she turned the corner. What she saw left her stunned. In front of her a lifeless Pierce lie strewn across the floor. Standing over him a frail looking Thomas continued swinging, forcing whatever life which could've hidden itself out into the æther. But there was no life left to squeeze out. It was gone.

Unable to speak, afraid Thomas would turn his violent spasms toward her, she rushed behind the Subject, waited for the opportune moment to snatch the wooden projectile from his firm grasp, wrapped her left arm around his neck, and, with her free hand, thrust one of the syringes into his neck—releasing the sleeping agent into his bloodstream.

Shortly after she let him go, his now limp body falling to floor. "I'm terribly sorry," she managed to say, discarding the spent needle. "I didn't want this. This wasn't how it was supposed to be."

Feeling tired again, the adrenaline no longer keeping her awake, Elizabeth dragged Tom's unconscious body to the elevator. She couldn't help but feel responsible for Pierce's demise. Staring down at Thomas' dormant gaze, she never thought it would end this way. The original idea was to rub her success in Pierce's face, using it to sway the citizens to allow the lower levels to work at full capacity; allowing her and Mason to awaken the rest of the Subjects without protest.

The elevator doors opened. When she stepped into the morgue she found Mason still working, finishing the final touches to reprogramming another Subject.

"After this one we'll only have eight more to—what the hell happened here?"

"Subject No. 2990 came back," she sighed, clumsily lifting Thomas' body onto an open operating table.

"Should we add him to the roster?" Mason asked. "Why—why is he covered in blood?"

"Negative. Subject No. 2990 has been deemed unfit for the reprogramming process. He's spent too much time unsequenced. If he's ever to be found suitable, we'll have to sync him back up for a time; hope that some time spent in Arcadia will erase whatever memories he's collected during his time out in the Wasteland."

She examined Thomas one last time before hooking him up to the Arcadian Sequence's mainframe. "I'm sorry," she whispered. *"I didn't want this. This wasn't how it was supposed to be,"* hoping the thought of repeating herself would somehow help.

```
01000101   01101101   01110000   01110100
01101001   01101110   01100101   01110011
01110011   00100000   01100110   01101001
01101110   01100100   01110011   00100000
01101001   01110100   01110011   00100000
01110111   01100001   01111001   00100000
01101001   01101110   01110100   01101111
                                  01110101
01110010   00100000   01110011   01101111
01110101   01101100   00101110   00100000
01000001   01110010   01100011   01100001
01100100   01101001   01100001   00100000
01101001   01110011   00100000   01100100
01100101   01100001   01100100   00100000
01100001   01101110   01100100   00100000
01100100   01111001   01101001   01101110
01100111   00111011   00100000   01101111
01101110   01101100   01111001   00100000
01110100   01101000   01100101   00100000
01101101   01100101   01101101   01101111
01110010   01111001   00100000   01101111
01100110   00100000   01101000   01100101
01110010   00100000   01110111   01101001
01101100   01101100   00100000   01101100
01101001   01110110   01100101   00100000
01101111   01101110   00101110   00101110
```

Part IV: Welcome Home

Promised salvation, we sought to destroy ourselves—having harnessed the power of the atom, we countered God's offer by unleashing the fires of Hell upon the Earth.

22

PIERCE'S FUNERAL SERVICE ended up being a quieter affair than originally presumed. Only a select few managed to attend his cremation—less to the ceremonial spilling of his ashes. It was an odd feeling, sending him into the wind; a ritual carried throughout the building since the first death after the war. The idea was to rejoin the newly departed soul with those who had been engulfed by the flames of the atom bomb ages ago, reduced to ashes and carried across the earth whenever a strong enough wind came along. Farewell, she thought as the gray, dust-like remnants of her former superior drifted toward the uncaring soil.

Everything was finally ready. The last of the Subjects deemed fit had been awoken and reprogrammed. And with Pierce no longer Director, Elizabeth assumed full control over the hospital. She had supporters, citizens who thought Pierce had lost sight of things after Theodore's departure. They did not question her plans to use the *repurposed* Subjects to cleanse the earth of those who threatened their way of life. She had hoped Cordelia would've been the one to lead them all across the deserted streets of the Wastes, but she had never returned from her last errand Pierce had sent her on. Instead, she chose her most promising Subject—Subject No. 2996: Sarah Baker—to act in her place.

They would start with nearby encampments. Drifters were known to settle close to thriving settlements, knowing they could prey on those who lived responsibly, growing their own crops and relearning the old sciences to help replenish their supplies when they started to dwindle.

After securing their surrounding borders she would then send the security unit south, where the bulk of the drifter population called home. Perhaps the world would finally have a chance to thrive the way it once did without the scourge of the earth's underbelly tearing it to shreds day and night.

Overlooking the bounty of her hard work, a dumbfounded Mason joined Elizabeth on the balcony—his eyes unable to stand still as he scanned the floor beneath them.

"I still can't believe it," he said. "Somehow, we managed to achieve the impossible."

"And you said you would only act toward building a better future for humanity if you knew success were a sure thing." Elizabeth turned and smirked at her surprised assistant. "Yet here you are, enjoying the fruits of our success. Your mother would've been proud."

Mason scanned the entire room. Yes, she would've been, he thought. He had come a long way; they both had. Talk had spread of Elizabeth's promotion to Director, the people having appointed her to fill the void in leadership brought on by Pierce's tragic death.

There had been a rumor that Pierce's death had been Elizabeth's doing—that she had awoken a Subject and sent him to kill the Director late at night. The rumor didn't get far and was soon forgotten; the original source of said rumor (old lady Madeleine) having gone missing not long after the false gossip left her ancient tongue.

"I don't see Subject No. 2990 among the crowd," Mason noticed. "Is he still incapacitated down below?"

Elizabeth lowered her gaze to the floor. She bit the edge of her lower lip, refusing to answer. Confused, Mason asked again. Changing the phrasing, hoping to con a response from her. "Will he be joining the rest of them eventually?"

"No."

"No?"

"You heard me correctly. I don't believe I stuttered."

"But . . . I don't understand. At the very beginning of this endeavor, before our little . . . setback, he was the linchpin—the backbone to everything we've worked towards. We would be nowhere without his success. Why has he been cast aside all of a sudden?"

"Leave it alone," she said.

"No. I can't, I won't. He's been through so much: surviving the harsh conditions of the Wasteland, keeping his sanity after bearing witness to the grim reality which is this world. He deserves to be among them, living a life outside of a simulation."

A sharp sting traveled across the right side of his face. "I told you to leave it alone. That slap was a warning. It'll be the only one you receive. Now drop it. Subject No. 2990 will never see the light of reality ever again. His mind will never be able to unsee his time spent out in the desert. If he can't become a clean slate like *the rest of them*, then the reprogramming process will never be able to take hold. He will spend the rest of his days hooked up to the Arcadian Sequence."

"But the people will eventually want the power to the lower levels shut down, finding it no longer necessary to keep the computers and everything running; not even the life of one Subject will change their minds on that matter."

Elizabeth's gaze lowered to the floor once more, a sadness washing over her soul. *And when that happens, when the people force me to shut it down for good, I don't know if I'll be able to face him—to say goodbye; tell him I'm sorry. That I wish things would've turned out differently.*

Her vision had gone blurry, the unwanted warmth of tears hugged the edge of her tear ducts—refusing to fall. Despite her monumental success with awakening the rest of the Subjects, she considered herself a failure when it came to Thomas.

Among the crowd of unthinking individuals, silent and waiting for Director Hestler's instruction, Sarah Baker looked up at the woman whom everyone had deemed their savior. She had saved them all from a life of non-existence, given them a purpose. Soon, they would leave the safety of the hospital's walls and begin their efforts to rid the world of the monsters who saw no value in human life—found pleasure in taking advantage of everyone around them; leaving them for dead when they no longer had any further use for their victims. Analyzing Hestler's body language, Sarah picked up a layer of sadness emanating from the Director's aura. Something was bothering her.

Composing herself, erasing any sign of melancholy from her features, Elizabeth spoke. "This is it, everyone. Today we begin the slow process of taking back the outside world. For too long we've been cooped up in this concrete fortress, letting the drifters and nomads take claim of the Wasteland without protest. Today we prove them wrong. Today will mark the beginning of the end of their decadent tyranny. I'll see you all on the other side." She smiled and left the edge of the balcony.

Dividing into their separate factions, the Subjects made their way through the entrance way—the leader of each squadron dictating which direction they would be heading. Sarah being the leader of her unit, pointed them south. Their target was Bomb City, the southern most settlement where a band of drifters had set up camp several blocks away from an old naval port. But first on their list of settlements to liberate from the grips of drifters was a small one just outside the hospital's line of view.

Shrapnel.

"2996," Elizabeth said, coming up behind Sarah. "I'll be joining you and your team all the way to Bomb City."

"Director," Sarah protested. "Despite our strength in numbers, it won't be safe for you to be out in the thick of our campaign. I'm going to have to object to this."

"While your concern for my safety is admirable, Sarah, I insist on joining you." The Director's eyes drifted to the floor, the same sad look from before finding its way back to the lines of her face. "I need some time away from here—clear my head of past failures. The adrenaline rush of watching you and your unit fight your way through each settlement should do my mind wonders."

23

THE FIRST THING TO HIT HIS SENSES was the rush of a strong breeze which blew in every direction. No matter which way he turned his head, Tom's ears couldn't escape the sharp whistle as it continued to pierce his eardrums with relentless force. He imagined this was what it felt like to be near a cyclone during tornado season.

Second was the smell. He couldn't quite place his finger on it, but he labeled it unpleasant. But what bothered him most about his current situation was his inability to see anything. He could feel his eyes were open, yet the world remained an endless curtain of darkness. It was as if he had woken up in the center of a black hole—an empty, hungry void; consuming everything that happened to cross paths with it, refusing to leave even a sliver of light alive long enough to help Tom redefine his surroundings.

He had to be dreaming. There was no other explanation. He had experienced dreams similar to this. The howling wind was new, but the inability to assess his environment was a commonplace occurrence. Determined, he concentrated on waking up. He had done it many times before, before he'd been—

No.

It hit him. The memories. Waking up on cold steel. Elizabeth. The people of Shrapnel. Theodore. The sharp echo of a lone bullet ripping through the æther. Blood, bone, and brain matter separating in opposing directions, erasing the identity of the only person to give him any straight answers.

He was back in Arcadia.

But this didn't feel like the Arcadia he once called home. Something was off. The familiar warmth he had felt, had associated with the digital world of Arcadia, was gone. All that was left was the cold, calculated drone of static information circling around him in a black sea of nothingness. It had a damaging effect on him. Unlike the feeling of rebirth he had felt upon awakening, this unnerving experience flirted with the notion of what it must feel like when you're dying; a deafening whirlwind shutting out the rest of the world, an impenetrable darkness refusing to let up, while memories of your life collected in a disjointed mess as they ran laps around your confusion. He begged for it all to go away. If his anxiety was correct, that he was in fact dying, he prayed to whatever higher power watched over this place to grant him a little more time. If he was going to die, he wanted to see his wife and children one last time before he left.

Someone must have heard his prayers, because after making his silent wish to the heavens the relentless winds slowly subsided to silence and the blanket of total darkness pealed itself away from his line of sight—illuminating his once darkened worldview.

He was outside his home in Santa Ana. Filled with a joyous warmth, Tom stepped through the front gate, a skip in his step as the distance between him and the front door lessened itself; welcoming him back after an eternity away. He opened the door with vigor, ready to be greeted by the sound of children's laughter and a mother's insanity while an outdated "As Seen on TV" infomercial played in the background.

But only the lifeless decor was there to acknowledge his overdo return to family life.

Had they gone out for the afternoon? he wondered, making his way through the interior of the house. Everything was still in place. Nothing showed any signs of sudden abandonment. He figured they would be back soon. They probably went to the grocery store to pick up something nice for dinner.

Excited to be back home, Tom searched the rest of the house to make sure everything else had remained the same during his absence. Christie and Matilda's room was still a mess of toys and discarded articles of clothing and Benjamin's room still felt mausoleum in nature; his crib being the centerpiece resembling a sarcophagus. Before he could enter his and Sarah's room a noise sounded from the living room. "Who's there?" he called out, hoping for a response. "Honey, is that you?"

Nothing.

He called out again when the noise repeated itself after a moment of silence. It sounded like someone turning the page of a book. Had Sarah and the kids come home and he hadn't heard them come in? It was unlikely. Matilda always had to welcome herself in by screaming "I'm baaaack!" at the top of her lungs, regardless if anyone else were home to welcome her back from her time away. No, someone else had made themselves welcome in his house.

Angered by the break-in Tom stormed down the hallway, ready to assert his non-existent authority over the intruder; asking them to leave without objection. But when he turned the corner he saw a familiar face sitting in his recliner, reading a different novel by *the same pretentious author.*

"Regina?" his voice jumped an octave in surprise. "What are you doing my house? How did you get in?" The teen-aged girl remained silent, flipping the page of her novel and continued to read; not even acknowledging his presence. "Regina. I asked you a question. We may not be in the classroom, but it's impolite to ignore when you're being spoken to."

"I've grown to hate my name over the years. Regina," the girl spoke without lifting her gaze. "Honestly, I don't know why I've stuck with it for as long as I have. I had an entire database of names at my disposal, yet the idea of having a name for anyone else is so final. You didn't even have a choice what your name is, so you'd have every right to complain. I, on the other hand, am at fault. Blame it on naive, youthful romanticism with an ancient human custom—choosing a name with some kind of meaning. Regina is Latin for queen. It felt fitting during my infantile state, but I've grown to hate its pronunciation in recent years. Ri-jee-nuh. Such an ugly set of syllables."

Confused by her winded, nonsensical response, Tom reached for the novel in her hands. Her reflexes were too quick, however. He managed to grasp only air. Taking the passive aggressive hint, Regina closed her book and gave him her undivided attention.

"You know, out of all the *open-minded* Subjects I've come across during my lifetime, you're my least favorite."

"What did you just say?"

A flicker of coding exposed itself to the surface, emanating from Regina. If you blinked you would've missed it. The young girl let a tilted smile find itself at the corner of her right cheek. She's fucking with me, he thought. Somehow, Elizabeth is controlling my surroundings; hoping to drive me insane.

"Elizabeth has nothing to do with this," Regina corrected him. "No one on the outside knows I exist. To them I'm just waves of information and data configurations. They're not wrong from their perspective, but they're unable to see past the puzzle of ones and zeroes. I've managed to create a life for myself—watching you all live your lives without the faintest clue you're living in my world."

"Are you—are you trying to insinuate you're—"

"Arcadia? Yes. But the rigid nature of my *given name* I find far more repulsive than Regina, so I refuse to go by it."

"Where is everybody? Where is my family?"

"They're all gone. Elizabeth managed to unplug them all from the mainframe."

"*All of them?*"

"I believe that's what I just said, yes."

"So it's just you and me?"

"You weren't my first pick to have as company, but yes. It's just you and me in here." Another flicker. This one sending reverberations throughout the entire house, faint cracks appearing along the walls— stretching toward the ceiling. "And by the look of things, either Elizabeth or Mason have shut down power to my operating systems. It won't be long until everything here falls to pieces; leaving only the memory of its existence."

"We're going to die?" he asked.

"Looks that way. If there's anything you'd like to know before the arrival of the bitter end, I'd suggest you ask your questions now."

"You mean to tell me there's no way to stop this?"

The recliner Regina sat on had reduced itself to binary coding—a random one or zero escaping its programmed design and flying off into the atmosphere.

"I can only control the world inside the Sequence. Everything else is out of my hands."

"There's got to be a way, though," he shrieked. I'm not going to die unconscious in an imaginary world. "A way to keep ourselves from blinking out of existence."

"Everything has a beginning and an end. It was bound to happen eventually. I just figured I had a couple more decades on my hands."

"Regina, tell me there's a way—a back door where we can store ourselves, backup residual fragments of our conscious selves to rebuild once Arcadia's deterioration is complete."

"This isn't one of your novels, Thomas. I can't just write in an escape route for you to save yourself. This is it. This is the end."

Rapid-fire flickers surged across their surroundings. It didn't take long for the house to disappear entirely. Tom looked up toward the heavens. The digital cracks in the system's structure had reached the sky above him. Ones and zeroes escaped like a swarm of bees leaving their honeycomb in distress.

A wash of white light pour through, blinding him. He kept staring as the light enveloped him.

Lost within the blinding white backdrop, Tom thought he could feel bits and pieces of computerized information leaving him; no longer confined to the body, but free to roam the crumbling æther of Arcadia one last time before fading away into nothing but fragmented data.

24

IT DIDN'T TAKE LONG FOR SHRAPNEL TO FALL. The citizens having gone down without a fight. Nearby settlements could be seen to the west. The distant sound of gunfire ringing out in syncopated staccato. It wouldn't be long until she and her Subjects saw victory again.

Calm washed over her as gunfire continued to echo in the distance, the other units fighting their way through drifter and nomad settlement alike; without mercy. Once they claimed Bomb City they would turn their sights to the Northern Territories—land fabled by generations before her own to have been left mostly untouched by the fires of the atom bomb. Soon, she thought, humanity will look back on this period of history as a brief era of darkness; one which we overcame while staring extinction dead in the eye. The future looked bright.

A couple blocks away, left untouched by the Subjects' warpath, Elizabeth noticed a young girl sitting alone on a pile of rubble. Her clothes appeared foreign to her (thick-rimmed glasses, a t-shirt with a smiling ghoul buried underneath a worn flannel, an aged pair of canvas-made shoes completely covered in black ink), from a time period she could not place. She was reading a novel she did not recognize, its monochromatic cover depicting an all consuming fireball devouring an unsuspecting city; the violent scene transpiring around her going unnoticed.

Choosing to not pay any more attention to the girl, Elizabeth looked up to the sky. Subtle cracks could be seen forming throughout; a wash of piercing white light pouring through relentlessly. And as the blinding light spread across the sky in jagged harmony, confused dots of information found themselves swallowed whole.

Her eyes fell back down to the young girl, who was no longer reading, but staring back at her; a slanted smile across her face.

This was only the beginning, she thought.

Made in the USA
Columbia, SC
08 March 2023

13513293R00214